MATE TO THE DEMON KINGS

LACEY CARTER ANDERSEN

To my PA— you are not only a dear friend, you are a source of light in a world that sometimes has too much darkness. Thank you for believing in me, even when I don't believe in myself.

~ Lacey Carter Andersen

Want to be part of the writing process? Maybe even get a taste of my sense of humor? Teasers for my new releases? And more?

Facebook Group: https://www.facebook.com/groups/laceysrealm
Facebook Page: https://www.facebook.com/authorlaceycarterandersen
Pinterest: https://www.pinterest.com/laceycarterandersen/
Twitter: https://twitter.com/LaceyCAndersen
Website: https://laceycarterandersen.net

SECRET MONSTERS

1

*CONCEALING A MURDER IS FAR MORE DIFFICULT THAN MOST
people could possibly imagine.*

Greg Manthen tapped his pen against his desk, silently seething as he thought about the one thing that might reveal what he had done. The one piece of evidence he hadn't considered.

It simply needed to be dealt with. And his patience was wearing thin.

Where is it? And what in God's name is taking so long?

When his assistant, Carson, lightly knocked at his door and entered, he glared at the older man without a word. Most men in Greg's position would scream their displeasure, but not Greg, he liked to watch his victims squirm.

The short man ran a nervous hand through his white, balding hair and straightened his skewed tie, as if doing so would suddenly make him presentable for someone as important as Greg.

It did not.

"Well?"

"They finished with it," Carson whispered, then scurried to stand in front of his desk.

Greg raised a brow. "So are you going to show it to me? Or stand there all day?"

His assistant glanced nervously at the door behind him. "There wasn't much they could decipher... she'd burned the journal almost past recognition."

Greg slammed his palm angrily on the desk, making the man jump.

Carson set the paper in front of him and took two steps back. "Anything else, sir?"

"No. You're dismissed."

He barely heard the door as it closed, grasping the paper and pulling it close with an eagerness that bordered on desperation. His team had deciphered all that remained of Elaina Davens' journal and typed it neatly on a paper.

Looking at the sheet, he read what little had been found:

THEY'VE LIED TO ME. *About everything. Level 10 demons are no worse than we are. The line between them and the angels is paper-thin.*

They're------ than I ever imagined.

They'll kill me if they ever discover what I know.

This changes everything.

GREG STARED at the paper for far too long before finally setting it down. He'd been right to betray Elaina. She'd discovered the truth. A truth that would have turned their world upside down and destroyed everything.

She had needed to die.

And once I burn this, and the charred remains of her journal, there will be nothing to suggest her death was anything but an accident.

The secret of what he and his team had done would remain a secret forever. There was nobody. No weapon. And no evidence. There was no crime, as far as humankind knew.

He smiled. *I actually got away with murder.*

IN A DEMON REALM, Elaina hid in a cave, praying to survive another night. This place wasn't meant for humans. The air was toxic. Low level demons roamed, searching for anything they could feed on, and a human without a weapon, a human too weak to use the powerful spells she'd been taught as a hunter, would be the perfect prey.

And so, she hid in the deadly white powder of the realm, feeling more lost and afraid than she ever had in her life. Death seemed to be hovering above her with a smile, promising her death would be slow. Because as powerful as the demons she loved were, they couldn't reach her here, no matter how much they might want to. She only had one hope, and it was a slim hope. Her best friend, and fellow demon hunter, Sharen would have to save her.

But Sharen didn't know where she was.

Sharen didn't know the truth about demons or the truth about the institute they worked for.

Hell, her best friend might not even know Elaina was *alive*.

And then, there was the whole divide between them that had grown bigger and bigger. Yeah, Sharen had married an asshole. But Elaina knew she should've tried harder to pretend to tolerate the man. Elaina shouldn't have let that abusive jerk get between them.

Sharen had needed her, and Elaina had failed her. How could she expect her friend to be there for her now?

"It's your own fault for letting that bastard trick you," she whispered to herself, her teeth chattering.

In all her times crossing into demon realms, she'd never felt cold before. She didn't know if that was because when she led her students through the portal, they struck fast, and ran. Or if it had something to do with the fact that the longer she stayed, the more the poisonous world sickened her.

Is it cold? Is it the sickness? She had no idea.

"A--At least I destroyed the journal," she whispered to herself, her dry lips cracking as she smiled.

It was the one thing that she'd been able to do before that bastard Greg Manthen had captured her. And as much as it pained her to lose all her journal entries documenting her discovery of the secrets of the demon realm and its connection to the human realm, she was grateful that Greg wouldn't be able to use it against anyone she loved. Especially her demons.

But even they wouldn't stay safe forever. Not without her in the human realm with them to guide them. Every moment she spent trapped in this place brought both her and the demons she loved closer to death. She had to escape, no matter the cost.

She curled further around herself, shivering. "Sharen, follow your instincts," she whispered. "Find out the truth."

A demon roared in the distance, as if to remind her that all hope was lost.

2

SHAREN'S PHONE BUZZED. IMMEDIATELY, HER PULSE PICKED UP, and her focus snapped away from the student's presentation to her phone. There were only two people who called her. One of them was the man who ripped her heart out, and the other one was her best friend who was dead.

So... there was really only one person who could be calling her now.

Willing herself not to assume the worst, she slid her phone off her desk. Swiping the screen, she read the text from her ex-husband.

I WENT BACK and got more of my things.

SHE STARED IN DISBELIEF. Somewhere deep inside, her heart squeezed painfully.

But she pushed the feeling aside. In both her professional and personal life, letting her feelings distract her was dangerous. If she wasn't strong all the time people got hurt.

People died.

Even Elaina.

So, she reached for her anger. Anger kept her safe. Alive. It was the only thing that made her keep going after her best friend's death.

I broke my own rules. I opened up to this man, and look where it got me. Now she knew the truth, as much as she wished she could be soft and vulnerable, at least in her personal life, she couldn't. So, she accepted that she'd be "The Ice Queen" in all areas of her life.

No matter how exhausting such a role could be.

I can handle this, as long as my ex didn't touch my secret stash of books.

Sharen had started seeking out ancient books after stumbling upon one half-buried in a demon-realm. The lettering of the first book had been hard to read, but she'd discovered spells that she'd never been taught in class, or even heard whispered about. Since that day, she'd bought any book she could find about magic, spells, demons, or different realms. Most seemed more fantasy than reality. But a few fascinated her by describing things that felt... possible.

Shaking herself, she stared back at her phone. *If he touched my books, it might just push me over the edge.* Slowly, she typed back.

WHAT THINGS? You took all your stuff when you left.

TWO MONTHS AGO, she'd walked in on her husband and her sister in bed together. Since that day, her personal life had been a mess. It wasn't that she was shocked that the cold man she'd married was cheating on her. The truth was her marriage had been in shambles before their honeymoon was over. *Because that was when he stopped pretending to be who I wanted and showed who he was deep down.* But having her sister betray her? It was like a knife that didn't stop twisting in her belly, no matter how much time passed.

And yet, all that pain, all that misery, was nothing compared to her best friend's death.

Her phone buzzed again as she stared numbly at the hand that held it. Unconsciously, her gaze went to the simple gold band she still wore, before swiping the screen once more.

I took the TV, stereo, and some kitchen appliances. We need them for our new place.

At least he left what really mattered. But her relief was quickly replaced by anger. She clenched her teeth and dropped her phone back on her desk. *Those were mine! Bought with my hard-earned money.*

Closing her eyes, she willed herself not to completely lose her shit. He had taken everything from her. And he had the nerve to take more? If her job didn't require that she keep a low-profile, she'd have called the cops and thrown his ass in jail a long time ago.

But as it was, all she could do was seethe. Silently.

And plan to finally have my locks changed.

God did she hate him.

Looking up, she stared out at the sea of faces. It was weird to think her "students" were only a few years younger than her. How did they look so youthful, while she felt so old?

And then, she realized something else. Most of the class wasn't paying attention to the presentation.

Her jaw clenched so hard it ached. This wasn't some bullshit English class. If they didn't learn what she was teaching, they died. And the new group of students this year was one of the worst she'd seen in a long time. She was having a student review basic information with them, because they desperately needed the extra help.

And they don't even care enough to pay attention!

Sharen tapped her fingers on the desk and glared, her focus turning to one student in particular who oozed arrogance. "Smith, there something boring about Katie's presentation?"

The freshmen jumped, guiltily hiding his phone at the same time. "No, Mrs. Bran."

Moving in one swift motion, she stood, and the room grew eerily still. Even her seniors and juniors in the back looked up from their textbooks.

"Lily," she said, drawing out the senior student's name.

Lily stood, her stance that of a well-trained military officer, which she practically was. "Yes, Mrs. Bran?"

The twenty-year old's golden hair was secured in a practical, low bun at the back of her head. She wore no makeup, but with her brilliant hazel eyes and high cheekbones, she didn't need anything to look more model than warrior. But people who missed the muscles tightening her young body, were fools because she could kill a man, or more accurately, a demon, faster than any student in the room.

Sharen circled the almost-bare teacher's desk, linking her hands behind her back. "Explain to Smith, and the rest of these worthless monkeys, what happens if you get your symbols wrong."

Lily took a second to phrase her words exactly as she thought best, something Sharen had grown to appreciate about the girl. "For one thing, you could go into the wrong demon's territory. Which would be bad on many, many levels. If you got stuck, for instance, other teams might not be able to find you, because we'd be logged in to The Program as having gone to a different territory." She looked to Sharen with an unspoken question: *should I keep going?*

Sharen gave a short nod.

Lily's pale complexion grew pink as a fiery determination filled her eyes. "You freshmen haven't battled yet, but those symbols that seem to mean very little in your textbooks will be the difference between life and death. You draw yourself into a safety circle, using the right symbols. You get them wrong, and a demon could be feasting on your flesh in the blink of an eye."

All the students had turned around in their seats, to stare up at the beautiful girl as she spoke so vehemently. But still, it sickened Sharen to think that in six short months, she'd be losing a good portion of her Demon Hunters at graduation, and would be left with the new students who showed very little promise, even after a half year of studying.

"Tell them about Brian."

For one second, shock registered on the blonde's face, before she expertly covered it up. "On his first trip into a demon's territory, he mixed up his first and second symbol. We found him at his location... a demon had eaten half his stomach."

A murmur rose from the freshmen and sophomores.

Some looked panicked. Some had obviously heard the story before.

"And what did the news report about Brian?"

Lily took a deep breath, likely trying to forget the image of Brian's mangled body. "They said he'd gotten drunk and stumbled into a river. They said he drowned."

"Very good. Sit down."

The girl complied.

"But sometimes you can do everything right and still die."

Her gaze snapped to Rorde, who leaned arrogantly back in his chair.

The twenty-year-old sorcerer made her skin crawl. No one in the classroom was aware of the extensive record he'd had as a minor. Of the violent crimes that he'd committed at an age when most kids were still scared of the dark. But Sharen knew, and she firmly disagreed with the Director allowing him to join their program and her team.

"You could always die crossing the street tomorrow," she answered him curtly. "But at least you won't die with demons feeding on your insides."

He rolled his eyes.

She strode to his desk and placed her hands on it.

After a second, he looked up. His aristocratic good-looks still not enough to hide the dangerous quality of his gaze, nor the cruelness of his expression.

"I've lost a student every single year. At least one, if not more." She cocked her head. "I haven't lost one yet this year though. I wonder who it'll be? The team members who know their shit, or the ones sitting in the back of the class acting like arrogant pieces of shit?"

A couple of choked laughs came from behind her.

Rorde glared. "I'll hope we all return safely. Especially you."

Is that a threat? "You do that."

Now, back to my point.

Sharen started slowly pacing in front of the freshmen and sophomores, some who would be entering demon territory before the end of the year. "There it is kids. Some jobs you mess up at, you get fired. You mess this up, you die. And along with that, no one ever knows the sacrifice you made so they could sleep safely in their beds."

The room descended into silence.

"Now, Smith," she said, eying the boy who likely only got accepted into The Program because he was the size of a small mountain. "How do you create a Circle of Protection?"

Defiance lit his eyes. "You draw a circle around you, and write three symbols inside."

"What symbols?" She asked.

He leaned back in his chair and folded his arms over his broad chest. "Protection, Luck, and Life."

"Correct," She said. But just as a cocky expression twisted his lips, she added. "In what order?"

He frowned and cleared his throat. "Just as I said it. Protection first, then Luck, then Life."

Sharen leaned over and placed her hands on the tiny desk connected to his chair. "Congratulations, you're dead."

Blake gave a short laugh from the back of the class and put his arm behind Lily's chair. "If you don't know that by now, you'll be the first to die."

Smith paled.

Normally she'd correct a student for speaking out, but Blake was the other team captain. He and Lily were the best, and one of those rare college engagement stories that

Sharen thought would actually work out. And when he spoke, the other students were more likely to listen.

"Now then," Sharen said, turning around to face the brunette patiently waiting to continue her presentation. "Katie, why don't you finish up. I think these monkeys could use a little more help."

The demon-meat paid adamant attention the rest of class, scribbling notes like it just might save their lives, which it might. *Good.* Her gaze shifted away from them to her team in the back of the room. The seniors had that nervous silence they always got the night before they crossed over. Only, it was more than that this time. Tonight, an orange moon streaked the sky, and for some reason, it made them all a bit jumpy.

Sharen moved through the room, answering questions, and offering subtle reassurance. Even though she feared for the new recruits, she still respected the hell out of them. Not everyone could risk their lives to keep others safe.

A shrill bell rang overhead. Everyone jumped a bit, including Sharen.

The students remained sitting, staring at her.

"Alright, class. Study and train. You know what to do. Now, get out."

When they were gone, Sharen's team stood and filed down the stairs. They waited in front of their teacher, in a quiet line.

I'm going to miss these kids. And she would. Even though she had to keep a secure line between herself and them, they were the closest things she had to friends. And they were amazing at what they did. *Amazing people too.*

"Let's head down and get this over with." Sharen headed for the door. "Lily and Blake, with me."

The team captains flanked her as they made their way

down the hall. The other eight students walked a short distance behind, except for Rorde who was so close Sharen could feel his breath on her neck.

Sharen rolled her neck, trying to shake the feeling of his breath on her skin. "What do you think of them?"

Blake cast a glance at Lily. "They're slow learners, but maybe they'll pick it up after they cross over for the first time."

Sharen looked at the boy. He'd come *into* The Program knowing the basics of creating a Protective Circle. He'd toned his body and practiced with a trainer, entering her classroom with the grace and skill of a warrior twice his age. Those kids had no chance of ever being as good as he was.

"Perhaps," Sharen said with a shrug.

Lily gave her a small smile. "Also, I wanted to tell you something. The Director approached me about taking on a role as a Leader after I graduate."

"Really?" Sharen couldn't say she was surprised. If anyone could do it, Lily could.

"I told him I wasn't interested."

Sharen froze, shaking her head. "Why? You'd be excellent at it."

"Because as much as I admire you, I could never do your job."

Sharen frowned.

"The thing is, and I mean this respectfully, I've watched you give up everything for this job. Your friends. Your family. All for a bunch of students you have to scare into learning enough so they don't die. And, to risk your eternal life in a way none of us have to... I just couldn't do it."

Sharen felt flustered as she started to walk again. Lily fell silent but kept pace beside her.

Would I have become a Leader if I had the love of a good

man? If I knew how to steal a little happiness from this world? Maybe not. Maybe I would've done my time and had a normal life. Lily deserves that after all she's done for this world.

"I think... perhaps you made a good choice."

Sharen glanced at the young woman out of the corner of her eye and was glad to see she looked relieved. She didn't want Lily to feel like she had disappointed her by not following in her footsteps, but she also didn't want her to realize that sometimes Sharen regretted her choice too.

They'd almost reached the steel elevator when her cell phone buzzed. Turning it away from her team, she read the expected message.

And my alimony check better be in the mail tonight.

An ache grew in her chest. She couldn't believe she actually had to pay her ex every month. It seemed like a bad joke. If anyone knew what her personal life was like, they'd probably lose a lot of respect for her. Because as much as she should feel nothing but hate for her ex and her sister, she missed both of them.

I'm pathetic.

She realized, too late, that she'd stopped walking. Her students stood silently, waiting for her next move. Tucking her phone in her pocket, she walked to the stairs and typed the code into the panel. A few seconds later, the doors slid open and they filed inside. She hit "Z" on the elevator, then they all held still as the green lights scanned each individual, ensuring they had the proper badge. The elevator jerked into movement a second later, traveling down at a fast speed.

"Don't worry." Lily gave a shy smile, unaware of what really troubled her teacher. "At least we don't turn twenty-one until after graduation, so you have a little more time with us."

Sharen tried to push away thoughts of her failed marriage. Lily was right, she could thank God for their ages. Once these kids turned twenty-one, crossing over became too dangerous. Twenty-one was somehow a "magic" age, where demons could possess their bodies. Or find ways to use them to enter their realm.

Each university around the world had one team, and only one adult, the teacher, was allowed to enter the other realms. The rules stated that he, or she, needed to stand next to the exit from the realm. They weren't allowed to directly engage a demon, and their students knew if things got dicey, their teacher would be the first to leave. It wasn't the best system, sending the kids in to do the dirty work, but it was better than sitting back until the demons got strong enough to enter their realm, and *then* fighting them here.

The elevator doors opened to another white hallway hidden beneath a soundproof layer below the surface of the more "normal" classrooms. They came to the familiar door, where Rorde, without being told, typed in the code. The doors slid open, and he cast her that familiar superior smile. One that said, *only you should know the code, but I do too.*

"I have a photographic memory," he said, staring directly at Lily.

"So you've told us. A lot," Sharen responded curtly.

Rorde had a thing for Lily. It seemed like everyone knew it except her. And Sharen had done everything humanly possible to keep him far from Lily. The sorcerer wasn't good for her. Even ignoring the fact that she was already engaged to one of the smartest, nicest men most people would likely meet in their lives.

The sorcerer glared at his teacher and opened his mouth.

But before he could speak, her phone rang. Pulling it

back out of the pocket, she stiffened at the unfamiliar number. "Everyone, file in. I'll join you in a minute."

Staying in the hall, she clicked the button to accept the call.

"Sharen?"

Her breath left in a rush. "You called."

The woman on the other line went silent, her breathing heavy. "Is this a secure line?"

"Yes."

"Checked recently?"

Sharen clenched the phone harder. *What could she have to say that's this important?* "Yes."

Another long pause. "I looked into Elaina's death."

Her heart raced, filling her ears. "And."

"It seems she went into a demon realm without her team."

Sharen felt a cold numbness wash over her. "That's impossible."

"That's what her official report says."

Sharen spun in the empty hall, clenching her free hand and pressing it against her forehead. "You can't possibly believe that! We all trained together! You know how good she was! Not even a complete moron would go into a demon realm alone, and sure as hell not a Leader."

"Sharen, listen to me. I know her death was hard for you. It was hard for me too. But if that's what her official file says, you have to let this go. Pursuing it could only mean trouble. And you don't need any more trouble in your life."

She took several deep breaths. There was no way she was going to let this go, but she also wasn't going to drag her friend into it. "That's... good advice. Sorry. And thank you for looking into it for me."

"You'll let it go?"

"Of course," she lied.

"Good, now I got to go. Be safe."

"Be safe," Sharen repeated back, then ended the call.

Rubbing her face with hands that trembled, she ordered herself to get a grip. She had a room full of people depending on her. She didn't have time for a meltdown.

Later, she promised herself. *But for now, let's go kill some demons.*

3

SHAREN STRODE INTO THE ROOM. ABOUT A DOZEN CHAIRS faced a large screen. To the side of the screen, a large black chair faced a simple-looking computer.

"Take your seats," she ordered.

Everyone hurried in.

As she made her way to the front of the room, Rorde spoke up. "We going to try P-90-5478 tonight?"

The suspicious demon realm we came across last time.

Her eyes narrowed as she sank into her chair. "Did you *Search* it?"

Sharen hated relying on him for information, but he was the only one on her team who could use magic in their realm. It was a powerful tool. A tool she'd be a fool not to use.

But it didn't make her like it.

"Yes," he answered her slowly, avoiding her gaze. "I believe the reason we detected a demon, then not, is because it may be a demon so weak it can't keep itself in that realm. I think now would be the time to strike."

His answer didn't sit well with her. "You sure it isn't a powerful demon trying to lure us to it?"

To her complete annoyance, he smirked. "Powerful demons completely hide their presence. It wouldn't allow its shield to keep slipping."

That was how it usually went, but most weak demons simply kept a constant, feeble presence.

"I don't like it," she said, after a time. "I think we should try—"

"But this is our chance to stop it before it gets too powerful, not going would be a mistake," Rorde argued, then looked to Lily.

Her skin tinged pink. "I agree with Rorde, but it's your call."

Rorde beamed at the younger woman.

Blake turned Lily's face towards him. "I don't usually agree with The Bug, but who could argue with this pretty lady." He brushed a kiss against her lips.

Sharen glanced away in time to catch the look of pure torture on Rorde's lips. *Good, the sooner you accept that she isn't for you, the better for everyone.*

Now, visit the realm we've already found something suspicious in? Or a different one?

Sharen fiddled with her wedding ring, then shrugged. "Okay, we go to P-90-5478." Then, she turned to the screen. "Computer, show me P-90-5478."

The screen flicked on. For a moment, everything was dark, then the tiny floating green shapes that represented different realms on the odd map popped up. In a nauseating motion, it slowly zeroed in on the realm in question, passing red squares that they, or other teams, had entered and found *too dangerous*, and yellow squares the teams had simply found empty.

At last, they came to the square in question. They couldn't see anything of the actual realm, but the system gave a universal way for all the teams to communicate what they found as they crossed over.

"Computer, record the following: Team Scorpion will enter P-90-5478 at approximately," she glanced at the clock in the corner of her screen, "10:30 pm. A Level One demon is suspected, although it has not been confirmed."

The computer beeped, and the information appeared on the green square.

"Alright team," she turned back to them. "Let's suit up."

Her team left the room in an orderly fashion, standing next to their partners. There was one fighter and one symbolist in each team. Each duo consisted of a boy and a girl, because the girls typically did better with creating fast, powerful symbols, and the boys were better with brute force. Rorde's team was the exception. He was both a sorcerer and a symbolist, so he was partnered with Valentine, a boy with the build of a linebacker.

Again, Rorde typed in the code and let the group into the Portal Room.

Sharen gritted her teeth.

The students walked to the back wall where there were at least ten uniforms in each size. Rule Number One, never bring anything personal into another realm. Sharen picked up a random uniform in her size and went behind a screen to change. She dressed quickly, then stepped out to find her students dressed and ready to go. Their white uniforms, with silver scorpions sewn onto the backs, looked brand new, as always. They'd all donned white sneakers, again from a huge collection lined under the uniforms.

Next, Sharen walked to the cubbies. Twisting her ring off, she went to drop it in her usual compartment, but found a gold band already there. She almost moved it, no doubt Lily or Blake had dropped it in by mistake, but instead she just put it in the cubby next to it, along with tucking her phone and wallet in the back corner. Turning, she almost slammed into Rorde.

"Careful, we wouldn't want you to get hurt."

Creepy. "Thanks."

She went to stand in front of the students. "Everyone, check yourselves for personal items."

A second later, Rorde's partner, Valentine, stood up. Pieces of his long blonde hair fell over his face as he pulled the silver cord off from around his neck. The boy, who no doubt had Viking in his blood, slunk past her, as she glared, to drop his necklace off.

Someone mumbled. "Rookie mistake."

And it was. If a demon had got his necklace... well, he'd be the bitch of a demon for the rest of his lifetime. *Idiot.*

Sharen waited until everyone took their seats before speaking. "Alright, we all know how this goes. Get in and get in position, without being seen. Put up your protective circles, and then Rorde will draw the demon out. Symbolists strike first, warriors only if it gets close. And as always, never follow a demon into its den. We all understand?"

"Yes, Captain!" they all shouted at once.

"If things start to go south, look to me or your captains for guidance. Questions?"

The room was silent.

"File up!"

They all went to the opposite wall from the wardrobes and pulled their weapons off the racks on the walls. The Splicers shone beneath the fluorescent light, the combination of smooth steel and sharp edges creating a weapon that was both beautiful and dangerous. Sharen picked up a weapon at random, automatically sliding her hand into place. The weapon was the size of her forearm and fit like a glove. A creation of pure brilliance, it was a sword and a magic discharger, all rolled into one.

Sharen stopped ogling her weapon, the one she rarely got to use, and passed her students, who waited in two rows. She went to the wall at the back of the room, with its massive block of black stone. *Demon Stone.* With a practiced hand, she curled her fingers around the thick, white chalk and drew a large door onto the black stone. Above the stone, she drew the sweeping symbols, and at last the name of the realm.

The door began to glow, slowly transforming from black, to white, and then to red. A soft gurgling sound was followed by a slowly swirling circle of red and white, like the caps on ocean waves in the shape of a doorway.

She dropped the chalk in its bin and stood back. "Let's go."

Blake and Lily led, matching expressions of fierceness on their faces.

The other students followed in quick pairs behind them. And at last, she herself stepped through.

No one ever got used to the sensation. Of being too hot and too cold. Of being stretched and squeezed. Of being weightless and so heavy the weight of your own body might crush you. But the uncomfortable sensation only lasted a moment before she stumbled out into the demon realm.

It was like every other. Hot as hell, even though it probably wasn't. White sand and rocks covered the landscape, where white plants like long, twisted mushrooms grew between boulder-like rocks. The sky, as always, burned brightly, with three suns so large they appeared close enough to touch.

Next to her, Rorde's Splicer glowed, and deep red symbols appeared on the side of the blade. Valentine's weapon glowed as well, less elegant blue symbols appearing. All the students stood still, equipping their own weapons with whatever shot they preferred the most.

Closing her eyes, she created symbols in green. Her weapon would fire simple strikes that would explode ever-so-slightly on impact. She could create something even more powerful, but it'd be like killing a fly with a grenade, pointless.

Lily and Blake broke off from the group, and each pair followed the next after a minute, spreading themselves out evenly. Rorde and Valentine were the last to go, since it was their job to keep an eye on their teacher. Everyone worked like one organism, creeping up the closest stack of boulders on their right.

Her captains reached the top of the boulders first, sinking low onto their bellies, then glancing back to signal they'd spotted the demon.

Sharen released some of the anxiety building in her chest. She hadn't liked this mission. But if the demon had already been spotted, it was likely she'd be home in time to get a decent night's sleep.

She, flanked by Rorde and Valentine, moved further from the exit, mostly to get a good view of the battle, but still staying close enough to escape in case of trouble. They scaled the boulders closest to them and lay on their bellies. A demon, definitely a Level One, sat in the center of a clearing in the middle of the boulders. Near it, the large hole signifying its den had been dug out of some of the rocks surrounding it.

The demon itself was young, judging by its small horns, and probably no more than Rorde's size. It used its sharp teeth and nails to dig between its toes, eating whatever it found of interest.

Sharen sensed the others creating their Protective Circles, just as Rorde created one around them. In this realm, it wasn't necessary to draw them, only to imagine them just as they should be. It was a difficult skill to master, but her symbolists were the best.

A tingle spread through them. Lily's signal, and suddenly, the symbolists opened fire.

The demon barely had time to look up, before the multicolored lights slammed into its flesh, slicing it into bits.

Silence held after the attack.

Rorde closed his eyes. His slimy magic tugging at her flesh, and then, he opened his eyes. "All clear."

Her team stood up and cheered.

Not the most exciting battle, but exciting battles were rarely a good thing.

They made their way slowly back down the rocks when a terrible stench struck them. One of rotting bodies and death.

"Back, back!" Sharen screamed, shoving Rorde and Valentine backwards.

The students scrambled onto their rocks and threw up their Protective Circles in a terrified rush.

Sharen flattened herself back onto the rock, safely in Rorde's shield and watched, her stomach twisting.

The air shimmered, and suddenly the clearing near their portal was no longer a clearing. What seemed like one hundred demons, or more, of every size, shape, color, and level crowded the space. Directly across from their portal, on the other side of the area filled with demons, a huge mountain rose, blocking out all three suns. The clearing disappeared into shadows.

A den with an opening as large as the side of a house stood quiet and dark, with three thrones in front of it.

On the thrones, three Level 10 demons sat smiling.

Sharen trembled. She'd never seen a Level 10 demon before, but her mentor had said she'd know it when she did. And she knew it. They looked almost... human, but with red skin and foot-long horns standing out on top of their head. All three of their features were symmetrical, handsome.

Okay, ridiculously handsome. Seeing them took her breath away, which was crazy. No man had ever made her feel this way; it made no sense for a demon to. *Or three demons.*

The one in the center was the largest of the demons. With an eight-pack tightening his sculpted stomach, and massive, thickly-corded arms. He had dark hair around his pale white horns and a face that was dangerously attractive.

"Welcome," the demon's smile widened. "I'm Alec, and I've been waiting a very long time for you."

His minions cheered, grunted, and roared.

"These are my brothers, Kade and Ryder. We together rule this realm and many others. And we are only too pleased to welcome you to your new, permanent home."

Sharen swallowed, and curled her hands into fists. "Conceal my words from the demons."

Rorde nodded, and his oily magic raced over her flesh.

"When I give the signal, fire at the roof of the den. It should crumble on their leaders, giving us a chance at escape. Strike anything down that gets in your way, but race for the portal. We can't win this battle."

Her students raised their fingers ever so slightly, crossing one over the other, to show their understanding.

She nodded, then went back to staring at the demon.

"Some of you," Alec continued, "will enjoy their time here more than others."

His black eyes slid over the students, then landed on Sharen.

Shock registered on his face. "What's this? A woman?" His gaze burned over her flesh. He turned to his minions, pointing at her. "None of you are to touch her. Understand? She's for my brothers and I alone."

Sharen's stomach turned. He would possess her, and use her body to exit through the portal and into their realm. The chaos such a demon would havoc... dark days would follow.

She had to get free. No matter the cost.

Pointing her weapon at the roof of his den, she turned to her soldiers. Locking eyes with Lily, she nodded.

Their weapons discharged silently but boomed as they hit the roof of the den. The ground shook as the den caved in on top of the Demon Kings. Their minions raced to their aid, and Sharen stood, half-climbing, half-running down the hill.

Valentine kept pace with her, the others just shortly behind them, but she had no idea why Rorde had hung back. They were nearly to the portal, when the demons seemed to realize what was happening. They leapt toward the students, who blasted and slashed out with their weapons. Valentine severed the head of a demon who stepped just in front of them.

Sharen skidded around the flailing creature and darted the last few steps to the portal, but paused. Pushing her strength into her weapon, she created the symbols for a powerful spell. The blade on her Splicer glowed a blinding red. Even as her students escaped through the portal, even while she knew she was being foolish, she turned back to the horde of demons.

Rorde was surrounded. One of his spells created a small

shield around himself, but terror filled his eyes. How long could he keep them at bay?

Why the hell didn't he follow us when we ran?

Gritting her teeth, she fired, praying his shield was strong enough. The blast was like a volcano exploding. Demons went flying and smoke filled the air, blocking her vision.

She needed to escape. Everyone else had made it through. But had Rorde made it?

Squinting her eyes, she tried to see through the black smoke, but there was nothing but shapes. *Damn it. Damn it.*

When a demon's claws curled around her arm, she slashed out, cutting his handoff. She ignored his screaming, knowing that she already stayed too long. Risked her life in a way that could cost her job at the least, and her eternal soul at the worst. It was time to go. Inching backwards, she prayed for Rorde's soul, and leapt through the portal.

The horrible feeling of traveling back to her realm only lasted a moment, and then she was smashing into chairs as she rolled on the ground. Rising shakily to her feet, she stood by the side of the portal.

I'm sorry, kid. She might not have liked him, but no one deserved the torment he would soon endure. But leaving the portal open any longer was too dangerous.

Rising on her tiptoes, she went to erase the first symbol.

"No," Lily shouted. "Rorde!"

She hesitated, then raised her hand again. *We can't risk it any longer.*

But it was in that moment that Rorde came rolling into the room.

With quick movements, she erased the symbols, and the portal closed with a disgusting sucking sound.

The room was filled with the sounds of their heavy breathing.

"What the hell was that?" Blake shouted.

Sharen stumbled to a chair and sat down. "My thoughts exactly."

Blake turned to Rorde. "You said it was safe!"

Lily put a hand on his chest, but Blake towered over Rorde, who lay sprawled on the floor.

"Your job is to make sure this shit doesn't happen!"

"It wasn't his fault," Lily said, shooting Rorde an apologetic look. "He can't always be right."

"But—"

"Blake!" Sharen silenced him with a single word.

Rorde looked to her, his face pale. "Thank you for—"

"We don't need to discuss it." She cut him off.

And it was true. If her superiors found out what she'd done...

Sharen opened her mouth, planning to stop the useless blame-game, when she spotted the blood spreading down Lily's neck.

"You're hurt," Sharen said, pointing at Lily. "We better get you looked at."

Blake's anger fled as he glanced at his fiancé. "Sweetheart, why didn't you say so?"

She shrugged. "I think we're all a bit hurt."

"How bad is it?" Sharen asked bluntly.

Lily gave a pained smile. "It looks worse than it is. I'll hit the med-area soon and be patched up without issue, I'm sure."

Sharen nodded. *She knows a flesh-wound from a serious one.*

"Maybe I can help," Rorde said, struggling to his feet.

Blake sent him a glare. "I think you've done enough."

Ignoring the argument, Sharen turned to the console. "Computer, label P-90-5478 as red. Put the following notes: Team Scorpion discovered three Level 10 demons and no less than one hundred minions. It appears the demons laid a trap for us, and they seem to be trying to acquire an adult human."

The new information filled the screen.

"Contact, Director Manthen."

The students shifted behind her, no doubt trying to look more orderly and less frightened. When the Director didn't answer right away, they began putting their weapons back against the wall, and their chairs into place.

"This better be good," Director Manthen said, his overly large head coming into focus, along with his messy hair and bare, hairy chest.

The room grew quiet.

She took a deep breath, then explained what happened.

The Director swore. "I'll make sure the other teams know, including our Realm Enforcers. No doubt, the Level 10 demons are hoping to get a human body before they come over. But if no one else enters it, they'll get desperate and come over on their own... even if doing such a thing will greatly weaken them. It'll make them easier to kill, but hopefully, the Enforcers can figure out the most likely place they'll cross over."

Without another word, the Director signed off.

Sharen spent the next few hours checking over wounds and waking Doctor Marshall to stitch up anyone who needed it. Luckily, they'd gotten out without any broken bones.

When the last student left, she felt weary beyond words. Shuffling to her cubby, she reached in and found her phone and wallet... but no ring. Her finger suddenly felt bare without it.

Carefully searching the other cubbies, she eventually had to accept that it wasn't there.

She sighed. Blake or Lily had probably taken hers by mistake. She'd have to get it back on Monday.

Great. Something else to look forward to.

She walked home, to her tiny house just off campus. Without undressing, she kicked off her shoes and lay down in her empty bed, completely exhausted. Sleep closed in like a rushing wave, and she gave in happily to its pull.

4

ALEC'S FRUSTRATION RODE HIM LIKE A WILD ANIMAL. He should've been angry that their first opportunity to leave the demon realm had gone horribly wrong. After all, they'd spent more years than he could count crawling from the darkest depths of the lowest levels of the demon realms solely focused on returning to earth.

On getting back the lives we lost.

And yet, he wasn't upset that the opportunity had slipped through his fingers. He was upset that they'd lost the beautiful woman.

Which is absolutely insane.

He froze in his pacing, imagining her. She was tall for a woman, with dark hair and stunning green eyes. *And with curves in all the right places.* She had stared down a horde of demons, and three demon-kings, and... defied them. Instead of freezing in terror, she'd attacked them. And escaped.

Why does the thought make me want to smile and roar in anger at the same time?

And that wasn't all, it was also the way she made him feel.

Human.

Like a cure to a vicious virus, just seeing her had awakened within him and his brothers a reminder of what it was to be human. Every moment since her appearance brought out new and strange changes.

We're even starting to sound different.

And think differently.

What does this mean?

He'd only looked at her for less than a minute. It seemed ridiculous the effect she'd had on him... and yet, the feeling wouldn't go away.

"My tattoos are coming back." His brother, Ryder, had taken off his shirt. And sure enough, there beneath his red flesh were the dull lines of the tattoos he'd had in life.

Alec tugged at his own shirt, revealing his stomach. His tattoos were returning too. *Strange.*

"What about you?" Alec asked Kade.

His twin glared at both of his brothers, but after a tense moment, pulled his shirt up. *Tattoos.* "We should've ignored the awareness of humans."

Why does he always have to be such a ray of freakin' sunshine? Sensing humans in this realm was unexpected, and didn't go as planned, but it's the best thing that's happened to us in a long time.

Alec continued his pacing. "Why would we have possibly ignored the chance at getting out of this damned place sooner and with our powers intact?"

Kade crossed his arms over his chest and leaned back against the cave wall, closing his eyes. "Don't pretend you didn't feel the same thing I did when you saw that woman."

Like she's part of us.

Like she belongs to us.

Ryder's expression grew thoughtful. "I feel about her... well, the same way I do about the two of you."

Alec laughed, glad for a distraction from his turbulent emotions. "God, I hope not!"

Ryder picked a rock off the floor and chucked it lightly at him. "You know what I mean!"

The rock struck his shoulder with no real force and clattered to the ground at the foot of their crude bed. "I know what you meant to say." *I wonder if Kade's pissed because he felt it too.* "There was something about her."

"Something we need to forget," Kade said, his words harsh. "We leave her alone. To live her simple life where demons are the enemy, angels are good guys, and what she's doing is for the greater good of the world. We keep going through the realms, and we get free. Seeing her today changes nothing."

An uncomfortable silence stretched between them.

Which, of course, was broken by Ryder. "Or we get out, find her, and teach her what it feels like to share a bed with the three of us."

The idea made a shudder run through Alec's body. *Even with this connection, even if we could hide what we are from her, is there any world where we can be with such a woman?*

A cruel but logical thought answered almost immediately. *No.*

He sighed, running a hand through his dark hair. "Unfortunately, I'm with Kade here. The woman ran from us. She didn't want us. So seeing her changes nothing."

Opening his mouth to say more, he felt a wave ripple over him. *Whoa.*

"What the hell was that?" Kade asked, frowning.

Alec moved without thinking, striding out of their cave, and climbing up the tunnel to exit out into the open demon realm. The vicious suns beat down on him, but he didn't care. He moved as if pulled by a powerful magnet.

He heard his brothers following closely behind.

Weaving through the horde of lower level demons, one hissed at him and he growled, sending the other creatures scrambling out of his way. Because he and his brothers were so powerful the darn things treated them like kings. But they were only staying there just long enough to recharge their powers before going to the crossing point. Otherwise, the Enforcers would sense them and send them right back to the lowest level.

Dealing with the creatures was annoying. Being treated as kings... not so much.

Another ripple ran through him, and he adjusted his direction.

The sense of being pulled intensified. It hummed of desperation and need, but also, something he hadn't felt in so long. A raw kind of loneliness that called to him.

At last, he froze. It took him a second to see the shimmering object in the white sands. Kneeling down, he plucked the gold ring up.

Instantly, he knew that it belonged to the woman. And she was calling to them.

Fuck. Arousal uncurled within him. So overwhelmingly powerful that he knew if he didn't take the woman soon, he would lose his mind.

He stood, and reluctantly allowed each of his brothers to hold the ring.

"What does this mean?" Ryder asked, his voice filled with awe.

It took Alec a moment to find his voice. "Normally, we could use the ring to bring her back to this world. To obey us. To allow us back to the human realm."

"But..." Ryder handed the ring back to him.

"Because she's calling for us, all we have to do is respond."

"So respond!" Ryder's expression filled with hope. "I've never been this turned on in my life. I'm not sure if she's sending me images of what she wants me to do to her, or if they're my own fantasies, but," he shuddered, "I need her. Now."

Kade closed his hand over the ring. "Are we sure about this? Responding to her could put her in danger." His breathing was hard. And even though Alec could tell he was trying to hide his need, it was clearly written in the hard lines of his face.

Alec jerked his hand away. "What danger? We have a plan—"

"I can't believe both of you could be this stupid!" Kade shouted, suddenly furious. "Don't you recognize her? Don't you realize who she is?"

Alec's entire body tensed. "Who?"

"Sharen!" Kade exclaimed.

An image came to him, of a human woman named Elaina trapped within a realm, begging for their help in getting home to her husband. And of the three demons who must be missing her, their friends.

Damn it. Their simple plan just got a hell of a lot more complicated.

5

Sharen opened her eyes sleepily and moaned softly as she ran her hand along the hard, muscular chest beneath her hand. *Muscular chest?*

Shooting into a sitting position, she stared around herself in confusion. She was no longer in her room, but a massive, bright cave of some kind. Looking down she realized that she was lying in a bed.

With the three Level 10 demons from the realm.

Her words caught in her throat. They were naked. Erect. And smiling at her.

They also didn't look nearly as frightening as they had before. The red-tint of their skin had faded, looking more tan than bright red. And rather than radiating an animalist need, they almost seemed casually relaxed.

It made absolutely no sense.

"What is this?" she asked, in total shock.

One of them smiled, a smile that was full of mischief. "It's just a dream, my love. I'm Alec, by the way."

Her breathing came faster and faster as her gaze moved

down his muscular chest to his long, thick cock. She had partied a bit in her younger days, but she'd never seen a cock as big as his. She swallowed, unable to explain the heat awakening within her body.

Beside him, another demon spoke. "I'm Kade."

He was slightly thinner than Alec, but it was immediately clear that they were twins. The same dark hair and dark eyes. The same face that looked chiseled by some horny woman.

"I felt your stare in our realm. I knew you wanted us. Have you ever had sex with a demon, demon-hunter?" Alec asked, cocking a brow.

She shook her head, unable to speak.

The third demon, his hair slightly paler around his horns, and his face kinder... softer in a strange way, but obviously their brother, ran a hand along her arm. "I'm Ryder, what's your name?"

It took her a long minute to force the word past her lips. "Sharen."

He titled his head. "Sharen, have you ever had a man worship you? Do anything for you?"

Her answer came easily. "No."

"Have you ever wanted one to?"

She nibbled her bottom lip. "I imagine that's why I'm having this dream. Because I'm lonely. And the reason you're all saying exactly what I want to hear is because... well, that's what happens in dreams."

Alec leaned up and cupped her bare breasts.

She gasped, realizing for the first time that she was naked.

"Then, take what you want from us, sweet human. That's what we're here for."

Her insides clenched. It felt wrong. Even in a dream. Mingling with demons was trouble.

When he leaned forward and sucked on her nipple, all logic died. It felt so damn good to be touched like this. She ran her fingers through his hair and clenched his horn, pulling him closer.

He murmured in satisfaction and sucked harder.

Kade leaned forward next and took her other nipple in his mouth. She grasped him as well, and held them close to her, overwhelmed by emotion. *It's been so long since someone made me feel... desired.*

Ryder moved behind her. He shifted her kneeling legs further apart and reached under her, his large hand cupping her womanhood.

She held her breath.

Very slowly, he parted her. His stroking shockingly gentle. Patient. As if he had all the time in the world.

She felt herself growing wetter. Her muscles tensing. When she began to grind against the hand that stroked her, a finger entered her core.

She moaned. Wanting more. Needing more.

Alec moved his mouth from her breast, and their eyes met.

He stroked her hair gently back from her face. "Let us make love to you."

She couldn't look away. He was so beautiful. There was a power beneath his skin that drew her to him like a moth to a flame. And yet, she couldn't think of a better way to go, no matter the danger.

Nodding, she tried not to think about what it would be like to have three massive demons inside of her. This was a dream. She could explore her inner-desires without consequence. She refused to be afraid here.

Alec lay down and pulled her on top of him. He was so hard beneath her hands. Every inch of his flesh was delicious muscle. She touched him, her fingertips grazing his nipples.

He tensed, watching her hungrily.

"You like that?" she whispered.

Leaning down, she took one of his nipples into her mouth and sucked. He groaned and thrashed beneath her.

His hands clutched her ass cheeks, pulling her harder against his erection. He spread her further apart, and his shaft began to rub in the outer folds of her wetness.

She shuddered and her lips broke from his nipple. "Alec... it's been too long. I... I can't handle that."

In response, he kissed her. His mouth was hard, demanding, desperate.

Hands gripped her breasts, stroking her nipples.

She bounced eagerly against the shaft that sent ripples of need through her body. It was so big. But she needed it inside of her. Needed to know what it felt like.

When she sensed one of the demons behind her, she was shocked when his finger began to stroke her ass. Breaking the kiss, she turned to see Ryder kneeling behind her on the bed. His grin wicked.

"Have you ever had a man in here?"

She shivered with anticipation. "Yes."

His eyes darkened. "I may have to kill that man."

One of his fingers moved inside of her, and she gasped. "Oh, God..."

As he plunged in further and further, sending the muscles in her ass tightening in protest, he spoke softly. "For now on, this is for me and only me. Understand?"

She nodded, overwhelmed by the possessiveness in his voice.

"You will never be lonely again, Sharen. You will never want for anything again."

A second finger joined the first, and she found herself shifting to take him deeper. The promises in this demon's eyes... they were things she wanted to feel. To explore.

Someone touched her cheek. She turned, meeting Kade's gaze.

"How many men have you fucked in your life?"

She shivered, bouncing against the fingers buried in her ass and the shaft rubbing in her wetness. "Enough."

He chuckled. "And did all these men satisfy you?"

She was breathing hard. "Not even close."

"Would you like to be ours? To share our bed and us each night? We would always ensure you were satisfied."

She groaned as Ryder shoved another finger inside her, and her answer came easily, "Yes."

His gaze darkened. "Then open your mouth, sweet Sharen. Take me deep. Deeper than you've ever taken a man before. I'll fuck that sweet mouth of yours until I fill you with my cum. Would you like that?"

A shudder ran through her. She was a demon-hunter. Used to being in charge. Used to running the show. But deep inside she knew, as much as she loved to kick ass at her job, she wanted nothing more than to feel safe, loved, and possessed in her personal life. She'd always wanted an alpha man. A man who threw her on the bed and fucked her until she couldn't walk.

And these demons? These demons could give her exactly that.

"Yes." She parted her lips and watched in fascination as he rose to his knees and positioned his long, thick shaft close to her mouth. It was hairless and absolutely delicious looking.

He wrapped his hand into the back of her hair and pulled her close. Gripping his shaft in the other hand, he ran his tip along her lips, painting them with his precum. She trembled with a need to take him deep in her mouth. But he moved slowly, only putting his tip inside. Not caring, she sucked his head, drawing a groan from him.

His hands wove harder into her hair, and then he eased himself further and further inside. His masculine salty flavor filled her mouth and she sucked eagerly. When she started to gag, he pushed himself deeper. She almost protested, but when she looked up and saw his eyes half-closed, his jaw locked, and an earth-shattering expression of barely controlled need... she allowed him to slide deeper and deeper.

As she truly began to gag, the fingers in her ass pulled out. She whimpered around the cock in her mouth, and then felt the slick tip of Ryder's cock rub against her ass. Tensing, she waited. Slowly, oh so slowly, he pushed inside her.

She almost panicked, almost pulled away.

And then Kade began to ease his cock into her womanhood.

Instead of being afraid. Instead of pulling away. She moaned and leaned back into them, taking their shafts inch by inch deeper.

Her eyes rolled back as they came to their hilts. She could barely breathe. Couldn't think. She was so incredibly filled with them. By them.

It felt... amazing.

When they slid back out and plunged back in, she cried out around the cock in her mouth. Her entire body shuddered and began to tremble. Her orgasm building with an intensity she felt like the waves of an explosion.

Kade began to plunge faster and faster into her mouth. She took him, watching as his expression grew more intense.

The cocks inside her followed suit, moving faster and faster. Their breathing filled the room. Her heartbeat pounded in her ears.

She gripped Alec's shoulders and forced herself harder against them, drawing groans from the demons. Her body clenched them tighter. A ripple ran under her skin, and she knew she was about to come.

She almost warned them, but suddenly, Alec roared beneath her, and his hot cum filled her womanhood. She gasped as his movements became frantic, and his warm seed coated her insides.

Her body spasmed, and then, she came. As she screamed, Kade came into her mouth, silencing her with his cum. She swallowed, lost in waves of ecstasy, and felt the deliciousness of Ryder as he cried out and spurted into her ass.

She continued to ride them, her muscles spasming as her inner-muscles clenched them, milking them of every last drop of their seed. Her head spun. She felt herself shatter into a million pieces of pure pleasure. Of light.

Time seemed to have no meaning. She was so filled with happiness. Every part of her body and mind relaxed.

When they rolled her between them and pulled the blankets over her, she finally looked up. Her body continued to shake, to twitch uncontrollably. And as she stared at them, their gazes worshipping, she burst into tears.

Panic twisted their expressions.

Alec reached forward and brushed her cheek. "God, did we hurt you? We're so sorry. It has been longer than you can imagine for us... we tried to be gentle, and we curse ourselves for failing."

"Sharen?" Kade asked, panicked. "Where does it hurt?"

Ryder swore. "I knew we should have taken her one at a time at first."

At last, her crying grew manageable. Around sobs, she spoke, "no, it didn't hurt. It was nice. It's just... just..."

"What?" Alec asked, his voice soft.

"It's been so long since someone touched me... kindly. I forgot what it felt like. And it's been years since I... since I... orgasmed. I thought there was something wrong with me. I thought that's why he left..."

"Who left?" Kade asked, an edge to his voice.

"My husband," she blinked through tears, sharing her secret shame. "He and my sister—" she couldn't finish.

"I'm going to kill him too," Ryder quietly promised.

"No," she shook her head, wiping away tears. "This is silly. Ridiculous. I'm a demon-hunter. Dreaming about sex with my enemies. And now I'm crying? This is insane."

The demons exchanged a look.

A long minute passed before Alec spoke, "but what if we aren't enemies? What if everything you thought you knew was wrong?"

She frowned, wiping her still-wet cheek. "But you are."

He took a deep breath that moved his whole chest. "Sharen, everything you know of demons. Of our realm and the angel realm, is wrong."

She stared. "This is just a dream."

He sighed. "Do you know what the difference between Level 10 demons and angels are?"

She folded her arms over her naked chest, suddenly feeling uncomfortable. "Demons are bad. Angels are good. It's pretty simple."

Ryder laughed, a sound that was harsh. "No, Level 10 Demons simply made a mistake they weren't forgiven for."

She shouldn't ask. Her dream was already strange enough, but she couldn't help herself. "What did you do?"

None of them spoke for a long, painful second.

Kade rubbed his forehead as if trying to chase away a headache. "We killed some men."

Her gaze narrowed. "And you didn't think that deserved being kicked into the demon realm?"

Ryder studied her. "Do you think it's always wrong to kill?"

"Well..." *Do I?* "No."

Ryder grinned. "I knew I liked you."

"Just know," Kade said. "The men we killed deserved to die."

Alec stiffened suddenly. "We're running out of time."

"Time?" Sharen asked, frowning.

Alec reached beneath his pillow and pulled out something. Taking her hand, he slid a ring, a simple band made of a metal so dark it was almost black. "This is for you."

"A ring?" she asked, frowning and staring at it.

He nodded and reached under the pillow again. "You gave us a ring, so we gave you one."

When she saw her wedding band between his fingers, her heart stopped. Every hair on her body stood on end. "I... lost that."

"No, your sorcerer left it for us."

She began to tremble. How had her mind come up with that? All of this was starting to feel too real.

Alec squeezed his fist around her ring and closed his eyes. As she watched, he whispered unintelligible words beneath his breath. When he opened his hand once more, three rings lay in his palm. His brothers reached for them, and each demon slid a ring on their fingers.

"Now, it's official."

She shook her head, goosebumps erupting along her skin. "Why does this feel so real?"

Alec rubbed his thumb along her cheek. "That, our beautiful bride, is because it is."

6

SHOOTING STRAIGHT UP IN BED, SHAREN CLUTCHED HER blanket to her racing heart. But as real as the dream had felt, her room was just as she left it. Instead of the acidic scent of the demon realm, she inhaled her favorite scent: vanilla. Her gaze scanned her simple window where early morning light was just streaming passed the white curtains, and over the end tables and dresser. Nowhere did she see a large bed with three sexy, naked demons.

It was all just a dream. A crazy, hot dream.

"I'm losing my mind," she whispered to herself, pushing her damp hair back from her forehead.

And I feel disgusting. Ugh.

Sighing, she climbed out of bed. She was still wearing her clothes from the day before and was sorely in need of a good shower. Stripping off the wrinkled outfit, she strode through her minimally decorated bedroom and into her bathroom.

Turning the shower on as hot as she could handle, she stood beneath the powerful stream and groaned. Her muscles were so sore. Her entire body seemed to melt as the glass doors of her shower grew heavy with moisture and steam filled the air.

She scrubbed her hair with shampoo and condition, then shaved. By the time she started rubbing her favorite vanilla moisturizing body wash into her skin, she was finally feeling more like herself. Visiting the demon realm always brought weird dreams, but never had a dream aroused her.

Freezing, she felt her nipples harden beneath the spray of the water. Everything about the dream was wrong. Demons weren't hot studs bent on pleasuring human women. And they weren't just a bit different than angels. They were the enemy.

Lifting her hand into the spray, she let the water wash off the soap. Her gaze moved to the dark band on her finger, and she froze.

A chill seemed to seep through her, straight to her core. She pulled her hand closer to her and touched the ring.

Breathing harder and faster, she felt her vision blur. It hadn't been a dream? Then, she'd really been in the demon realm. She'd really had sex with the three hot demons.

And she'd really left her ring there, tying them to her forever.

What will they do with that kind of power?

She sensed movement on the other side of the shower glass.

"Sharen," Alec's deep voice seemed to stroke her flesh. "We made breakfast. I've got coffee for you, but we weren't sure what you like in it."

Painfully slowly, she opened the glass door and stared at a man. He looked like the demon king, only his flesh was tan, and he no longer had horns. Intricate tattoos curled along his bare chest and arms. She followed the designs down to where they stopped just above his sweatpants.

"See something you like?" he asked, in a teasing voice.

Her gaze jerked back up to his face. "How—how is this possible? You can't be here. You're a demon. You're—"

"Sweetheart," he moved closer to her. "I know this is a lot to take. We were going to give you more time, but when you reached out to us through your dream last night, we couldn't refuse you. Our beautiful bride needed us, and God knows we needed you."

She shook her head, wrapping her arms around herself. "No, I didn't call for you."

He frowned. "You were lonely. You wanted a life surrounded by people who loved you. Your soul called to us, and luckily for your forgotten ring, we were able to answer your call."

"I'm a demon-hunter," she said, her voice taking on an angry edge. "Don't you think I'll tell someone? Aren't you afraid I'll kill you?"

His frown pulled into a slight smile. "Not even a little bit. Now, if you don't want to experience round two of last night, better get dressed before my brothers see you. We have a lot to talk about."

"Like what the hell this is?"

"I wish, but no. We need to talk about your friend, Elaina."

She stiffened. *What did he know about her best friend's death?*

"Why do you want to talk to me about her?"

He stared. "Because she said you were the one person we could trust to help. And the one person who could save her."

Her stomach twisted. "Save her? How can I save her? She's dead."

"Is that what they told you?" There was an edge to his

voice that was almost frightening. "No, she's not dead. But they did trap her in a demon realm."

Could Elaina really be alive?

"Who trapped her in a demon realm? And how do you know she's not dead?"

He stared. "Because her husbands are still here in the human realm desperately trying to save her. And, because we've seen her and spoken to her. Apparently, your superiors suspected she was involved with demons. They didn't realize that her husbands were demons, but their suspicions were enough to exile her. But she's running out of time. We need to get her out of there, before it's too late."

This could all be a trap.

Demons can never be trusted.

So why do I believe him?

"I'm going to get dressed, and then you're going to tell me everything. And I mean *everything*."

I just hope I'm not making the worst mistake of my life.

And yet, staring at the beautiful demon, she was pretty sure if she was making a mistake, it would be worth any price she paid.

7

HOLD IT TOGETHER, DAMN IT!

Sharen stared at her reflection in the bathroom mirror, getting angrier the paler she became. *Do not fall apart, or I swear...*

Or what? She took her hands off the sink and tugged her white towel closer before it could fall. Was she really threatening herself?

Great. I've completely lost my mind.

But with every second that passed, her heartbeat seemed to fill her ears more, and her head felt lighter.

I've made the biggest mistake of my life... I brought demons into this realm. And I have no idea how to fix this.

The demon named Alec knocked at the bathroom door, his deep voice running down her spine like fingertips. "You sure you're okay, sweetheart?"

She forced a response past her lips. "Yes."

"As soon as you're dressed, breakfast is ready."

A demon is making me breakfast. Strike that, three demons are making me breakfast.

Don't freak out. "Okay."

After a few seconds, she sensed that he'd left. Dropping her towel, she dressed without thinking. Her hands shaking so hard it took her three tries just to get her shorts on.

These demons have my ring. They used me to enter this realm. They own me now, and everything they do here is my fault.

Panic rode so close beneath her skin that she was panting, frightening thoughts flashing through her mind against her will. *Is this a panic attack?* She'd never had one before, but if there was ever a time for one, this was it.

The dream I had last night wasn't a dream. I actually had sex with three demons.

And it was so freaking good.

Doesn't matter! I still brought demons here. And the second I find out if they actually know something about Elaina, or if this is all a trap, I'm sending them right back where they came from.

Elaina. Her best friend's name calmed her in an instant. Elaina was what mattered, not all of this. She could handle three demons if it meant helping her friend.

It's the least I can do.

Picking up her hairbrush, she could suddenly think of nothing but Elaina. They'd gone through training together. While most of the rest of the demon-hunters were bad-ass "cool kids," they'd been awkward as hell in social situations. But while they never seemed to quite fit-in on Earth, when they were fighting demons, they were incredible. Confident.

While they might not have been blessed with true magic that they could use on Earth, they were incredible in the demon-realm. There, magic-welders became powerful through the knowledge of spells and the ability to focus, even in chaotic situations. And she and Elaina, they knew more spells than any of their peers.

Just two nerds killing like we were born to do it.

Beyond that, their combat abilities amazed others. No one expected two awkward women to be able to kick ass the way they did. But, they'd both had their own private reasons for always being able to fight as if their lives depended upon it.

Everyone knew we'd both become Leaders.

They'd connected so seamlessly that Sharen had felt like she'd known Elaina her whole life. They'd become more than friends, they'd become each other's family. And for someone like Sharen, a person who felt like an outsider in her own family, she'd desperately needed someone like Elaina.

And then I met my ex and ruined everything.

She suddenly realized that she'd been brushing her dark hair for God only knows how long. *Enough freaking out, Sharen! Time to put on your big girl panties!* Pulling her hair into a ponytail, she glared at herself in the mirror.

You're a damn demon-hunter, act like one!

Without her weapons or the magic she could harness in the demon-realms, she felt completely out of her element. But it didn't matter. She'd deal with this the way she dealt with everything: head-on. In uniform or out of it, they wouldn't find her to be some frightened human who'd let them destroy the world.

I have to keep it together, for Elaina.

There was a soft tapping at her bathroom door. Alec's sensual voice came, "you planning on coming out? Or are you going to hide in there all day?"

Squaring her shoulders, she put on the emotionless mask she hid behind in difficult situations. *I can do this.* Opening the door, she looked up, up, up into the face of the tall demon. He gave her a reassuring smile that transformed his face from dangerous into one that was sexy as hell.

Without his red skin and horns, he was without a doubt the most stunning man she'd seen in her life.

Swallowing, she tore her gaze from his eyes. Which was a mistake as it immediately went to the large bulge in his pants. Breathing hard, she forced her gaze slightly higher. His sweat pants were pushed so low she could see far past his eight-pack and down to a level that was so tempting it made her thighs squeeze together. And the sight of his bare chest, which was strangely enough now covered in tattoos, made her remember every second of touching him the night before. Every inch of him screamed sex. Even his tousled hair and dark eyes looked like a man who did nothing but tempt lonely women into bed.

No one should look that good.

Biting her lip, she remembered what it was like to kiss him. To touch him. To have him inside her. Against her will, her body seemed to heat up

"You thinkin' about skipping breakfast, sweetheart, and getting right to dessert?"

Her inner-muscles clenched. *Damn it. It's not like I've never been hit on before!*

She scowled up at him. "That's the worst line I've ever heard."

He chuckled, a sound that slid along her skin like velvet. "Can you blame me for trying? You were looking at me like I'm your favorite new treat. Which I don't mind, in case you were wondering."

Sharen felt her cheeks heat. How did this demon know that flirting was her kryptonite?

You don't know anything about what these Level 10 demons are capable of. Don't forget that. They could have all kinds of abilities you never imagined. So be smart. Stay calm and ask the right questions.

"Why do you look different here?" *Demon magic maybe?* She frowned. "Actually, you even sound different here..."

"Because the human parts of us are coming back to life here."

Against her will, her gaze slid back down.

"Want to see what other ways we're different?"

Her heart raced. "Let's just get this over with." Squaring her shoulders, she did her best to push past him.

He chuckled again. "Whatever you say, boss."

Instead of turning around to glare at him, she continued through her bedroom out into the rest of her tiny home. Ryder stood over her little stove, using a spatula to push the bacon around. On her kitchen island, pancakes, eggs, and even more bacon were piled high.

As Ryder began to hum, her gaze snapped back to him. He looked *too* damn good. Unlike Alec, who screamed sex, he looked like every woman's fantasy of a sexy down-to-earth man next door in his jeans and plaid shirt. Like Alec, there were changes about him since she last saw him in the demon realm. Not having red skin or horns was the first thing, but the second was that his slightly long sandy brown hair had been styled, and he sported a dusting of facial hair.

When he turned his baby blue eyes onto her and gave a shy smile, her heart sputtered, and her thoughts scattered. "Hungry?"

His question seemed to hang between them, and she knew he was asking about more than breakfast. *Don't let him get to you. He isn't just some melt-in-my-mouth, hot man, he's a demon.*

Who might be playing with the memory of your best friend to keep you from sending him right back where he belonged.

"It looks like you guys made yourselves at home."

Ryder had the decency to look apologetic. "We thought you might have worked up an appetite after last night."

A flash of a memory came to her. Of him stroking her folds gently as he eased into her from behind.

This demon was pure trouble. *One minute he seems all sweet, and the next he's just as much of a dominating alpha as the other two. I better watch out for him.*

He dropped the spatula loudly against the pan. "If you don't stop looking at me like that right now, I'm going to have to fuck you against the counter."

"I'm not looking at you like anything!"

He scowled and flipped more pancakes in a pan. "Alright, but I never want anyone saying my wife has needs I'm not meeting. Because, honey, I'll meet your needs any time you want."

Wife? Geez. I can't even think about that right now.

She hurried to the stool in front of her kitchen island and climbed onto it, watching the demons as Ryder cooked and Alec washed dishes. Both chatted cheerfully, as if this was their favorite morning ritual.

She felt like she was having an out-of-body experience. Before yesterday, demons were vile little creatures she'd made her mission to stomp out. To kill. And keep the world safe. Now, apparently, demons had become the best sex of her life. And her husbands? None of it made sense.

The truth was that she had no idea what she was thinking or feeling. For now, she had to put aside what the discovery of intelligent, and seemingly non-violent, demons meant to her and to their world because she needed to focus on her goal.

And because finding these demons means my superiors have been lying to me. Either because these demons aren't as dangerous as they led us to believe, or because they are even more danger-

ous. But either way, it was a problem for another day. It was her best friend that took priority.

There were so many things about Elaina's death that hadn't made sense. That had every instinct screaming inside her. But she wasn't sure if she believed the demons about Elaina being alive, or if she just *wanted* to believe them. She just knew that she would never forgive Alec and his brothers if they were lying to her about her friend.

Never.

Yet, even if she was angry with them, could she actually send them back to their realm? They defied everything she'd ever been told about demons, and she felt a connection to them that made no sense. It wasn't just that they were hot and made her feel things she thought had been long dead. It was... something... more.

Whoa. I can't deal with this right now. I just need to stay calm and find out about Elaina. The rest can wait.

Instead of pelting them with difficult questions, she decided her best bet was to play it cool. Start slow. So, she reached for the pancakes, and piled scrambled eggs onto her plate, then grabbed the crispy bacon and started eating.

"So, where's your brother?" she asked, hoping she sounded nonchalant.

Ryder spoke over his shoulder. "Taking care of some business."

Okay, that wasn't elusive at all.

Alec sat down beside her and put a mountain of food on his plate, then used the syrup to coat everything on his plate.

For some reason, it intrigued her. "Do demons like sugar?"

He frowned. "No, *I* like sugar. I always liked sugar. And the crap they grow in the demon realm isn't exactly tasty."

She looked back down at her food and felt strangely guilty. Even though it made no sense.

Of course demons eat crappy food. They were thrown into a horrible realm for being bad people in our world.

Ryder smiled at her, his soft voice breaking the tension. "This is a nice little place you have here. Do you want to keep living here? Or would you like something bigger?"

She bit into a piece of bacon and studied him over the coffee cup that he'd placed in front of her. "Why would I need something bigger?"

He poured himself a mug of coffee. "Well, we all don't mind living in a cozy house. But it might get a little crowded."

She choked on a piece of bacon and started coughing.

Alec pounded her lightly on the back until she was able to take a sip of her warm coffee.

"You okay?" Alec asked, frowning.

The second she caught her breath, the words came pouring out. "What in the hell makes you three think you're gonna live here with me?"

Ryder laughed, a deep sound that made her nipples harden. "We're married now. What makes you think we'd live separately?" He reached across the counter and brushed the back of her hand with his thumb. "We could never be away from you."

She ignored the tingle that ran through her body at his touch and pulled her hand out of his reach. "We met yesterday. How do you even know you would enjoy being around me? Or do you guys not even care about that? Is this all just some sick game to stay in the human realm?"

Both men stiffened, but Alec was the first to speak. "Sharen, if we were using you to get into the human realm, well guess what, we're here. We don't need you anymore.

But we *want* you. We didn't have to pledge ourselves to you. But we all felt the same thing. The connection between us was so powerful, you were able to reach for us through your mind and bring us into your dream. A connection like that's rare. Do you really want to waste it?"

She took a deep breath. But couldn't think for the life of her what she wanted to say.

What's wrong with me? These are demons. So why don't I just tell them to get lost?

Suddenly unsure of herself, she changed tactics. "I want to find out what happened to my friend. You guys said she was still alive?"

But before anyone could answer, her front door opened. And Alec's twin, Kade, came walking in, carrying a TV. Kicking the door closed behind him, he moved across the room as if the massive set weighed nothing at all. He set it down on her wooden floor, and then looked up, his dark gaze meeting hers. A small smile curled his lips. "Looks like sleeping beauty is finally awake."

She swallowed. Hard. And tore her gaze away from his.

"How did it go?" Alec asked, his casual words holding a slight edge.

A hardness came over Kade's features. "We had a little chat, and the situation is handled. Oh, and the back of her car is loaded with the rest of her stuff."

Sharen stared at him, feeling confused. "Who did you have a chat with?"

Looking at the TV more carefully, her eyes widened. "That's mine!"

Kade nodded and walked over to her. Before she could even comprehend what was happening, he pressed a soft kiss to her lips. "Don't worry, babe. Your ex won't be bothering you again."

My ex? Oh shit. "You visited him? Is he okay?"

Kade folded his big arms over his chest and widened his stance. "Why do you care about him? He was an asshole who treated you like garbage. After last night, I could tell he fucked with you a lot, but I wanted to find out how bad. So, I paid him a visit. He spilled his guts about your entire marriage, and I got to tell you, he deserved exactly what he got."

Her heart raced, and it was hard to breathe. She hated her ex, but no one deserved to have their stomachs split open from a demon. Or their heart eaten out. "Did you kill him?" she whispered.

There was a tense moment when not a single one of them moved.

And then they burst out laughing.

Alec stood from his chair beside her and wrapped her in a half hug. "He just scared him a little, sweetheart. And made sure he wouldn't be bothering you again. Guys like that need to be put in their place. And Kade was only too glad to do it. Actually, we all wanted to go, but figured you'd need us here this morning."

She nodded, sucking in deep breaths. "You guys are acting like demons never kill anyone. "

Kade snorted. "Yeah, demons kill, but not half as much as humans do."

Shaking her head, she reached for her coffee with hands that shook. "I don't get you guys. Don't demons usually come to this realm to wreak havoc? Not that I'm complaining! But why threaten my ex? Why waste time with breakfast and all of this?"

Kade looked at the two other men, his expression irritated. "Haven't you guys explained it to her yet?" Before they could answer, he put his finger under her chin and tilted her head up. "We are back on earth to enjoy the lives we deserved before they were taken from us. And we're here, making you breakfast and scaring the shit out of your ex because you are our everything now. Our soul mate. Our wife. We will do anything for you."

Whoa. Why is it suddenly so hard to breathe? His dark eyes seemed to stare straight into her. It was strange that after all her time dating, no man had ever made her feel the way these three demons did.

Before she could respond, he leaned down and kissed her.

Someone set her coffee down as he pulled her out of her chair and into his arms. Her thoughts floated away as his hot tongue slid into her mouth, and the kiss deepened.

She whimpered, her hands moving to his hair, pulling him closer.

When he picked her up, their kiss broke for less than a second, and then he was kissing her once more, carrying her through her house. A minute later, he was laying her on the bed.

"Again?" she whispered, barely registering anything but that they were inevitably going to have sex again.

He leaned over her, his eyes even darker with arousal. "You're telling me you don't want us?" Reaching down, he brushed his thumbs lightly in a circle around her hard nipples. "I bet you wore this just to drive us crazy."

Looking down, she realized for the first time that the white tank top she'd worn had gone almost entirely see-through when she'd put it on still-damp from the shower. And her boy shorts without underwear suddenly seemed like the most ridiculous idea in the world. *It's been so long since I thought of myself as an attractive woman. Does this... does this really turn them on?*

The thought made something inside her come to life. She'd let her ex make her feel like an ugly, old woman, but she wasn't. And if she needed proof, all she needed to do was to look at the three handsome demons who seemed like they couldn't get enough of her.

She sensed the other demons as they came into the room.

Kade moved back from her.

She could've gotten up, but she didn't. Nor did they come towards her. *They're waiting for me.*

"If we do this..." she began, feeling her cheeks heat. "It doesn't mean I'm accepting all of this 'wife' nonsense."

One corner of Kade's mouth twitched up. "Agreed."

But still, they didn't come toward her.

It gave her time to remember what it was like to be touched by them. To be with them. She longed for that feeling of closeness, for a release from the tension that seemed to eat at her day after day.

Feeling her arousal grow, she shifted on the bed. "Uh, what are you waiting for?"

"Just making sure you're sure." Alec's gaze ran over her like a caress.

"I'm sure," she whispered, so softly she wasn't certain they'd hear.

But, they obviously did, because Ryder immediately pulled off his shirt and slid off his pants, revealing his massive erection. "We're going to make love to you now, Sharen. And you're going to enjoy every second of it."

His hurried movements were almost comical, but there was nothing funny about the need he awoke within her. Suddenly, she was imagining licking every inch of his hard, perfect body.

When Alec knelt between her legs and pushed her

thighs apart, she let him, watching with anticipation. One of his hands slid slowly up and pushed aside her boy shorts. A second later, she cried out as his thumb began to rub her wet folds.

He moved slowly. Unrushed. And as embarrassing and strange as it should have been, she instead found that she was rubbing herself against him.

When Kade pulled down her tank top and began to pluck at her nipples, she felt her orgasm building deep within her. His hot mouth lowered and captured one of her sensitive nubs, causing a moan to slip past her lips.

Her eyes opened when she sensed Ryder over her. Trembling, she reached for his naked cock and brought him into her mouth.

He made a sound, almost a growl in the back of his throat.

The noise thrilled her. Taking him deeper and deeper, she hummed around him.

He swore, thrusting into her as he gripped the back of her head.

She moved her hips in rhythm with the cock that moved in and out of her mouth. Alec sucked on her clit, and she cried out around the shaft that continued to pump into her.

At last, Ryder shouted, "enough! I need her sweet ass!"

There was yet another moment she could have protested. But instead, she watched as Alec and Kade stripped off their clothes. Alec lifted her and then sat at the edge of the bed, with her straddling him. His erection pressed against her wet folds. And without waiting, she wiggled, positioning him just right, and then took him inch by inch inside of her.

Gripping his shoulders, she paused, waiting to gain control over her senses. When she felt Ryder behind her, pressing the tip of his cock into her from behind, she felt a secret thrill. The night before flashed through her mind. As frightening as the idea of two men at a time once was, now she knew exactly how it would feel. She knew exactly how many amazing pleasure points would be pressed at once.

And she wasn't disappointed as his massive shaft slid into her.

All along she was aware of Alec already in her channel. But with them in each of her openings, she was filled in a way that was truly incredible.

When they began to slide in and out of her, she went wild. Kade barely had to tug her head down before she opened her mouth and sucked on him with abandon. She rode the men and sucked Kade like she'd waited for that moment all her life.

The incredible sense of them, filling every inch of her. Of their groans of pleasure. Of their loose handle on their control. It was all too much.

As her orgasm exploded, she rode them like crazy, taking Kade so deep in her mouth she choked around his girth. When Kade exploded into her mouth, she didn't slow. She sucked him as he dug his hands into the back of her hair, crying out around his shaft.

When she felt hot cum fill her womanhood and her ass, she finally tore her mouth from Kade and screamed, gripping Alec's shoulders as she rode the waves of her orgasm.

It was as if the world had faded into a fluffy cloud of pleasure. For too long, she lay sandwiched between the men. They fondled her breasts, stroking her nipples. They touched her face and kissed her swollen lips. And when a minute later, she felt the fires within her reawaken, she was shocked to realize that the men inside her were growing harder.

Her eyes flew open, and Alec's intense expression filled her sight.

He was fondling her breasts as he slowly leaned back on the bed. "Damn," he murmured. "I could fuck you all day."

As if to prove his point, his hands went to her hips, and he began to thrust in and out of her once more. Ryder did the same. His cock hitting her differently in this angle. The feeling was... more than a little pleasant.

When Kade turned her head toward his erection, she smiled wickedly and licked his tip. He cursed and plunged himself further into her. As their thrusting found a rhythm once more, she gave herself up to the sensations. Within moments, her orgasm was upon her once more. She came like a flash of lighting, glorying in the feeling of her inner-muscles squeezing the cocks within her until they were coming too, filling her with their hot seed.

When she swallowed the cum in her mouth, she collapsed onto Alec.

Ryder pulled out of her from behind, and somehow, the three big men were all lying on the bed. She leaned up and was amazed by the way they looked at her, as if she was something precious. Something special.

I'm in trouble.

8

THEY SHOWERED TOGETHER, SQUEEZING INTO HER TINY bathroom. It could've been comical, but there was nothing funny about the three tattooed hotties rubbing Sharen down in warm water. By the end of it, she was deliberately rubbing herself against their erection, until Ryder growled into her ear that they were about to go for round three.

That got her thinking.

As much as she might want to spend her time lying in bed, making up for years and years of bad sex, she had a job to do. So, she slipped on a bra, underwear, dark jeans, and a black tank top and went to eat the rest of her cold breakfast.

When the men were reasonably dressed, they all sat, or stood, around the kitchen eating like there was no tomorrow.

The food went surprisingly fast, and then they arranged themselves on her sectional, drinking hot coffee and regarding each other with open interest. Alec had pulled her legs into his lap and was rubbing her feet in a way that made her toes curl.

Ugh! Focus!

Pulling her legs away, and tucking them under her, she set her coffee on the table. "Guys, uh, as fun as that was, we need to talk."

Ryder smirked. "About how you'd like it next time?"

Damn it, she was blushing again. "No, about... well, everything!"

Alec chuckled. "Sweetheart, you know what we're doing here. We know you being a demon-hunter and all means you'll need some time to get used to the idea that we aren't evil and that we aren't going anywhere, but we can give you time. Alright?"

There were a thousand things she wanted to say. Like that the demon-hunters in this world might find them and that they could all be in danger. But what she should have been saying was that she would be turning them in. That *she* would be telling the authorities about them.

But somehow, she couldn't force the words past her lips. Nor could she tell them that she refused to be the instant wife to three demons.

I must be lonelier and more pathetic than I thought because I'm actually thinking about keeping these three.

That was a whole other issue, and one she had no intention of diving into at that moment. But there was something they needed to talk about: what had happened to her best friend.

"Tell me about Elaina."

The demons exchanged a glance.

After a tense moment, Kade spoke, his tone serious, almost annoyed. "You already know that Elaina is trapped in a demon realm because your superiors suspected her involvement with demons. What else do you need to know?"

Does this guy always have such an attitude?

She glared at him. "Look, just because I'm not calling the

authorities right now doesn't mean I suddenly think demons are the good guys and my fellow Hunters, the ones keeping the people of earth safe, are suddenly the bad guys."

"Don't forget the asshole angels," Kade muttered.

Asshole... angels? She'd have to come back to that later.

Ryder, or Mr. Hottie Next Door, as her brain had started to think of him as, phrased his explanation as if desperately trying to be gentle. "Sharen, the people you work for do some good. They keep out the really dangerous demons, but they aren't perfect."

She hated that she didn't immediately jump to the defense of The Universal Protection Department.

Ryder continued, running a hand through his hair in frustration. "The people you work for know more about the realms than they're letting on. They know what you've figured out, that not all demons are bad. They also know that not all angels are good."

"Is that what I think? That not all demons are bad?"

All three men studied her.

"I mean," she continued, choosing her words carefully. "You said you killed some people. Just because you don't seem like murders doesn't mean you aren't."

Kade raised a hand to stop the other two before they could keep talking, and his tone left no room for argument. "The men we killed deserved to die, and we sure as hell didn't deserve where we ended up, but there's no point in arguing. You'll figure this all out when you talk to Elaina."

Sharen sat up straighter. "Where is she?"

"Trapped in a realm," Alec said.

She glared at him. "You told me that. Which one?"

He frowned. "We don't know how you guys identify realms. We just know how the realm she's trapped in *feels*."

Are you freaking kidding me?

She stood, feeling frustrated. "So, I'm just supposed to believe that my superiors trapped my best friend in a strange realm and that you need to *feel* for it? How do I know this isn't a trap?"

"A trap?" Alec asked, studying her like she'd lost her mind.

"Yeah, a trap!" She put her hands on her hips. "The only way you can tell me which realm she's in is if I lead you into a top-secret area where we identify different realms? I'd be insane to let a demon in there!"

Alec stood, staring her down. "Then, don't! Do you think I want to get involved in this crap? I don't. I came here to live a normal life. Getting mixed up in this could get us all captured and thrown right back where we fought so hard to escape! We told you because Elaina's husbands are friends of ours and because frankly, we hate the idea of her dying like that."

Sharen stiffened. "Dying?"

The more they spoke, the more real it all felt... the more she believed them.

Reality was starting to come crashing down around her, making her muscles tense as if preparing for a fight. Instead of Elaina feeling like a ghost who haunted her, she was starting to feel real again. Alive.

And she needs my help.

Something within her changed, and she turned determined eyes onto the demons, waiting.

Alec's anger melted away. "Sweetheart, sorry, I shouldn't have said that."

"Tell me." Her words held an unspoken threat. "I already lost her once, I can't do it again. I won't, not if I can do something about it." She took a deep breath, trying to take the edge from her words. "Please."

Alec swore and sat back down, crossing his arms over his chest.

After a long moment, Ryder spoke, "humans aren't meant to survive in our realm. She's been eating our bad food, trapped in the heat, and hiding from the lesser demons. She's got another couple of days, max."

Sharen felt as if a bucket of ice water had been thrown on her. *Of course, Elaina can't survive much longer in the demon realm. It's a miracle she's survived this long.*

I need to save her. Fast.

Alec leaned back against the couch, his irritation clearly visible. "So, who can you contact to rescue your friend? I know you feel an obligation to save her, and we feel an obligation to our friends, but I don't like any of this. Our presence should mean that your life is happier and safer. Not more dangerous. And getting mixed up in this, it's the last thing we wanted for you."

"I was the one who said we shouldn't tell her," Kade said, crossing his arms over his broad chest and glaring.

She looked at them as if they'd lost their mind. "You're asking me who has access to a portal room and would break every single protocol to rescue a woman who is supposed to be dead? I hate to tell you, but I'm the only one."

Alec's expression froze. "There's got to be someone else who can help her."

Even if I could convince someone that all of this is true, no one else would be reckless enough to enter a demon realm without an entire team to defend them. Especially not a Leader. And only a Leader has access to the portal realm.

"There's no one."

Alec gave an angry bark of laughter. "Well, there's no way in hell we're going to let you go into a demon realm."

Her brows rose and her words came out, cold and controlled. "Who said you *let* me do anything? If I want to save my friend, you three aren't going to stop me."

Alec stood again, his expression thunderous. His hands curling into fists.

And yet, Sharen wasn't afraid of him. Deep down in some unexplored place inside her, she knew this man, this demon, would never hurt her. And the knowledge made her feel strangely confident.

"Do you have something to say?" she asked, trying to look as arrogant as hell.

He made a sound, almost like a growl.

Ryder leapt to his feet, placing his hand on the other man's chest as if to hold him back. "Let's just take a minute and calm down."

Very slowly, she rose and leaned closer. "If you don't help me do this, any chance of something real happening between us is gone. I'll kick you out of this house and never think of you again. So what are you going to do?"

But before Alec could answer, Kade spoke from his spot on the couch, his tone dangerous. "We can't return to a demon realm. It took years to manifest the energy to even reach the realm you found us in. We can show you what realm it is and that's it. So, if you do this, you do it alone."

"Which is not going to happen!" Alec shouted.

Her gaze met and held each of theirs. *They're not going to help me.* "I'll keep the secret of what you are." Their expressions remained the same. "I'll... I'll agree to be your wife." She saw her words hit them and knew she'd found their weakness. "If you do this for me, I'll give myself fully to you. But I meant what I said, if you don't, you'll lose me forever."

Tension seemed to crackle through the air like lightning. *They're demons. They have my ring. They can force me to do whatever they want, so I just have to hope what my gut is telling me is right. That these three want me to love them willingly, not by force.*

Ryder spoke after a long minute. "It'd be too dangerous for all of us to go to one of the facilities. But... I'll go with you."

"Ryder—" Alec's tone was a warning.

The other man spoke softly. "Her soul called to us. Because she's a fighter. Because she has the heart to love all three of us. A woman like her could never find peace leaving her friend to die. We can't feel this illogical love for her because of who she is deep inside, and also stop her from being that woman. You both know I'm right."

Alec's tough expression crumpled, and he turned to look at her, his dark eyes holding her gaze. "If you stayed with us, you'd be safe and loved. You'd want for nothing. Do you really want to risk your life now, when we've finally found each other?"

She didn't hesitate. "I don't want to. I have to."

Alec sat back down, digging his hand into his dark hair and hanging his head.

"I guess we can't just tie her up. Can we?" Kade said, the hurt in his eyes so powerful it took her breath away.

Ryder brushed her cheek. "If only."

For some reason, everything they said made her heart ache. These men seemed to profess their love for her so easily. All because of some connection they were so sure of. She wanted to scoff at it. To call them liars. Or hopeless romantics. But the truth was, she felt a connection to them too.

And if I let myself for one second think about what I'm about to do, I might lose my nerve.

So I just can't think about it then.

"At least I'll be there with you. Most of the way." Ryder gave her a smile that didn't quite reach his eyes.

Her stomach twisted. *Oh yeah, this isn't just about me breaking rules to save Elaina. I have to take one of the demons with me.*

If she took them to the control room, she'd be breaking every rule she'd ever been taught. She'd be risking her life, but more than that, if these demons were lying to her, she was taking the chance that they could cause complete chaos. They could use her and the portal equipment to allow a limitless number of powerful demons onto earth.

No sane person would take this risk.

But if they were telling the truth, and she did nothing, she was condemning her best friend to death.

So, the question was, did she trust them enough to endanger all of humanity?

9

WE COULDN'T GO TO THE SCHOOL DURING THE DAY. THERE were too many people around, and there was no way that the teachers and staff would fail to notice the massive Ryder beside her. So as much as it killed her, Sharen told the demons that they'd have to wait until nightfall to save her friend.

They didn't seem to mind. Instead, she watched them as they explored life as... human-like people again. She followed them to the backyard as they breathed in the fresh air, and even stopped to pick flowers and smell them. Within a few minutes, Sharen felt better than she had in years. It was like all the things that she'd forgotten to appreciate were suddenly impossible to ignore.

"Are you a gardener?" Ryder asked, kneeling down by some wild flowers.

She shook her head. "I have someone who tends the garden. With how much I work, there's no time to do anything. Actually, I'd normally already be at work, offering to tutor students and going through research about the realms."

Ryder frowned, his gentle blue eyes onto her face. "But surely you can't work all the time?"

She shrugged, feeling strange.

Suddenly, Alec lifted her chin. "Do you like working so much?"

It took a minute to remember to speak as she looked up into his handsome face. "I don't know. Sometimes. But a job like mine, filled with training constantly to keep my body in shape, training with my students, teaching classes no one appreciates, and diving into dangerous realms... it's draining."

He nodded and pressed a soft kiss to her lips. "I worked a lot in life too. I barely made time for my brothers, or even... even my sister. And I regret it more than I can ever say."

"Regret sucks to live with," Ryder said, touching the petals of a flower.

Alec moved away from her, staring out at the cloudy sky at her side. "If you don't want to work all the time, don't. Life is too damn short."

Kade breathed in deeply and spread his arms at his side, tilting his face to the sun.

She couldn't help but smile. "You guys really missed this realm, huh?"

Ryder set the flower down and ran his fingers along the grass. "You have no idea. But now that we have a second chance, we're not going to waste it. As long as we don't use our powers, the angels won't be able to find us. We can live a peaceful life, and this time enjoy as much of it as we can."

Wow. They're pretty damn excited just about my boring backyard. I wonder how they'd acted if we did something that was actually fun?

Suddenly, a strange idea hit her. "Do you guys want to go to the fair? There's one in town that I've been passing, and I kind of wanted to--"

"Yes," Ryder said, not even letting her finish.

She laughed, along with Ryder and Alec, and even the stoic Kade gave a smile. So, even though it seemed crazy, she loaded the demons into her car and they headed to the fair. There, she bought them a ridiculous amount of tickets. Being a demon-hunter paid damn well, but she'd never had the time or the energy to spend money on anything, so today she didn't hold back.

Like kids ditching school, they raced around as if it was the best day of their lives. They ate cotton candy, hot dogs, and a bunch of unhealthy things that tasted amazing. The guys played games and won her prizes. They went on rides and laughed like idiots.

And it was strange, because she learned so much about them so quickly.

Alec and Kade were competitive with the games, which she wasn't surprised by, given that they were twins. She and Ryder exchange a lot of looks that said they both thought Alec and Kade were being ridiculous, and it felt amazing to have secret looks with a person. Since she and Elaina had drifted apart, Sharen hadn't had that with anyone.

Not even with her ex-husband.

A strange memory came to her as she rode in a bumper car with Kade. Kade was driving, chasing his brothers around, and she was so happy that it felt like a strange dream. So strange that her thoughts wandered to long forgotten places. Two years ago she'd tried to convince her ex to go to the fair with her. He'd scowled at her and said he had better things to do with his time.

Sharen looked at Kade. The giant man was stuffed into a little bumper car, his teeth gritting together as a little boy crashed into their car and pointed, laughing at Kade. *Would I ever have to convince these guys to do anything with me? I doubt it.*

When they'd ridden every ride, and eaten everything they could eat, they made their way back to the car. The sun setting in front of them.

Ryder put an arm around her shoulder and leaned in, planting a soft kiss on her cheeks. "Thanks, sweetheart, for the best day of our lives."

She looked at him. *How is this man a demon? How is there anything bad inside of him?*

She wanted to ask him who the men were that he killed. She wanted to ask him why he and his brothers had killed them. But she didn't. Because even though he thought this was the best day of his life, she was pretty damned sure it was the best day of her life too.

As they sat in the car, Kade spoke, his tone gentler than before. "How dangerous is it to sneak into the facility?"

She switched the engine on and grabbed the steering wheel, her knuckles whitening. "This time of night, it's not very busy. I go in and out all the time, barely spotting a soul, and everyone is used to seeing me. I'm not worried about it."

Maybe she was nervous, a little. But worrying the guys wouldn't do any good.

Ryder stretched his hand out and took one of my hands off the steering wheel, then squeezed it gently. "I got you. If anything goes wrong, I'll take care of you, I promise. And when your friend is safe, every day can be like this, if you want."

Three demon men had stumbled through her dreams and into her life, and everything felt too perfect. Maybe she was still dreaming. Maybe there was a dark side to them she couldn't imagine. But the truth was that somehow all of those possibilities felt less painful than being alone, or even feeling alone with her ex.

It's a fact. I've officially lost my mind.

10

HOURS LATER, SHAREN WALKED DOWN THE HALLS OF HER school, her breathing ragged. The day spent laughing and enjoying life felt like a dream... and now the nightmare had set in.

Beside her, Ryder seemed to fill the entire hall with his massive frame. He'd hidden his tattoos under a grey sweater they'd picked up on the way home, along with dark jeans and black boots. In his new clothes, he looked like an incredibly handsome human, but he also could've passed for a Hunter. Which was what they'd going for.

But even so, she worried about someone realizing what he was.

The only way to detect a demon in this realm is if they use their magic. Otherwise, they need to cause trouble for us to find them. That was the thing that bothered her about her demons' plan. If they actually just intended to live normal lives, chances were they would never be caught. The idea fascinated her.

And terrified her.

How many Level 10 demons were walking around her without her even realizing it?

She typed in the code for her classroom and led him in without saying a word. He needed one of her student's badges to be allowed below the normal classrooms, and she was sure at least one student had to have left their badge by mistake.

Moving around the room, she checked in the desks and the floor. *Nothing.*

"Damn it!"

"Is there another way?" Ryder asked.

He was leaning against the back wall, arms crossed over his chest in a strangely casual way given that he was sneaking into an enemy building and trying to infiltrate their most secure areas.

"No," she said. "We need a badge."

He opened his mouth, but before he could speak, the classroom door opened. Rorde came in, his hair a mess. He was wearing the same clothes as the day before, and there was a franticness to his movements that worried her.

"Mrs. Bran!" He froze, wide eyes going between her and Ryder.

"Rorde, what are you doing here? You don't have class today." She moved closer to him, her gaze going to the badge on his shirt.

"I—I," he took a deep breath, closing his eyes. "I did something bad."

Oh, right. He was the asshat who left my ring behind.

She stiffened, realizing for the first time that it probably wasn't a mistake.

"Listen, Rorde—"

"I left your ring in the demon realm yesterday... uh, by mistake."

Schooling her expression into a calm one, she reached out and gripped his shoulder. "I think you might be a bit too stressed out because I'm wearing my ring right here."

She moved the finger that still wore the dark one the demons had put on her hand.

He frowned. "No, that's impossible. You had a gold ring. It looked the same as Blake's, and I..."

You've got to be kidding me. He risked my eternal soul to try to get rid of Blake, so he could move in on his fiancé? This sorcerer just keeps getting worse.

"Blake and Lily have their rings. I have mine. You must have gotten mixed up."

"I didn't," he said, shaking his head.

She leaned in and gave him a hug. "Why don't you go home and get some rest?" Pulling back from him, she put her hand behind her back and gave a reassuring smile. "The stress gets to us all sometimes."

His gaze went to Ryder.

Does he recognize him? Shit. I didn't think about that.

"But—"

"Get some sleep, and that's an order."

He hesitated a moment longer, then muttered, "yes, ma'am." Turning, he walked out the door of the classroom.

She let out the breath she was holding.

Ryder, to her surprise, was glaring.

"What?" she asked, feeling uncertain.

"Is there something going on between you two?"

Her mouth dropped open. "Rorde? He's a student!"

"You hugged him."

"To get his badge!" she exclaimed, holding it up.

His scowl deepened. "I don't like seeing other men touching you."

"But you don't mind your brothers touching me?"

He walked slowly toward her like a predator.

A chill ran up her spine. *Here's the sexy man beneath his casual boy-next-door surface.* She licked her lips, unable to look away from him.

Stopping just inches from her, he seemed to radiate a maleness that had her transfixed. "I like watching my brothers with you. It turns me on. But I don't want to see another man touching you."

She nodded, mesmerized as he leaned forward and kissed her so intensely that when he pulled back, she had to hold onto him or fall.

He chuckled. "Come on. Let's get this over and done with, so I can fill your sweet ass with cum again."

Wow, that's... hot.

Nodding, she clipped the badge onto his broad chest, facing it the wrong way so that no one would realize it didn't belong to him. Heading back into the hall, they passed a few students who cast Ryder curious glances but seemed unconcerned as they saw a teacher leading him down the hall.

At the elevator, she typed in the private floor below the regular school building and the sensors scanned over them before it started down. Ryder said nothing, his expression guarded.

Something strange fluttered in her stomach. *They're tricking you!* Her brain yelled, but she pushed the thought aside. Elaina would take the risk for her.

"What are Alec and Kade doing right now?" she asked, as the elevator dinged open.

"Arranging our new lives," Ryder said, a slight smile touching his lips.

They walked side-by-side down the empty hall. "How are they planning on doing that?"

"We've decided to run a business. To invest in some stocks. To make use of our... talents."

Why does that make me nervous?

"What talents? And where did you get all this money?"

He raised a brow as they stopped at the door to the map of the realms, and beyond that to the room with the portal door. "Level 10 demons can be very, very convincing."

She froze, her fingers hovering over the control panel. "Is that why I've taken you here even though every logical thought is telling me not to?"

His brow rose. "Sharen, if we were secretly trying to trick you, would I tell you about our ability right at this moment?"

The truth tumbled past her lips. "I don't know."

He sighed. "There's nothing more we want from the demon realm. If you want to walk away right now and forget about Elaina and just enjoy our lives together, we can do it. I'll go in a heartbeat."

Her hand trembled as she typed in the code. *God, I hope I'm not wrong.*

When they moved past the rows of chairs to the computer screen, she pulled up the strange spinning map of red, yellow, and green shapes. At first, she moved through them slowly, watching his face as his gaze slid over them. But then, he pushed her hand aside and started spinning through the shapes faster and faster.

"There!" he said, abruptly stopping the screen.

A large red shape stared back at them.

"It's labeled red." She took a deep breath. "That means someone went in and decided it was too dangerous to go back in."

"Or your superiors labeled it that way so no one would ever find Elaina."

It made logical sense, but still, her stomach turned.

Everything about this is wrong. And yet, when she pictured her best friend, snorting when she laughed too hard, or screaming at a scary point in a cheesy horror movie, she knew she could never live with herself if she walked away now.

She memorized the realm's number, went to the portal room, and typed in her code. When she entered the next area, she immediately grabbed her white suit and went behind the screen to change. Stripping down, the last thing she expected was to see Ryder appearing beside her.

She stifled a small shriek, but his gaze was locked on her naked body. Instantly, she felt herself heating up.

"Turn around," he commanded.

There wasn't time. "No, someone could come in. What we're doing is--"

"I need to fuck you. To touch you. It's the only way I can possibly let you go." He paused. "Please."

She shivered at the raw need in his voice.

"Turn around," he commanded again.

Her nipples pebbled as she slowly turned around.

"Put your hands on the wall."

She obeyed.

The sound of his zipper going down had her wet, needy. She spread her legs further apart and waited.

But she didn't have to wait long.

He moved behind her, positioning the tip of his cock at her womanhood. At first, he simply slid in her wetness, coating himself. She tried to hold herself still, but her entire body trembled.

And then, she heard the door to the portal room open.

Stiffening, she tried to turn around, but Ryder pressed her back into place.

Two voices, the familiar ones of the guards, came. They were arguing about some football game they'd bet on as they slowly circled the room.

She had to bite back a shocked scream as Ryder slowly slid into her womanhood from behind. One of his hands moved around to cover her mouth, while the other one teased her clit. He thrust in and out of her, faster and faster. Absolutely silent.

The fear of getting caught should have stopped her enjoyment, but for some reason, she only felt her body responding faster. The guards were feet from them, just on the other side of her screen, when she felt her orgasm coming to its peak.

Clenching her teeth together, she willed herself not to make a sound as her inner-muscles squeezed his cock so hard she felt him swell and cum. He continued to ride her, his hot seed driving her over the edge.

She came, silently, her orgasm shattering inside her body. Leaving her tingling and completely satisfied.

Collapsing against the wall with him still buried inside her, she listened as the room to the portal opened once more and then closed.

"Ryder, that was—"

"Incredible?" he nibbled her earlobe. "I know. Now, get dressed. You're going to get us caught.."

"ME get us caught?" She swatted at him as he laughed and moved back into the room.

Scowling even though the sex had been incredible, she dressed quickly. But even her scowl felt out of place now and slowly faded away. She wasn't sure if she believed in all that soulmate stuff, all the stuff about them having a connection, but she couldn't deny that some part of her heart had never been happier. When she was dressed, she put on the plain white shoes, dropped her ring into the bin, and grabbed her weapon.

She turned and stared at the large black demon-stone. All she had to do was draw the doorway and write the realm name at the top, and she'd be on her way. To a demon realm. Alone. That was labeled dangerous.

I need to shut my damn thoughts down before they drive me crazy! "I guess it's now or never."

"None of us would blame you if you decided not to do this," Ryder said, his voice no louder than a whisper.

She straightened her shoulders. "Don't worry. I got this."

"I know you do, but you can't blame me for trying."

Picking up a piece of chalk, she wrote the sweeping numbers and letters of the portal name, then drew the massive doorway. A second later, the portal opened, revealing dark crashing waves in the center.

Taking a deep breath, she moved forward.

Ryder caught her arm.

She looked back at his tortured expression. *He wishes he was powerful enough to go with me, and still be able to return to the Earth.*

So do I.

"You're really sure about this?"

The concern in his eyes, no, the pure love in his eyes, erased all her doubts in one perfect moment. "I'm sure. I'll be back. Promise."

His hand dropped, curling into a fist. "I'll wait right here."

Turning, she gripped her weapon tighter and stepped into a dangerous realm.

Alone.

11

SHAREN STUMBLED OUT INTO THE HEAT OF THE DEMON-REALM. The awful feeling of going between realms left her feeling shaken, but she couldn't let it slow her down. Instead, she armed her weapon with a powerful magical spell that burned black ancient symbols into her blade.

A spell few Hunters knew existed.

Reading does have its benefits. She thought with a humorless smile.

The arms length weapon almost hummed with magic, as if awakening from a deep slumber. In the light of the three suns, the edge of her blade looked extra sharp, and the dark glow that radiated from it gave it a nightmarish quality. She gripped the long hilt and moved it, rotating her arm as she gave herself a moment to grow accustomed to it.

Feeling slightly more confident, she inched away from the portal opening. *Breaking such an important rule feels wrong. I'm leaving the safety of the exit. Cutting myself off from escape. Opening myself up for possession.*

Her stomach twisted. *But I won't let that happen.*

Taking a deep breath, she wrinkled her nose. Sulfur

scented the air, so strong she could taste it. *Something I never get used to.* Her gaze swept over her surroundings, looking for any signs of danger, but all was quiet.

She inched further, staring at the endless land that stretched before her. Between the oppressive heat and the three suns, bright mirages appeared to shimmer in the distance. The landscape was white, like every demon realm, but with more caves than usual carved into the hills. The white-bulbous plants that grew in bulbous tangles gave everything an alien quality.

The caves could mean a number of demons live here. Normal protocol would be to proceed slowly and cautiously. To not attract attention until all possible dangers have been identified.

But this isn't a normal situation. If I follow protocol, I'll never find Elaina in time.

And I could become lost.

She shuddered at just the thought. Without a team to slowly spread out from the portal site, getting lost was a real and very frightening possibility. The only thing she could do to have any hope of finding her friend in a place that stretched out in all directions was absolutely reckless.

Please don't let this get me killed.

"Elaina!" she shouted into the silence. "Elaina!"

Moving slowly further and further from the portal, yet always keeping it in sight, she shouted her friend's name over and over. Nothing moved. Nothing reacted to her voice.

And so, she shouted louder and louder.

Soon, she would either discover her demons had told the truth and find Elaina, or she'd bring whatever demons had been deemed too dangerous to fight right at her. She was taking a leap of faith, and for some reason, she wasn't half as terrified as she should have been.

When she'd married her ex, she'd felt like marrying him

was a leap of faith. She'd told herself that love wasn't logical, and so she'd pushed every instinct to the side and married him anyway.

This time, however, fear told her that the demons had lied. Logic told her this was a trap. But her instincts? They told her that there was something real between them and her. And so, she was taking another leap of faith with love.

She hoped she wasn't going to come crashing down yet again.

Nearly thirty minutes had passed, at least that's how much she estimated, when she saw something stir from a cave forty feet or so in front of her. The entirely white creature moved slowly and strangely, half dragging itself toward her. She pointed her weapon at it and held her breath, watching as it moved closer and closer.

This was not a demon.

But she had no idea what it could be.

As it got closer, she caught sight of two bright blue eyes. Heart racing, she felt hope grow within her. When it was about ten feet away, she realized that it was indeed her friend, dusted in white powder.

Sharen felt tears choke her throat as she raced to her friend, and pulled her into her arms.

Elaina sobbed. "I didn't think you'd come. I didn't think they could convince you to trust them."

She stroked her friend's matted hair, not caring when she felt tears sliding down her cheeks. "I'm here now. But we have to hurry, I've already been here far longer than protocol allows."

Elaina pulled back, her own tears had made paths down her pale cheeks. She was far thinner than Sharen had remembered, her cheeks hollow, and her white dusted clothes were tattered and hanging off her tiny frame.

"Let's go," she said.

Sharen pointed her weapon in front of them and wrapped an arm under her friend's waist. Elaina leaned heavily onto her.

"The... food.... here," her friend explained between pants, "pretty sure... it's toxic... to humans."

As they moved closer and closer to the portal, Elaina seemed to move faster. A small smile even curled her lips. But then, when they were just feet from it, the portal vanished.

"What the—?" Sharen stared at the empty space in disbelief.

Why?

Her logical thoughts filled her head with a roar. *You stupid, stupid woman! You were the only one who knew they were demons! Of course they tricked you into their realm and sealed you in here! Now, you'll both die here, and they're free.*

"I can't believe—" The ground began to shake beneath her feet. Sharen looked at her friend's horror-stricken face. "What's that?"

Elaina spoke, her voice filled with terror. "The demons."

12

RYDER HID BEHIND THE CHANGING SCREEN IN THE PORTAL room, trying to keep his breathing even. Sharen was trapped in the demon-realm. She could be in trouble. He needed to open the portal back up and make sure she could escape when she needed to.

But he couldn't do anything with the two guards chatting casually just feet from him.

If they make me wait too long, I might just have to break their skulls.

He swallowed the growl that built in his chest. But panic was clawing under his skin. In life, all he'd ever wanted was to find a woman who could be his match. Things hadn't been so easy. His unique relationship with his brothers meant that they'd have to find a woman who not only wanted one of them, but wanted all of them.

And they weren't exactly easy to love.

They were demanding, harsh at times, and probably a bit too cocky. But with Sharen, he'd just *known* she was meant for them. He'd always wanted to believe in soulmates and love at first sight. But love after death seemed to be a hell of a lot different.

Their connection felt... like magic. Like something so powerful that none of them could fight it, even if they wanted to.

The guards continued yammering on, fighting about some game, and about who owed who money. Ryder's stomach sank further.

He'd been in his mid-twenties when he died. The memory of bullets ripping through him had dominated his thoughts of what it meant to be human for so long. But with each level they climbed through the demon realms, more memories came back to him. Now, all he wanted was to taste the crispness of a breeze, to lie on his back in the ocean, to feel the rain on his face.

He didn't want to be in Hunter-territory. He didn't want to be near a portal leading to the horrible place he'd fought so hard to escape. But most of all, every part of his being screamed that he shouldn't have let Sharen go.

What if she gets hurt? What if you lose her? The thoughts clawed viciously at his mind.

He could never forgive himself.

When the guards finally left, he leaped to his feet and hurried to the demon-stone. With his hand shaking, he picked up the Soul Chalk and wrote the name of the correct realm. In the doorway Sharen had drawn, the white and grey waves came swirling into life.

He dropped the chalk and drew back from the stone. Sweat beaded down his back. He hated this place. Hated to see the stone and feel the chalk. They made him think of pain. Of things he struggled to forget.

Come back, Sharen. Please, come back.

But then, a feeling came to him. A new and different kind of fear. It almost felt like... Sharen's fear.

His heart pounded.

If he entered the portal, he would not be able to return through it. He wouldn't have the power. It would shred him to pieces, killing him again. Making him return to the darkest, lowest pit of the demon-realms. And without his brothers, he might never get back to earth.

He'd never get to feel the rain. Never get to breathe in the scents of life, green and nourishing. He'd never get to surf, or swim in the ocean. And he'd lose his best friends. His family.

But if I don't go through, and Sharen's in trouble, could I really stand here and not save her?

He stood frozen, feeling his eyes sting.

Either way, he'd lose everything.

13

SHAREN TURNED AND WATCHED IN HORROR AS HUNDREDS OF demons came running over the hills toward them. She began to fire her weapon at random. Where she struck, a ball of fire blasted a deep black hole into the earth, taking out dozens of demons with every blast.

But no matter how many she killed, there were always more.

As they got closer, she pushed Elaina behind her and clenched her weapon more closely. They would not survive this, but she'd be damned if she didn't take as many of the fuckers out as she could before she died.

Time seemed to slow as they grew closer.

I gambled on love, and I lost.

I was wrong.

They always meant to betray me.

I was a fool.

The words seemed to circle around in her mind, and suddenly, a strong hand pulled her back. Ryder stood before her, his red skin glistening in the light.

His roar came like a thousand angry lions, and the demons stopped in their pursuit.

"Go through the portal! Now!" he ordered them. "This isn't my horde. They won't listen for long."

Sharen grabbed Elaina, but Ryder shoved Sharen through first. She went tumbling into the waves, the awful feeling of being stretched and pulled, of being too hot and too cold came and went in a flash, and then she was crashing into the chairs in the room. A few seconds later, Elaina barreled straight into her.

She helped her friend up, then turned to wait for Ryder to come flying through.

But everything happened faster than she could comprehend. One moment the portal was there, the next, Elaina was erasing the address above the door.

The portal closed.

"What the hell?" Sharen shoved her back, and Elaina hit the floor.

"He's still in there! What are you doing?"

Elaina caught her hand, which she promptly pulled free. "He told me to."

"*Who* told you to?" Sharen asked, grabbing the chalk with hands that shook and praying she remembered the right address.

"Your demon," Elaina said quietly. "He said he didn't have enough power to come back, so I should close the portal as soon as I got through, and then he shoved me in."

Sharen froze, feeling tears prickle her eyes. *Did he sacrifice his freedom for me?* "That can't be true."

Elaina stared. "It takes demons years and years to gather enough power to cross over."

"So... so how do we get him back?"

Her friend was quiet for too long. "We don't."

14

LIKE HELL I'LL GIVE UP!

Sharen went to her cubby and pulled out her ring. "I'm going back in, and I'm going to leave him this. He can use it just like last time."

As she ran back to the portal, her friend caught her arm. "Sharen, I have three demons I love too, but this is insane. That horde will have torn him apart by now. If you go back in, they'll just kill you too. Don't do this!"

There has to be a way to take on that many...

She froze. There had been a spell. In an ancient book. It was a dangerous, reckless spell, one she'd never been brave enough to try, but maybe it could stop the demons.

But there had been so many warnings in that book. And the pages had been stained with blood. As much as she'd liked experimenting with spells in her younger days, she'd avoided that one like a dead body.

And yet I've never forgotten it.

Perhaps somewhere in the back of her mind she always knew it was a contingency plan. A spell to try when death seemed certain.

"You're not thinking of trying something from one of your damned books, are you?" Elaina knew her too well.

Sharen shook out of her friend's grip. "Don't worry about it."

"This is insane. You can't—"

"I'm one of the best fucking Leaders in our school has ever seen. I'll kill every one of those assholes before I let them lay a finger on me or him." She headed for the portal.

Elaina followed closely behind her. "Just wait. Maybe he got away from them. Maybe if you go to his brothers they can find a way to help. But one thing I'm sure of, if you go in there, if he isn't already dead, he will be. Seeing a human female will drive those bastards crazy, and he'll have to protect you."

She whirled around and glared at her friend, shouting. "Am I supposed to just leave him there? Huh? Is that what I'm supposed to do? Just let him die!"

Tears ran down Elaina's cheeks, creating more lines in the white powder that covered her body. "I'm so sorry."

A flash of bright light filled one end of the room for one horrifying second before the angel appeared. He was a beautiful man, with flowing locks of hair, and intense green eyes. But in his hand, he held a dangerous looking sword.

Sharen stared, unsure what else to do. Angels fought the demons alongside the Hunters in the human realm, but she'd never been face-to-face with one before. All she knew was that they were powerful.

"What are you doing here?" Elaina asked, her voice shaking.

The angel's lips curled into a cruel smile. "Why, killing the demon-whores, of course."

15

His blade caught the edge of Sharen's weapon, sending sparks flying.

The angel looked surprised. "You're faster than most humans," he said, then a cruel smile twisted his lips. "But I'm faster."

In a blink of an eye, he used the broad side of his sword to smack Sharen behind her knees. Playing with her.

She crumpled to the floor, only just raising her Splicer in time to catch the blade he slashed out at her stomach.

Elaina was dragging herself toward the weapons on the back wall. Sharen shook her head. *She's going to get herself killed!* But her friend couldn't see her.

"You know, I almost couldn't believe it when the Director said a couple of Hunters had fallen for demons." He grinned. "I didn't think anyone could be so stupid."

The angel slashed out again, but Sharen rolled and climbed back to her feet, glaring at her opponent. *I need to get to Ryder. I need to save him in time.*

"And I can't remember anyone telling me, not in all my

training, that there were demons that could talk. That had empathy. That were... human-like. Why is that?"

He swung his sword around, as if to show off. "Humans aren't very bright. It's always better to keep things simple. Demons bad. Angels good. That's enough for your tiny brains."

I need to kill this asshole if I'm going to save Ryder. A fact that she was feeling less and less guilty about by the second.

But for the life of her, she'd never heard of someone killing an angel before. *Is it even possible?*

"Just let us go," she said, narrowing her eyes at him. "We aren't going to cause any problems."

"And I bet your demon husbands won't either, huh?"

He twisted his blade and struck, cutting a deep slash into her arm.

Sharen hissed, jumping back. Ignoring her injury, she kept her eyes trained on him, willing him not to look behind him to where Elaina was slowly sliding a weapon down from the wall.

"You angels think you're so perfect. But look at you, attacking humans is beneath you."

He scowled. "Sometimes angels save lives, and sometimes we take the lives not worth saving. You've killed enough demons to know what I mean."

Asshole.

Elaina looked like she could barely hold her Splicer as she crept up behind him and raised the blade over her head.

"Oh, and you're so innocent! I've heard all about how much you angels like to sleep with humans. To feel *alive* again." she accused him.

Anger filled his expression, but just when she thought he was going to attack her with all his strength, he turned around and buried his blade into Elaina's stomach.

Her mouth opened. Blood poured out.

No! No!

Sharen rushed toward her as the angel pulled his blade out of her stomach. She attacked him, striking, kicking, dodging... but nothing helped. He was just too fast. Too good.

Ryder was being killed by a pack of demons in the other realm.

Elaina was bleeding to death before her.

What could she possibly do to save them?

And then, it hit her.

I can die.

16

SHAREN LET HER SWORD TUMBLE FROM HER FINGERTIPS. SHE and Elaina had helped demons. They would go to the demon-realm when they died. And once there, Sharen would do everything in her power to bring her friend and Ryder back to the human world.

All she had to do was die first.

"What's this?" the angel asked, raising a brow. "Have you decided to give up?"

She gritted her teeth and nodded.

His awful smile returned. "That was the smartest decision you ever made. Because, unlike your friend," he looked back at where Elaina had collapsed onto the floor, blood still bubbling up from her lips, "Your death will be quick."

Fighting every instinct inside her, she curled her hands into fists and waited for the blade to come down onto her. But behind the angel, a bright light came and went in a flash.

He turned around, frowning. "Surcy, what are you doing here? I said that I would deal with the traitors."

The angel before him was a young woman, with long

golden-brown hair and gentle eyes. Unlike the male angel, her wings were a stunning black. She curled them behind her. But even though she wore a simple tank top and jeans, she radiated an ethereal quality that marked her as something other than human.

"Oh, Frink, I simply came to watch you."

His spine stiffened. He turned back to Sharen.

Her heart began to race once more. *This is it.*

A flash of steel, and a second later, the male angel's head toppled from his body.

Sharen looked at the female angel, eyes wide. The woman held her blood-soaked blade.

Their gazes met and held.

"You're on our side?"

The angel smirked. "A demon-hunter and an angel. Who would have thought we'd suddenly be on the side of the demons, right?"

Sharen felt dizzy with relief. And then Elaina coughed.

Racing to her side, she knelt down in the growing pool of blood around her. "Come on, stay with me!"

The angel knelt down too. "I can get her to safety and heal her."

Even though trusting her is hard, I don't exactly have another choice.

Sharen almost nodded but stopped. "Take her. There's something I still need to do."

The angel shook her head of long, beautiful hair. "Our enemies know you're here. They're coming for you even now."

"One of my demons is trapped in the other realm. I have to... have to save him."

The angel's eyes widened.

"He doesn't have the power to come back through, but I—"

"I can help you with that too. At least a little. I make no promises." She reached out and touched Sharen's chest. A golden light spread, glowing just beneath Sharen's skin.

"That might give you enough to bring him back here, but it'll be dangerous."

Along with my magic in the demon-realm, we might just have a chance.

Sharen nodded. "Thank you."

The angel didn't say another word. One minute she was there, and the next both she and Elaina were gone.

Hurrying to the door to the room, she used her Splicer to pound the control board until it sparked and the lights died. *That should stall them from getting in here.*

Turning back to the portal, she scribbled the name of the portal on the dark stone, and it opened.

Ryder may be dead.

The horde may be waiting for me.

I'm risking everything for a demon who I barely know. A demon my foolish heart thinks I might love.

But do I?

Taking a deep breath, she stepped through.

17

SHAREN RIGHTED HERSELF AS SHE CAME THROUGH THE PORTAL and into the demon realm. Her head spun, but she gripped her weapon with certainty. Ready for a fight.

Bring it!

But to her surprise, no demons attacked.

Her gaze snapped to the battle a hundred feet in front of her. Ryder, his blood-red skin shimmering with sweat, fought the vicious Level 1 demons with absolute certainty. He'd called his demon blade to him, and his dark steel seemed to sparkle as he slashed out at the creatures. Many died at his feet, but more quickly replaced the dead ones.

He continued fighting, but his movements were clumsy. Like a tired warrior. When two demons leaped onto his back, he staggered onto his knees.

Shit.

Her instincts screamed to join him in battle. To use her Splicer to shred the beasts to ribbons. *But even together, we aren't enough to stop them. I need to try the spell.*

Time to do something dangerous as hell.

Closing her eyes, she imagined the ancient spell, praying

it was as powerful as the book had warned. She had no idea what it would do, but hopefully, it would be enough.

It has to be.

This magic... felt different than any she'd tried before. She sensed power gurgling out of her, the sensation prickly. Wrong. But she didn't stop repeating the spell, no matter how her heart raced, because there was no other magic she knew that had any chance at defeating the horde.

Of saving Ryder.

Her pulse pounded loudly in her ears. She had to focus on the spell. Not on the hungry demons just a short distance from her. Not on the possibility that Ryder could be dying.

In her training, she'd learned that distractions killed.

And I'm not dying today.

Her weapon warmed in her hand. Opening her eyes in surprise, she watched as her Splicer glowed, a deep blood red. After a second, flames erupted along the sharp edge, dancing dangerously.

The blade seemed to pulse. As if it had a heartbeat of its own.

Whoa. She'd never seen anything like this before.

Taking a deep breath, she turned her focus onto the hundreds of two feet tall demons. The dark red creatures were everywhere, encircling Ryder. He fought gallantly. Even with demons on his back and his chest. Gashes covered his red flesh, and there was a wildness to his expression that said he knew he wouldn't survive the day's battle. And yet, he kept fighting.

Hold on, I'm coming!

Pointing her weapon to the side of him, she decided she couldn't risk attacking the demons directly, not with Ryder so close. First, she needed to see what the spell would do.

Willing the magic to obey her command, she fired.

Flames raced along the ground from where she stood, leaving a bright trail. Beneath the fire, the white sands melted, caving in. Black smoke billowed above the hungry flames, darkening the bright sky.

She took a step back, shocked by the heat, by how the heavy scent of smoke filled her nostrils. The demon world always felt so surreal. Like a nightmare. But at that moment, it felt more real than any other moment of her life.

As if the human realm was a dream.

It took the demons a minute to notice, and then the flames reached them. They screamed, high-pitch wailing sounds that made every hair on her body rise. The little creatures went tumbling into the abyss created by the flames, falling into darkness.

The demons attacking Ryder stopped. Their gazes went to the ever-widening gash in their world, and raw panic twisted their strange faces.

That's right, time to run, shitheads!

The flames continued to spread, melting the earth, and widening the cavern. And for the first time, she realized that she had no idea how to stop it. Or how to control it.

But that's a problem for another time. All that matters right now is that I save him.

Ryder.

As if he heard his name in her thoughts, he turned and looked toward her. Their eyes met across the flames. Shock filled his expression, followed by a terrifying desperation. He tore through the remaining demons and circled around the cavern. A few demons followed him, but he turned, picking them up and tossing them into the flaming abyss with a roar that seemed to shake the ground.

When he reached her at last, to her surprise, he picked

her up and pulled her into his arms. "What the hell are you doing here? And what happened to your arm?"

My arm? Adrenaline had almost made her forget the cut from the angel's blade. "It's just a scratch." *Best not to think about that now. What matters is saving Ryder.*

His hold on her gentled. "I told Elaina not to let you return. I have no hope of getting back through."

To her surprise, she felt tears prick the corners of her eyes. "That's why you were an idiot to come here in the first place!"

"I had to save you," he whispered against her hair. "But you returning for me changes nothing, if I step back through the portal, it'll tear me to pieces... sending me back to the lowest level of our realms. You have to go back without me."

Pulling away from him, she touched her chest, which still glowed softly with the angel's powers. "An angel helped me. She gave me enough magic to hopefully take you back to our world."

He touched the glowing space on her chest, his expression one of wonder. "Angel magic? I can hardly... why would one help us?"

She smiled. "I guess a couple of demons stole her heart too."

Behind them, a demon leaped onto Ryder's back.

Sharen cried out, and acted without thinking, driving her Splicer through its neck. The demon hit the ground without a sound.

She looked back at the horde. Most were still panicking over the growing flames spreading through their world, but a few were staring right back at her.

"We should go," he said. "Now."

She nodded and turned to the portal. "Our enemies may be waiting on the other side."

He stood straighter. "And the angel's magic might not be enough to take me through in one piece."

Her eyes widened. "Are you sure—"

"There's no other choice."

He took her hand, squeezing it in his much larger one. Something wondrous coursed between them, something that made her feel an unfamiliar fluttering in her heart. Looking at him one last time, at his stunning face, she sent a prayer that what she was doing would save his life.

That he would arrive in one piece.

And then, they stepped through the portal.

18

Sharen stumbled onto her knees, her head spinning. She'd gone through the portal too many times. More times than she ever imagined possible in such a short period of time. It left her feeling weak, strange.

Next to her, she heard someone hit the ground.

Ryder!

Turning, she froze. He lay on the ground. His eyes closed. His body limp. Even though the wounds on his flesh were already healing.

"Ryder?" Dropping her Splicer, she reached for him, touching the side of his neck.

There was no pulse.

"No!" Panic clawed at her lungs, but she laid him on his back and started CPR. Over and over again, she pressed on his chest, creating a rhythm she'd practiced countless times. Then, leaning over him, she breathed into his cold lips.

Outside the door to their room, someone began to pound.

Please, please, Ryder, come back to me!

Something unfamiliar warmed within her chest, and he

suddenly took a deep breath. Sitting back on her heels, she watched the rise and fall of his chest, wiping at a stray tear that ran down her cheek.

I owe that angel more than she could ever imagine.

"Ryder?"

He didn't respond to his name. Shaking him, she prayed for yet another miracle, but he didn't react.

Okay. I can do this. I can get him out of here.

But first, I need to make sure I don't bleed out. Her arm was starting to ache, and she wondered if half of her light-head-edness was coming from losing too much blood. Grabbing one of the white suits from a peg off a wall, she used her Splicer to cut it into strips and quickly wrapped her arm. Even so, the dark blood running down her arm made her stomach churn. *That's a lot of blood.*

Outside the portal room, the pounding grew louder.

Instinctually, she shifted into a crouch, picking her Splicer back up. The pounding continued, but the metal doors held. *But for how long?*

"And there's no other way out," she whispered to herself.

Scanning the room, she prayed for a large vent. *Anything.* But there was no other way out than the door. *So, I guess I'll have to fight them. I can do that.*

But she didn't have to just fight her way out, she had to carry the massive demon beside her too.

There's no way you can carry him.

"Logic, you're a bitch," she muttered to herself.

Reaching for Ryder, she forced him into a sitting posi-tion and wrapped his arm around her shoulders. "Moms lift fucking cars when they need to. I can lift one giant demon."

Clenching her teeth, she tried to rise with him. Several times they fell back over, but she finally managed to drag him to the door. Panting, she went back to her weapon. As it touched her palm, she felt a spark.

Freezing, she opened her palm. The angel's golden magic still glowed softly. *What does that mean?*

More pounding at the door drew her gaze. Hurrying back to Ryder's side, she tensed, watching as the doors were slowly drawn apart. On the other side, she caught the sight of a room full of security guards.

Shit. If only...

She imagined one of the first spells she practiced with. One that knocked out an opponent and left them confused and disoriented. To her shock, her Splicer began to glow a light blue.

I can use magic in this realm!

I really owe that damn angel...

A smirk twisted her lips. The odds had just evened out, at least a little bit. Crouching over Ryder's body, she waited until the doors were fully opened. The security guards had their guns drawn, but they parted.

The Director stood in the center of them. He wore a grey striped suit, his large belly straining the buttons in the center of his jacket. His thinning hair was combed back, as always, and his hazel eyes held a familiar hard edge.

"Sharen, *tisk tisk tisk*, I'm disappointed in you."

Do you think I'm going to play your game old man? Sorry, but I'm not your puppet anymore.

She tightened her grip on her weapon. "Why? Because I discovered your little secret?"

His large lips curled into an unkind smile. "We all have secrets, Sharen. Only a naïve fool would believe otherwise."

Her gaze slid to the security guards. "But you don't think humanity deserves to know that not all demons are bad? That some of them are more like us than even the angels?

That we have no right to keep them imprisoned in their realm?"

To her shock, he laughed. "Is that what they told you? Oh, you are a naïve, little girl aren't you?"

"You said they were little more than wild animals," she said, her voice rising with each word. "How do you explain intelligent human-like demons?"

He tilted his head. "Do you have any idea what the most dangerous animal is?" When she didn't answer, he continued. "Humans are. And Level 10 demons are more dangerous than anything you can possibly imagine."

Her weapon glowed more brightly. "I don't believe you."

His gaze slid to her weapon, and his eyes widened. "I know you're probably feeling scared and confused. You have every right to be. Level 10 demons plant ideas in your mind and feed them like a fungus. You aren't the first Hunter to succumb to their manipulations." He took a small step toward her. "Put your weapon down. Give us the demons, and you'll be forgiven."

She narrowed her eyes. "Is that what you did to Elaina? You showed her forgiveness?"

His confident expression melted away, deepening the frown lines around his mouth. "I won't talk about her." His gaze moved to Ryder. "I remember him... and he had two brothers right? The story of what they did was all over the news, but then, you were probably too young to remember it."

Her heartbeat sped up. *Don't let him get to you.* "You're changing the subject."

"You don't want to hear what they did." He was smiling again. "They ran into a room full of men and killed them all. In cold blood. They'd never even met them before."

She gripped her weapon more tightly. "You're lying!"

"I'm not," he said. "And that's what bothers you the most. You don't know." He cocked his head. "So this, Sharen, is your last chance to end this. Your last—"

She fired, striking him, her magic exploding out onto the guards like fireworks. Curling over Ryder, she continued to fire, even as bullets whizzed around her.

One struck her shoulder. She clamped her teeth down on a hiss and continued shooting.

These fuckers have no idea how much pain I can take.

A buzzing filled her ears. The scent of burnt flesh reached her nostrils. Still, she didn't stop.

She couldn't stop.

I have to save him. I have to.

Time seemed to slow. Bullets moved leisurely toward her, and she frowned, easily shifting her body to avoid them. *Is this the angel's magic?* She didn't know, but something seemed to change within her. To stir.

After too long, she realized everything had grown quiet. She blinked, as if awakening, and stared at the room full of guards. All lay at various angles on the floor.

I... beat them? Shit.

She rose from her crouched position. None of the guards moved.

No time to rest. They won't be knocked out for long. An hour or two at most.

Even though her legs trembled, she clutched her weapon more tightly and reached for her demon. *I can do this.* Dragging Ryder to his feet, she staggered under his weight, moving around the bodies as she headed for the door. But just as she was feet in front of it, the door began to open.

You've got to be kidding me...

19

LILY AND RORDE STOOD ON THE OTHER SIDE OF THE DOOR. Sharen pulled back her magic, waiting. She didn't want to hurt her students. The idea sickened her. *But I'll do it if I have to.*

Please let them just get out of my way.

Their gazes widened over her, lingering on her blood-drenched arm, and then moved to the room full of bodies. Lily was the first to speak, "what happened?"

"I have to go," Sharen said. "Before it's too late."

A painfully slow second ticked by.

Lily's hazel eyes flashed with something. "Rorde, help her carry that man."

"Man?" Rorde sputtered. "I told you, it's the demon from the last realm. It must have got her ring. She's under its control."

One of her sculpted brows rose. "Mrs. Bran, are you under his control?"

Sharen shifted Ryder on her shoulders, not sure how much longer she could hold him. "No. I can explain everything. But I have to go *now*."

Lily nodded. "Help her."

Rorde swore. "Are you two out of your fucking minds?"

Moving as fast as lightening, Lily caught him by the throat and shoved him against the doorframe. "I've trusted Mrs. Bran with my life a hundred times, and I'm going to do it again now, so you either get out of the fucking way, or you help us."

Rorde shook his head.

Lily made an annoyed sound and smacked his head back, knocking him out cold against the doorframe. Dragging his body in, she laid him down among the other bodies. With a cold efficiency, she moved and placed Ryder's other arm over her shoulder.

"My car's just outside."

Sharen shook free of her shock. *I knew I liked this girl.*

They started down the hall, huffing as they shouldered Ryder's weight. In the elevator, they hit the button, and Lily stared at her.

"Can I get a little info about what's going on here? Because I'm thinking it's a hell of a story."

I've only got a few minutes with her. And after she helped me, she deserves the truth.

Sharen held her gaze. "They've been lying to us, Lily. Not all demons are bad. Not all angels are good."

To her shock, Lily simply grinned. "Glad to hear you think so."

She stared in surprise.

The girl laughed. "Half-breeds understand a hell of a lot more than humans do about the complicated problems with labels, and the struggles of the different realms."

Wait... what?

"You're a half-angel?" Sharen asked, shocked to her core.

Lily winked. "Who said I was an angel?"

The doors opened, and they shuffled out on instinct. Sharen's head spun with confusion as they approached Lily's car. There were actually half-breeds running around? How was such a thing possible?

I really didn't have a clue about my own world. Not a clue.

They made it to a gray car, parked right outside. The lights were on, and rock music was blaring inside. As they made their way around the front, she spotted Lily's fiancé, Blake, in the front seat. They shoved Ryder inside, and Lily climbed in the front, while Sharen sat with her demon's head lying in her lap.

Blake turned down the music. "Uh, what's up? I thought you were here helping Rorde with some emergency."

How much does he know about all of this?

"Things have changed," Lily said, her voice too calm. "Let's head for Mrs. Bran's house." She looked back at her. "Right?"

She found her voice. "Right. Just turn left. It's a few miles down Main Street."

Blake did as he was told, but his eyes stared back at her in the rearview mirror. "So, what's with the... hopefully drunk and not dead guy?"

Lily spoke before she could answer. "He's a demon."

Her fiancé hit the brake, causing the car behind them to honk and swerve. "You're kidding me, right?"

The young woman shook her head. "Just keep driving. We need to get as far from here as possible, and we need to shut up while Mrs. Bran explains." Lily gestured at her. "Start talking."

Blake muttered something, but started driving once more.

So she talked, giving them the PG version of what happened as they bounced along the road to her house.

When she finished, her *very* abbreviated tale, Blake spoke first.

"We're all going to be thrown in jail for the rest of our lives. You know, if they don't just kill us."

Lily laughed. "I'm going to have a friend delete the security footage, so no one will know you and I were there, except Rorde, but I'll handle him." She picked up her phone and started typing, while continuing to talk. "Mrs. Bran needs to get the hell out of town, but we'll be fine." Then, she set down her phone and picked up a paper and pen.

Sharen heard the sound of ripping paper, and Lily started to scribble something down. The car grew uncomfortably silent, and her thoughts started to invade her mind. *Lily's right.* When the Director and his men came to, they were going to start a massive search for them. Helicopters, Hunters, police cars, the works.

There's no way we'll be able to escape this city.

Goose bumps erupted on her flesh. *What if we did all of this for nothing?*

They stopped in front of her house, and Lily folded the paper and handed it to her. She stared at the girl in confusion.

"Read it when you get inside. It's important."

Blake turned fully around in his seat, glaring down at Ryder. "Okay, I can't just sit here silently any longer. That thing is a demon. We just helped a demon escape its realm. This is against everything we've learned. We've become criminals. And neither of you see a problem with this?"

Lily placed a hand on his shoulder. "We'll talk later. I'm sure I can help you—"

He shrugged her hand off.

A pained look came over her face, and then she glanced

back at her teacher. "Read the note. And don't waste any more time."

"Thank you," she said, shoving the paper into her front pocket.

Getting out of the car, she went around to the other side and pulled Ryder out, staggering under his weight. The second the door closed, Blake sped off. She didn't blame him for not wanting to be involved, but she hoped he came around to the idea that not all demons were bad. Otherwise, she doubted his marriage to a half-breed would work out.

Lumbering toward her door, she barely made it halfway before her demons came pouring out. They took the weight of their brother from her without a word, and they all rushed inside. She locked the door, and they laid Ryder on the couch, before turning to her.

"What happened to him?" Alec asked, his dark eyes filled with concern. "And what happened to your arm?"

She ignored his second question. "He went through the portal to help me."

Alec's face paled. "How is he still in one piece?"

Her throat felt raw as Kade knelt down beside his brother and bowed his head.

"I—" There was so much to explain, but time was ticking away with each moment. "Don't interrupt me. We need to pack and go."

"Wh—?" Alec began.

"I said don't interrupt." She took a deep breath. "One angel helped me. She gave me magic to bring him back safely, but I haven't been able to wake him. She also killed another angel who stabbed Elaina, and slashed my arm. The Director of our organization found out somehow, and he and his men tried to attack us. We escaped, but they should be after us soon."

Alec's expression was thunderous, but Kade spoke first. "We don't have time to pack. We need to get in the car and go. Now."

"Go where exactly?" Alec asked, his voice tense.

But neither of them had an answer.

Instead, she scrambled to her room and grabbed her duffel bag. Opening her safe, she threw her various weapons, a few daggers and a couple guns in, and her stash of money, about three grand in total. And then... she reached for the four aged books in the back. Her most precious treasures. Putting them gently in the bag, she felt a small measure of relief. As she stood up, Lily's note fell out of her pocket.

Heart racing, she unfolded it, hearing the sounds of Kade and Alec arguing in the living room. Scribbled in the note was an address, and the following words:

A safe place for people who know the truth.

"Guys," she shouted. "I know where we're going."

20

"You're sure we can trust her?" Alec asked, running a nervous hand through his hair.

Sharen nodded. "She's a half-breed. And she's the reason we got out of there alive."

Kade moved to pick up Ryder. "It isn't like we have another plan."

Alec made a frustrated noise and went to help his brother.

She looked one more time around her house. A home she would likely never see again. And then, she stared at her demons. In so many ways, they were still strangers. Their world was still a mystery to her, and why they had been condemned to the demon realm. But no matter how illogical everything she had done for them so far had been, her heart told her she was making the right decision.

They headed toward the door. Her hand reached for the light switch.

The smallest sound came from behind them. She turned, swinging her bag out in front of her. The angel's sword sliced through it, her possessions spilling out and crashing to the floor, just as her demons spun around.

Frink, the angel that had died just a short time ago, pulled back his sword. His dark hair moved strangely slowly around his inhumanely beautiful face. And his expression... it was murderous.

"You died," Sharen whispered.

Behind her, her demons set their brother down.

The angel sneered. "For the second time."

Alec shifted her behind him, and Kade moved in front of her. But still, she could see the angel between their massive shoulders.

"Angels are like cockroaches, you can never kill them." Alec's voice held a coldness that made every hair on her body stand on end.

A warmth crawled along her skin, and suddenly, both her demons held swords with blue flames dancing along their edges. *Demon magic.* Sharen's heart sped up. Every demon-hunter in the area would have felt their magic. *They'll be coming for us too now.*

The angel's green eyes flashed with rage. "We're cockroaches? You die and are sent to a world without light. In a pit in the deepest part of the demon realms. But you crawl out, don't you? Like an infestation. You work together, using your filthy magic, to conceal yourselves as you move higher and higher through the realms. And then, when you get high enough to pass through into the human world, you gather your strength. Or," and his gaze snapped to her, "you trick some weak-minded human to let you through earlier. *We* are not the disgusting vermin of the world, *you* are."

Alec roared, his skin suddenly shifted to a pale red. "And who decides if we go to that dark hole or to the heavens? What monstrous being?"

"You'll never know that, you murderous demon."

Kade's voice came soft and deadly. "Five men raped and beat our little sister, and they got less than a year in jail, 'because they had so much potential.' They didn't have potential. They were monsters who deserved to die. Our sister had potential. Our sister who faded away, terrified of the day they'd be released, needed to feel safe again." He moved his sword, rotating it in a way that made the angel take two steps back. "Killing them was the best thing I did in my life. And when their friends jumped us, and killed us, the last thing we deserved was to be punished for extracting the justice our sister deserved."

The anger in his voice, paired with his calm exterior, made her pulse pick up. Kade may have been Alec's twin, but he was a different man altogether. While Alec roared, Kade whispered, and yet, both their voices carried.

And now I know why they were sent to the demon realm.

She finally understood why she felt so connected to them. So safe with them. Old horrifying memories clawed at her, but she pushed them back, filling her mind with good images instead. Using the tools a therapist had taught her long ago.

I don't connect with them simply because of the night I was hurt by someone I trusted, I connect with them because we're all fighters. These were deadly men, just like she was deadly in so many ways, but they fought for justice too. Her horrifying experience at a young age made her become the strong woman she was now. And the moment these men chose to protect their sister, regardless of the consequences, they became warriors in the fight against evil too.

We're the same.

And now, I need to find some way to keep them safe.

Her gaze moved to the angel. "Did you know that's why they were thrown into the demon realm?

Perhaps their admission will mean something to this angel.

The angel smirked. "Doesn't matter why they were condemned there." He gripped his sword tightly. "Because I'll be sending them back."

She opened her mouth to speak again, but the angel launched himself forward. His blade striking Alec's. Instantly the angel leapt back, but Alec and Kade followed him as one. They forced him to move back further and further, and then they were all circling around her tiny living room.

Kade spoke, over his shoulder to her. "Get him to the car! Be ready!"

Her hand curled into a fist. Her body demanding that she fight too. Her training whispered a thousand ways that she could attack the angel, that she could hurt him. But when she glanced down at Ryder's pale face, she knew what she had to do.

Grabbing one of her daggers from the mess of her belongings, she clutched it tightly in her hand, and shoved her money in her front pocket. Glancing at her books, she promised herself that she'd find a way to take them with her. Then, she struggled yet again to heft Ryder onto her shoulders. Breathing hard, she grabbed her keys off the ring on the wall and opened the door.

As she stumbled down the sidewalk to her sleek blue car, she heard the sounds of a battle behind her. Metal clashing against metal. Heavy breathing. And cursing.

Can they defeat an angel? Is such a thing even possible?

Clicking a button, she started her car, and then hit the button next to it to unlock the doors. Shoving Ryder as carefully as she could into the back, she closed the door.

Which was exactly when her phone rang.

Pulling it out of her back pocket, it was her friend within the department. *Vanessa.* Fingers trembling, she accepted the call.

"Sharen, run!"

"Why?" she asked, ice trailing down her spine.

"They've sensed powerful demon magic near your home. The Hunters are closing in, but they're still minutes away. You need to get out of there."

Without responding, she ended the call.

Pulling her dagger from her sheath, she raced for her house, heart pounding. Inside, her demons were wounded. Deep red blood darkened Alec's chest, and Kade's leg was slashed in multiple places. The angel was in no better shape, but she didn't give a shit about him.

Gripping her weapon, sweat trickling down her back, she crept forward. And then, she leapt onto her enemy's back. The angel stiffened as she took her dagger and slid it across the creature's throat.

Jumping back, she rolled and held her dagger out in front of her, prepared to defend herself from his attack. Her pulse raced as Alec moved to the angel, and with a flick of his wrist, severed the angel's head from his body.

A second later, Kade lifted her into his arms, crushing her to his chest.

"What were you thinking?" Alec asked, but his voice was filled with fear, and wonder, not anger.

Tears stung her eyes. "The demon-hunters are closing in. If we don't go now, we won't get out."

Kade released her, and Alec's gaze met hers, a thousand unspoken words in his eyes. She nodded, and they turned and ran. Only, she slowed just long enough to scoop up her books.

In the car, she placed her books on the seat next to her, shoved her key in, and her tires squealed as they pulled from the driveway, heading for the highway. Her gaze went to the rearview mirror. The shadows around her house shifted, moving. Hunters who worked in the human realm were different than the ones that hunted in the demon realms. Most of them had magic. And one of their skills was to blend into the shadows.

She recognized their magic. In her head, she counted twelve Hunters before she turned onto the next street.

"Are they there?" Kade asked from the backseat, staring down at his brother.

She nodded.

"How many?" Alec asked from beside her.

"I counted a dozen."

"Fuck," Alec muttered, then hissed, shifting beside her.

Her gaze went to him. His blade, no longer glowing with blue flames, rested against his knee. But his hands were pressed to his stomach, his expression one of pain.

"We need to get you three to the doctor."

Alec met her gaze, and a strangely sexy smile curved his lips. "You happen to know any doctors who work on demons?"

"Not to mention," Kade added, "the fact that we have Hunters, angels, and the government currently tracking us."

She rolled her eyes, trying to match their light attitude, even while her stomach twisted. "I'm just saying... all three of you look like you could use some help, you know, before you bleed-out."

Alec shrugged his broad shoulders. "We'll live."

Flying through a yellow light, she raced to the turn off to the freeway. "Did you get stabbed in the stomach?"

"A little. But as long as we take it easy, we should both heal. It takes a lot to kill the undead."

She laughed, feeling the knot in her stomach loosen.

"What did I say?" Alec asked, a smile in the question.

"I just always thought of the 'undead' as, well, zombies, vampires, all that made-up crap."

Alec laughed. "Nope, demons and angels are their own kind of undead."

After a quiet moment, Kade spoke from the backseat. "And vampires aren't made-up."

She looked back at him, raising a brow. "I think we'd know about vampires, if they existed."

Kade gave her a defiant look right back. "Like the general public knows about demons?"

She opened her mouth, then snapped it shut. *He has a point.* "Okay, let's put a pin in that. What do you guys think are the chances we're safe now?"

An uncomfortable silence stretched between them.

"Babe, I hate to tell you this, but I don't think we'll ever be safe." A darkness came over Kade's expression. "I knew we shouldn't have come into your world."

Her eyes widened in surprised. "You didn't want to cross over?"

Kade looked out the window, his expression unreadable.

Alec reached over and took her hand. She watched him as the street lights of the freeway moved over him.

"We all wanted to return to the human realm," Alec said, his words slow and guarded. "But Kade wanted to ignore the connection we felt to you."

She watched the baffling demon through her rearview mirror as he sat silent in the backseat. "Why?"

Alec sighed, his handsome face twisting as he leaned back, and then winced. "It's confusing. You see, to reach the human realm, the perfect number of demons is three. In order to get past the Guardians at each cross over point, and the Hunters patrolling, one demon must always use his powers to conceal the others. It's too hard to conceal more than two other people. And takes a lot of strength. With three demons, you can take turns. While one of us hides the group, the other two must guide them. And at cross over points, one demon must use his magic to create a hole to slip through."

He took a deep breath and winced again, shifting slightly. "The thing is, most of the time when a trio of demons reaches a place that connect to the human realm they've bonded in a way that... unites their souls. It's why most of the time three demons share one mate. But with us, we shared women before we died. Becoming demons and working together to escape that dark," he shivered, "pit of screaming demons, was natural. We became closer. Our souls worked together in an even deeper way, but we always knew we would share one woman."

I've heard of sharing a woman in bed, but sharing a woman in life? That's new.

She looked at the dark ring on her finger, and curled her blood-splattered hands more tightly around the steering wheel. As strange as the notion was, somehow, it was her reality. She couldn't imagine a life without one of her demons. They were... hers, in all ways.

After a few moments, Kade spoke, tension lacing each word. "Yes, we all knew we would share a woman, but I didn't want to endanger anyone. Especially not the woman we would love. They disagreed. *Obviously*."

Alec glanced over his shoulder. "Ryder and I thought we could keep you safe. Just live a normal life."

The mention of Ryder silenced them all for a painful moment.

"But of course," Alec said, his voice barely above a whisper. "We were wrong."

"And it might cost our brother his life." Kade stared down at Ryder, a raw vulnerability to his expression that twisted her heart.

What happens if he doesn't wake up? She suddenly felt a cold rush sweep over her skin. Her mind ran over the short time they'd shared together. His touch still seemed to linger, not on her skin, but somewhere deep inside. Somewhere that used to ache with loneliness.

She felt Alec brush her cheek.

"Why are you crying?"

Am I crying? She looked at his hand. Sure enough, liquid reflected back on his fingertip.

"I was just thinking about Ryder. What if... what if...?" She couldn't even say the words aloud. This time, she felt the tears that trickled down her cheeks.

"Don't even think of it," Kade said. "He's survived a hell of a lot more. He'll survive this." But he sounded like he was trying to convince himself as much as he was trying to convince her.

Ahead of them, she turned on her blinker and switched over several lanes to get onto the loop that would take them on the right freeway, and out of the city. They drove around the tight loop, having to slow on the sharp turn, and came out... right into a complete shock. The freeway in front of them was closed off. Speed traps had been laid out, to shred their tires if they drove over them.

Screeching to a halt, her heart in her throat, she stared at the dozen black Hunter cars that had blocked off the road just beyond the speed trap. Hunters stood on the other side of the cars, guns pointed directly at her. And on the roofs of the vehicles, angels with pale white wings crouched low.

"Fuck."

Alec grabbed his sword from the floor. "Kade and I are going to take care of this. You hit it in reverse and get Ryder—"

Behind them, black cars came to a halt. More Hunters, in dark leather outfits, exited their cars. They drew guns, pointing them at their vehicle.

"What now?" she asked, desperate, her mind spinning as she tried to think of a way out.

"Now?" Kade said. "We turn ourselves in. We'll be sent back to the lowest realm, but at least you'll be safe."

Something squeezed her heart. "No! This isn't over!"

She tightened her hands on the steering wheel.

Alec shifted her car into park.

"What the hell?" she shouted, spinning on them. "We got this far! There has to be a way! There *has* to be."

"There isn't." Kade's voice held absolute certainty.

A desperate idea came to her. She looked down at her chest. Did she still have the angel's magic? She no longer glowed. But anything was possible, right?

Right?

I'm with you, a soft, familiar voice whispered in her mind. *I'll give you everything I have.*

But then a dozen unfamiliar voices chimed in, whispering *and me* as one.

Heart pounding, she felt warmth spread through her chest and into her limbs like nothing she could've imagined. The feeling was overpowering, and terrifying. It seemed to slow her pulse.

And then, her thoughts quieted and the world grew oddly still.

Allies in this war have lent me their strength. Given me their magic. I won't let them down.

She knew what she had to do.

An image formed in her mind. A way to channel their magic into something that was both powerful and destructive.

Thank you, she thought, unsure which immortal being had given her the idea.

Taking her dagger from the seat between her and Alec, she gripped the hilt. *I might not survive this. But my demons might.*

"Sharen..." Alec said her name, his voice holding a warning.

I won't let them send you back to the darkest realm in the demon world. I won't let you spend another lifetime trying to crawl your way out.

"You said we were giving up, so let's give up."

"But your dagger..."

Throwing her door open, she jumped out of her car. A bright light flashed onto her.

"Hands in the air!" Someone shouted.

She obeyed, moving slowly toward the Hunters, all of whom pointed weapons at her. The dozen or more angels rose into the sky, the sight of them breathtaking. Their wide wings were so white they seemed to glow. As one, they dropped to the ground in front of the cars. All had long hair, all moved with an animal's grace as they stayed crouched, staring through their curtains of hair with eyes that seemed to watch her every move.

Behind her, she heard the other doors to her car open. Instantly, the attention snapped to her demons. *Good.*

Reaching for the angels' magic, she imagined what she wanted. A tingle ran along her skin. A warm ball of magic grew within her until she felt it pulsing through every inch of her being. Then, it changed, shifting within her as if it was a part of her.

I can do this. The knowledge made her heart slow and her focus sharpen.

With a strength she didn't know she had, she drove her dagger down, slamming it into the road.

Like an explosion, a wave rolled out from where she stood. It sent the road and everything on it, including the vehicles, Hunters, and angels, into the air. They went flying, in all directions.

Shocked, she looked behind her. Kade and Alec stared back at her, their mouths hanging open. Their vehicle untouched. But behind them, the road was broken, gone, as were the vehicles that had blocked them in. Nothing but dirt surrounded them. Dirt, and small patches of black road. It was truly as if a hurricane had picked up everything around her, in a swirling mass, and sent it flying in all directions.

Moving on legs that felt numb, she climbed back into her car, as did Kade and Alec. No one spoke. She shifted the car into drive, and she started forward, bumping off their small patch of road and onto the brown dirt. She made her way toward their destination, trying her best to find the smoothest path. All along wondering when the angels and Hunters would gather once more.

But with the destruction her spell had caused, she imagined it wouldn't be any time soon. She felt a ping of sadness that she'd been forced to hurt her fellow Hunters. But then, Alec took her hand, and Kade touched her shoulder. In that moment, her heart seemed to swell.

"I think you might have some explaining to do," Kade said, squeezing her shoulder gently.

She opened her mouth, but a softer voice cut her off. "What did I miss?"

Her breathing stopped as Ryder slowly sat up, looking around in confusion.

Alec answered him, his voice filled with happiness. "Just the fact that we married a bad-ass."

Ryder rubbed his head. "Hate to say it, but I already knew that fellas. Now, where are we headed?"

She answered, feeling foolish as happy tears gathered at the corners of her eyes. "To a city called Shady Falls. To a new life."

Ryder collapsed back against the seat. "Well, I'm exhausted. Wake me when we get there, okay?"

She laughed. *He's going to be fine. And maybe, just maybe, we all will be.*

Her phone rang again, spoiling their happy moment.

Stiffening, she released his hand. *Whatever this is, I need to know. Even though it's probably trouble.* She pulled her phone from her back pocket, careful as she drove around another random chunk of road.

"Don't answer it," Alec said, his hand closing over the one that held her phone.

Glancing down at the phone, she saw the number was unknown. *I bet I know who this is. Maybe she can help us.* She ignored Alec, shaking her hand free of his, and clicking the button to accept the call.

It was, as she suspected, her friend within the department. "You're working with them." Vanessa spoke without hesitation, her voice a statement rather than an accusation.

The truth spilled from her lips. "Yes, I am. But I haven't lost my mind. Actually, I've finally started to figure things out. And what I'm realizing is that I've been lied to, for a really long time. And they're lying to you too."

Her friend, Vanessa, was silent for a long moment. "Why do you think we spent your life shaping you into the perfect Leader?"

Why doesn't she sound more worried? Or even shocked?

Sharen felt ice run through her blood. *Because maybe she isn't.* "What are you talking about?"

Her friend's voice came, cold and calculated. "Did you really think it was a coincident that the week after your trial ended, and they gave that piece-of-shit a slap on the wrist, you were recruited into the program?" She laughed, a harsh, awful sound. "No one makes a better soldier than someone who has been wronged. Who has been turned into a victim, but wants to be strong."

She can't actually be saying...

She felt sick. So sick she feared she'd hurl. "They arranged all of that?"

"*We* arranged all of that. And the best part? You never even knew what you were. You filthy, little half-breed. But I want to tell you, so there is no mistake, we will never, ever, let you go. So run little half-breed. Our Hunters like a challenge."

Then, the line went dead.

Alec snatched the phone from her, removed the battery, and tossed it out the window. His expression said everything. He'd heard their conversation, and even he had been shaken by it. Her gaze slid from him to the end of the apocalyptic disaster area she had created, and back to the road leading out of town. Her car bumped back onto it, even as her mind spun, turning over the psycho's words over and over again.

I'm a half-breed? Me? If what she said was true... what am I, angel or demon?

And how much of my life was orchestrated? My rape, but

what else? How many moments, how many friendships, were all part of their plan?

And why? What's so special about me?

"Sharen, are you okay?" Alec asked.

Something dark moved through her, replacing her shock with a dangerous anger. "Yes, but I've come to a decision."

"And what's that?"

"I'm going to take down The Universal Protection Department. And every one of those bastards."

21

ONE YEAR LATER...

SHAREN MOVED through the shadows of the city, her pulse racing. Taking a deep breath, she crinkled her nose. The air was crisp, cool, and tinged with the scent of rain... and coppery death.

Removing the cloth from her pocket, she wiped her hands and dagger free of blood, then put the cloth away. Instinctually, she touched her other pocket, relieved when she felt the outline of the tiny item that had been worth killing for.

Now, we have everything we need.

The strange warm spot within her grew hotter, as if to whisper, *yes, we do.*

She closed her eyes, stretching out her awareness. After a second, she breathed a sigh of relief. She neither detected Hunters or angels nearby. *Hopefully by the time they find the body, I'll be long gone.*

Continuing to walk through the shadows of the alleys,

she moved through the city undetected. Nearly an hour later, she came to her destination. The alley looked just like any other, except it held a secret.

Between two abandoned warehouses, she ducked down a short passageway that ended in a brick wall. But just before she reached it, she stopped and faced the wall of the building. Pushing aside one of the red bricks, she revealed a tiny key pad. Typing in her code, she slid the hidden door open and moved into the darkness of the room beyond, sliding the wall closed behind her.

Weaving through the boxes of neatly lined supplies throughout the room, she came to the big black stone in the center of the room. For a second she stared at its flawlessly smooth surface. Dozens of people had died to secure the stone. And yet, she hoped it would save hundreds of thousands of lives.

At least now that we have the last piece of the puzzle.

Going to the small glass enclosure before the stone, she typed in a different code. It opened, empty. Waiting. Reaching into her pocket, she pulled it out, her hand shaking. Then, carefully, she set down the Soul Chalk.

When she was a Leader, she never thought of how precious Soul Chalk was. It had seemed that there was a limitless supply of them. But now she knew better. This chalk was more important than she ever imagined possible.

Closing the case, she sealed it safely inside. A strange weariness moved through her. It was a feeling she never grew accustom to. Going to the other side of the massive room, she pushed open a doorway into a bathroom lined with open showers. The white tiles practically shone beneath the fluorescent lights.

"I guess there's one good thing about having a demon who loves to clean."

She winced as she pulled off her clothes. Looking across the room, she caught her reflection in the wall of mirrors. She was absolutely filthy, and covered in dark bruises. And big red marks that would soon be new bruises.

My demons won't be happy.

Shivering in the cold room, she went to one of the dozen or so handles on the walls and turned on the shower. Standing to the side of the water, she waited until it heated up and then moved beneath the jet.

"Oh yeah."

"I thought you were only supposed to make sounds like that with us."

She whirled around and stared at Ryder. He was wearing his typical clothing, a plaid shirt and jeans that hugged his incredible ass. *At least his typical 'out of the office' clothes.*

Ever since her demons took over a very successful company, they'd been spending their time bouncing between work and their secret project. She knew they were exhausted from it, but it was the only way they'd have the cash to fund their very expensive work.

They need more fun in their lives.

"Mind if I join you?" There was a twinkle in his eyes as he asked.

"Sure." The word came out soft and tired.

His expression changed. "You okay?"

She wanted to feel nothing but happiness that her sexy demon wanted to join her in the shower. But after her day, she couldn't seem to summon the proper emotion.

I can't let him see how much this work is impacting me.

She turned back to the water, lowering her head so that it could wash over her. Pressing her hands to the shower wall, she willed herself to forget what it had been like to take a life. No matter how much she told herself that killing an enemy didn't matter, it did. To her.

How can so many lives be lost in a battle the world doesn't know exists?

Strong hands grasped her shoulders and spun her around. Ryder's gentle fingertips tilted her head up so that she was forced to meet his gaze. For a minute, they looked at each other. Their mouths so close she could feel his warm breath rushing over her flesh. And then, he brushed the gentlest kiss against her lips.

"Let's get you washed up."

His touch was strong, yet soft, as he bathed her. He scrubbed her body with soap, and washed her hair. All while she closed her eyes and let his hands give her the strength to forget about the things she couldn't change.

A war I'll continue fighting, no matter the cost.

She'd communicated twice with Elaina since she'd joined The Rebellion of The Forgotten. Her friend was on the run from the Hunters and the angels. Always just a step ahead of them. And the angel who had helped them? It sounded like she'd been captured.

If only I could save them all.

"I think we should dress and head home," Ryder said, folding her in his arm from behind. His warm body curling around her in a way that made her feel safe and loved.

Her body tingled pleasantly as she opened her eyes. "But we finally have the last piece. We can cross over."

It just needs to be tested.

He smiled. "We can do it tomorrow. I think for tonight you should have a good meal, maybe a foot rub, and relax with your husbands."

That sounds, her eyes stung with unshed tears, *amazing.*

Unable to help herself, she turned and threw her arms around his neck. "Thank you," she murmured into his skin.

Without another word, he shut off the water and carried her from the room. Drying her with a soft towel, he dressed her, and then himself. Even though she protested, he picked her up and carried her to his black Bentley parked just around the corner.

Sending a quick text, he threw the car in gear and drove a few blocks to the brand new high-rise. Tossing his keys to the valet, he carried her through the luxurious lobby, to their private elevator, and up to their penthouse suite.

The first thing she smelled as the door opened was her favorite Italian restaurant.

"Did we get baked lasagna?" she asked, her exhaustion replaced by excitement.

Alec rounded the corner, striding out of their kitchen. He wore nothing but boxers, a sight that was as mouth-watering as the food. "Baked lasagna, chicken parmesan, and ziti. Your favorites!"

She grinned as Ryder put her into her chair at the table. "You guys are the best!"

Her gaze slid over the rest of their massive apartment. "Where's Kade?"

Alec spooned food onto their plates, avoiding her gaze as he sat down beside her. "He's trying to be patient."

"Patient?" she asked, frowning.

Ryder sat down on her other side, digging into his food.

"Yup," Alec said, popping a piece of lasagna into his mouth. "He's hungry for something other than food."

Tearing her gaze from the table, she looked to her bedroom door, swallowing hard. Suddenly, something sounded better than food.

"Is he just lying there?"

A gruff voice came from the bedroom. "Naked, erect, and ready. So eat quickly and get your sweet ass in here."

She must have started to rise, because Ryder tugged her back down. "Eat first."

When she failed to pick up her fork, Alec smirked. "Trust me, you'll need your strength for what we have planned."

He's got a point, my boys like it rough.

Besides, it's fun to make Kade wait.

Taking her time, she ate until she couldn't eat another bite, then polished it off with a glass of expensive white wine. *Moscato my favorite.*

"How was work?" she asked, as Alec poured her another glass.

He grinned. "Running a company is about as much fun as you can imagine."

She smiled back. "Had to deal with a lot of *tools*, I take it?"

He laughed. "I can't believe they call demons evil! Some of these humans make *my* skin crawl."

Ryder poured himself another glass of wine. "Sharen got a piece of Soul Chalk today."

Alec turned to her, his expression shocked. "How did you manage that? I thought the Hunters guarded that stuff like gold?"

I don't want to think about that. "Doesn't matter, I got it."

Both demons went silent for a long minute.

"Sharen," Alec paused. "You don't need to do anything that you don't—"

"It was fine."

Her husbands exchanged another look, then returned to their food. No longer in the mood for wine or conversation, she rose from the table and went to the bedroom. Stripping, she told herself that all she wanted was to be fucked hard. To forget about her day.

She crawled onto the bed, easily identifying Kade's big shape.

Without hesitating, she straddled him.

He cursed. "You keep up with that, and I won't last long."

"I just want it hard and fast."

Kade rolled so that she was under him, but to her shock, he simply pinned her beneath him, and then stood staring at her in the dim light. "Want to talk about it?"

It was her turn to curse. "No. I think I made it pretty clear what I wanted."

Kissing the sensitive space between her shoulder and neck, he trailed his lips slowly up to her ear. "That might have been what you asked for, but it's not what you need."

Using his knees, he spread her further, pressing his length against her womanhood. But to her annoyance, he didn't slam into her.

Wrapping her legs around his back, she tried to pull him inside her, but he refused, holding himself stiffly above her.

"Damn it!" she shouted. "If you won't fuck me, get off of me!"

Instead, he kissed her, gently, slowly. For a minute her thoughts swirled away, and then he slowly moved down. "You want to save the world," he whispered against her flesh. "You want to change the world." He pressed a kiss to the space between her breasts, then cupped her breasts. "But changing the world takes time. And more than one person."

She bucked beneath him. "Don't tell me what to do!"

He kissed his way to her nipple, then sucked softly, before pulling free. "I'm not telling you what to do, little human. I'm telling you what not to do. Don't make yourself miserable. Don't let the bad things you do define who you are."

When she tried to shove him away, he only moved to her other nipple.

Panting, she curled her hands into his hair. "And how many bad things before I become no better than them?"

He released her nipple, tearing a whimper from her lips. "We'll never let that happen. So, hon, give yourself a break. Enjoy today, because you never know what tomorrow will bring."

Damn it, he's right. I can't just distract myself with angry sex. I need to let this go, or I'll go crazy.

So, she tried to let it go. Tried hard.

But when he made it to her womanhood, she stopped having to try. His beautiful, amazing tongue did that for her. He licked slowly, pressing hot kisses to her clit, and making her toes curl. Her hands wound into the sheets above her head as her muscles tightened, her orgasm building and building.

"Is there room for us?"

In the doorway, her other incredible husbands stood watching. Alec with his dark, dangerous beauty. And Ryder with his boy-next-door good looks. She never grew tired of their company, their touch, or the feeling of them inside her.

Moaning as Kade licked her clit, she whispered. "There's always room."

Alec and Ryder stripped for her, right there in the doorway. Her gaze moved up their long, thick legs, to their long, thick cocks. She lingered on them for a moment, biting her lip as Kade continued his cruel touch. When her gaze moved higher, to their six-packs, massive arms, and almost impossibly beautiful faces, she felt lost in a dream. A dream where three demons made love to her as if she was the most important person in the world.

Alec and Ryder moved to the bed.

Immediately, Alec thrust himself into her waiting mouth. One of her hands moved up to cradle his balls as he slid in and out of her. On her other side, Ryder took her hand and curled it around his shaft. Eagerly, she stroked her husband, enjoying the feeling of him swelling in her hand.

When Kade sucked her clit, she cried out, gasping. She was so close to her release, but she wanted more than just his mouth, she wanted her husbands inside of her.

"How do you want it?" Alec asked, sensing what she couldn't seem to ask for.

A naughty shiver ran down her spine. "Upside down?"

"Fuck yes," Ryder groaned.

They launched into action. Kade moved from between her legs. Alec lifted her ass high into the air, and she put her hands out in front of her to steady herself.

The first time they'd put her in a headstand on the bed, she'd thought they were nuts... but very quickly she'd realized the benefit to such a strange position.

Alec and Ryder stood above her. All four of their hands on her legs and thighs, holding her into place. And then, very slowly, Ryder lowered his cock into her womanhood, thrusting his long shaft down further and further.

Her inner-muscles clenched him tight as she bit down another moan of pleasure. He felt so good inside her. So right.

Just what I need.

When Alec parted her from behind and squeezed into her, she stopped breathing. Inch by inch he slid into her. The feeling of his big cock and her tight ass was almost too much, but she'd learned to keep her orgasm at bay, knowing her patience would quickly be rewarded.

When Kade placed his cock close to her mouth, she opened her lips and took him in. He groaned, gripping the back of her hair and forcing himself deeper.

As the three men thrust into her together, she almost came undone. In her position, she could scarcely move. She was entirely at their mercy, and somehow, she loved every second of it.

Their groans filled her ears. Their tight grip on her legs kept her spread wide, allowing them to slam into her deeply, and thoroughly. As she felt her orgasm building higher and higher, she sucked harder on the dick in her mouth.

When she felt Ryder shudder above her and explode into her womanhood, she lost all control and tumbled off the edge. Bucking the best she could, she rode the cocks within her as her inner-muscles squeezed them tightly. Her vision wavered as Alec came into her from behind, his hot seed filling her. And then a second later, Kade came straight into her mouth.

They held her still for a couple long moments, sliding slowly in and out of her as they panted. But at last, they released her, laying her gently on the bed. Covering her up, they curled around her, encasing her in their warmth.

This was everything she needed and more.

Trying to change the world was exhausting, but the three demons in her bed made it all worthwhile. Because at the end of the day, she got to go home to them. They were her world, her everything, and she gave thanks every day that they were in her life.

So imagine her surprise when Kade's phone began to vibrate on the nightstand, and an instant later he was springing out of bed.

"I thought we don't work when we're home," she said, flashing him a smile.

How many times has he told me that same thing?

But instead of smiling back at her, he didn't look up from his phone. He just stared and stared.

Uh oh.

"What is it?" Alec asked after a moment.

Kade passed the phone to him, frowning.

This can't be good.

"What does that mean?" Alec said, his voice filled with frustration.

"I don't have a clue." Kade folded his big arms over his chest. "Maybe nothing?"

Feeling impatient, she snatched the phone from Alec and read the words. *She's back. They let her live. But something's wrong.*

Her hand trembled as she lowered the phone.

"What's going on?" Ryder asked.

Without looking up, she answered. "Surcy, the angel who saved us... the one they took... she's back."

But what did they do to her?

"Back from where?" Kade took the phone, looking confused.

"From the angel realm."

From being punished.

"What does this mean?"

I don't know.

22

KADE STOOD BY THE WINDOW, STARING DOWN AT THE CITY. Tension made every muscle in his body acutely uncomfortable. He rolled his neck until it cracked, but still, the tension remained.

And I know exactly why.

Being back on earth was everything he'd imagined and more. His business-knowledge, teamed with his demon ability to encourage others to obey him, had given him everything he'd never had as a human. He had a beautiful penthouse suit, sports cars, and the respect of many, many people.

But the one thing he wanted was the one thing he couldn't have.

Sharen safe.

She was hell-bent on changing everything. She wanted to help other demons. But that meant her going back through the portal. Alone. And as strong as the others thought he was, he wasn't sure he could let it happen.

If I lose her, this second-chance at life means nothing.

Turning back to the bed, he stared at her sandwiched

between his brothers. His chest ached. The bruises on her body looked painful. And she'd lost weight.

I should destroy the demon-stone. And the Soul Chalk. I should make it impossible for her to continue down this reckless path.

And yet, if he did, he knew she wouldn't give up. She'd just hate him.

So what am I to do? How could he hope to protect her?

Staring back out the window, he knew it would be another long night. Because as much as he wanted to curl back around the woman he loved and go to sleep, he knew he wouldn't.

He wasn't sure he'd ever sleep again. Not when he could feel death coming for her.

23

GREG MANTHEN KNELT BEFORE THE IMMORTAL BEING KNOWN only as Caine. *He's going to kill me.*

Letting his gaze subtly move up, Greg stared at the being who looked like nothing more than a man. He had dark hair, strong cheekbones, and a well-defined body. A woman would have called him handsome. But as he turned his eyes to roam over his subject, kneeling before him, the cruelness in his gaze sent every hair on Greg's body standing on end.

What must it be like to have the power to destroy a person with a touch? And then, to decide how they spent eternity?

"So," the being said, drawing out the word. "Not only were my plans for the half-breed ruined, but an angel was corrupted too?"

Tread carefully. Don't anger him.

Sweat ran down Greg's back, and he glanced slowly around the room at the dozen angels watching him from the shadows of the empty warehouse. "That's correct, my lord."

The tension was palpable. The angels, with their inhuman beauty, didn't fool him. He knew what they were.

Most were little more than brainwashed murderers, under control of the magical being who silently ruled the world.

"This is... disappointing." Caine circled him slowly, staring off as if lost in thought.

Greg tensed, waiting. If he were killed, this creature would no doubt send him straight to the demon-realm, where a number of enemies would be prepared to make his eternity a painful one.

Convince him! Convince him not to kill you!

"Yes, but I think it worked out for the best," he rushed out in desperation.

"Do you?" Caine's deep voice held a dark amusement.

Please, please let him listen to me. "The angel could be useful to us."

"She will be useful to me. Of that, have no doubt."

Greg's voice rose against his will in desperation. "We never would have discovered that Surcy was a traitor if Sharen hadn't needed her help, so it was for the best."

The being smiled, a joyless, frightening smile. "Mistakes have consequences." He leaned toward him, and Greg instinctually cowered back. "From this day forward, Greg Manthen is dead. He no longer exists."

"Please—" he whimpered.

"The half-breed must be watched, carefully. Her role in the coming war is still yet unknown. You will not harm her, but you will watch her. And, you will become someone she will never expect."

Hope blossomed within Greg's heart. *I won't be dying today.*

Closing his eyes, he shifted, wincing as his bones cracked and his skin shrunk. When he opened his eyes, he had a new face and a new body. Panting, he looked up at his lord, praying the creature would approve.

Caine's brow rose. "That will do, shifter. That will do. Now, find the girl."

Greg turned scrambling from the old building, even though his body ached from his Change. He had just lost the cushiest position he'd ever had. Being The Director had brought him wealth, power, and a life of endless pleasures.

Sharen had taken that from him.

And now, he would make certain she paid for it.

~ FIND OUT **what happens to Sharen and her demons in Unchained Magic.**~

UNCHAINED MAGIC

1

SHAREN PLACED HER BOOTED FOOT ON THE LEDGE OF THE building and looked down at her city, Shady Falls. The sun was just starting to rise, painting everything in reds and oranges. But below her, it wasn't the sun's light that painted the alley in red.

There was blood. Everywhere.

Closing her eyes, she inhaled deeply, tasting the coopery scent with her superior sense of smell. The killing had been recent enough that the blood still glistened in the dawn's light. *My demons will want me to wait for them to investigate.*

But if she waited, a human was bound to stumble across the crime scene. And once the police were involved, there would be little any of them could do. It was now or never.

Time to put my new abilities to use.

She let her gaze run over the alley, looking for the perfect spot. Then, taking a deep breath, she leapt off the edge.

The ground always came faster than she expected. But she struck the pavement, falling into a crouch, trying to be as soundless as possible. Looking over her shoulder to the entrance to the alley, where early cars were already starting to drive past, she waited. When she was certain no one would see her, she headed toward the massacre.

Everywhere she looked, she saw blood, but there was no body, and she didn't see any signs that a body had been dragged away. *The victim wasn't human.* Since demons and angels didn't leave behind bodies, it had to be one of them.

She hoped it'd been an angel.

The cocky bastards.

As Sharen surveyed the mess, her gaze skittered and then froze. Inching around the gore, she reached out and plucked the silver item from a pool of blood. It was a tiny silver car.

"Shit!" she shouted, clenching it in her hand. "Shit! Shit!"

Storming away from the mess, she kicked the dumpster, over and over again, denting the entire side of it in, as if a car had smashed into it rather than the tip of her foot. Several minutes passed of her kicking and swearing before her anger was finally spent. Collapsing with her back against the mangled dumpster, she shoved away a tear and stared at the blood-drenched car again.

She knew exactly who it belonged to.

This can't be real...but it is.

More blood. More death.

It haunts me.

She hated that she thought of her parents, even after all these years. Hated that her mind immediately went back to the day she'd gotten home from the first grade. She'd raced down the street to her house with her A+ paper in hand.

So full of happiness. So unaware that in seconds my life would change forever.

Hurrying up the steps to her porch, she'd turned the handle on her door. Even now, she could hear the groan it made as she pushed it open. She could remember the scent of her mother's lavender candle that always seemed to fill the air.

And then...then she'd seen the room. Painted in blood. Her parents' bodies lying in the center of her living room. In crystal clarity, she saw her paper float to the floor, the big A+ staring up at her. A smile drawn next to it.

A simple, innocent thing. Just like this car.

But just like back then, there's no time for sadness. No time to slow down. Because the world doesn't wait for grief. It just keeps on turning.

Rising, she stuffed the toy into her pocket. With hands that shook, she pulled her black hoodie up and headed for the street.

Little Brian had been killed, which meant his mother and sister had too.

Her heart ached painfully. She smacked into someone's shoulder on the street. They muttered something she didn't hear, but she just kept walking.

The world seemed painfully bright and her head spun. A family of demons had been slaughtered in the streets, but the day kept on going as if their lives meant nothing at all.

Brian with his bright smile. His silly laugh. And his excitement about everything. Gone.

She wiped at a stray tear that tracked down her cheek. *I'd told Brian he was safe.*

I fucking hate myself sometimes.

But as much as her sappy heart wanted her to curl up and bawl, she pressed forward. The only thing that would help now was to keep going.

Because once a demon was killed, it'd take them years to

journey from the lowest levels of the demon realms back up to the realms close enough to cross over to Earth.

Brian and his family were beyond her help now.

As she was walking past another alley, she caught a flash of white. Freezing, she turned. Two angels with white wings were laughing together.

Keep walking, Sharen.

But her feet propelled her toward the angels, and a blade slipped into her palm.

You can't possibly take on two angels. This is suicide. Stop! It won't bring back Brian and his family.

More old memories came to her. Of the angry kid in foster care who fought and fought. A child more afraid of her own sadness than the beating she'd take as a result of her sharp tongue and quick fists.

Turn around, Sharen. Show yourself that you've changed. But she kept moving toward the angels, her rage growing with each step.

"What's so funny?" she challenged.

The two massive angels stopped talking.

One of them, a man with a military cut and dark eyes, turned to look at her. "Our joke isn't of any interest to you."

Her lips curled. "Try me."

His gaze moved down to the dagger in her hand, and he raised a brow. "I know who you are."

"Do you?" Her pulse was racing, filling her ears.

"Yeah, you're that damned Hunter. The one who switched sides."

Then you know I spent years learning to fight. Years being taught how to kill.

You're an idiot for still looking so damn smug.

She smiled. "It looks like you know everything, so here's

a question. Any idea what killed a couple of kids and their mother a few alleys from here?"

"Oh, you mean that demon spawn. Me and Jason here took care of them."

Her steps froze.

Take deep breaths. Don't do anything stupid.

His satisfied expression widened. "And we did it *slowly*. You know, to discourage them from leaving the demon realm again."

A scream tore from her lips, and in a blur of motion she drove the dagger through his forehead.

The other angel jumped back, forming his soul blade in his hand.

As her first enemy hit the ground, she reached behind her, tossed back her hood, and pulled out her sword. "Did you help kill them?"

He looked uncertain. "It's our job to rid the human realm of demons."

Swinging her sword out, it struck his. They leapt back from each other, both of them circling and looking for an opportunity to strike.

"You know you can't defeat me," he said.

That's because you think I'm just a Hunter.

"Try me."

He drove his blade toward her chest with a strength and quickness that would have ended the life of a human. But Sharen? She darted out of the way, rolled, and buried her blade into his stomach.

His mouth opened and blood poured out.

Yanking her blade back, she let the angel fall. Then, ignoring her racing heart, she sliced off his head.

One of the few ways to kill an immortal being.

A sword's blade was suddenly at her throat. "Drop your weapon," the first angel hissed into her ear.

Damn it.

She let her weapon fall to the concrete. The sword echoed through the alleyway, far too loudly in her ears.

"See, Hunter, that's the difference between you and us. Jason there will be back on Earth within a few hours. I bet it'll take you years to crawl out of that hole of a demon realm."

Except that I'm not a demon.

She swallowed, her fingertips reaching for the other dagger she kept hidden in her sleeve. Just a little further and—

The angel moved the sword back, just a couple inches, preparing to sever her head from her body. But instead, his weapon tumbled from his fingertips.

Turning, her enemy hit the ground, his head severed.

Behind her, Kade stood, wearing a thunderous expression, his blade in hand. And to her shock, his dark irises were almost entirely red. "What the hell were you thinking, Sharen?"

I haven't seen him this close to losing control in a long time.

Probably not a time to piss him off, if I can help it.

She knelt down and collected her dagger and sword. With careful movements, she used the angel's shirt to wipe her weapons free of blood before she hid them again.

"Are you going to answer me?" He was practically shouting, but his eyes were growing dark once more.

Standing again, she looked at him, her gaze moving up, up, up to his handsome face. His human-looking eyes reminded her of storm clouds, heavy with rain. The harsh lines of his face hinted at the well-disciplined warrior who trained beside her each day.

A lover. A partner. And one pissed off alpha demon...which I have no intention of dealing with right now.

"What do you want me to say?"

He glared. "I want to hear something that explains the idiocy of attacking two angels alone!"

"I don't have to explain myself to you or anyone else!"

Shoving his shoulder, she stormed back out onto the sidewalk of the street. She barely looked where she was going. She just plunged forward.

Kade caught her arm and pulled her back around. "Are you trying to get yourself killed? Or are you just trying to prove to us that you don't need us?"

"Neither." She yanked her arm, trying to break free of him, but his grip was relentless.

"This shit has got to stop!"

"Or what?" She stopped fighting him and took a step closer. "You're going to leave me? Huh? Go ahead! You won't be the first person."

His expression gentled. "I'm not your ex. I've told you that a thousand times. I'm not going anywhere."

It was hard to speak around the lump in her throat. "You might not be my ex, but I'm still me."

His grip tightened. "Good, because I fucking love you just the way you are. Crazy angel-fighting badass and all."

Damn it, why does he have to say crap like that? She jerked her arm free of his grip.

Something hit the pavement.

Their gazes moved down at the same moment, but Kade was faster. He plucked the little silver car off the sidewalk. In the morning light, the staining of blood stood out. "Where did you find this?"

She shook her head, unable to form the words.

His arms were around her in an instant, his big hand

stroking her hair. She buried her face into his jacket, breathing in the spicy scent that was all Kade.

"I'm so sorry," he whispered into her hair.

She couldn't form the words to tell him it didn't matter. That demons were dying every day. That she was a Hunter, a killer, and a warrior. And that death didn't bother her.

Because as much as she hated it sometimes, he would see right through her. He knew how she reacted to death. How it brought up old memories. How maybe it made her change from a strong woman to a complete disaster.

It reminds me that I'm still damaged, no matter how much I think I've moved on from the shadows of my past.

"Let's get you home."

His voice was so damn gentle that she felt her eyes sting. *God, I love you for how much you care about me. How much you take my bullshit and still love me. But as much as I want to spend the day curled in bed with you, I need to continue fighting.*

Releasing his jacket, she cleared her throat. "I can't. Today I've got plans."

"Sharen…"

She shrugged and forced the words past her lips. "It doesn't matter that Brian and his family are dead. I still have to go through the demon stone."

"You don't *have* to do anything."

Her gaze held his. "Yes. Yes I do."

Sharen was the only one capable of going through the demon stone without being trapped there forever. *At least the only one with the ability to harness magic on the other side insane enough to go through alone and working for the Rebellion of the Forgotten.* Sure, there was her old student, Lily, who was secretly working for their side, but she had her own responsibilities as a double-agent within the Organization.

So that just leaves me.

Her plan was to save demons. *But some days I feel like I'm the one who needs saving.*

2

SHAREN TYPED IN THE PASSCODE OUTSIDE THE REBELLION'S headquarters, a warehouse that looked abandoned from the outside. She shoved the door open, and Kade held it while she stormed inside.

She was used to the massive space being filled with boxes of supplies and weapons, but she was still getting used to the many demons and other beings that had joined the Rebellion and now occupied the space.

"Commander," a demon said, rushing up to her, saluting.

She sighed. Many of her newest recruits were ex-military. Even though she'd told them a dozen times that saluting her wasn't necessary, they couldn't seem to break the habit. As a result, all the demons treated her like a military leader, a position she had no interest in taking.

"What is it?" she asked, frowning.

The short man named Henry stood up taller and dropped his hand. "Two demon families have failed to check in."

Don't start crying again. "Brian's family was killed by angels. Have someone check on the other family."

"Yes, ma'am."

As she strode past him, someone called out her name. She turned to the side of the room now filled with a dozen different computer desks. Ryder circled the demons who worked relentlessly, searching for information. They hoped to learn more about the angels' weaknesses, and about other ways to help the demons.

Sharen headed toward an outspoken demon named Isa. "What's up?"

"A demon used their powers around three in the morning. I hacked into the hunters' system and discovered that he was apprehended rather than killed."

She frowned. "Any details as to why?"

The older woman shook her head.

"Keep searching."

"Yes, ma'am." She turned back to the screen, her gaze intense.

Before Sharen could turn to go, Ryder pulled her into his arms. She got a flash of his smile before he was kissing her. For a second, she forgot about everything, about her responsibilities, about the people she'd failed to help. She could do nothing but kiss the handsome demon until he pulled back.

Her eyes were closed, and her hands clung to the front of his shirt.

"Damn, you look beautiful," he growled into her ear.

A shiver went down her spine, and she opened her eyes, unable to hold back her smile. His light brown hair was even messier than usual, and the red plaid shirt he wore had several buttons undone at the top.

She just stared at him for a long moment. Alec and Kade

might have been her rocks in this stormy time in her life, but Ryder was like a tropical island, a vacation away from it all. He didn't ask her what was wrong. He just tried to make her happy.

"You don't look so bad yourself."

His hands slipped down from her back to cup her ass. "How about you meet me in your office for a little *meeting*?"

She laughed. "Sorry, but I've already got other plans."

She sensed Kade approach behind her and knew what he would say before he said it. "She intends to go through the stone again today." His voice held disapproval, and she could picture his stormy expression behind her.

A look of concern came and went in a flash on Ryder's face. "Well, don't tire yourself out too badly. I plan on hitting this tonight, and hitting it hard."

She stood up on her tippy-toes and pressed a kiss to his chin. "I think you're the one who'd better save your energy."

He laughed. "God, I love you."

Her heart warmed. "Right back at you."

Turning away from him, she moved past Kade, her back straight. She needed to be tough and not show weakness. Soon, she would be jumping into a demon realm alone, and the last thing she needed was to carry Kade's doubts with her.

"Sharen!"

Darla raced up to her, clenching a pile of papers. "I think I have my latest spell down."

The youngest witch in the Rebellion, Darla was barely eighteen, with reddish-blonde hair and a face full of freckles. She was also a witch with a whole lot of power and very little experience.

"Which spell?" Sharen tried to keep the concern out of her voice.

"To force angels out of any hosts they possess." Darla

grinned. "It's not an easy spell, but I think, based on all my research, it'll work."

That would be useful, but it sounds dangerous as hell.

"Have you actually tried it?"

Darla's grin wavered. "Well, no, but in theory it should work."

In theory.

"Well, keep up the good work. I'll hope we never need to use it, but I'll be glad to have you around if we do."

The girl beamed and took off back to the far corner of the warehouse used as the research nook. She and two other witches spent all their time researching the ancient books the Rebellion had managed to gather. So far, they hadn't learned much, but Sharen had no doubt that with time the witches would prove useful.

Going to her office, she slipped into the darkness. Taking off her hoodie, she sank into her chair, resting her head on her desk.

A soft knock came at her door.

She took a deep breath, gathering strength to face yet another person who needed something. But before she could give the order to enter, Marval appeared before her.

Sharen snapped into a sitting position. She hated it when the vampire surprised her. Even though she'd met with him many times before, she always felt like she needed to prepare herself for him. When he caught her off-guard, she didn't get that chance, and it meant that she was a little rattled at their meetings. But even though she logically knew why he unnerved her; it didn't change the fact that she needed to act like she had her shit together.

So, she tried damned hard to pretend she did.

"Yes?" she asked, lifting a brow.

For a long minute he didn't answer. Just studied her. So,

she studied him right back. The vampire appeared young, but he was in fact the oldest being in the Rebellion. Old, powerful, and capable of learning things that no one else could. Which was why she'd put him on a private mission. *Figuring out what the hell I am.*

"I found out more information."

"Go on."

He sat down, his dark eyes fixed on her face. He had an aristocratic beauty that hovered over him like a cloak, even as he leaned back in his chair in a casual way. And yet, he might try to look relaxed, but he didn't pull it off. He was a creature who hummed with power and strength, so much that it felt as if he might attack at any moment.

Not that he would. He was on their side, after all.

"Let's start with what we know and what that means."

She nodded.

"You're getting stronger and faster, but your abilities come and go, which is unusual in every way. If you were part demon or part angel, you would have always had these abilities."

"So, there's never been a case of a half-breed developing powers later on in life?"

Marval touched his dark beard, rubbing it as if lost in thought. "Only under special circumstance. Typically, if powers develop later on in life, it's because their abilities were sealed with magic earlier for some reason and then unsealed. Yet, you've indicated not being aware of any such things. Of course, then there's the fact that your abilities are inconsistent."

She felt her irritation rise. "Okay, so we've established that I don't seem to fit the pattern for normal half-breeds. Is there anything you *have* figured out?"

He regarded her for an uncomfortably long time before

speaking. "You cannot manipulate others with your words like a demon. You cannot fly or teleport like an angel. You cannot use magic like a witch, nor shift like a shifter. You don't need to feed like a vampire."

"Right," she said, her teeth clenching together in frustration. "There's a whole list of things that I'm *not*, so what I am?"

He leaned forward. "You, Sharen, are like nothing I have seen before, but this I am sure of: you have an ability that I cannot connect with any supernatural being I've come across before."

An ability? "What?"

He nodded solemnly. "Others follow your lead, almost without question."

Her irritation rose once more. "That's not a power."

"Perhaps not, but—"

"Marval, I appreciate all you're doing, but I have to go through the portal today. Keep researching and come back to me if you actually find something."

He rose. "You may feel that your ability to lead is not a power, but I've lived for hundreds of years and no one has ever convinced me to join a cause. Until you. Think about that."

The vampire left, vanishing from her office as silently as he entered.

She put her head back down on her desk. *I don't know what I am. I don't know what I'm doing. But I've got to keep going. I have too many people counting on me to stop.*

Yet, she didn't move for several silent minutes.

3

Sharen stood before the portal, Soul Chalk in her hand. The busy room had grown silent, and most of the people had come to gather around her. The seven-foot demon stone, made of a massive block of stone darker than any dark found on Earth, towered in front of her, radiating danger.

Riverly stood at her side, tablet computer in her hand. She gestured to the screen. "The Hunters have marked this realm too dangerous to enter. They found five demons, just recently." She spoke the words softly and adjusted her glasses when she was done speaking, before looking meekly toward Sharen.

"Five god damn demons," Kade hissed. "We couldn't have found a more dangerous realm to enter."

Sharen spun to face him, biting down a string of curses. All eyes were on her, and most of the people looked frightened. "A realm with five demons means there are five people we can save."

"And what if they don't want to be saved?" Kade's big arms were crossed over his chest, his eyes filled with anger.

"They'll want to be saved," one demon said, his voice barely louder than a whisper.

Kade's angry gaze swung to the man. "Didn't you think she was a hunter trying to trick you when you met her? Didn't you nearly kill her?"

The demon's cheeks turned bright red. "But she convinced me to believe her. She'll convince these demons too."

Sharen stood up taller, looking out at the three dozen or so faces that stared back at her. Each time she went through the portal it brought hope to the Rebellion. It moved them towards their goal to save as many innocent demons as possible.

If she didn't go, the hope of the Rebellion died with her.

None of the demons were capable of crossing back over without being torn to pieces, and the other magical creatures refused to go to a place they weren't trained to survive in. They couldn't wield the same magic she could in the demon realm, and they weren't about to risk their lives in such a dangerous place.

That left only her, and they needed to know they could count on her.

Sharen hid her own emotions behind a smirk. "If you guys think I'm afraid, think again. This war won't be won in a day. It'll take time. But I'm more than willing to save demons one trip to the demon realm at a time. And before we know it, they'll all be saved."

The room suddenly swelled with emotions. Her people looked relieved, hopeful. Their faith filled her with a rush of strength. *I can do this. But first...*

She moved down the steps with absolute certainty, stood on her tiptoes, and planted a light kiss on Kade's lips. His eyes widened in surprise, but she didn't give him a chance to respond. "I love you, but you've got to trust me that I'll be okay."

His features gentled. "I'll try."

She smiled, winked at him, and climbed back up the steps. As frustrating as her demon could be, she knew he was just worried about her. She didn't want to step through the stone without making sure they were okay. Her cause might be important to her, but nothing was more important than her husbands.

Now, time to focus!

Turning to the demon stone, she drew a doorway carefully onto it and scribbled the name of the realm over the top. Instantly, the realm opened and swirling waves of grey moved into the doorway she'd drawn, beckoning her to enter.

"Sharen!"

She looked back.

Ryder had come to stand beside Kade. And both her demons looked concerned.

But Ryder simply nodded and said, "Be safe."

She held his gaze. "I will."

Riverly, her assistant, handed her a splicer. Sharen gripped the handle on the half-circular blade, took a deep breath, and stepped through. The horrible sensation of stepping through realms filled her. She was blazing hot, freezing cold, squished into nothing, pulled too far.

And then she came out into the demon realm.

It took her a second to find her bearings. But when she did, she took a deep breath. Three painfully hot suns bore down on the white desert that stretched around her in all directions. Small white plants, like cacti or stunted trees, dotted the landscape. She only spotted a few caves in the hilly landscape, but knew from her past trips that there were likely many, many more concealed all around her.

Meaning, there's a lot of places to hide. Danger could come from any direction.

Her pulse sped up. As a hunter, things had been so different. She'd been the leader of a team. As much as she hated it, there was something a hell of a lot safer about travelling into such a dangerous place with a team rather than alone.

For years, she'd hovered by the portal, as protocol dictated. All leaders stayed in the safest position, because they were over the age of twenty-one and could be possessed by a demon. Their younger students were put in the more dangerous positions, since they could be killed, but demons couldn't use their bodies.

Now, however, she didn't have the luxury of hovering safely by the portal. She had to be careful, but she also had to take risks she never would have before.

Clenching her splicer more tightly, she called her magic to the weapon. It was a simple spell, meant to stun but not kill. It spilled out of her, sending a tickling sensation along her skin. The spell made her weapon glow green, but the light was the brightest along the sharp edge of the blade that curved just above her knuckles.

Magic and weaponry at its finest.

She took a deep breath. *I'm ready.*

"Demons!" she shouted, feeling sweat run down her spine.

Moving forward, she continued to shout, waiting and hoping, but she saw no one.

When she was as far from the portal as she felt comfortable, she paused and scanned the horizon. Her shoulders sank. Either the hunters' map had been wrong, there weren't demons in this realm, or the demons had already left. Either way, they were gone.

Turning around, she started back toward the portal before she froze. Five demons had melded out of nothing and now blocked her escape.

Shit!

"Hello," she called, her heart hammering. "I'm Sharen, and I've come to help you."

The five beings were massive, like many of the demons. Their white horns stood out from their heads with sharp points and their dark red skin glistened under the lights of the suns. None of them returned her greeting.

Keep trying. "I'm with the Rebellion. We are dedicated to saving demons from the demon realm and fighting against the hunters and the angels."

One of the demons, a man with dark hair and pale eyes, cocked his head. "You're also a hunter."

"I *was* a hunter. I've turned my back on them now."

"How do we know this isn't a trap?" He grinned, a cold replica of a smile that left her with no doubt as to where he stood. He would not be an easy one to sway. "It would be easy for you to lead us through the portal where we'll arrive at Earth weak and unable to use our powers. We would be easy prey for you and your buddies to exterminate in one fell swoop and send us straight down to the lowest level of the demon realm."

"This is not a—"

He stepped closer, menace in his every movement. "Do you have any idea how many years we spent in darkness crawling from those miserable pits? You think we'll risk it all to trust you?"

Her legs trembled. "Others have come before you, and they were scared too. They had to take the risk to trust me.

Yes, there is a portal behind you, but if you try to exit without me, you'll be torn to pieces." She could tell from the look in his eyes that he wasn't buying her story, but the others seemed to waver, so she continued. "You have to ask yourselves, is it worth the risk? Would you really rather spend another year crawling up through the realms to reach Earth, or will you take a chance with me?"

His pale eyes narrowed. "Or one of us could simply possess you." He looked to his compatriots and they seemed to swell as one. She had no hope of fighting all five of them.

She swallowed hard, reminding herself that he could do just that. "My team is waiting for me on the other side. You'll never survive it."

He smiled. "You'd be surprised how well I can convince them that I'm you, especially if my life depends upon it."

Sharen took a deep breath and tried again. "You're making a mistake. If you cross over with me, my team is waiting to help you. We'll hide you from your enemies and get you established on Earth."

He shrugged. "I'd rather do all that in a nice, comfortable human body." He gestured toward her. "Bring her to me; she's mine!"

Fuck.

The demons raced toward her. She struck one with her magic, sending him flying back onto the ground. She had time to strike one more before they were upon her.

One swung at her, but she ducked. The next kicked toward her and she used her blade to slice his leg. But her movements...they were slow. *Human.*

This is the fucking moment my extra strength and speed fail me? This has to be a joke!

The demon she struck cried out, jumping back. The

other two demons circled her as she held her splicer out in front of her.

"You don't need to do this," she panted. "This isn't a trap."

One of the demons leapt at her. She sliced him across the face and he stumbled back, swearing.

"Listen to me," she whispered. "I just want to help you."

Suddenly, there was shouting behind her. The two demons she fought sprang further from her, terror in their eyes.

Glancing behind her, Sharen felt her stomach flip. A team of hunters was coming toward them, and she recognized their leader.

Rorde, my former student.

Rorde was an asshole sorcerer who she couldn't stand, even when she taught him. He stood in the center of the other hunters, his dark hair perfectly neat. His black-as-coal eyes were nothing more than two dark pools, and his awful mouth was curled into a smile.

"Ready to die, bitch?" he shouted, gesturing for the students around him to continue forward. "Teach her how we repay traitors of humanity, boys!"

She wanted to kill the bastard right there and then, but she wouldn't be able to kill him and protect the demons.

If we don't get out of here now, we're done for. If the hunters kill me, my people will never know what happened to me. My demons will suffer and the war will be lost.

Turning, she beckoned to the demons in front of her. "Last chance. Come with me."

Their gazes said it all. They wanted her body, not her help.

One of them reached for her, but she struck it with her

magic and slammed her splicer into the face of the other one. Both of them hit the ground, unmoving.

Racing past them, she barreled toward the portal. Only one demon remained in her path, and she was determined to get him out of her way, one way or another.

"Come with me!" she shouted.

He looked between her and the hunters. "Yeah, right..."

Her splicer heated in her hand as she sent her magic blasting out at him, but he avoided her spell, moving with the grace and agility of a shifter. When she reached him, she gritted her teeth, ready to fight for her life.

Even without my extra strength and speed.

Something hit the back of her leg, a spell that sent fire burning through her clothes and onto her flesh. She screamed and fell, just feet in front of the demon.

She saw a flash of his red flesh and then his hands closed around her throat. He pressed until he forced his body into hers. She fought him with every ounce of her being, but he overpowered her.

Her body stood, but she had no control over it. The demon turned her to look back at the hunters racing toward them. He raised a hand, flipping them off.

No! She struggled harder inside herself, but she was trapped, unable to even move her lips to scream.

"Stop fighting it," he whispered. "This is your new life. You'd better get used to it."

Turning back to the portal, he stepped through.

4

Kade's stomach twisted and turned with every second Sharen was gone. God, he hated not being able to cross over with her! Seeing his woman risk her life made him crazy. Every protective instinct within him roared to life, demanding that he act.

But she acts like I'm just an ass.

Sharen didn't understand, couldn't understand. He had failed everyone he'd ever loved. He would not fail her.

For an instant, he was drawn back into a memory a lifetime ago. He pictured his little sister, spinning in her new pink dress. She said the pink dress made her a "princess," but she never realized that with three big brothers, she was always a princess.

Always my princess. He grinned at the thought.

He tried to imagine her older, her smile filling her entire face. Her pigtails were long gone, but the image faded. He would forever see her as a little girl who saw the world in brilliant colors, who thought she could fly in his arms.

His smile faltered as he recalled seeing her in the hospital, her face battered and her heart cracked into pieces.

What she went through, it changed her forever. And I see that in Sharen. I see her changing, and I would do anything to keep that from happening, to keep her from seeing the darker side of the world.

As he paced the small space, a demon crossed his path, drawing him from his thoughts. He didn't care that he was irritating everyone trying to work around him. He growled low in his throat until the other demon scrambled away.

His Sharen was alone in a demon realm. Her idealistic views on demons caused her to throw herself into danger time and time again. But one of these days, he knew she would see the truth. Not all angels were bad, and not all demons were good.

I just hope she can learn the truth in the least painful way possible.

He heard footsteps behind him and then his brother Ryder's voice. "She'll be okay. She always is."

Kade spun and growled, but Ryder simply smiled.

"She's stronger than you give her credit for," his brother said.

"She's only human!"

Ryder raised a brow.

"You know what I mean!" Kade was trying to keep himself from shouting and failing miserably.

"She's smart and strong. And amazing. We've got to trust her."

Kade's fist clenched so hard he heard his knuckles crack. "You think I don't know she's all those things? But here's the thing: that's not enough."

Ryder's expression faltered. "She's been fine every time before."

"Yes, and she'll keep being fine until she's not. Where

will we be then?" Kade said the words, his greatest fear, driving his point home.

"Fuck." Ryder swept a hand through his light brown hair. "You've got to stop this, man. You'll drive yourself crazy."

"I can't stop. Not until she lets me keep her locked up safely at our apartment." He felt every muscle in his body tense. "I can't lose her."

Ryder came closer, putting a hand on his shoulder. "That's the thing, Kade. She's never going to let that happen. You know that. But I'll tell you this—if you don't start supporting her, you might lose her anyway."

Kade froze. *Lose her?*

His breathing rushed in his ears. Yes, he and Sharen fought a lot, but could it actually end with her walking away from him?

The world spun around him. *Never.* He could not, *would not,* let that happen.

"Just have faith, okay?"

Kade's gaze zeroed in on his younger brother's face. There was a reason Ryder was so relaxed. As a human, he'd spent his weekends surfing, his nights cooking romantic meals for women who drooled over him, and his workweek doing just enough to get by. Ryder had never been high strung. He'd always believed everything would work out, because it usually did for him.

But that's not the same life Kade had lived as a human.

My sister, hurt because I couldn't protect her. My wife, who grew tired of her soldier husband. Her little daughter I wanted to be my own, but never was.

And the day I came home to my empty house and realized I had nothing. Nothing but the ability to kill the men who hurt my sister.

He closed his eyes, fighting a wave of pain. He could never go through that again. Never be a man with nothing to live for and no one to love.

The portal purred as the gray waves grew larger and faster. Sharen came flying into the room, her face pale and tight with fear.

He pushed past the horde of demons and rushed to her, catching her as she crumbled to the ground. Staring down at her, he felt uncertain. What should he do? How could he help?

"Did you save any demons?" Riverly asked from behind them. "Should we shut the portal?"

Sharen shook her head. "Shut it. Hunters are coming."

Instantly, Riverly raced up the steps and erased the specific realm code. The portal vanished and the room grew quiet. The others drew closer, waiting for Sharen's explanation.

And here it comes. She will spin a story that might sound like a failure, but somehow she'll inspire everyone in the room.

Even if deep inside I know she's putting on a show for the others.

"What happened?" Ryder asked, kneeling down beside her.

His brother's voice was calm as always, but worry lingered behind his question. Sometimes Sharen's missions went wrong. Actually, they usually went wrong, but he couldn't think of a time she'd come back looking this frightened *and* without a demon to show for her trouble.

And normally even then she was spouting orders and reassuring everyone.

"Nothing," she said, her eyes narrowing. "The hunters came, and I couldn't save the demons."

That's all she's going to say?

"And what about your leg?" Ryder touched her leg.

Kade's gaze went to her injury, where her pants leg had melted away, leaving behind a nasty-looking burn.

She's hurt! His pulse sped up. *How the hell did that happen?*

"I got hit with a spell. I'm fine." She tried to stand, but her knees buckled.

Ryder swept her into his arms. "I'll help you shower."

Kade watched as she stiffened in his brother's arms. "No way. I'm—uh fine," she said, looking even more terrified.

Huh? Kade's body tensed. "You're not fine; let him tend to your wound."

She elbowed Ryder's chest. "Seriously, put me down. My leg will heal, but I'm ready to get out of here."

Her gaze shifted over the room, her expression uneasy.

That was when he knew. Kade acted in an instant. Pulling her from Ryder's arms, he dropped her down onto the ground, pinning her arms over her head and her body down beneath his.

"Get out of her."

She froze. "I don't know what you mean."

"What the hell are you doing?" Ryder asked, confused.

"She's been possessed." Kade hated speaking the words aloud, hated knowing that some slimy creature was inside her. *This demon will die for this.*

"Get out of her now, or you'll regret it," he threatened softly.

She turned angry eyes onto him. "I don't know what you mean."

"Darla!" he shouted.

A minute passed before the high voice of the young woman came to him. "What is it—uh—Mr. Kade?"

"You said you knew how to force a possessed being out of someone. Get this demon out of Sharen, now!"

"I, uh, I only studied how to get angels out of—"

"Just fucking do it!"

Sharen struggled harder beneath him. A string of curses and threats exploded from her lips, but Kade's hold was iron tight. This demon would not escape with his woman.

Darla began to whisper soft words. Kneeling down next to them, she touched Sharen's face in a strange pattern. First her forehead, then her cheeks and chin. There was almost a pattern, but not quiet.

At first, nothing happened. Kade's anger rose higher and higher as the demon who possessed Sharen smiled in triumph. And then, Sharen began to shake and writhe beneath him.

"Kade," Ryder whispered. "What if Darla doesn't know what she's doing? What if—?"

"Shut the hell up and let's get this animal out of our Sharen."

Ryder grew silent, but he sensed Kade's agitation spike with each twitch Sharen made. She twisted and tried to lift her body off the ground, but he wouldn't allow it.

Kade refused to react in any way. He refused to let the demon see how much seeing Sharen like this was killing him. Instead, he kept his expression like stone and held her without flexibility.

As Darla continued her spell, Sharen threw back her head, screaming, her chest raised up. He felt a crowd gathering around them. People whispered in concern.

"Should I stop?" Darla murmured.

"Keep going," Kade bit out, his words strong and certain.

"Kade." Ryder put his hand on his shoulder.

Kade jerked away from his touch. "You heard me, woman, keep going!"

Darla's words came, faster and louder. A golden glow surrounded Sharen and she began to spasm, her entire body seizing and jerking. As a black ooze flowed out of her mouth, Kade finally let her go. Within seconds, a blond-haired demon lay on the floor beside Sharen's still twitching body.

The demon gasped in deep breaths. "I'm sorry. I didn't know—"

Kade pulled his sword from off his back and cut the demon's head clean from his shoulders.

The room descended into silence, the only sound made by Kade's sword as it clattered to the floor. He dropped beside Sharen, cradling her into his arms.

Please be okay. Please be okay.

At last, her jerking calmed and her eyes opened. "What...happened?"

"It's okay." He stroked her sweaty hair back from her face. "The demon's gone."

Her expression grew confused. "Did you save him?"

Kade tensed. "Save him? He possessed you!"

Their gazes locked and he couldn't look away. The dark green depths of her eyes called to him, beckoning him to get lost in them. But he saw something else within her large, familiar eyes—sadness and disappointment.

Two things I never wanted her to feel.

"He was scared," she whispered. "We all get scared sometimes."

Kade felt as if he'd swallowed a stone. She couldn't have thought he'd let the demon live, not after he hurt her.

"Where is he?"

"Dead," he said, the word a challenge.

Rage flashed in her eyes. "You killed him."

"Yes, and I don't regret it."

She struggled out of his arms and he let her leave.

Ryder caught her arm as she tried to stand on her injured leg. Her gaze moved down to the dead demon, and it was then that Kade realized that the entire warehouse was staring at them as the scene unfolded.

"The mission was a failure," Sharen said, her voice carrying through the silence. "I couldn't save any of them."

That was all she had. She had nothing positive, nothing uplifting. No hope.

Just...sadness.

And then Sharen limped away with Ryder at her side. Sadness moved over the people. As Kade watched their faces, it was as if a light had turned off within them. The sight of it was heartbreaking.

Slowly, they returned to work, but no one spoke.

This isn't my fault. It's the damned demon who possessed her.

As angry as he was at the demon, the worst part was knowing that tomorrow Sharen would go through the portal all over again.

Maybe this is true hell.

His hands clenched into fists. *There has to be something I can do to stop this, but what?*

What?

And then an idea came to him, a dangerous, terrifying idea. His hands uncurled and his heart raced. It was...possible.

He could protect Sharen!

All it would cost him was his life.

5

BACK AT THEIR APARTMENT, RYDER EASED SHAREN INTO THE shower and crouched behind her so he could care for her injury. He washed the back of her leg gently with his large fingers. The skin was pink, but the blisters and burns were gone.

"You're already almost entirely healed."

Like a demon or an angel. Ryder forced himself not to frown. *We need to figure out what the hell is going on with her. She's changing. Every day seems to bring something new, and I don't know what we're supposed to do about it.*

She finished scrubbing the soap out of her hair and glanced down at him. "Good, because I've got too damn much to do to be injured."

"Like going on another mission..."

She sighed loudly. "Something like that shouldn't happen again. It was just...bad luck."

"Bad luck?"

He stared at her, knowing that even she didn't believe the words she was speaking. Unfortunately for her, he could see right through her careful mask.

"Yeah," she continued, sounding too casual. "A team of hunters just happened to enter the realm right after I did. If they hadn't, I would have gotten away."

Ryder didn't want to say it, but he did. "I've never been one to believe in coincidences much."

She rubbed soap on her arms, but her hands moved slowly. "All right, fine. I didn't tell the others. But I thought the same thing."

He waited, knowing what she'd say next.

"But the thing that really bugs me is how did they know I'd be there? Have they picked up on a pattern to how we're doing things? Are they tracing us somehow? Or...or do they have a spy in the Rebellion?"

Ryder thought for a long time before he responded. "Either way, we need to be careful going forward."

She nodded. "You're right, of course. I'll be more careful when I cross over tomorrow."

He stood. A thousand things popped into his mind, but he said none of them. Sharen wouldn't listen if he told her to slow down or to relax. She'd be angry if he told her that she was still reeling from being possessed and needed time to process all that she'd been through.

Instead, he said nothing.

He turned her around to face the shower wall and rubbed her tense shoulders beneath the hot stream of their apartment shower. Her head rolled forward and she groaned, a sound that made his cock harden.

He loved to take care of her. To make her feel loved and precious.

She needed that. She *deserved* that.

He worked every muscle on her shoulders, then moved to her back, and then slowly down to her lower back. She braced herself against the shower, breathing hard. He heard a crack.

"Damn it," she muttered. She pulled her hands back from the shower wall and revealed the tiles clenched in her hands. She set them down on the bathtub ledge.

"It takes a while to get used to the strength," he reassured her, rubbing her back again.

She shook her head, sighing loudly. "Yeah, but do my messed-up powers have to leave when I need them the most and then show up just long enough to ruin things in the apartment?"

He chuckled, thinking of their broken toaster. "Just don't think about it."

She nodded and let her head roll forward again. In moments, the tension in her lower back began to ease again.

How can any woman be so sexy without even knowing it?

God, did he want her. Staring at the hard lines of her body, he gloried in every inch of her. In the months since joining the Rebellion, she'd added far too many scars to her human body, but he loved every one of them. Yes, each scar meant that his woman had been hurt, but it also meant she had survived.

My tough warrioress.

As he leaned forward and kissed her shoulder, his gaze went to the fading bruises on her wrists. His chest ached at the memory of how Kade had to hold her down. He thanked God that Kade held fast. Ryder doubted he could have hurt her, even if it was to save her.

She spun around and slid her arms around his neck. Instinctively, he leaned down. The instant their mouths touched, fire leapt between them. Arousal and need awakened within him, drawing a groan from his lips. Her skin felt so soft beneath his hands, her mouth eager and ready.

He deepened their kiss, moving his tongue into her mouth. The instant their tongues slid along each other, she pressed herself harder against him. The tight nubs of her breasts pressed into his chest.

His hands slid down and grabbed her ass, cupping the soft cheeks and pressing her more tightly against his arousal.

She broke their kiss. "Come on, Ryder, give it to me."

His hands tightened on her ass. "Your wish is my command."

Just the thought of easing inside her made his muscles tense. This was exactly what they needed.

The door crashed open. "Almost done in..."

Ryder turned to see Alec standing in the door, grinning at the two of them.

"Got room for one more?" Alec asked.

Sharen nodded. "Better hurry, I'm already ready."

Kade's twin pulled his tie loose before he started working on the buttons on his suit. In moments, he was naked. Alec joined them in the big, open shower and kissed her softly on the lips.

Then Ryder picked her up.

Instantly, her legs wrapped around his back. She sighed, slipping her arms around his neck. For a second, all Ryder could do was stare at the flawless lines of her face. He loved her high cheekbones and her stunning green eyes, but most of all he loved the way her expression relaxed when both of them touched her like this.

Our wife is the most beautiful creature I've ever seen.

Alec moved behind her. "I've got the best damned timing in the world."

They touched her together, running their hands along every inch of her flesh. Alec cupped her breasts while Ryder trailed kisses down her throat. Her hot breath came out in pants, and her nails dug more deeply into the flesh of his shoulder.

Ryder rubbed his hard length in her wet folds, loving the way she shuddered with each stroke. He gritted his teeth, desperate to keep control as he carefully maneuvered his tip inside her. Then he pressed deeper, further and further as her tight body held him in a grip that made every nerve in his body scream with need.

When he reached his hilt, he took deep breaths, waiting for his brother. But he didn't have to wait long. He felt her body tense as Alec entered her from behind. She gasped and her head rolled back.

They thrust in and out of her in a rhythm they'd perfected long ago, taking their time to draw out her desire. As she began to bounce on top of them, chanting the word *yes, yes* over and over again, Ryder's careful control crumbled away.

His demon side roared to life. He took her harder and faster. His grip tightened on her hips. When her inner muscles squeezed him and her nails dugs deeper into his back, she came, screaming his name.

He snapped, coming so hard it made his vision swim. God, this woman was incredible!

As he continued to thrust, loving the way her body drained him of every drop of his seed, he had to use every ounce of strength he had not to collapse to his knees.

Alec came behind her with a groan, and as he thrust harder, her body held Ryder tighter. He bit down on a string of curses, loving the pleasurable pain these moments brought. When his brother finished, they continued holding her beneath the spraying water, which had grown cold some time ago.

"Better?" he whispered into her hair.

She nodded.

Slowly, they eased her back onto her feet.

They showered again, quickly, and she went back into the bedroom to change. As Alec finished drying off, Ryder caught his arm.

"What is it?" His brother's dark eyes narrowed, zeroing in on him.

Leaning closer, he kept his voice low. "She was possessed today."

Alec's expression froze. "She was *what*?"

"Her trip through the portal went wrong. A witch had to perform an exorcism."

"Fuck!" Alec spun around and punched his fist through the wall, sending plaster raining down. "This has to stop! She has to stop!"

Sometimes I forget that even though Alec and Kade are different in so many ways, they both have the same damn temper.

Must be a twin thing.

Ryder grasped his shoulder. "Enough. Don't let her hear you. She's been through enough."

"And how much longer before one of these trips of hers ends in her death, huh? How much longer are we going to sit by, helpless, letting her risk her life?" Red bled into his pupils as the demon within him roared to life.

"Stop it! Now! Do you have any idea how close you are to losing control? Do you want to ruin everything by bringing every angel in the area straight to us?" Ryder's own anger flared to life.

The red faded from Alec's eyes. "Sorry. I just...I love her."

Ryder smiled, a smile that hurt. "I know. Me too."

After a second, Alec leaned against the wall, closing his eyes. "Does Kade know?"

Ryder took a deep breath, adjusting the towel around his waist. "He helped get the demon out and then killed it. They're sort of pissed at each other right now."

Alec laughed, shaking his head. "What else is new?"

A comfortable silence stretched between them for a long moment.

"Seriously though," Alec asked, opening his eyes and holding his gaze. "How long can we keep this up?"

Ryder shook his head. "For as long as she needs us to."

The worst thing is that she's right.

Ryder's thoughts moved to his time spent in the demon realm. It had been...awful. He'd felt himself changing day after day and he hadn't known how to stop it.

He was used to a world of beauty. On earth, he had always been the person who valued each and every day. He'd awaken in the mornings to watch the sun rise over the ocean, sometimes already lying on his surf board. He'd listen to the waves and feel the kiss of the sun's rays on his skin.

His world had been filled with peace and appreciation for all that the world had to offer. But after his death...he'd gone to a place devoid of life.

He shuddered, not wanting to remember the dark pits where light couldn't reach. How long had he stumbled around a foreign place completely blind? How quickly had he learned that he'd need to kill to survive?

Too fast.

And without beauty, without life, Ryder had felt himself fading away.

Until Sharen.

"Alec?"

His brother raised a brow. "Yes."

"Would you abandon the Rebellion if Sharen did?"

Alec was silent for too long. "I don't know. But I would abandon it if I knew it would keep her safe."

Ryder nodded. "When I think about leaving other people like us in that place..."

"I know," Alec said.

And yet, we aren't the ones risking our lives.

He knew the exact same thought had entered his brother's mind, because he turned and headed for the bedroom. His shoulders were slumped and he walked slower, as if the weight of the world rested on his back.

But it doesn't. I'm here. I'm always here.

When Ryder entered the room, he found Sharen in bed, fast asleep. He and Alec dried off some more, then climbed in next to her. But even though Alec fell asleep quickly, sleep eluded Ryder.

A few hours later, he still lay awake when he heard a soft sound in the living room. He watched as Kade came to stand in the doorway of the bedroom. His brother stared at Sharen for the longest time, then turned and went out to the living room.

Ryder wanted to go out and tell him not to sleep on the couch, that Sharen wasn't really mad at him, just the situation, but he knew it was pointless.

Some things just take time.

Just like saving the demons.

And figuring out how the hell we're going to help the Rebellion while keeping our wife safe.

That question kept Ryder awake long past the sunrise... which he didn't watch. He simply lay awake, letting the question roll through his mind.

Becoming a demon had changed him. In fact, he

couldn't remember the last time he watched the sunrise. But then, in his old life he'd never laid awake watching a woman sleep, falling more in love with her with each moment that passed.

How is it that even when I feel like I've lost myself, I don't regret it because I found her?

Despite everything, he finally fell asleep with a smile on his face.

6

SHAREN LEFT THE HOUSE EARLY AND STARTED HER MORNING jog. It was the only thing she could do to try to calm down. The events from the day before were driving her crazy. And what was worse, she had been prepared to unleash her frustrations on Kade when she woke up, but he was already gone.

Normally, they'd yell. Maybe she'd throw things. And then they'd calm down, both of them refusing to admit that they felt a little better.

But I should know better than to think I know what Kade will do.

When he disappeared, it usually meant that he couldn't handle whatever feelings he was having and needed time to sort through them. She hated when he left, but she also knew he needed the space.

Kade might be a demon, but he had inner demons he couldn't conquer. His fear of losing her drove him crazy, but she couldn't stop what she was doing because of his past. She had to be true to herself.

And I have to let him deal with that fact in whatever way he needs.

So, she went jogging, pushing herself harder and harder until the little sounds around her were silenced by the wind rushing around her. Until the shadows that chased her lessened. Until she stopped picturing the dead demons lying beside her. And until she stopped feeling him possess her body.

At last, out of breath, she collapsed onto a park bench and stared out at her favorite park.

Will I ever stop obsessing over my mistakes?

"Anyone sitting here?"

She jumped at the sound of the man's voice. She looked up to see a man not much older than herself, with long blond hair and pale green eyes. Something about him made her feel uneasy.

"No."

He sat down beside her.

She started to rise, but his voice stopped her.

"Don't leave on account of me."

She froze. "I'm not."

"Come now, Sharen, let's at least be honest with each other."

Ice ran through her veins, and her gaze swung to him. "Who are you? What do you want?"

He smiled, flashing bright rows of teeth. "I'm a hunter. Like you once were."

Her gaze moved over the people in the park. A woman jogged. A couple walked a dog. *Am I already surrounded?*

"Calm down, it's just me. I'm here for a little chat."

A need to run or fight washed over her. Every muscle in her body tensed.

"Running would be a very big mistake, Sharen, because

then I'd have to tell the others where you are. If that happens, you and your demons will have to pick up and run again. Do you want that?"

She didn't answer him. Instead, she countered, "Why are you here?"

He patted the seat next to him.

Reluctantly, she eased back down, poised at the edge of the bench.

"My name is Alderon. Perhaps you've heard of me."

Her breath quickened. Alderon was the name of a half-fae warrior who was in charge of the Guardians within the demon realms. His job was to ensure as few demons as possible were able to reach the higher realms and cross over to Earth. And from what she knew of him, he was a very dangerous man.

"I thought you stayed in the demon realms."

He smirked. "Even the Great Alderon needs a vacation every now and then."

Her lips curled. "And this is how you spend your vacations?"

Leaning further back on the bench, he looked out at the park as if he truly was just relaxing for the day. "Do you know what makes me such a good hunter?"

She gritted her teeth together. "You're annoyingly relentless?"

He laughed. "I heard you were funny. I'm glad the rumors were true. But no, Sharen, it isn't that I'm annoyingly relentless. Obsessive might be a better adjective to describe me. Yet, it's not just that. You see, I have the unique ability to track others. And when the Department of Universal Protection asked me to find you, I easily agreed."

Sweat trailed down her back, and she wiped her palms

on her pants. "And yet, you've implied that you're here alone."

He glanced at her, his pale eyes eerie. "Yes. I did come alone. And I haven't told anyone I found you yet."

"Why?"

"Because," he stretched out the word. "I'm also a man with a strong moral compass, and something about this feels wrong. One of our best hunters simply ran off with three demons? There must be more to the story than that."

She stared, unwilling to tell him anything of her life story.

He nodded, as if he expected her silence. "Something also feels rotten about all this. I checked your file. It was wiped clean. But when I did some digging, they had a strangely long, detailed history of your life."

Her heart raced. *Because they've been controlling my life for God knows how long.*

"And," he continued, "I can't say I've ever heard a story of someone with as miserable a life as you've had."

"So, what are you saying?"

All amusement fled from his expression. "I'm saying that I need to know what's going on here before I decide what to do with you."

What the hell am I supposed to say to that?

"I don't know everything myself."

He sat up straighter. "Then tell me this. Why has nearly every person in your life been on the Department's payroll?"

Her stomach turned. She'd suspected it. Vanessa, her ex-friend within the organization, had practically told her. But to realize how much of her life the Department controlled was terrifying.

"You want to know?" she asked, her anger rising. "You really want to know?"

"That's what I came here for."

She stood, her hands curling into fists. "They controlled every aspect of my life. They orchestrated every terrible moment. And I have no idea why the hell they did it."

He studied her. "Your parents' deaths. Your adoption to that god awful family. Your rape. Your—"

"Yes!" A string of curses exploded from her lips. "Is that what you wanted to hear?"

He rose, his demeanor strangely quiet. "And you have no idea why?"

Her jaw tensed. "No."

Except that I'm not human.

"Then I'm going to find out why."

She stared at him. "Are you joking?"

"Not even a little."

"Why?" She frowned at him. This had to be a trap of some kind.

He shrugged. "Like I said. It's important to me that I'm working for the good guys, and I can't logically wrap my brain around what I've been seeing since I looked into your case."

Shoving his hands into his jean pockets, he turned to go.

"Wait!" Her brain scrambled to make sense of this man. "So you aren't telling them where I am?"

He looked back at her and smiled. "Not yet. But if that changes, and I decide to, I will give you a 24-hour head start. Deal?"

She wasn't sure she could trust him, but she didn't have a choice. "Deal."

Turning away from him, she took a long and confusing way back home, constantly checking over her shoulder. She was certain no one followed her, but when she took the elevator up to their penthouse suit, she didn't feel relieved. She felt...afraid.

If they catch us, we're dead.

And yet, I can't just abandon everything I've done here.

Even though her stomach twisted, an idea formed in her mind. *If I tell my demons, they'll make us go.*

So I won't tell them.

She thought of Alderon. Did she really trust him with all their lives?

Closing her eyes, she ran over the scene in the park. *I—I do trust him. Even though it's probably foolish.*

The elevator doors opened and she headed toward her home. She tried to walk with confidence, but she couldn't ignore the little voice in the back of her head whispering, *But what if you're wrong?*

7

KADE STOOD BEFORE THE DEMON OF SACRIFICE, HIS HEART aching. This was the last place he wanted to come. But he would do anything for the woman he loved.

Even this.

The demon sat on a throne of bones, her grey eyes cold and cruel. More bones littered the ground at her feet, skeletons of the men who had bowed before her in the past, men who knelt at the very spot he stood now.

At her sides, eight demon guards wore armor made of bones, ready at her slightest signal to end the lives of anyone she chose. Kade hated that there wasn't one inch of beauty or happiness in this place. The guards, the bones, and the woman all radiated death and sadness. He wouldn't condemn his worst enemy to a place like this.

And certainly not her.

This far beneath the ground, a chill hung over everything. It settled on his flesh and then sunk deep to move through his veins. Demons were rarely cold, but in that moment, the chill seemed to squeeze his very heart.

"It has been a long time," the Demon of Sacrifice said, crossing her legs.

Her movement caused her long black skirts to float around her body like living things. It was beautiful. And horrifying. The demon was becoming more a creature of fantasy and magic each time he saw her, which meant she was losing her humanity. Eventually, she would have nothing left.

Trying his best to conceal his disturbing thoughts, he moved forward and knelt before her. "It has been."

"Have you told them about me yet?" she asked, never one to mince words.

Kade looked up at the familiar lines of her face. "No. But I want to."

She shook her head full of long dark hair, the same color as his own. "I told you, they can never know."

His chest ached at the secret he'd kept all these years. His brothers deserved to know the truth, and yet, it wasn't his secret to tell.

"Why are you here?" she asked, her tone gentling.

He took a deep breath. "I need to see the King of Hell."

Her eyes widened, but she said nothing for a long time. "Why? Why would you ever take such a risk when you've finally made it to Earth?"

The words wouldn't form on his tongue.

"It's for love," she said, sounding surprised, perhaps awed.

He nodded, and for an instant, all he could see was Sharen, her face bruised, and the scars on her body. She couldn't keep going on the way she was, saving one demon at a time. Regardless of the risk to him, he had to stop it, and this was the only way he knew how to.

The Demon of Sacrifice slid off her throne to kneel before him. "Are you certain this is what you want?"

He locked gazes with her. "I would give my eternal life to stop her pain."

She reached out and stroked his cheek. "You, Alec, and Ryder are the only good men in all the realms. The rest are monsters that should be wiped out. Their bones crushed beneath my feet."

He touched her hand, pressing his much larger one to hers. "One day, you'll know this kind of love."

Her teeth clenched together and she rose angrily, towering over him. "I am the Demon of Sacrifice. When a man harms a woman, she need only ask for me, and I will come with a vengeance. I will watch his blood run and offer her my help in all things. In my many years, both in life and death, I have met many monstrous men. But I have only met three good ones. Do not try to convince me there are more out there."

Kade felt tears sting his eyes. "The day we sought vengeance for you...I'd hoped it would give you some peace. Some healing."

Her expression was like stone. "Accept the truth: nothing will ever bring me peace."

He hung his head. "We failed you."

She grasped his arm and pulled him to his feet. "No, the men who raped me killed the girl you loved. But seeing what you did to them? That gave me the strength of will to become so much more."

"Kayla—"

She shook her head. "Kayla is dead. Only the Demon of Sacrifice remains. And you may have anything you ask of me, no matter how foolish it seems." Closing her eyes, he felt her power wash over him. A portal of bluish-grey magic spiraled in the center of the room. "Enter it and find the Demon King's city not far from it. Only you can see the portal. You may enter it only once, and you may exit it only once. In three days, it will close forever."

He nodded. "Thank you."

She sat once more on her throne of bones. Her expression was cold, but beneath it he could feel her sadness.

Oh, little sister, how did we fail you so badly?

With his entire chest aching, he turned to the portal. If the demon king agreed to his plan, Sharen would never again have to risk her life so recklessly.

And if he failed? He'd be condemned to the demon realm for eternity.

No one had ever escaped twice.

8

SHAREN STARED OUT THE WINDOW OF THEIR CAR AS THEY drove the short distance to the refuge. It was only fifteen minutes outside the city but felt like a world away. Her demons had used a great deal of the funds from their business to purchase the large estate and acres of woods around it. This was the place they kept most of the demons while they adapted to the human world once more and learned not to use their magic.

Alec took her hand, squeezing it gently. "Thank you for agreeing to come with me. I think seeing you will cheer them up."

She raised a brow. "Don't think I don't know what you're doing. Trying to get me to take a day off."

He smiled, which only made his stunning good looks completely breathtaking. "You got me."

She stared for a long moment. Sometimes it amazed her that he was Kade's twin. Both men had the same dark hair and brown eyes that were so dark they were almost black, but while Kade's hair was cut so short it was nearly a military style, Alec's haircut looked as if it cost a hundred bucks, which it nearly did. And while Kade preferred jeans and t-shirts, Alec always looked ready for a night out on the town. Even today he wore a sports coat and a white shirt, unbuttoned low in front.

Her insides tightened. A man shouldn't be allowed to be as handsome as Alec. It was as if someone had given him classic good looks, then sprinkled in some bad boy.

The perfect recipe for Mr. Panty Dropper.

She smiled.

He turned to look at her. "What is it?"

She shrugged. "I was just thinking about what you'd look like with a mustache."

"A mustache?" He touched his square jaw. "Not a chance. You can't hide these good looks with hair."

This time, she laughed. "You sure are humble."

He raised a brow, his smile widening. "It's hard to be humble when a beautiful woman follows you around smacking your ass and demanding sex."

"*Demanding* sex!" She hit his shoulder. "Like hell!"

He threw back his head and laughed, the sound deep and satisfying. "Come here, my little sex kitten. Why don't I unbutton my pants and you can just—"

She reached across him and grabbed his erection.

A strangled sound exploded from his lips. "That was a joke!"

"Let's see if you're laughing when I take you into my wet mouth and—"

"Hell!" he said. "Want me to pull over the damn car?"

She unbuckled and leaned forward to lick his tip through his pants. "No, we're on a deadline."

Then she rebuckled and turned to look out the window as if nothing happened.

"Are you, I mean, this is a joke, right? Now I'm horny as

hell and can't stop picturing those sweet lips wrapped around my cock."

She looked back at him and grinned. "I wonder who will be chasing who tonight."

He groaned and rubbed his face. "Remind me not to joke around with you. You're one cruel woman."

She smirked and leaned back in her chair. God, her demons kept life interesting. And they were the perfect distraction from all the things that had been spinning around her head lately.

A couple minutes later, they turned off the main road and started down a small, unpaved road that served as the private driveway to the estate.

Alec cleared his throat. "So, have you heard from Kade?"

Way to ruin my good mood. "No. But you know he does this when he's angry."

He disappears for a few days, to God only knows where. She pulled her hand from Alec's, crossing her arms in front of her chest. *Not that he has a reason to be mad. I'm the one who should be mad.*

"Maybe you should give him a call."

She scoffed. "Not a chance."

"Sharen—"

"Don't say my name like that!" She glared at him, the fighter within her roaring to life.

"I'm just saying." His tone was growing angrier with each word. "He did what he had to do to keep you safe."

"He didn't have to kill the demon, he could have—"

"Left him alive so he could hurt you again?" he challenged.

She reached out and struck the dashboard with her fist. "Why the hell can't you guys have some faith in me? I wouldn't let that happen!"

Why can't anyone just believe in me? Why does everyone think I'm such a useless burden?

When she struck the dashboard again, her hand cracked right through, leaving a fist-sized hole. "Damn powers!" she shouted, then followed up with, "Damn idiot demons who think they know better!"

He slammed on his brakes and whirled on her. "We love you because you have so much damn hope. So much faith that everything is going to work out. But you get to be idealistic, because we're practical. We take care of the things that you can't. So as much as we want to follow recklessly after you, we have to use some common sense to keep you alive."

"Keep me alive!" Now she was full-on shouting. "I can take care of my God damn self!"

"Everybody needs somebody!"

I didn't need my ex. I didn't need my parents. I didn't need that foster family that told me every day what a waste of space I am.

"I don't need anyone! And I'm not some idealistic idiot who just does whatever the hell I want, leaving you guys to pick up the pieces!"

He looked forward, his hands tightening on the steering wheel. "I kill myself at the fucking company to fund your dreams. Getting that demon stone. Getting that equipment. And those books. None of it's cheap. And Ryder? He's working like a madman to turn the lost souls you save into functioning, helpful parts of the Rebellion. And Kade? He handles everything else. He puts himself in dangerous situations to get the information and sources we need to make this thing run."

"And what?" she challenged. "I do nothing?"

He looked at her. "None of this would be possible without you. You're our guiding light. Our hope for a better future. I'm just saying, you could try to understand how exhausted we are, and how much it's killing us to let you put yourself in danger every fucking day. It's driving us mad. Especially Kade."

She glared. "Why do you guys have this need to keep me in a safe little box?"

Alec grew quiet for a long minute. "Well, because we love you. And maybe you don't need us, but we need you. And...because we failed at keeping the woman we loved safe once before."

She stilled. "Your sister."

They rarely spoke of the girl who had been raped. She knew they had killed the men responsible for hurting her, and that they'd been jumped and killed before they could get out. But she knew little else.

"What happened to her wasn't your fault."

He hung his head. "We've told ourselves that a million times. But the truth is, we failed her twice: once by letting her get hurt, and again when we died. She had no one. And by giving in to our reckless anger, we got ourselves killed. She was left alone. Even though we've searched for her, we have no idea what happened. Did she go on to live a happy life? Did she get married or have children? We don't know. But what we do know is that we failed her. And we don't want to fail you."

I'm such an idiot. Why do I get so caught up in other things that I forget my tough demons have a softer side?

Reaching out, she pulled his face to her and planted a soft kiss on his lips. "I'm not your sister. I've chosen this life. I know it's dangerous, but I can't stop. I can't live knowing innocent people are suffering in the demon realm."

Alec pushed her dark hair back from her face. "We know

we can't stop you. I'm just saying, maybe give us a break when we act like possessive, alpha assholes."

I hate when he's right. "Okay."

"Can you call Kade?"

She bit her lip. Usually it was a game between the two of them of who would break first. He usually did. But Alec was right, maybe she needed to stop taking her frustration out on the man she loved.

"All right." Then she lowered her voice. "But also, I do need you guys."

He rolled his eyes. "Of course. Because without me, you'd have to take out the trash yourself. And without Ryder, you'd have to cook and clean. And without Kade? Well, who would fix every damn thing in the house?"

She laughed. "I could always *hire* someone you know."

One of his brows rose. "But would you make them do their chores in nothing but a sock?"

She couldn't help herself. "It depends what they look like."

He growled low in his throat. "Better call Kade before I decide to start beating up random good-looking repairmen."

Trying to hide her smile, she unbuckled and pulled her phone out of her back pocket. Hitting Kade's name, she listened to the ringer, holding her breath.

But it went to voicemail.

She frowned. "He didn't pick up."

Ending the call, she stared at her phone. *Kade always picks up his phone, no matter how mad he is.*

"Maybe he's in the shower." Alec spoke the words, but his tone held doubt.

She called him again. Nothing.

Her pulse sped up. "Any idea where he went?"

"Not a clue."

Alec closed his hand over hers again and pulled her closer to press a light kiss along her knuckles. "We'll call him again after our visit. I'm sure he's fine."

She nodded, even though every instinct was screaming inside her.

They continued down the private road until they felt the magical barrier. It tingled over her flesh for a moment, then vanished. They'd had to pay a witch an ungodly amount of money to create a barrier around the estate that would hide the demon's magic from the angels. It wouldn't hide all of it... If the demons went wild, the angels would feel them, and the barrier had to be enforced again by magic every few weeks, but it gave the demons some level of protection from discovery.

A minute passed before they reached the massive brick fence. Typing in the code, the gates parted in front of them. Driving through the wild grounds of the estate, it took them a minute to exit out to the neatly trimmed lawn and the mansion. On the lawn, demon children played ball.

Her fears slipped away in the face of their happiness. The kids looked like any other human children, but she knew they would always be different. Death did that to a person.

But at least they're out of that awful place.

That was the other thing. Earth wasn't truly the place for them either. They belonged in the angel realm. She had no idea what their lives would be like as immortals living on Earth. She hadn't yet thought that far into the future. All she knew was that for now, they were safe.

Alec parked the car out front. More demons poured out of the house, men and women, both old and young.

Taking a deep breath, she opened her door and came out into the fresh air.

There were lots of hugs and excited questions, but then the kids reached them. She knelt, wrapping her arms around them, breathing in the sweet scent that was solely that of children.

Pulling back, Beth's face came into view. Her lovely dark skin, her stunning brown eyes. "Have you heard from Brian? How's he liking the big world?"

Ice settled in her stomach. How had she forgotten that they would ask her? She still felt too raw to talk about the boy. In her mind, the alley flashed in her thoughts. All the blood. The little car that was still in her jacket pocket.

Alec cleared his throat. "We should discuss that inside."

As she stood, the atmosphere changed. The adults looked at her. And they knew. She could see it in their faces.

Their hopelessness tugged at her like a living thing, and suddenly, she felt exhausted.

Alec wrapped his arm around her waist and pressed a kiss to her hair. "Come on."

As they made their way up the steps, she fought back tears. *How can I make them believe they have a better future in this world if I'm starting to doubt it too?*

9

KADE HADN'T FORGOTTEN THE DEEPEST PARTS OF THE DEMON realm. The smell of sulfur, thick and suffocating, hung in the air. He made his way from the portal, hidden by his sister's magic, and stared up at the dark sky. The tiny sparks of fire drifted down from the darkness, the only thing close to rain in this world, except the sparks always fell, the only source of light.

As he continued on, he weaved between boulders. This far down, everything was covered in several thick feet of ash. He shuffled through it, kicking up a small cloud as he moved.

As he came around a corner, a creature was waiting for him. The demon was massive with dark hair and rugged features. One side of his face was covered in scars that had once been burns. And even from a distance, he radiated anger. What was more, he wore the white uniform of the king of the demon realm.

I expected to meet one of his men, but not quite this quickly.

"Hello," Kade called, clenching his fists. Down here he could call his soul blade to him without fear of attracting angels, and he'd do it in a heartbeat if the demon showed himself to be a threat.

"I am a defender of the king, and you are trespassing on his lands."

Kade stiffened. *This man will take me right to the person I want to see, if I do this right.* "I apologize. I wasn't aware. But I'm here from Earth to see the king."

The demon's gaze ran over him. "It's not often demons return here when they've escaped. It's against the king's rule."

"I'm aware, but my mission here is an important one."

The demon shrugged his massive shoulders. "So be it."

To his surprise, the man didn't grab him. Instead, they walked next to each other and toward a river of flowing lava, as if this was the most normal thing in the world.

"I'm Kade," he introduced himself.

The demon raised a brow. "Jaxson."

After a minute, the stoic demon spoke again. "I have a feeling, and tell me if I'm wrong, but I think the only reason a demon would ever do something so stupid is for love. Am I wrong?"

Kade sighed, running a frustrated hand through his dark hair. "You're not."

The demon nodded. "I just hope you know what you're in for."

They reached the river. "I guess that depends. Has the king ever granted a favor to a deserter before?"

Jaxson grinned. "Nope, but there's a first time for everything."

Great. Just great.

10

Alec couldn't bear to listen to Sharen explain what happened to the demon family for another second. In moments like these, she didn't want his comfort or help, and it drove him crazy. What was he supposed to do to fix this for her?

He left the building and stormed outside, walking without thinking. *How is it that Ryder can always make her feel better, and I can't?*

He kicked at a rock, his frustration building. Sharen had been on the edge of tears. He'd thought bringing her out here would give her a break from the constant portal jumping and disappointment. Now, it seemed, he'd made things worse.

I'm horrible at relationships if I can't even comfort the woman I love when she's sad.

"How's business?"

He whirled to spot an old demon sitting on a bench near the house. The man had long grey hair and shrewd eyes.

What the hell is wrong with me? I shouldn't be so concerned with Sharen that I forget to watch my surroundings.

A demon can never be too careful.

"Fine," Alec responded, watching him cautiously.

The old man raised a brow. "I'm Dave."

"Alec."

He laughed. "I know who you are."

Alec stared for a long minute, not sure what to say. Alec was a businessman, dominating every meeting and running things with an iron fist. He'd gone to college, unlike Kade, who'd gone straight into the army, and Ryder, who had drifted about, following whatever interested him. Alec's success in the business world had taught him to never stop until he was the best.

But outside of work, he felt a bit lost. He'd never been one for small talk.

"Why don't you come sit with me?" Dave said, indicating the other side of the bench.

I don't have a good excuse to say no. Alec withheld a sigh, but moved slowly over and sat down.

"So Brian and his family died?"

Alec looked to the man in surprise. "How did you know?"

The old man shrugged. "I saw the look on your woman's face. I didn't need to go inside to hear all the awful details of it."

"Yeah, they died."

The man reached into his sweater and pulled out a bag of bread crumbs and began throwing them onto the lawn. Not even a second passed before birds flew down and started eating. It was a strangely quiet moment, even though they were discussing the murder of a mother and her children.

I guess I'm numb to death now. Is this man as well?

"So what are you guys going to do about the angels?"

Alec stiffened. "What do you mean?"

The old man snorted. "Well, clearly you can't just keep sending us out into the world to be slaughtered."

"That's why we try to keep you here long enough so you stop using magic without thinking. So you stop doing things that would draw attention to yourselves."

He laughed. "That's not possible for most of us. At least those of us who were in the demon realm long enough to lose most of our humanity...gave into the demon side that grew more powerful with each day we remained in the demon realm."

"It wasn't hard for us," Alec said without thinking.

Dave threw more bread. "Let me ask you something. Do you ever thirst for blood? For death? For carnage?"

"No."

"Even when you were in the demon realm?" the old man pressed.

"No." Alec froze. "Well, maybe. It's hard to remember those times."

Dave nodded. "You aren't struggling the way many of us are for two reasons. For whatever reason, you and your brothers were able to hold onto most of your humanity. No matter how much the demon realm called for you to let the human within you die and accept being a demon, you didn't."

"We're Level 10 demons," Alec interrupted. "That's not how it works. Level 10 demons are mostly good people. Most of them should never have been in the demon realm to begin with."

The old man chuckled. "I'm surprised how little you know for such a powerful demon. Yes, most Level 10 demons were good people. The key word there being *most*. Some of them were awful people who never had a chance to follow through with their dark desires. But then there are the Level 10 demons who *were* good people when they died, but the demon realm twisted them. Darkened their souls. There are few people who can withstand the call forever."

Alec shook his head. "That can't be true. I don't remember a call."

Dave threw more bread. "Some of the purer souls aren't as susceptible to it, but believe me, there's a call, and it's hard to resist. And it isn't as easy to let go as you might think. Most of us here are struggling. We thirst for destruction and chaos, for death and violence. We crave all the things that make us more powerful. Frankly, I'm not sure we'll be able to stop ourselves when we're released onto humanity."

"No." Alec stared, unable to believe his words.

The old man turned to him, raising a brow. "How do you think Brian and his family were discovered by the angels? Purely by chance? I doubt it. They used their magic. They called the angels to them. And if I were to guess, they were probably doing something bad."

"I don't believe you."

"Be logical," he said. "What brought the angels?"

Alec felt his pulse racing. "My brothers and I have never felt the need for death, chaos, or destruction. We came here to have a chance at life again, like we thought all of you did."

He shrugged. "Some of us will be able to do that. Some of us won't. But not only are your souls purer than most of ours, free of demon's desires within us, but you have Sharen."

"What do you mean?"

"There's a reason demons prefer possession of a human when they cross over. You three are linked to Sharen. To a human. And that link will help keep your humanity alive too."

Alec felt sick. He rose, unsure what to say or do.

The old man shook his head. "We can all use our strength, quickness, and ability to convince...along with our natural gifts, to avoid the radar of the angels, but sooner or later, most of us will give into our darker side. And so, you'll need to figure out a solution to the angels. A way to stop them from coming after us."

None of this can be true. Alec thought of himself in the demon realm. Foggy memories began to come back to him. Of his throne. Of the masses of lower level demons who obeyed him without question...or died for their insolence. He'd never thought about how different he'd felt since coming to Earth. He just imagined that it was escaping the demon realm that quieted the demon within him. It'd never occurred to him that it wasn't this easy for all the demons. He'd just found their lack of restraint annoying.

Alec shook his head. "We can't take on the angels. All of you will have to simply work harder. We'll keep you in the sanctuary longer, but—"

"Eventually, we'll all give into our other half. It's what we are now."

His stomach turned. "Sharen believes—"

"That we can all be saved." The demon smiled, and for the first time, Alec saw that his teeth were sharpened to points. "We can't be. We weren't meant to be demons, but that's what we are now. She can pretend we can be human all she wants, but we can't be. This isn't a permanent solution."

Alec stared. "We *can't* take on the angels. We won't win."

The demon was quiet for a long moment. "Perhaps with so few of us. But what if we build an army?"

Something about his suggestion made Alec's pulse race. "We can't unleash an army of demons onto this world."

"As my father always said, 'Shit or get off the pot.'"

Alec frowned. "What the hell does that mean?"

Dave grinned. "If this Rebellion is about saving demons, then save them, but know there are consequences. Know that you're changing this world in a way that can never go back. If demons are allowed free range, some will blend in and live normal lives like you and your brothers. And some will unleash death and destruction."

"No," Alec said. "We're only letting the good Level 10 demons out."

The man raised a brow. "And how do you know if we're all good? Do you have any idea what I was thrown into the demon realm for?"

His stomach turned. "No."

The man grinned again. "And you don't want to know. Trust me. Or you wouldn't want to leave me here with all these innocent lives."

Alec's fingers twitched, his need to call his soul blade to him like a fire burning through his blood. "And what's to stop me from killing you right here?"

He shrugged. "Nothing. But you should know, I've turned over a new leaf. Not everyone here has. If you notice the dead animals throughout the sanctuary, you'll know I'm speaking the truth."

Alec grabbed his blade from the sheath at his back and pulled it free. "Who?"

The man leaned back on the bench. "I'm not certain. But one thing is sure: you guys need a better plan. A way to tell the good ones from the bad ones. A way to keep us safe out in the world and to be sure our demon side won't endanger humanity." His gaze moved to Alec's sword. "Put your blade down. It might make you feel better to kill me, but it certainly won't help your situation."

Alec turned and hurried across the lawn. The old man was playing with his head. He had to be lying. There was no way they'd unknowingly released danger into the world.

But only a few minutes into his walk, he picked up the scent of blood. Following it, he came out into a field. On one edge of it a deer had been slaughtered, ripped apart in a way no animal would ever do.

He stared in shock. *This can't be happening.*

His sensitive ears picked up another sound further in the woods. Clutching his sword, he moved deeper into the trees, where the sunlight didn't quite filter through the thick leaves.

It only took a moment to find what he was looking for. Beth, the sweet little girl they'd rescued not long ago, was clutching a squirrel. As he watched, she tore one of the legs from the creature, who screamed helplessly.

"Stop it!" he shouted, the words pouring from his lips.

She turned, her eyes blood red. She growled low in her throat and dropped the suffering animal.

"Try to harm me and die," he whispered.

A moment later, she froze, and her eyes slowly returned to big brown ones. Her lips pulled into a frown. "Sorry, sometimes I just can't help myself."

Then she turned and ran back to the manor.

He knelt down where he stood, pressing his knuckles to his mouth.

What have we done?

11

Sharen stared at Alec in complete disbelief. "I don't believe it."

Alec ran a frustrated hand through his dark hair. "Why would I lie to you?"

She leaned back in her seat in the car, staring out the window at the trees that were flying by as Alec sped along the road. There was no way some of the demons they rescued were bad. No way that they were a danger to humanity.

No way Beth would torture small animals.

"This isn't possible," she whispered.

"You think I like it any more than you do?"

She clutched her arms around her chest. "So they're all evil?"

"No." He reached over and squeezed her knee. "Some of them are. Some of them are good. We just need to find a way to determine who is who before we bring more demons over."

"And how the hell are we supposed to do that?" Her

words were angry, bitter, but she felt on the verge of something awful.

"I don't have a clue, but we'll figure it out."

She shook her head, hating that tears stung her eyes. *I'm not this woman! I don't cry at every little challenge in life!* But as a hot tear rolled down her cheek, she had to accept the truth. She felt completely crushed. Completely hopeless. She wanted so badly to make things right, to save the innocent demons.

And now? Now she might have unleashed monsters onto the world.

Are the fucking angels right? Are they the good guys and we're the bad guys?

"No!" She turned to Alec. "No, this can't be true. There has to be more to it than this."

As they entered the town, her thoughts spun. She had to know for sure. But how was she supposed to do that?

For too long she sat, feeling numb, feeling lost. And then, as she gazed out her window, she saw something familiar. "Stop!"

Alec turned to her, frowning. "What is it?"

"Just stop. Pull the car over."

He did and she unbuckled, rushing out of the car.

She sensed Alec behind her, but she ignored him. As she moved to the front of the alley, she stared, feeling her heart clench. Moving slowly, she came to the spot. Most of the blood had been cleaned up. The area had clearly been swept over by the police.

But there has to be something I missed.

Stretching her senses out, she still caught the coppery scent of blood. And other scents, of filth, sweat, and garbage. But then she caught something else.

Moving without thinking, she walked through the alley. When she reached the other side, she looked at the tall brick apartment building. There! Rushing forward, she pushed opened the doors of the apartment, found the stairs, and rushed up them, taking each step two at a time.

"Sharen—" Alec began behind her.

She tuned him out, continuing to walk until she rushed out the stairwell.

When she came to a random door on the third floor, she froze. There was nothing unusual about it, and yet, she knew this was where she needed to go.

She knocked, even though she didn't expect anyone to answer. After a moment of silence, she reached out and shoved the door. The wood splintered and cracked free of the lock.

Thanks, powers, for actually being here when I need you.

Taking a step into the room, she immediately knew something was off. The apartment was a strange mix of an old woman's taste, flower furniture, plants everywhere, photos of grandchildren covering every wall, and tiny fragile figurines. Then she saw new items that didn't make sense. She found children's toys and clothes and a sink stacked up with unwashed dishes.

She walked past the coffee table, where little cars had been arranged as if racing. When she moved to the fridge, her heart was in her stomach. Turning the handle, she opened it.

Inside was the old woman's dead body.

No. No. No.

"Fuck!" Alec muttered behind her.

Breathing hard, she closed the fridge door and moved back. "They did it. Brian and his family killed her."

"Why?" Alec asked the question she wondered herself. "We helped get them an apartment. We got her a job. There was no reason to kill the old lady."

Going to the window, she already knew what she would find. Directly below them was the blood-stained alley.

"They used their magic to kill her, for whatever reason, and they brought the angels down on them." She said the words numbly.

Turning, she walked right back out the apartment door. She moved down the street until she found a phone booth. Inside, she dialed the police and told them where they would find the old woman's body.

The least she deserves is to be found by her family. To have a proper burial.

Hanging up the phone, she stared at Alec. "I want to go home."

He took a second to answer. "I thought we were going to headquarters."

To face everyone when I feel like falling apart? I can't do that, or they'll lose all faith in what we're doing here.

"I want to go home."

To her surprise, he didn't immediately jump into action. Instead, he studied her, his expression thoughtful. His eyes filled with helplessness.

"We don't *know* what happened," he said, reaching out to touch her arm.

She shifted out of his reach. "Maybe you don't, but I do."

All hope rushed out of her, leaving her feeling weak and empty.

As if the world sensed her pain, rain began to fall. Cool, soft drops from a sky with only a scattering of clouds.

Turning, she headed back to their car.

Whatever happens now, I swear no one else will die because of my mistake.

But how she would stop it, she had no idea.

12

KADE KNELT BEFORE THE DEMON KING'S WHITE THRONE, waiting to be acknowledged. The king ignored him, speaking to a demon near him in a hushed tone. So Kade let his gaze run over the high ceilings of the white palace and then back to the young man who occupied the throne. He had dark hair, dark eyes, and a strange quality that spoke of his immortality. It was as if he was too perfect-looking.

Inhuman.

And the most unexpected thing? Every demon in the realm had bright red skin and twin white horns on their heads, including himself. But not the king. As much as he had an inhuman quality to him, he was the only one who actually...resembled a human.

Not something I would have expected from the king of demons.

At last, the king turned to him, the man at his side shuffling away. "So this is the demon who trespassed on my lands after doing the forbidden...returning to the human realm." His voice boomed through the massive throne room, echoing so much that even some of his guards that stood along the wall flinched. "What do you have to say for your-self, demon, before I toss you back into the Pits?"

Here goes nothing.

Kade held the man's gaze. "I've returned to ask you for help."

The king raised a brow. "Surely you jest?"

"No, I do not, my lord." He took a deep breath. "I am a member of a rebellion on Earth. We know that something is going on with Caine and the realms. We know that innocent people are being tossed into the demon realm incorrectly. And so, we are working with a human who is helping us save innocent demons."

As Kade spoke, the demon king's gaze narrowed. "Are you so certain that these people are innocent?"

"We know there are innocent people incorrectly thrown into the demon realm."

The king looked away for half a second.

He knows I'm right.

"None of this explains why you're here."

Kade's hands clenched into fists. "I'm here because the woman I love believes in our cause so much so that she risks her life each and every day trying to save these lost souls. But she can give every ounce of herself and it won't be enough. Every day more innocent demons will be sent here. Every time she tries to save someone, she risks her life. So, I have to believe that there's a better way. And I think if anyone can help us, it's you." The demon king leaned back in his throne, not speaking for a long time. One of his hands hung over the arm of his throne, his fingers moving in small ways, but otherwise, he remained perfectly still.

"Everyone!" His voice boomed over the room. "Get out!"

The demons hesitated for half a second, looking shocked. But then, one after another, they trickled out. The throne room door closed behind them like a crack of thunder.

"Rise," the king commanded.

Kade obeyed.

The most powerful being in the demon realm rose and moved down the steps toward him, stopping no more than a foot away. "I am going to tell you things that no other demon knows. And you will keep these secrets. Do you understand?"

"I give my word."

The king studied him for a long second, then nodded. "Did you know that two hundred years ago there were no Level 10 demons?"

Kade stiffened. "I did not."

"And did you know that all of the demons older than two hundred years have no memories of the days before that time?"

"I did not," Kade whispered, feeling the hairs on his body stand on end.

"Myself included," the demon king continued. "All I know is that the first time a Level 10 demon appeared in my realm, I was confused. Within those demons, I sensed goodness. I knew my job was to ensure that the evil paid. That the cruel suffered in my realm. But what was I to do with beings that felt as if they should be angels rather than demons?"

Kade shook his head, not sure if he was expected to answer him.

The king held his hands behind his back and began to pace. "I couldn't help them, or I'd risk bringing the wrath of Caine upon me. So I did the only thing I could. I did nothing. As they climbed the realms to escape this prison, I didn't stop them. I did nothing outwardly to support them, but in ignoring their actions, I helped them the only way I could."

He stopped pacing and met Kade's gaze. "But there's change in the air. My demons with the ability to prophesize have warned me. A war is coming, and there are whispers that Caine will be overthrown."

Kade closed his mouth, realizing that it had been hanging open. *This is deeper than I ever imagined.*

"So now a demon comes to me with a desire to help free the good demons, and I must ask myself: do I do nothing once more? Or do I do *something*?"

Kade held his breath, waiting.

The demon king moved closer to him, so close they stood only inches from one another. A second later, a strange black pen appeared in his hand. "Roll up your sleeve and give me your arm."

Kade obeyed.

The king pressed the pen against his skin.

Kade hissed, shocked as it burnt his flesh. Gritting his teeth, he held perfectly still as the king scribbled something onto his arm.

At last, the king pulled the pen away and it disappeared from his hand. "This is the location of a realm that no one knows exists but me. In three days, I will ensure that every innocent demon is there. Your human can return them to Earth. But after the three days, the location will fade from your arm and from existence."

Kade stared at his arm, then back at the king. "Thank you."

The man nodded. "But you know, this is just the beginning. You will not be able to hide that many demons. Caine will feel their presence. This act will be the beginning of war. Can you handle that?"

I would do anything for Sharen.

"Yes."

"Then go. But if you should return to me again in death, do not expect to leave."

Kade bowed low and then hurried out the door. The smell of burnt flesh followed him as he headed out into the demon city, but his heart also felt lighter.

War with the angels would be difficult, but it was better than what they were doing now. He and his brothers could help protect Sharen this way. And one way or another, all of this would end soon.

Hold on, Sharen, I'm coming!

13

SHAREN LAY CURLED UP IN THE BOTTOM OF THE SHOWER. SHE didn't have a clue what to do. When she'd joined the Rebellion, she'd been so sure of herself. The other humans that were helping the cause had found ways to track where some of the demons crossed over. They went to any location that appeared on their radar and tried to help the demons. She'd been the first one to suggest actually going over and getting them, and she'd been one of the few that could do it.

Everyone had been ecstatic. They'd thought this would change everything. *Now what do I tell them? What do I do?*

Turning off the shower, she lay in the two feet of warm water that had pooled in the tub. She felt like she was being ripped apart.

On the sink, her phone rang. She frowned at the unknown number, but went with her gut and answered.

"What's cookin', good lookin'?" Her best friend Elaina's voice swept over her, instantly bringing her comfort.

"I haven't heard from you in over a month."

Her friend's tone changed to a more serious one. "That's

one of the problems with being on the run...not enough time to call the people I love."

Sharen laughed, although the sound was tinged with sadness. "I miss you. I'm completely lost, and I don't know what to do."

"Tell me what's happening. I only have a minute, but I'll help, if I can."

Sharen rushed through an abbreviated version of what had happened and held her breath.

"Wow! Well, shit, that is a problem. Humm... First things first. You need to calm down."

"Calm down?" She looked at the phone. Had she heard Elaina correctly? "Calm down about unleashing evil into our world?"

Elaina laughed. "You forget that you can't control what these demons do. You can do your best to only save the good ones, and you can try to teach them how to be human again, but then it's up to them."

She shook her head. "But—"

"Hon, just do the best you can. That's all you can do."

Sharen sat in silence, not knowing what else to say.

"How are your demons doing?" Elaina said, abruptly changing topics.

She swallowed hard, trying to switch tracks while her heart was on the floor. "Kade got mad at me and took off. Alec is acting like I'm made of glass. And Ryder? Well, like usual, he's pretending everything is fine."

"So nothing has changed."

Sharen smiled, a small smile. "Not much. I just wish they could...they could...I don't know."

"They can't do anything other than what they're doing, because they're as lost as you are. They want to be tough demons, but not every situation can be fixed with super strength or speed. Trust me, my demons struggle with it too, but give them a break, I'm sure they're trying."

Sharen leaned against the back of the tub. "Why does everyone keep telling me that?"

Elaina laughed. "Well, I need to go, but take a deep breath, Sharen. The amazing thing about you is that you can find hope in even the darkest of situations. I know you can fix this, or at least find some peace...with the refugees and your demons."

She swallowed around the lump in her throat. "Thanks."

"Talk to you soon," Elaina whispered and the line went dead.

Sharen stared at her phone and took a deep breath. She would try again. She dialed Kade's number, her heart hammering, but just like before, it went to voicemail. She ended the call, worried more than ever. *What if this is more than Kade ignoring me?*

The water suddenly felt ice cold. Rising from the tub, she set her phone on the sink and grabbed a towel. Hurrying into her room, she dried and dressed as quickly as she could. She might not be able to solve all of the concerns from her demons, but she could find Kade and make sure he was safe.

Out in the living room, she heard a key turning in the lock.

A second later, Kade came in. He looked...filthy. Ash streaked his brown hair and his skin. His blue shirt was blackened in several spots and his jeans were a mess. Her gaze moved up to his face. The lines around his dark eyes looked deeper, but there was also something unexpected in his gaze... Hope.

She felt something rush through her. Something beautiful.

"Where have you been? I've been worried sick." She gravitated to him, then reached up and stroked his cheek.

He leaned into her touch, his eyes closing. "I've been to hell and back."

Her heart hammered. Was he being literal? "Why?"

Those piercing eyes of his opened once more. "For you. Always for you."

She didn't understand, but she took his hand. She led him to the bathroom and filled the tub once more with steaming water. He made quick work of removing her clothes and then moved to his own. He undid the buttons on his shirt and tugged it off, then slid off his pants. To her surprise, his clear arousal strained through his boxers.

She looked up at him. "Clearly you aren't too tired from your little trip."

His normally stoic expression changed, a slight smile touching his lips. "Never too tired for you."

Removing his boxers, she stood, and they moved into the bath together. The water blackened around them. She took her time, washing his hair and his body. Then she drained the water and filled it up with clear, fresh water.

She leaned against him in the bath, closing her eyes, feeling his arousal behind her. When his arm came around her, she glanced down and gasped. On the underside of it were strange symbols.

"What the hell is this?"

He kissed the back of her neck. "The solution to our problems."

The skin around the burn was red and painful-looking. And the symbols...they looked like a strange tattoo that shimmered slightly in the light.

"What does that mean, Kade? What happened to you?" She sucked in a deep breath, fighting her urge to flip out.

"While we were here trying to figure out how the hell to stop bad demons from crossing over and destroying humanity, you disappeared to what? Get a tattoo?"

He laughed, his other hand moving around to cup her breast.

She wanted to slap him away, but she was too damn focused on the symbols. "This isn't funny."

He rolled her nipple between his thumb and finger, drawing another gasp from her lips, but this time one of pleasure. "That's because you don't know what it is."

"Kade!" she shouted, shifting, only to feel his erection growing harder behind her.

"Fine." He pressed kisses along her shoulder as he spoke. "This was given to me by the demon king himself. He has agreed to send all innocent demons to this realm location in three days' time, so that we can save them all at once. So that we'll know for sure the good ones from the bad."

She whirled towards him. "Are you serious?"

He nodded.

This is...this is incredible!

"You idiot!" she exclaimed, throwing her arms around his neck. "How dare you go see the demon king! How dare you put yourself in danger like that! And how dare you not tell me!"

He held her closely, tenderly. "Sorry."

She clutched him tighter. *If anything had happened to him, I'd never forgive myself.* "And...and...thank you."

Not just for this. For everything. For caring about me. For caring about this cause. For being the man I never thought I deserved.

Pulling back from him, their eyes locked. She leaned forward and they kissed.

Like always, magic surged between them. An explosion

rocked through her, awakening every nerve in her body. She parted her lips and his tongue dove inside, exploring every inch of her mouth.

She shuddered, feeling her nipples bead into tight nubs.

As if sensing her arousal, his large hands closed over her breasts and he grabbed them possessively. The feeling sent heat pooling at her core.

He parted her legs and slid her closer until she straddled him. After that, his hands returned to her breasts, touching them as if he knew how hot each stroke of his fingers made her.

She rocked against his erection and rolled her head back as his tip brushed her hot core.

He used the opportunity to lean down and suck one of her nipples.

She sucked in air, grabbed the back of his head, and drew him closer. His mouth felt like heaven as he took her nipple deep into his mouth, licking it, and even gently biting it.

Desire built within her like something dangerous. She needed him inside her, and she couldn't wait another second.

She let her hand run over the hard lines of his chest and stomach before she reached down and gripped his length.

A groan tore from his lips. "Sharen..." The way he murmured her name was a warning, but she didn't care.

Positioning him at her entrance, she slowly took him inside her. *All of him.*

Even after all these months, it was difficult to fit his massive length inside her. He was so hard, filling her so completely that her mind became empty. Only pure sensation remained...the most amazing feeling in the world.

When he bottomed out inside her, she released him and braced her hands on his shoulders.

He reached between them and stroked her clit, looking up at her as if she were the most extraordinary thing in the world.

Her body spasmed around him as he stroked her and she began to slide up and down his hard length. A string of curses exploded from his lips, only encouraging her more.

She took him faster, harder. And each time she came down on him she saw stars.

Her nerves sung, her body screaming for release.

Throwing back her head, she barreled over the edge. Her orgasm, like something untamed, overtook her. She shouted Kade's name, riding him until his hot seed filled her. But she continued to move against him until they both slowly stopped.

He held her close and stroked her hair. "I love you."

She kissed his shoulder. "I love you too."

After a long minute, he whispered, "If this is what you do every time I put myself in danger, I'll have to do it more."

Pulling back from him, she punched him in the stomach. "Don't you dare!"

They both grinned at each other, lost in the perfect moment. The door to the bathroom opened and Ryder and Alec stared at them, not looking the least bit surprised.

"We need to talk," Alec said.

She frowned. "Now?"

He nodded. "Now."

What the hell has gone wrong now?

14

SHAREN DRIED OFF AND SLIPPED INTO NEW CLOTHES. WHEN she finished brushing her hair, she took a deep breath, wondering what the heck her boys were so upset about now.

Probably nothing.

They did have a tendency to overreact. When she opened her bedroom door, her three demons stood in a circle in the center of the living area. In the middle of them, a man was bound, his mouth duct taped.

She froze. *What the hell?*

The man sat up slightly and looked toward her.

She recognized him in a heartbeat. "Alderon?"

All three of her demons looked at her like she'd suddenly grown another head, but Alec spoke first. "You know who this is?"

Her mouth clamped shut. *I guess I'm passed a lie at this point.* "Yes."

Alec got that look. The one that said he was pissed. He stalked toward her, a threat in his eyes. "How do you know this *fae*? This man who followed me home?"

She was shocked by the venom in his voice. "What's your issue with fae?"

"Answer the question, Sharen!"

She sighed. *They aren't going to like this one bit.* "He's a hunter."

"Fuck," Kade muttered. "We'll have to kill him."

Sharen stiffened and hurried toward the man on the floor. "You can't just *kill* him. He hasn't done anything wrong."

"He knows where we are." Kade crossed his arms in front of his broad chest, and she could see that in his mind his decision was already made. "And he'll bring the others. Leaving him alive isn't an option."

Sharen ignored Kade, kneeling down and ripping the duct tape off the hunter's lips.

Alderon winced. "Thanks."

She tossed the duct tape on the floor. "Did you really think following him was a good idea?"

The man tried to shrug, even with his hands bound behind his back. "Honestly, I didn't think the demon would notice."

"Pompous ass!" Alec snarled.

Alderon had the nerve to shoot her demon an arrogant look. "And I wasn't trying to conceal myself too carefully. I assumed if you spotted me, you'd know exactly why I was following you."

All eyes were on her.

Crap.

She cleared her throat. "I ran into Alderon yesterday. He agreed to look into my past and to keep our location a secret."

"Sharen!" Alec ran angry fingers through his hair. "What the hell were you thinking?"

Her gaze swung to Ryder.

He shook his head. "Sorry, babe, but I'm with Alec on this. Hunters can never be trusted."

"You guys trusted me." Her words dropped like stones into the silence.

After a long minute, Kade spoke. "Why did you trust him?"

She tried not to look at the man duct taped in front of her. "I don't know. But I did. And sometimes I need to trust my instincts more than my head."

"I hate to interrupt this...whatever it is," the fae said, "but maybe now that we're all on the same page you could untie me?"

"Not a chance!" Alec muttered.

Sharen bit back her irritation. She wouldn't waste her time arguing with them. *Damned demons!* Pulling a dagger out of her boot, she cut him free, ignoring Alec's stream of curses.

"Did you come here to give me a 24-hour heads-up or did you discover something?"

Alderon sat up and started pulling the duct tape from his wrists with a hiss. "The latter."

Her pulse picked up. "Go on."

He pulled the shreds of duct tape off his ankles, looking strangely graceful as he did so. "There were several names connected with you. Lindsay Grace. Tally Summers. Sosha Arthur. Jenee Collens. Kathleen Thomas."

She frowned. "How are those names connected to me?"

He finally shook the last piece of tape onto the carpet and then turned his strange pale eyes to her. "None of the women lived at the same time. None of them came from the same family line, or even the same country. The only similarity between them was that when one woman died, another one was born."

"I don't understand."

"When Lindsay Grace died, Tally Summers was born. When Sosha Arthur died, Jenee Collens was born. And so on."

Sharen's head spun with his revelations. "So what does that mean?"

Alderon gave her a gentle smile. "I'm not sure yet. I plan to research the names, but I wanted to check with you first to see if any of them sounded familiar to you."

She shook her head. "Not even a little bit."

"I thought that might be the case." He shrugged. "That's all right. The mystery deepens."

Suddenly, Alec grabbed Alderon by the arm and hauled him to his feet. "Now that your friendly chat is over, I think it's time we handle this situation."

Sharen stood and held Alec back with a hand on his bicep. "Let him go."

His muscles tensed beneath her touch. "Dammit, Sharen, we can't just let him go. He knows where we live."

"I don't care. He and I have a deal."

Alderon cleared his throat. "My superiors know the mission I'm on and where I went. Killing me is the fastest way to bring suspicion down on you."

"He's right," Kade said, surprising them all. "It isn't enough just to kill him. We'll have to kill him and leave town."

Sharen looked from Alderon's unreadable expression to her demons. "So what, now we kill humans in cold blood? He's done nothing to us. If we kill him, we're no better than what the hunters accuse us of being."

Ryder moved forward and placed his hands lightly on

her arms, pulling her closer. "I hear what you're saying, but are we really supposed to just let him go? And wait to be attacked? They know who we are and where we are. And, I'm sorry, but I don't trust this man with my life."

She took a deep breath, searching his eyes. "But do you trust *me* with your life?"

His expression froze. "Always."

"Then trust me with this." She looked at her demons. "I think he can help us. And I believe him when he says he'll give us a twenty-four-hour head start."

The room was quiet for a long minute, and then Ryder released her arms. "All right."

Alec shook his head. "I—damn it, all right."

Kade swore. "This is insane!"

He looked at her and his brothers, shook his head, and then stormed across the room and slammed the bedroom door behind him. Tension hung heavy in the air.

Alderon cleared his throat. "Well, thanks. When I got caught by these demons, I assumed I'd be ripped to shreds. The fact that I'm not, well, that's something else I need to think about."

The fae pulled free of Alec's hold and walked toward the door. She could sense frustration building through her demons, so she didn't take an easy breath until the man walked out the door and closed it quietly behind him.

"That man will betray us, mark my words." Alec walked to the kitchen and started pulling out pots and pans.

Alec must be livid. He always cooked when he was upset.

Looking at Ryder, she smiled softly. "You understand, right?"

He gave a sad smile. "I understand that you were willing to trust an enemy for valuable information, but I don't understand why you didn't tell us about him. Trust is a two-way street, and if you expect us to trust you, you have to trust us too."

Before she could respond, he walked away, leaving her feeling like a complete ass. Not telling them had made sense in her head, but now she couldn't think of anything she could say to make things better.

Relationships are a lot harder when you like the people you're with.

For a minute, her mind went back to so long ago that her memories were fuzzy. She saw her mom's face. She heard her dad's laugh. And there in the middle of them was a little girl in pajamas, the brightest smile in the world on her face, pouring her heart out.

Her smile faltered. That was a long time ago. With the only two people in her life who had deserved her trust. *Until my demons.*

They've never done anything to break my faith in them. I need to remember that.

But old habits died hard. No matter how hard she wanted things to be different, trusting didn't come easily for her.

Her phone rang in her pocket, startling her. Looking at the caller ID, she accepted the call and headed for the balcony.

"Marval, what's up?"

The ancient vampire spoke softly, emphasizing each word. "A hunter is on your tail by the name of Alderon."

She stiffened. "How do you know that?"

"He and I are...old friends. And it seems he and I are both looking into your past."

She put one of her hands on the railing and looked out at the dark city below. Without hesitation, she explained everything Alderon had told her, including the most recent information. "He says there's something suspicious about my file in the Department and he thinks there's more going on than we think."

After unloading, she took a deep breath and waited for his response.

"You may not hear from me for a time," he said, his voice excited. "I have a suspicion about what you are, but I need to do a little more research first."

The hairs on the back of her neck stood on end. "What do you think I am?"

His voice lowered, so quietly that she could barely make out the words. "If I'm right, it isn't safe to say it on the phone. Just...be careful, Sharen."

"Marval—"

"I have to go," he said, and the line went dead.

That was weird.

She stood on the balcony for a long time, enjoying the wind tugging at her wet hair. So many things had gone wrong recently, but as many things had also gone right. As much as it drove her crazy that Marval hadn't told her every-thing, she felt hope, knowing that he had a real lead. For the stoic vampire to be excited, well, that was something by itself.

"Dinner's ready!" Alec called.

Sharen smiled out at the city and came back into their apartment. But before she made it across the living room, the door to the bedroom opened.

Kade stomped out. "Did she tell you guys about my little trip yet?"

She stiffened. *How the hell did I not?*

Ryder was setting food on the table while Alec was washing dishes. But both men froze, then shook their heads.

Her angry husband gave one of his rare smiles. "Well, we better talk, because we have a lot to do and only three days to do it in."

Hope flared to life within her chest.

In three days, the innocent demons will be safe and the Rebellion will have accomplished its goal.

Now to make our plans.

15

CAINE STARED DOWN AT THE PATHETIC SHAPESHIFTER. "THAT'S all you have to tell me?"

The creature nodded, still kneeling before him.

If you weren't my child, I would have killed you long ago, you useless creature.

Caine began to pace the warehouse. The darkness of his magic spread out around him, not just cloaking his shape from form. It spread further, filling the whole side of the empty building. Normally, in front of his child was the one place he didn't hide his true form, but now that the war was beginning, he couldn't even afford that luxury.

The judge of all of humanity must take every precaution.

"But," the shapeshifter sputtered out, "this changes everything. We can stop them from saving the other demons. We can raid the sanctuary and kill the ones they already saved. We can end this now!"

"If only my mind was as simple as yours." *But none of this is simple.*

The Fate had told him that soon the war would begin. He hated that he couldn't simply kill any of his enemies. If he did so, he would never gain the powers of the Immortal Ten, and he wanted their powers more than he wanted anything else in this world.

And so, he would have to play this game. He would have to allow a war.

But he already knew he would win.

Like a chess game, I must always be ten steps in front of my enemies. They must not see me coming until every piece has been moved into place. Then, and only then, will I strike.

"I am yours to command, my lord. I can go back to the sanctuary. I can be the old man, or the girl, or return to Rebellion. Whatever you ask, I will do it an instant."

Another whimpering creature eager to obey me, how... expected. And yet, a mindless grunt is just what I need.

"My desire is simple."

The shapeshifter lifted its head. "What would you have me do?"

Caine smiled. "I would have blood...lots of it."

In his mind, he pictured the chaos he would unleash onto their world.

I may not be able to kill them, but I can make them suffer.

16

ALEC DROVE SLOWLY DOWN THE DIRT ROAD THAT LED INTO THE sanctuary. It was late at night. Only the brightness of the moon lit his path. He wanted to be home in bed, curled around Sharen, but he couldn't. She might be able to believe these demons were capable of turning over a new leaf, but he couldn't stop hearing the old man's words. He couldn't stop seeing the girl hurting an innocent animal.

And something had to be done about it.

"What if this doesn't go the way you've planned?" Ryder asked, breaking the silence.

Alec's hands tightened on the steering wheel. "It has to."

He'd thought over their options again and again. And this was the only thing that made sense.

"Sharen won't be happy." Ryder sounded...uncertain.

"When I told you the plan, you agreed to come with me. You wimping out now?"

Ryder turned and glared. "Not a chance, old man. I just wanted to make sure you thought this through."

"Geez, do you have a better idea?"

Ryder shot him a dirty look. "If I did, would I be here?"

Alec was sick of moments like these. Where there was no good option. Yet, that's how things usually seemed to go —always stuck between a rock and a hard place.

As they came to the brick fence, he unrolled his window and typed in the code. The gates opened with the smallest squeal. They continued as quietly as they could down the dirt road

His instincts were on high alert as he scanned the trees on both sides of them. Were demons watching them even now?

They stopped the car while still in the woods. Cutting the engine, they sat in silence.

"What if we're wrong?" Ryder's question surrounded them in the darkness

"We better pray we're not." He opened his door and grabbed his sword from the backseat.

Ignoring his brother, he silently closed his door, then headed toward the manor.

There were no sounds in the woods. No soft chirps of night birds. No fluttering of wings. As his ears strained, he didn't even hear creatures skittering about the forest floor.

His stomach sank. *Have they killed everything?*

When they came out of the woods, he paused for a second. Across the neatly trimmed lawn, the manor stood tall and silent, its windows dark. For some reason, whether because of their mission or because it was night, the building looked sinister, almost threatening.

They proceeded cautiously across the lawn. When they were nearly to the manor, he caught a flicker of light in the woods. *What is that?*

His eyes narrowed and his steps faltered. *To the strange light or to our mission?*

Every instinct within him screamed. Something was wrong. And yet, he continued toward the manor.

"Alec," Ryder whispered his name.

Alec shook his head. There was no time to second-guess themselves. They'd search the woods after they killed their enemies.

The concrete steps didn't make a sound as they started up them. At the door, his hand shook as he pushed his key into the lock. But instead of it clicking solidly into place, the unlocked door opened on its own.

Someone left it open. Why? Do they know we're coming?

They stepped into the hall.

"The floor," Ryder hissed behind him.

Alec's gaze moved down and he tensed. Blood had dried on the floor, leaving a small streak and a few drops leading toward the kitchen.

His pulse raced. *What the hell is going on?*

They checked all the rooms on the first floor, swords clenched tightly in their hands. But they found no one. Upstairs, they searched one room after another. All stood empty.

What the fuck is this?

Ryder turned to him. "This isn't good."

"No shit."

He turned, then hurried down the stairs and back outside. Turning toward the light in the woods, he moved with quiet but sure steps. He wasn't sure whether to pray they found the demons or not. If they left, they would likely create such chaos in the world that he would regret it for the rest of his life. But if they were in the woods doing some kind of sick ritual?

I'll have to kill them all.

As they moved closer and closer to the light, it became

obvious that it was a massive fire. Another few seconds passed, and they heard the murmur of low voices.

Please let me be wrong.

As they came to the edge of a clearing, they peeked out from behind a tree. He froze. The demons were...roasting marshmallows?

He stood a little taller.

Some of the adults were leaning over the little ones, helping them make s'mores. Others sat on fallen logs that had been dragged to encircle the fire. A man and woman kissed in the shadows. A mother nursed her baby on another.

"They don't look all that dangerous," Ryder whispered.

"No shit," Alec said.

They resheathed their swords. But still, he felt confused as hell. In his mind, he couldn't quite connect these demons with the dangerous ones the old man had warned him about.

Speaking of which...he didn't see David anywhere.

Coming out of the shadows, he waited for a few of them to notice him.

"Alec! Ryder!" A pretty blonde rose and hurried toward him, carrying a sleepy-looking toddler in her arms. "What brought you two here in this hour?"

Alec took a deep breath. "I need to talk to someone."

Her happy expression faded, replaced by a tense one. "Of course. Shall I go for a walk with you guys?"

He nodded.

She walked back and handed her little one to an older woman, who smiled and held the baby gently in her arms, rocking him. The joy in her face shone as she stared down at the toddler.

"That's Crissy," Ryder explained. "She's the unofficial leader of the refugees."

Alec nodded, grateful that his brother knew these people better than he did.

Crissy returned, and they all silently started through the woods. When they'd gone a distance from the others, she spoke. "So what's this about? I'm guessing it's not good."

"Why's that?" Ryder asked.

She smirked. "You guys are wearing all black. I can tell you're packing some extra weapons, unless you're just that happy to see me. And you both look like you're about to do some bad shit."

Ryder sighed. "I guess we're pretty transparent."

"How well do you know the people here?" Alec folded his arms over his chest and turned to face her.

She stopped walking. "Even though it's only been a couple months, they've become my family."

"That doesn't answer my question."

Her brows rose. "I know them."

"Then tell me," he locked gazes with her, "who are the good ones and who are the bad ones?"

Her brows rose even higher. "The *bad* ones? What the fuck does that mean?"

His jaw twitched. "Cut the crap."

"Alec." Ryder stepped between them. "Crissy, he just wants to know which of them are having the most trouble ignoring their demon side. Who is struggling with blood lust? Who feels the need for chaos the strongest?"

She stared at them for a ridiculously long time. "Is this a joke?"

"Do I look like I'm laughing?" Alec narrowed his eyes, daring her to lie to him.

"Fine." She put a hand on Ryder and slowly moved him

back from them. "Let's do this then. None of these demons are bad. They are *Level 10* demons. They were good people in life, and they're good people in death." She stopped talking as if she expected him to be satisfied. Alec stared at her until she continued.

"Yes, they are struggling not using their powers. Yes, they are struggling being educated on everything they've missed since being dead. Some of these people have been dead for hundreds of years, and you can bet that seeing televisions, cellphones, and computers is a transition. Now, excuse me if I sound pissed, but I am. You guys saved us. You guys brought us here. How can you stand here asking me this right now?"

Is she lying? Alec studied her face. If she was lying, she was a damn good liar. "What about David?"

Wrinkles formed on her forehead. "Who?"

He scoffed. "The old demon. He told me the truth about this place. About your unquenchable desires. And what all of you are capable of."

She laughed. "Two things. First, never say 'unquench-able desires' to a woman. It's freaking creepy. Second, there isn't a demon named David here. And third, and I know I said I just had two things, but I've thought of a third, we're just like *you*. Why the hell would you be worried about us?"

His head spun. "David. The old man with the long white hair. And the sharp teeth." He turned to Ryder. He knew these people. He had to know David. "The old man..."

Ryder shook his head. "I don't know him."

Maybe I should've given him more details about my conver-sation with the man. "But...well, how do you explain Becky? I saw her ripping legs off a squirrel. I saw her eyes were red. She hissed at me."

Crissy shook her head. "Bullshit. That little girl did no such thing."

He uncrossed his arms and advanced on her. "I *saw* it."

"I don't know what to tell you, but you're wrong."

Alec turned to Ryder. "Have you seen anything? *Anything* weird about the girl?"

His brother shook his head. "She just seems like a sweet girl."

Nothing made sense. He grasped for understanding. Something that would make it all make sense.

"What about the blood in the foyer?"

"Blood?" She stared for a second, then her mouth formed into an *O*. "One of the boys fell off the wall and got a good crack on the head. If he was human, he would've needed to be stitched up. But even though there was a lot of blood, we got him all taken care of. He should be fine by the morning." She looked a bit embarrassed. "Everyone was kind of in a rush to get out here before it got too late, so we did a crap job cleaning up. We figured we'd take care of it when we got back."

Ryder turned to Alec, raising a brow. "Well, that explains everything."

"Not what I saw," Alec whispered.

He'd seen the girl. He'd spoken to the old man. He didn't understand what was going on, but there was something very, very wrong.

"Listen guys," Crissy said, some of her attitude leaving her voice. "I can say with absolute certainty that everyone here is good. Not perfect. But these are good people."

Ryder nodded. "I believe you."

What? Even after what I told him?

The thing was, Alec's mind was screaming that his

brother and this woman were wrong. But his heart? That was the issue, because his heart begged him to believe them.

They stopped by the fire. Ryder ate a s'more and checked on the kid with his head wrapped. Even dressed in black and decked out in weapons, Ryder seemed to join the group with an easy smile that put everyone at ease. Within minutes, he was laughing, telling jokes, and talking to the group as if he was their best friend.

How the hell does he do it?

People shot Alec a few curious glances, but otherwise, left him alone. So he used the opportunity to watch Becky closely. In all ways, she seemed to be a sweet little kid... ridiculously hyper on sugar, but a sweet little kid.

Something is rotten here, and I'm going to figure it out.

When they got into the car later, Alec didn't turn on the engine. "What do you think?"

Ryder spoke, his voice low and threatening. "Someone wanted to stop us from helping these people. Maybe even get us to hurt them. And we're going to find out who it is."

"The old man." Alec's instincts tinged. "I knew there was something off about him. But how is it possible he was here? How is it that no one else knows him or has seen him?"

Ryder shook his head. "I don't know. But I think our plan for the evening was doomed from the start."

Find the old man. Question him. And kill him.

His sword suddenly felt heavier on his back. Whoever that man was, even if they could question him, Alec was certain they couldn't believe his answers.

"So what do we do now?"

Ryder buckled up. "Now? We tighten security around the refuge, and we watch our backs. Because even though we thought the hunters and the angels were our only enemies, I have a feeling the ones we don't know about are even more dangerous."

Alec felt sweat trickled down his back. *All this on top of changing our world forever.*

Switching the car on, they started back down the quiet road. As they turned back onto the main road, he caught a motion out of the corner of his eye just before a massive truck slammed into the side of their car.

ALEC BLINKED AWAKE. Was the world tilted? Warm blood ran into his eyes, but he couldn't lift his hand to wipe it away. The smell of gasoline and smoke filled his nostrils. Air bags clouded his face. But with great effort, he turned his head toward his brother.

Ryder's head had gone through the window. Blood coated his head and face. His eyes remained closed and his chest was still.

He tried to reach for him, but his body wouldn't obey him.

Outside his brother's window, there was motion. It took him a second to spot the two dark-winged angels. His heart sank.

We're dead.

17

SHAREN WOKE EARLY THE NEXT MORNING AND DISCOVERED Alec and Ryder were missing from their bed. Immediately, she felt agitated. Where would they have gone without telling her?

She shook Kade awake. He grumbled something and pulled the covers more tightly over his shoulders.

"Alec and Ryder are gone."

Slowly, he sat up, his eyes instantly open. His hair was a mess, his stubble bordering on a beard, and lines creased his face from his pillow.

"Gone?" He sounded confused.

Her worry grew. "They didn't tell you anything?"

He shook his head.

Frowning, she grabbed her phone and called Alec, but his phone rang and rang before going to voicemail. When she called Ryder, the same thing happened. "What the hell is wrong with you guys that you can't send a text before you take off to God only knows where?" She smacked her phone down on the table and sprang out of bed.

"They probably went to get donuts," he muttered.

She watched him climb out of bed and briefly forgot to breathe. Geez, as annoying as Kade was, she never got tired of seeing him naked. Who could possibly get tired of seeing a sea of beautiful muscles and a gorgeous cock?

"You don't seem too worried."

Her gaze traveled up to see his smug expression. *Damn, I hate when he sees me checking him out.*

She forced herself to focus. "I know it's probably nothing...but what if something's wrong?"

He shrugged. "Those two can take care of themselves."

Suddenly, her phone rang. Springing into action, she grabbed it. The number was restricted, but she answered it anyway.

"Mrs. Bran?"

She stiffened. "This is her."

Instantly, her gaze went to her dark wedding band. Why was her heart suddenly racing?

"This is Officer Smith. It seems that a vehicle registered in your name was involved in a car accident last night."

Ice ran through her veins. "A car accident? Was anyone hurt?"

It took him a long time to answer. "A semi-truck barreled into the side of your vehicle. Your car is in pretty bad shape. And the interior is covered in blood."

No. No. This can't be happening.

"The thing is, we didn't find any bodies inside, either in your car or the truck. It's as if everyone simply vanished."

Her legs folded beneath her, and she collapsed onto the floor.

Kade was by her side in an instant, wrapping his large arms around her.

"Where was the last place you saw your car, Mrs. Bran?"

She swallowed around the lump in her throat. "In my parking garage. It must have been stolen."

"If you're sure about that, we will open an investigation and get back to you as soon as we have some answers."

"Thank you," she whispered.

Hanging up the phone, she looked to Kade. "Our car was covered in blood. But there weren't any bodies."

"Sharen—"

"The only way there wouldn't be bodies is if the accident killed them. If they—"

"No." The word came out a growl. "It'd take a lot more than a car accident to kill those two idiots. There's got to be another answer. We just haven't found it yet."

Her stomach turned. "Maybe."

He rose, looking agitated. "Let's get dressed. We'll figure out what to do from there." She took the hand he offered and they moved toward their closets. Autopilot took over and Sharen dressed without thinking. She couldn't feel her fingers but numbness was beginning to creep through her. God did she want her demons to be okay. Even though all logic said they weren't.

Sitting on the edge of her bed, she put on her boots. When she looked up, Kade was dressed in a tight, dark shirt and jeans, his expression thunderous.

They took their SUV's keys off the chain and headed for the door. But when she opened it, the most shocking thing greeted her. Two massive angels were carrying her very beat-up-looking demons.

Kade growled and sprang forward, but Sharen caught his arm.

Time seemed to stand still as they stared at each other.

"We weren't responsible for this." The angel who spoke had short blond hair and dark eyes. He was older than most of the angels she'd seen, and he carried a gun strapped to his side.

"Come in," she said.

"What are you doing?" Kade asked, his voice rising. "You can't possibly believe them!"

She looked between Ryder's face, which was covered in deep gashes, and Alec's swollen face. "If the angels wanted to hurt them, they would have."

Stepping out of the way, she waited.

Slowly, the angels moved into the apartment, their dark wings folded tightly on their backs. They walked across the room and gently laid her demons onto the couches in their living room, then turned to face her.

"What happened?" she asked.

The older angel studied her for a moment. "We've been watching your demons for some time."

"Why?" Kade barked the question.

His dark gaze moved to Kade. "Because we wanted to see if they could truly exist in this world without trying to destroy it. There was an angel we knew...Surcy. She said some things that have disturbed us. And so, we watched without acting, to see if there were truly demons who were good."

"And?"

"And, they did nothing terrible." He shrugged. "We still hadn't decided exactly what that means, but last night we witnessed something strange. An angel possessed a truck driver and barreled into these demons' car."

The other angel, a man with black hair and stunning olive skin, cut in. "Which made no sense. An angel's job is to kill demons. This one knew he wasn't going to kill your demons, so why injure them so terribly? It made no sense.

And then what was stranger...he just left. Again, why? So, we got involved."

She stared between the two angels. "Why when you could have just left them?"

The two exchanged a look, but the older angel spoke first. "Because we think Surcy might be right. We think we might be fighting on the wrong side."

Her mouth dropped open.

"Liar!" Kade shouted. "This is just Caine's latest plan."

The older angel's brows rose. "Say what you wish, but we're done following your demons. We plan to seek out Surcy and ask our questions. So the next time these two are injured, we won't be there to save them. Might I advise being more careful?"

The angels started toward the door.

Sharen's brain seemed to unfreeze in a rush. "Wait. I don't even know your names."

"I am Steven, and that is Gene," the younger angel answered her.

"Well, thank you," she said, meaning it in her very soul.

Steven's expression grew thoughtful. "May I ask you something?"

Gene waited by the door, radiating annoyance.

"Of course."

"Why would Caine wish your demons injured when he could have killed them?"

She stiffened. *Good question.* "I don't know."

"I've heard it whispered that no one is to kill you or your husbands. Why?"

Her heart raced. "I don't know."

The younger angel shook his head and headed for the door, but when he reached his friend, he looked back. "If I were you, I'd try to find the answers to some of these questions, because there's nothing more dangerous than ignorance."

She nodded. "I will."

The angels left as quickly as they came, closing the door softly behind them.

Instantly, she ran to Ryder's side. He had two black eyes, a terrible cut on his forehead that was mostly healed, and several more red gashes on his neck and cheeks. Placing her hand on his chest, she listened intently to the gentle rise and fall of his chest. He looked like hell, but he was alive and breathing, which meant he was healing. *Thank God!*

That left Alec. He had severe burns on his arms, probably from the airbags. His face was swollen and his nose looked broken. Despite the terrible bruises beneath his eyes, his breathing was steady and even.

That's something. More than something.

She glanced up. Kade stood across the room, watching his brothers from afar, his arms folded across his chest.

"Will they be okay?" she asked, unable to stop the question.

Kade crossed the room and put his hands on her shoulders. "They'll be fine. When we get injured this badly, we sleep so that our bodies can heal us faster. They'll wake up soon, probably feeling like hell, but they'll be okay."

She wiped away a tear she hadn't even realized trailed down her cheek. Reaching out, she took one of each of their hands and held them in her clammy ones. It was heart-wrenching to see them like this, but she was thankful beyond words that they were okay.

"Do you really trust those angels?" Kade asked.

She took an unsteady breath. "Yes."

He shook his head and began pacing the length of the room. "I don't understand you."

Oh no, he's pacing. That's never good.

She frowned at his reaction. "What do you mean?"

"Sharen, you forget that we're in the middle of a war. Caine, his angels, and the hunters—they all want us dead. You know that, but every chance you have to trust one of them, you do. It makes no sense."

Sharen stared at Kade, willing him to understand. She couldn't look away if she tried. "From the moment I met you three, everything changed for me. A power greater than myself took over. I have spent my life fighting demons, training hunters, and being betrayed by everyone I loved. But when I met you, I realized I was wrong about demons. I was wrong about hunters and angels. And...well, I was wrong to believe I'd always be betrayed by everyone I loved. You and your brothers showed me that. So now, instead of always expecting everyone to hurt me...I guess I just hope for the best. It's that hope that helps me go on."

Staring at Kade, her demon with such a hard outer shell, she was prepared for many things. For starters, he would tell her she was crazy and foolish.

But instead, he knelt down and placed his hands on top of hers. Leaning closer, he planted a soft kiss against her lips. "Logic says that trusting our enemies is a mistake, so why can't I find one thing wrong with what you just said?"

She smiled. "I'm rubbing off on you."

He returned her smile with one of his rare ones. "And somehow that doesn't feel like a bad thing."

Alec suddenly groaned and her interest immediately snapped to him. His swollen eyes popped open and she could see bloody streaks through his white pupils. He struggled to talk. "Ryder—"

"Is safe," she reassured him.

The tension faded from his face, and then he sat up, groaning in pain. "The angels."

She put her hands on his shoulders, trying to push him back down. "They brought you safely to us."

He frowned and looked at Kade.

"She isn't crazy. They actually brought you here...and might just be on our side."

Alec lay back down, pressing his palms to his forehead. "I must have hit my head harder than I thought," he panted. "It sounds like you two are saying the angels helped us."

Kade chuckled. "We are."

Alec dropped his hands and looked at them. "Someone ran into our car. On purpose. And something weird is going on at the refuge. That David guy apparently doesn't exist, and the little girl apparently doesn't kill animals."

Sharen felt something tighten in her chest. "I don't understand."

Alec sighed loudly, his eyes closing once more. "That makes two of us."

She looked to Kade, feeling panic building in her chest.

"We need to figure out what's going on. And we only have another day to do it."

How the hell do we do that?

18

SHAREN WIPED HER SWEATY PALMS ONTO HER PANTS AND stared out at the busy park. She needed to get to headquarters. Today was the day she had to use the portal to rescue the demons. So what was she doing here?

She hated that when she found the note tucked under her door that she'd come without thinking. No matter how stupid it was. Because she hoped against all odds that today might not only be the day she helped the demons, it might also be the day she found out the truth about what she was and why she had such strange powers.

Alderon came around the path, walking at a leisurely pace. He stopped to pet a dog and flirt with the dog's owner, shifted out of the way of kids chasing a ball, and then approached her. His smile was easy, non-threatening, which immediately put her on high-alert.

"You left me a note." She held it up, watching him closely.

He nodded and sat down beside her. "Have you ever heard the name Surrena?"

She shook her head. "It doesn't sound familiar."

He spun to face her on the bench, an element of excitement in his expression. "She's Caine's daughter. A powerful, nearly-immortal being with the ability to change her identity."

She frowned. "What does that have to do with me?"

"That's where it gets interesting." He lowered his voice. "I think you might be her."

Her back went rigid. "What?"

No chance in hell!

He nodded enthusiastically. "I found her name in your file and started doing some digging. It all makes sense. I think all the women's names are actually..." He paused for a heartbeat before he continued. "I think they're all you."

No! Her memories instantly went back to her childhood home. She pictured the tire swing under the tree in the backyard, and the way she'd tell her dad to spin her *faster and faster*. She remembered her kitchen, the one her mom always exclaimed was falling apart. But Sharen never noticed, because she was too busy eating her mom's delicious cooking.

Is it possible they aren't my parents?

Her fists clenched. It wasn't! She had her mother's green eyes! And her father's dark hair! She might not have pictures of them after stupidly leaving the couple she had at her house before going on the run, but she'd never forget her parents' faces.

I'm their child. Nothing this man says will ever change that.

He doesn't need to know I'm not entirely human. She paused at the thought. Being a half-breed meant that either one of her parents weren't human, or... She shook her head, unwilling as always to even consider that possibility.

"Are you sure you're human?" he pressed, as if reading her thoughts.

"Wouldn't I know if I wasn't?" she shot back, trying to keep her voice steady and calm and failing miserably.

"Maybe, maybe not." His brows drew together. "I think they've somehow come up with a way to alter your memories."

The tire swing. The kitchen. Was it real?

She felt sick. "That's not possible. I have pictures of myself as a child. Not many. But I have them."

Somewhere.

"Are you sure they're you?" he asked, watching her closely. "You grew up with adopted parents paid for by the Organization."

Albert and Brandy, the two worst human beings alive. With hard fists and even harder words. They might have adopted me, but they weren't my parents.

She swallowed, trying to push away her nausea. "I had parents before them. Parents I remember. So none of this is possible. I can't be that evil being's child."

"That's not even the most interesting part," he continued without pausing. "Do you ever feel like your enemies are one step ahead of you? Like they know things they shouldn't?"

Do I?

Her heart raced. Something strange was going on. Things she couldn't explain. The hunters in the demon realm. The stranger in the refuge. The car accident.

But is it that they're one step ahead of us? Or something else entirely?

Even though she didn't respond, Alderon continued, "I think you might be sharing important information with Caine and his followers without even realizing it. I think you might actually be working for the other side."

She stood. "No."

He looked surprised, his excitement fading. "It's just a theory...but everything adds up. Caine has commanded that you not be killed, which only makes sense if you're important to him. You've been watched closely your whole life. And if I were to make a bet, I think you're not human."

"You don't know that!" she spit out.

He raised a brow. "Didn't you take a dagger and send it through the ground, creating some kind of wave of power that destroyed roads and cars, and even sent our hunters and angels flying? Don't bother denying it, because it's all well-documented."

Her head spun. "I could feel the angels' magic. I didn't do that. Their magic allowed me to."

He leaned back against the bench. "So, you aren't Caine's daughter? But you're able to harness the angels' magic? I'm sorry, but doesn't that seem like exactly the kind of thing the daughter of such a powerful being could do?"

"No!" She shook her head, inched backwards, and then spun, hurrying away from him. Panic clawed at her throat.

What he said couldn't be true. Could it?

"I'm not finished researching," he said, suddenly walking at her side. "But if I were you, I'd be careful. It seems to me right now the greatest danger to your little cause could be...well, you."

She whirled on him. "I don't know what you think you read, but I am not some twisted creature's child! And I'd burn in hell before I betrayed the people I'm fighting so hard to save!" *Before I hurt my demons.* "You've got me wrong."

His pale eyes gentled. "Sharen, I don't know what it is about you, but from the first time I saw you, I felt...different. The facts are telling me that you are his daughter, but for some insane reason I believe you. And I'm not the kind of man who believes anything but what I see right in front of me."

She took a step away from him, pulling her gaze from his. "I need to go."

He didn't follow her as she hurried away. Like before, she took a roundabout way back to headquarters, just in case. But her thoughts spun with each step she took.

What Alderon said couldn't be possible. Yes, there were some things that didn't make sense, but she'd never betray her demons. Never.

Still, her entire body shook and her teeth chattered. There was something about what he said. Something she couldn't quite put her finger on.

When she reached headquarters, her assistant was smoking outside the door. The young brunette stood taller as she approached.

Time to focus. "Is everything ready?"

Riverly nodded. "Yes, ma'am. The refuge has been set up with a number of temporary housing structures to hopefully accommodate the demons. We have buses parked close by to transport everyone. And the witches strengthened the magical barrier around headquarters. If anyone accidentally uses their magic, the angels shouldn't detect it."

Sharen let out a shaky breath. "Good."

At least everything is going right here.

"Ma'am?"

Sharen looked at the young girl, who nervously adjusted her glasses. "Yes."

"I just want to thank you."

She frowned. "Thank me?"

The girl nodded. "Before you found me, I didn't know what I was doing. I didn't understand why I was stronger and faster than my friends. I didn't understand why I was being followed. If you hadn't have saved me that day, the angels might have discovered I was a half-breed before you did, and I don't think I would've lived."

Sharen smiled and reached out to squeeze her shoulder gently. "No, thank you. I don't know what I would've done without you through all of this. You've truly become part of the family here. A valued part of the family."

She saw tears in Riverly's dark eyes.

I need to erase all the doubts Alderon raised inside of me. I'm not something evil. I'm doing something good here. No matter who I end up being, it doesn't change who I am deep down.

"Let's go inside and save some demons."

The girl smiled. "Yes, ma'am."

Sharen typed in the code with a smile. *Today is going to be a good day. I can feel it.*

19

SHAREN STOOD IN HER OFFICE WEARING HER DARK GREEN uniform. Turning to each of her demons, she hugged them tightly. "Everything's going to be okay."

She was overcome by a strange giddiness. Her people were finishing setting up the last few things, and then she'd be stepping through the portal. For some reason, everything seemed to be hitting her at once.

After today, there would be no more jumping into dangerous realms. There would be no more staying up at night and thinking of all the lost souls unfairly trapped in the demon realm. The fight would be...over.

Then she could focus on helping the demons. She'd figure out how they fit into this new world. That would be a whole new struggle, but one she would welcome. For a second, all she could see was Brian and his family. They would be waiting for her. She knew it. And this time when she rescued them, she was determined they'd never be in danger again.

And what if they killed the old woman? a tiny voice whispered in the back of her mind.

She stiffened. She'd find out the truth and deal with it later.

And then there were the other uncertainties of the situation. Would there be hundreds of demons? Thousands of demons? Tens of thousands? She truly had no idea what to expect.

But she was overwhelmed with a sense of hope. Of happiness. She felt it radiating out of her like a light, filling her with energy.

"I hate that we can't go with you," Kade murmured, drawing her back to the present.

She smiled. "I know, but everything is going to be okay."

Her gaze slid over her handsome demons. The bruises had nearly faded from Alec's face, and the gashes on Ryder's face were light pink lines. She knew they still hurt by the way they moved stiffly when they thought she wasn't looking, but she was thankful that they were healing so well.

Everything is falling perfectly into place.

Alec pointed his finger right in her face, his expression serious. "If anything doesn't go according to plan, and I mean *anything*, you get out of there. Do you—"

She couldn't help herself. Leaning forward, she slipped his finger into her mouth.

His eyes widened. "Sharen..."

Trailing her fingers down his chest, she curled her hand around his cock. It instantly hardened beneath her touch.

His breathing grew ragged. "How much time do we have?"

"An hour," Kade said behind them, his words husky with need.

"That should be enough time," Alec whispered, his eyes glued to his finger in her mouth.

She released his finger. "That'd give us time for two, maybe three times."

Ryder slapped her ass, drawing her gaze. "Are you saying we're too fast? Because I don't remember hearing you complain."

She laughed. "I'm just saying, we have plenty of time."

Alec reached for the button on his pants. "I think we're wearing a little too many clothes for what I have planned."

She grinned, reluctantly releasing his shaft. He unzipped his pants and they dropped to the floor.

Unable to help herself, she moved out of the circle of her demons. Moving to her desk, she stood in front of it. All three men watched her, their gazes dark, need radiating from them in waves.

Grasping the zipper on her uniform, she drew it all the way down. Pushing the sleeves off, she let it slide down her body. Another minute later, she'd kicked off her uniform and boots. Standing in front of them in nothing more than her white lacy bra and underwear, she smiled.

"What are you guys waiting for?"

They removed their clothes and in a matter of moments stood before her in nothing at all. Her hungry gaze slid across them. There was no doubt she was the luckiest woman in the world. Three beautiful men wanted her and no one else, and what was more, these three incredible men knew exactly how to touch her, how to make her feel...too much.

"Make sure you boys keep it down," she whispered, her voice shaking with anticipation. "This is an office, after all."

Alec closed in on her, standing just a foot in front of her. "I think one of us is overdressed."

Her heart sputtered. "Who? Me?"

He reached forward and ran his soft fingers along the

tops of her breasts. "You are so beautiful."

She couldn't catch her breath as she watched him.

His fingers moved to the latch at the front of her bra. His knowing gaze locked with hers, and he flicked his fingers.

She gasped as her bra fell apart, even though she knew it was coming. The cool air rushed over her nipples, causing them to tighten into hard nubs.

His naughty hands slid down the slides of her breasts, causing a tremble to overtake her body. When he cupped her breasts in his hands, she swallowed, trying to keep her calm, trying not to show him how much he affected her.

When he leaned forward, she arched her back, eager to feel her nipples in his warm mouth.

He chuckled, his hot breath brushing against her sensitive nubs. "I thought you wanted us to move slower."

Ryder stepped forward, linking a finger into the front of her panties. "No one ever said we were good at following directions."

Instead of tugging her underwear off, Ryder slid his fingers over the lace, then began to rub her slowly through the material. She bit her lip, hating that her legs shook.

When Alec finally closed his mouth around one of her nipples, a moan tore from her lips. His hand moved to pinch her other nipple between his fingers.

When Kade came closer, she watched him, wondering what he would do next. To her shock, he stood close to her, slowly stroking himself up and down.

Her entire body went wild for the three of them. Ryder was driving her crazy, his touch amplified by the silk lace. The more he moved, the more nerves he awakened, causing her to burn with desire.

And Alec's lips and hands on her breasts? They were amazing!

Digging one hand into his hair, she pulled him closer. She wanted more, needed more.

Watching Kade stroke himself brought her a different kind of arousal. She couldn't take her eyes off the man. He was so beautiful, all muscles and corded, powerful arms. An eight pack rippled down his chest and stomach as he stroked his cock—a cock that she knew was capable of magical things.

When she pushed his hand away, he let her. She stroked the big man, loving how he rocked into her grip, loving how his eyes widened in amazement.

No matter how many times they touched each other, it was always like this. Hot and beautiful.

Maybe it was because her demons spent so long in the darkness, in a place without pleasure and closeness, that now they never seemed to get enough of it.

Or maybe it was because before them she'd thought she was broken, unlovable, incapable of enjoying sex.

A woman tossed aside by my husband for my sister.

But if all her pain and heartache meant she appreciated what she had with her demons more, then it was all worth it.

When Alec released her breasts and sank to his knees, he pushed Ryder's hand away and yanked her underwear down. Before the thin material could hit the ground, his mouth was on her hot core.

She gasped, and he pulled her legs off the ground and around his neck. If Ryder hadn't grabbed her around the waist from behind, she might have fallen.

She gripped Kade's cock harder and thrust against Alec's delicious lips. He licked her softly, slowly at first. Then his mouth grew harder. He kissed, pressing his lips deeply inside her. When he licked her clit, she cried out.

There was no way she was going to last much longer.

Ryder moved behind her, and she barely registered his shaft as it rubbed against her backside. But then his tip dipped into her wetness, close to Alec's mouth, but not too close. It slid back and forth in her wetness several times before returning to her ass.

Gripping Kade harder, she took a deep breath as Ryder slowly eased into her from behind. Each inch of his length felt massive, too big, but she knew she could handle him. Her heart hammered against her ribcage as she felt him slide deeper and deeper, until at last he reached his hilt.

Ryder grabbed her hips from behind and pulled out for an instant before plunging back in.

She rode Alec's face while Ryder slammed into her from behind. Her arousal built like water rising, waiting to overflow. Alec found her clit and sucked.

The combination of Ryder behind her, Alec sucking on her, and Kade's gorgeous cock in her hand was too much. She shot over the edge, screaming incoherently.

When Alec stood and replaced his mouth with his cock, she was still tingling, her orgasm not yet spent. She felt like a live wire. When Alec eased into her, she didn't think she could take both of them. Not right then. Her nerves were too sensitive, her body too aware.

But when he slammed into her, and Ryder continued to pump into her from behind, she knew she was going to come again. And this time, it was going to be something dangerous and uncontrollable.

She began to chant the word "*yes*" her nails digging into Alec's shoulders. Behind her, Ryder groaned and came, filling her from behind with his seed. Her arousal grew, and when she felt Kade's hot cum shoot onto her hand, she threw back her head and let herself go.

She went wild. Riding them. Screaming. Her inner muscles squeezing Alec like a vise until he swore and exploded inside of her.

Her vision went white. Her limbs went limp.

She lay sandwiched between them, feeling amazing.

"You know," Ryder whispered, kissing her shoulder. "Some women just say they'll see us later."

She laughed, feeling happy and satisfied. "I'll have to remember that next time."

Kade turned her head and kissed her until her head was spinning again. "There won't be a next time, little human woman. Because after today, you'll never leave us again."

Staring at Kade, Sharen's heart swelled with love for him. For the three of them. There was nothing better in this world than feeling loved.

She smiled. "We had better get dressed."

Ryder pulled out of her from behind. "And tell the others we just had a hot sex session, because they probably think someone was dying in here."

Her cheeks heated. "We weren't that loud!"

Alec chuckled. "*We* weren't that loud. But you sure were."

Knowing she was probably blushing like a teenager, she let her legs drop back onto the floor and moved away from her demons. "Let's just focus on the mission!"

Ryder winked at her. "Yes, ma'am."

Getting dressed, she couldn't help but look at her demons again. After today, everything would change. And she was looking forward to a little time to just enjoy being with her husbands.

Maybe we'll even take a little vacation when everything is settled.

The future was looking bright.

20

SHAREN STOOD IN FRONT OF THE SWIRLING PORTAL, CLUTCHING her splicer. The weapon felt light in her grip, and she felt confident with it back in her hand.

Looking back at the room of over two dozen members of the Rebellion, she smiled. The room overflowed with hope and excitement.

"Everyone ready to save some lives?"

The room erupted into cheers. Her soldiers clapped. The witches shouted. And the demons hooted while cheering loudly.

Giving them one last nod and meeting her demons' eyes, she stepped into the portal.

The awful feeling of crossing over pulled her in every direction, stretching her, squishing her. One moment she felt fire course through her, and the next a cold chill that radiated through her very soul.

And then she stumbled out into the realm.

Before her vision adjusted to the blazing suns in the sky, she equipped her splicer with a simple spell to knock a person unconscious. It sent a stunning green glow dancing along the dangerous edge of her weapon.

She might be on a peace mission, but she'd be ready for anything.

Blinking into the sunlight, she waited only a moment for the world to come into focus. She was at the bottom of a tall hill of white sand. As far as she could tell, there were none of the caves or the white cacti-like plants that grew in most of the demon realms.

Everything was quiet. *Too quiet.*

Not the welcome I expected.

Her heart hammered, but she started cautiously up the hill. The suns beat down on her, and sweat formed quickly. She wiped it away from her eyes, still keeping one hand firmly on the hilt of the semi-circle of sharp metal.

When she was nearly at the top of the hill, she took a deep breath, preparing herself for anything. Maybe no demons would be there. Maybe it would be a trap.

Really, anything could happen.

But when she got to the top, she froze. Stretching out before her were thousands of demons, all sitting or standing across the white sands in all directions.

Her mouth dropped open, and she felt tears sting her eyes. They were there. The king of hell had followed through on his word. Her heart swelled as she slowly walked down the hill, feeling as if she were walking into a dream.

A light wind picked up, sending the white sand scattering. It also carried with it the smell of sulfur. She inhaled, despite the unpleasant scent, and moved a bit faster.

The demons' skin was bright red in the demon realm. And all the people had white horns. The men had larger ones, the women smaller ones, and the babies had little ones that were almost cute. They also all wore white clothes, made from the only plants that seemed to grow in the hot, dry place. Most of the demons were covered in a layer of the white sand that covered the ground, but even still, their red flesh stood out brilliantly against the endless sea of white.

As she got closer, a young woman with flowing blonde hair and a small baby strapped in a wrap around her back turned toward Sharen. The woman's gaze flickered to her, then away, then back. Her eyes widened.

Brian's mother!

Sharen saw her shout. But from the distance, she couldn't hear what she said. But the effect of it was instantaneous; the demons turned in her direction. Most froze in what they were doing. And then, a second later, the crowd began to move towards her.

She froze, swallowed hard, and waited. It was a strangely intimidating sight to see thousands of demons coming straight toward her.

Her palms grew sweaty. She wiped them on her pants and waited.

The demons came closer and closer, gathering less than twelve feet in front of her. They looked...uncertain. Concerned.

Are they afraid of me?

It took a long time for them to gather in a tight space in front of her, but at last the shuffling slowed. All eyes were on her.

Here goes nothing. She took a deep breath. "I'm Sharen. And I'm here to help you."

Brian's mother, Elle, stepped in front of the group. "They decided they wanted me to speak for them."

Even though you and your children had to experience death again just a few days ago.

Sharen felt a tinge of horrible guilt. "I'm so sorry," she said, her voice soft.

Elle held her gaze and slowly shook her head.

She doesn't want to discuss it? Because she doesn't want to relive it? Or doesn't want the others to know?

"Sharen!" someone shouted.

Brian came rushing through the crowd of people, and suddenly, he was launching himself into her arms. She just barely managed to grab him with one arm and hold the splicer out so he wouldn't hurt himself.

"Brian." She said his name like a prayer.

The boy pulled back slightly, and she stared. His messy brown hair was the same. His eyes, so big they seemed to fill his whole face, looked the same.

God had she missed him.

"I don't want to die again," he whispered.

"You won't," she promised.

He curled into her for one more minute before finally letting her go. Moving back to his mother's side, he stared back at her, a smile on his face.

"Our questions!" a man shouted, his voice laced with irritation.

Sharen stood straighter. "Go on."

Elle met her gaze again. "First, we want to thank you for coming. We thought when we ended up here there was no escape. Many of us were still trying to climb free of the demon realms, but we weren't confident that we'd ever be powerful enough to make it. Quite a few of us have been caught by hunters over the years, killed, and had to start back in the Pits again. We were starting to lose hope. Until you..."

We are pretending she never went to the surface. Weird.

But Sharen followed the young woman's lead. "I'm sorry for your struggles, but I'm glad I can help."

Elle spoke without hesitation. "We don't want to seem ungrateful, but we have some questions first."

Is this good or bad? "Okay."

The woman nodded, then spoke, her voice louder than before. "You used to be a hunter. How do we know this isn't just a trap?"

Shit. How do I reassure them? I don't seem to be very good at it. Clenching her hands, her ring bit into her palm. *My ring!* "I'm doing this because not so long ago I thought demons were evil, and it was my job to hunt them. Until I met my husbands." She held up her hand, and the ring seemed to glow in the light of the suns. "Now, I'm married to three amazing demons. I know them. And I know they aren't bad. Since that day, everything has changed for me. My focus is to right this wrong. To make sure innocent people aren't rotting in this awful place anymore."

Elle nodded, her lips curling into the slightest smile. Some of the demons whispered to each other, but the focus remained on Sharen.

"And what will happen when we get to Earth?"

Sharen spoke a little more confidently. "We have a refuge ready to go. You'll be protected there until we can help you adjust back to the new world."

Elle opened her mouth again, but a massive man behind her spoke instead. "I think that's all we really need to know. Let's get the fuck out of this hell hole!"

A cheer rose over the demons.

Sharen looked to Elle.

The woman smiled. "I guess he's right."

"This way, then!" Sharen shouted, her heart soaring.

Elle walked straight up to her, then lowered her voice. "We'll have to talk privately, later."

Sharen thought of the old woman, dead in her home, and some of her excitement faded. "Yes, we will."

Elle leaned in closer. "It's impossible to tell your enemies from your friends anymore."

The hairs on Sharen's arms stood on end. *Are you a friend or an enemy?*

"Lead on!" someone shouted.

Time to focus. We'll find out what happened when they died later.

Turning, she started back up the hill. Her mind was going a thousand miles a minute. Soon they would all get through. There were more demons than she expected. They wouldn't all fit in the warehouse, but they could start busing them to the sanctuary at once. The refuge would be tight too. They might have to get tents for a while. And more supplies. But—

As she stepped onto the top of the hill, someone kicked her hard in the face. She flew back, rolling down the hill. Someone caught her. It took her a second to look up into Elle's frightened face, then back at the top of the hill.

A hunter stood in his white uniform, staring down at her.

Raw terror streaked through her. Where there was one of them, there was more.

As if her fears brought them to life, two more hunters stood next the first one. Then two more. Then more. Within seconds, twenty hunters stared down at them from the top of the hill.

"What do we do?" Elle whispered above her.

And suddenly the baby on her back began to wail. The sound cut through Sharen's terror.

She struggled out of the other woman's arms and rose to her feet. "Everyone, get back."

"You can't fight them all," Elle said, her voice carrying above the silence.

Something warmed within her chest. "But I can sure as hell try."

"No," someone said behind her. "If we work together, we can defeat them."

She looked behind her. Many of the demons were inching backwards. But a few were pressing forward.

A massive demon came to stand behind her. "We're with you."

She nodded, her gaze returning to the hunters. As much as she wanted to fight them on her own, this wasn't about her pride. It was about saving as many lives as possible.

"Sharen." Someone spoke her name with venom.

A man pushed past the line of hunters. It took her only a moment to recognize Rorde.

How did he find me, yet again? The sorcerer bastard!

"That's Mrs. Bran to you."

His mouth curled into a cruel smile. "Your demons must be awful good in bed for you to turn your back on your own kind and side with these animals."

She smiled, even though her eyes felt cold. "It's a hell of a lot harder to do the right thing than the easy thing." She gestured behind her. "What do you think these people did to deserve to end up here?" She met the gazes of each of the hunters. "What did this tiny baby do? What did that old woman do? What did those children do? Ask yourselves something: what if we were lied to? What if not all demons are bad?"

To her surprise, her gaze met several of her students, and she saw the hesitancy in their faces.

"Think about it. Truly. I taught many of you. I killed and fought next to many of you. What made me switch sides?"

Rorde laughed. "What a joke! I know exactly why you switched sides! Those demons got your ring. And they own you now. You don't have a choice but to fight for them."

"No." She shook her head. "Listen to me." A wave went through her. Every hair on her body rose as goosebumps erupted on her flesh. *What is this power?* She shivered. "Listen to me. I'm here to save these people, not fight you. Please, let us go. Look into your hearts. Forget every lie you've ever been told. Look at these people. Do *you* think they are evil?"

Samantha shook her head of dark hair. "I can't do this. I won't fight Mrs. Bran."

Rorde turned to her. "Are you fucking kidding me? She makes a speech and suddenly you're running away. Are you really willing to give up being a hunter because of one mistake?"

The blue shield of power that surrounded Samantha faded, and she lowered her splicer. "It's not just the speech. She was our teacher. And...and I believe her."

Samantha looked at Sharen and her gaze gentled.

Sharen smiled. "Thank you for believing in me."

Red power hit Samantha. Her eyes widened, and she hit the ground. Her body rolled down the hill, and Sharen caught her at the bottom of hill, brushing the sand off her face. Her eyes were still open, but the life was gone from them.

Ice settled in her belly, and she looked up at Rorde who still held his splicer, his red spell lighting the weapon. "You killed her!"

Light danced in his eyes. "A traitor's life is worthless."

Sharen looked to the other hunters. "If what you're

doing is right, why do they have to scare you into obeying them?"

Several of the hunters looked uncertain, but they didn't move.

Rorde tilted his head. "You'll learn, Sharen. Your words mean nothing to us. Today you and these demons will die, and then this foolish Rebellion will be squashed. Forever."

She pressed a light kiss to Samantha's forehead and closed her eyes. "Rest in peace, Samantha. I'll come back for you soon."

Releasing her, she picked up her splicer from where it had fallen. "I know you think this will be easy, but you're wrong."

Dark magic oozed from her, a cloud that moved around her splicer like a living creature.

Rorde's eyes widened. "What the hell spell is that?"

She smiled. "It looks like you don't know everything."

He took a step closer to her. "Neither do you."

She frowned, and then saw motion out of the corner of her eye. Turning, she watched in horror as more hunters suddenly stood. There was more motion on her other side. More hunters, who had camouflaged themselves against the white landscape, stood.

Her heart pounded in her ears. There had to be hundreds of them, every hunter in the entire Department.

"Don't move!" she shouted to the demons.

Whirling, she spotted the hunters that were behind them.

We're surrounded.

Suddenly, bursts of magic exploded into their group. Screams tore through the air. Some of the demons began to run, but had nowhere to go. Magic struck them, knocking them to the ground. The smell of burned flesh and coppery blood filled the air.

She closed her eyes, gritted her teeth, and imagined the symbols of the spell. It was basic, but she'd never used it like this before. It hurt as it poured out of her, and she felt it draining her with each second that passed.

When she crumbled to her knees, she stopped feeding strength into the spell.

A golden bubble of protection surrounded a portion of the demons. Some of them seemed to have realized what she'd done. They pushed and shoved to get into the protection of her spell.

Breathing hard, she climbed to her feet.

She felt Rorde's spell coming just in time to roll to the side. A fiery magic hit the ground where she'd stood just seconds before.

Leaping to her feet, she blasted the black magic back at Rorde. A smoky mist came to life, filling the air for thirty or forty feet around the sorcerer. Many of her students struggled within it.

Her pulse sped up. It was a distraction, but it wasn't enough.

A terrible realization hit her at once. If she wanted to save the demons, she'd have to kill the hunters.

She'd killed hunters before, but not her students, not young people too scared to disobey their commands.

A shout came from her left. Hunters were running toward them. Magic exploded toward the demons. Her shield shuddered, but held.

The demons outside of the shield roared and ran toward the hunters. Many of them were struck down by multi-colored magic long before they got close enough to reach the hunters. If this kept up, none of them would even have a chance to fight.

Tears filling her eyes, she lifted her hand. The spell was one she'd never thought to use. One few hunters knew of.

She sent the blast of white light out toward the fifty warriors running toward them. In an instant, their shields vanished. Their steps faltered and they slowed.

Their faces were filled with confusion. She knew they wouldn't understand. Where were their shields? Why was it suddenly nearly impossible to lift their splicers? Why did their feet feel so heavy?

The horde of demons leapt onto them. She stared in shock as claws and horns ripped apart the humans standing frozen. Tears tracked down her face.

She turned back to Rorde and his hunters. They were carefully climbing out of the dark mist. When they emerged, they looked between the hunters being torn apart and the demons battling them.

She raised her hand.

"Wait!"

She stared at Rorde, her heart racing. "What?"

"Maybe there's another solution."

Please. "Speak."

"Maybe we could—"

Hunters shimmered into existence around her.

She screamed and her splicer struck the metal of another splicer. Every muscle in her body tensed as she ducked and spun. Her weapon struck two, three, four splicers. The hunters were relentless.

But they didn't know, couldn't know, that she wasn't human.

Her speed and strength was its own kind of weapon. She sliced the head from a young woman and cut the arm off a young man. More bodies hit the ground. She drove her weapon through the stomach of another.

Smith's face came sharply into view. He was her student, a cocky boy who never believed how dangerous the demon realm was. Blood poured out of his mouth.

"I'm sorry," she whispered, feeling more tears sliding down her cheeks.

She pulled her weapon out of his chest and turned toward the chaos behind her.

Her shield had fallen. The demons trapped in the center of the hunters were being killed off with a ruthlessness that was terrifying. Children who were struck by fiery magic screamed and hit the ground. Elderly people held up their hands as if they could stop another painful death, but it did nothing to slow the on slaughter of colorful bursts of magic.

"Accept it!" Rorde shouted above the sounds of battle. "You've lost."

She shook her head, turned to Rorde, and started to run.

His eyes widened. He sent bursts of magic toward her, but she struck each one away with her splicer.

When, seconds later, she smashed into him, she held the splicer to his throat. "Tell them to stop. Tell them it's over, or so help me God, I'll end your life."

Sweat ran down his forehead. "I'd love to, but I'm not the one in charge here."

She pressed her blade closer, watching as a line of blood opened on his throat. "End this."

He smiled. "Do it, Sharen. Turn me into an angel. See what kind of enemy I make when I'm immortal."

She started to pull the blade back.

His smile widened. "I knew you couldn't just kill me in cold blood."

With the slightest movement, she severed his head from

his body.

Two hunters leapt at her at once. She raised her splicer above her head, and both weapons caught hers just inches from her skull.

Her reflexes were like lightning. She moved faster than her enemies could follow, and body after body fell at her feet. Someone had cut her arm. She felt warm blood running down her leg, but none of it hurt. Adrenaline blocked any pain. She turned toward the demons. From where she stood, she saw it all clearly. Time slowed.

They couldn't win this battle. Even with her strength and quickness. No demons would survive.

She hated that her heart seemed to break. Hated that she felt such helpless rage.

I can't let this happen. I was supposed to save these people, not get them killed again.

Her demons had described to her what death was like for demons. Awakening in a pit of absolute-darkness, trapped in the oily blackness. Struggling beneath it, drowning and unable to see.

Sometimes it took hours, days, or weeks to escape it. Then a demon struggled through a place without light. Searching and searching for a way out.

To get to a realm like this one took years of climbing from the lowest realms to this one.

If these demons didn't escape now, she doubted they ever would.

So how do I save them?

Whispers filled her mind, but she couldn't make out their words. She stiffened, remembering this strange feeling from the last time she'd done the impossible. An overwhelming strength filled her, like air filling a balloon. It was power. Magic. From who or what, she wasn't sure. Last time she sensed it was angels. This time? This time she didn't know.

Her body began to tremble. To shake. The brightness of the demon realm grew brighter.

Kneeling down, she touched the white sand, her heart racing. Whatever this power was, she couldn't contain it much longer. It was begging to be released, but she didn't know how. Her fingers curled into the sand. She waited, but the magic continued to build inside of her. More demon bodies hit the ground. More hunters let their bright powers fly through the air to hit their targets. Some demons reached the hunters, trying to fight through their shields, but the hunters were untouchable.

More magic struck them. More bodies fell.

There was so much death. So many lives lost.

Her heart constricted. More tears rolled down her cheeks.

She commanded the power to help her. To help the demons. But it continued to build inside her.

"What do you want?" she shouted. "Help me! Help them!"

But the whispers only grew louder.

She screamed, the sound tortured.

Rising to her feet, she made a choice. A decision she could never go back on. If she couldn't save these demons, she would die with them.

The portal was behind her. The path clear. And yet, she walked away from it.

Her feet caused the ground to vibrate with each step she took. The foreign magic brimmed around her like a golden smoke.

She hated that she didn't know how to use it, hated that it was trapped within her.

Elle slammed into her chest, her wailing baby clutched in her arms. Brian's arm was grasped in her other hand as he cried. Blood coated the woman's face. Even her twin horns were painted in blood. "Take the children!" she shouted. "Save them!"

Suddenly, the baby was clutched in Sharen's grip. She looked between the baby and the woman.

"Please." Her words seemed to vibrate through the air. "You're our last hope."

Golden life blossomed from Sharen. It washed over the baby and spread out.

Sharen gasped. The warmth of the magic was like nothing she'd felt before, like she was giving birth to something alive and precious, like the baby in her arms.

The golden light spread out, coating the lands.

The hunters fell, one after another, until all were lying upon the sand.

Silence reigned. The silence of disbelief.

She looked to the demons who still stood and counted seventy-two. "The others..." she whispered, hating that her eyes burned. "I couldn't save them."

The bodies that littered the ground shimmered before they turned to ash. There was no breeze, and yet, the ash scattered and vanished within the sand.

Elle took her baby back, her eyes wide. "We...lived. Sharen, we lived! I thought it was impossible. I thought it was over." She rocked her baby. "We need to go, now. Before more hunters come."

Sharen looked at the hunters who littered the ground. Were they dead? Had she killed them all?

What's done is done. Elle is right; save those you can.

"Yes." Sharen took a deep, fortifying breath. "Yes. You're right. We have to go." She choked out the words.

Her heart ached to focus on the lives that had been lost, but her head made her turn and start back toward the portal. One of her students lay upon the ground. She stared at the body. His chest rose and fell.

A strange hope filled her. She hadn't killed all of them. She knew she should be worried that so many of her enemy had survived, but she was thankful beyond words that their blood wasn't on her hands.

Like the others. Like Smith and Samantha.

She looked back, grateful that demons trekked up the hill behind her. There were a handful of children, and some women and elderly, but only a few of the massive warrior demons had survived.

Most of them were injured. But all of them looked terrified.

War wanted death, and it got it, no matter if the person was old, young, big, or small.

She swallowed hard. When she reached the portal, she took a deep breath. "I've never taken this many demons over before. I think...I think it would help if we held hands."

The demons obeyed without question, lining up behind her.

When everyone was connected, she took one last look at the beat-up survivors. What would she tell the others when they saw how few had survived? She imagined their disappointment, feeling it deep within her soul.

It would kill them all to know how many lives had been lost that day. She just hoped that they could forgive her for her failure.

Taking a deep breath, she looked at the portal. It was time to face her people.

Without hesitating a second longer, she stepped through.

21

SHAREN CAME THROUGH THE PORTAL AND STARTED FORWARD, her head still spinning. She needed to get out of the way, to make room for the others. No matter that she couldn't see where she was stepping.

When she hit the box, she crumbled to the ground. Blinking for a moment, she realized her hand was lying in something wet and sticky.

The room slowly came into focus. And her heart stopped.

No one was there, but it was obvious that there had been fighting. Blood was everywhere. On the floor. The walls. And all the equipment.

She climbed to her feet.

Someone gasped behind her. "What happened?" It was Elle.

She didn't have time to answer. Where were her demons? Where were Alec, Kade, and Ryder?

Tearing through the room, she searched every blood-soaked corner of the warehouse. Crashing into her office, she looked, hoping against all hopes that they were there.

But the warehouse was empty. Not one person remained.

This couldn't be happening. She stumbled back into the main room. The demons she had saved were standing in the center of the room, gathered together like a frightened group of animals.

Numbly, she walked past them and erased the realm address on the demon stone. Instantly, the portal vanished.

"Sharen?" Elle asked, sounding concerned.

"We need to get you guys to the refuge. I don't know what happened here, but I don't think we're safe."

They seemed to accept her words. As she led them out into the alley, they followed closely together. She rushed them across the road on the other side of the building and led them to the parking lot.

Four demons stood around the buses, smoking and chatting.

When they saw her approach, they stiffened.

"Sharen?" one of them asked.

"Get these people to the refuge," she commanded.

She could tell they wanted to ask questions.

"Now."

They snapped into action, helping the people load the buses.

"Did you see anything?" she asked Charlie, knowing the answer before she spoke.

"See anything?"

"Anything strange?" she pressed.

He shook his head. "We've been here since you left. Why? Is something wrong?"

"We were attacked." She said the words without emotion. "Don't come back here after you drop them off. Stay at the refuge."

She turned, heading back toward the warehouse.

"Sharen!" Elle caught her arm. "Where are you going? You saw what happened there. They killed everyone. You need to come with us, where it's safe."

She shook her head. "I can't."

"Yes, you can," the woman pressed, bouncing her baby as she began to fuss.

"You go and protect your children," she whispered. "But I can't stop until I know what happened to my husbands."

Elle's eyes widened. "Sharen, you know what happened."

She jerked her arm from the other woman's grip. "I don't know what happened."

I'll find them. And I'll find who did this.

"Think about it. Someone knew where and when you were coming to get us. Someone knew where your headquarters were."

Sharen stiffened. "What are you saying?"

"I'm saying that you were betrayed. By someone. And until you find out who, you can't trust anyone. You can't go looking into what happened, because chances are you'll end up dead too."

It took her a long minute to answer. "Thanks, Elle. Now, go take care of your little ones."

"Please, Sharen."

She smiled, a smile that was so sad it seemed to break her heart. "I don't have a choice."

Turning, she started back toward the warehouse.

Elle is wrong. No matter the danger, I won't stop searching. I can't believe my demons are dead. I'll find them, and I'll punish the people responsible for this.

As a cool wind teased the air, she watched as dark feathers seemed to rain down from the sky. Looking up, she swore she saw a shape, but when she blinked, there was nothing but clouds.

Her hands curled into fists. There was one thing Elle wasn't wrong about. Someone had betrayed her.

And that someone was going to pay with their life when she found them.

22

RYDER GROANED AND PRESSED HIS FISTS AGAINST HIS EYES. A headache that was like a raging bull pounded through his mind. He stiffened when he felt wetness.

Drawing his hand back, he blinked into the small light that hung far above his head. When his gaze focused on his hand, he saw dark blood.

Memories came back to him, sharp and horrible. He sat up in a rush of movement, and his hands shot out, striking the bars of the cage that imprisoned him.

Gritting his teeth, he willed himself to bend the bars, but they didn't move. Not an inch. His breathing grew faster. He shuffled closer to the bars and pressed his face between them.

They were in a dark building with only a few bulbs dangling overhead. The only thing within the room were row after row of cages. Some of the shapes within the cages looked familiar, but he didn't spot his brothers among them.

He opened his mouth to shout for them, when he heard a noise. A whispering. Straining his ears, he listened closely.

"Sharen made it through the portal."

"Good." The voice that spoke caused every hair on Ryder's body to stand on end. It held power and darkness. Something that went beyond the deep, raspy quality of it. It was as if Ryder's very soul recognized something terrible about the man who spoke.

"But there was a problem," the other person whispered. The woman's voice was gentle, almost familiar. "Some of the demons survived."

"Survived?" The man's voice held nothing. Not surprise. Not anger. Just acceptance. "How is that possible? A group of frightened, weaponless creatures defeated the entirety of the hunter army?"

"I...it appears so."

The man didn't speak for a long time. "She used her powers. It's the only possibility."

"That was my thought," the woman rushed out, too quickly.

"And she's getting stronger."

Ryder heard footsteps, someone pacing back and forth.

"That cannot be allowed," the man said. "Something must be done."

"But, you see, that's why I imprisoned her people. She'll have to come here. She'll want to save them."

There was another long time when no one spoke, before the man's frightening voice came again. "I will consult the Fate. If Sharen becomes too powerful, I will be forced to kill her and her demons, regardless of the cost."

"Yes, my lord," the woman whispered.

"Either way," the man continued, "when she gets here, we'll have a very painful surprise waiting for her."

"Yes, my lord."

Ryder heard the sound of a door opening, then closing.

He waited for several long minutes, then began to whisper his brothers' names.

No matter what, they couldn't allow Sharen to step into a trap.

But even when his whispers turned to shouts, his brothers didn't answer. Nor did the bars on his cage bend.

To be continued...

WANT to read the final part in Sharen's story? Pick up Dark Powers.

DARK POWERS

1

A FEW HOURS BEFORE THE ATTACK...

THE SHAPESHIFTER ENTERED Sharen's office with the ease of someone who belonged there. He smiled and looked at his reflection. He'd taken on the face of a demon who worked for The Rebellion, one who just *happened* to have been killed on his way to work by a group of angels.

His smile widened as he moved to Sharen's desk and started rifling through her belongings. He found plenty, but nothing he could use. Nothing discussing The Immortal Ten or shedding light on what Sharen knew about her role in the war.

Frowning at his inability to find anything, he settled into her chair, placing his booted feet on her desk. Caine would not be pleased if he returned with nothing.

So what do I do now?

The office door opened and a pretty, young blonde came in, staring down at a pile of papers in her hands. She seemed entirely unaware of his presence as she headed for the desk.

Such a bad thing to be so unobservant. Dangerous even.

But a second later, she glanced up, then down, and then back up again, her eyes widening. "Henry, what are you doing in Sharen's office?"

Henry, is that this demon spawn's name?

He shrugged. "Relaxing."

Her eyes narrowed. "No one ever goes in here."

Fuck. He took his boots down from her desk. Before he'd watched the angels slaughter his target, he hadn't bothered to study the demon. He'd just taken his place. Now, he had no idea how to mimic the man, and the last thing he wanted was to tip off their enemies before the attack.

I was supposed to use this body to get information and then help catch them by surprise. I had better be successful in at least one of my missions.

"I know I shouldn't have come in here," he said, trying to soften his voice in a way he hoped was similar to the demon. "I just needed a few minutes to myself."

The young woman took a step back. "That's all you have to say? What's wrong with you?"

He rose from his chair. This was not going according to plan. *Not at all.* He couldn't give his father one more reason to kill him. "Nothing. I apologize for going where I shouldn't have."

She took another step back. "O—okay."

Oh, why couldn't you have been one of those simple humans who ignore their instincts when faced with evil?

He moved around the desk, trying not to alarm her any further. "What's your name?"

Her eyes widened. "My name? You're not Henry."

And you just signed your life away. Funny.

"What makes you think that?"

She trembled. "Because *Henry* and I are dating. *Henry* and I were supposed to meet for breakfast this morning, but he never showed up. So, who are you? *What* are you?"

He leaped towards her. She dropped her papers and turned to run. Her fingertips brushed the door handle when he reached around and covered her mouth.

She screamed, but his hand muffled the sound. His grip tightened around her body, holding her easily. She was no match for him and he barely felt her struggles. Leaning close to her ear, he whispered. "I've got a lot of pent-up up anger. And guess what? I'm going to take it out on you. I'm going to make you wish for death, but I won't give it to you. Not quickly any way. And when you're past the point of being anything but a shell of beaten flesh, I'm going to take your life."

He killed the woman slowly. First punching her face enough times to be sure she couldn't scream. And then, when his energy was finally spent, he stuffed her body into the closet. Smiling down at her, he thought of the way she'd looked when she was still alive. His body shuddered. His bones cracked and skin shifted, and then, he looked like the woman.

For a moment he felt relief, and then he thought about his failed mission and about Caine. Every ounce of relaxation beating the woman had brought him disappeared in an instant.

"Father will not be pleased when he discovers I learned nothing about their knowledge of the Immortal Ten," he told her dead body, glad to finally have someone to talk to. "The great *Caine* will likely come up with a new and terrible way to punish me. His *failure* of a son."

He started to pace, growing more and more agitated. "He

doesn't care that I've got everything planned... three perfect locations to put our precious bait, both the Hunter and angels in place. *And* that I thought of the only way to take the demons without killing them. No, all my father will think about is that I returned from her office empty handed."

He scowled. "I preferred being Greg Manthen to this retched role. He was a man of power and position. He was man who slept when he wanted, ate what he wanted, and killed what he wanted. Now, I'm what... shifting from one fucking demon to another. Slinking around in the shadows of The Rebellion. And all for what? My father hints at what his goal is, but doesn't care enough to just say it."

And it must be something important! Otherwise, he wouldn't be going through all this trouble. He'd just grab her with the others.

His nose wrinkled. "You have no idea how stressful it is to have The Judge of all of mankind as your father. It makes every day an awful one." He glanced at her again. "Not as bad as the day you've had, of course." Chuckling at his own cleverness, he felt a little better.

Time for the bloodshed!

Closing the closet door, he whistled under his breath as he made his way back to the main room of The Rebellion's hideout. Soon the attack would come, and every one of these bastard people would become pawns in his father's game. Caine, The Judge, the immortal being responsible for where people went when they died, would remain in power forever. This he was certain of.

DARLA LOOKED DOWN at her dead, broken body lying in the closet. Even in death she remembered how painful her last few moments of life had been. And now, her spirit was angry. If the creature who had killed her knew she was witch, he would've been more careful about how he disposed of her body, and about what he said when he thought no one could hear... but he hadn't. And now, she had a chance to do one final act before her spirit left her body.

Reaching with her ghost-like fingers, she touched her dead body. Her soulless eyes opened, and she pushed a message into it. When she finished, she felt cold, substance-less tears tracking down her cheeks.

As long as her body was found in time, the people she loved would be safe.

She closed her eyes and prepared for the afterlife, but minutes ticked by and nothing happened. More tears flowed down her cheeks.

Even in death, she couldn't find peace. There was still something left for her to do in this world. *But what?*

2

The Present...

SHAREN'S FEET pounded against the pavement as she ran, fiery rage burning through her veins with each step. She looked up and spotted a white-winged angel flying lazily across the city. She would catch the bastard and tear every feather from his wings until he told her where she could find her people.

And my demons.

Her heart lurched at just the thought of her demons. All she could picture was the blood-stained room she'd returned to after jumping through the portal. If they weren't safe—

Don't think of that. It's not possible.

Her demons hadn't wanted this life. They'd just wanted to return to earth and lead a peaceful existence. *She* was the one who couldn't just forget the truth about her world. *She* was the one who couldn't focus on anything but saving innocent lives.

They didn't deserve an ounce of pain. And yet, she had no control over that now.

I was willing to die for this cause. I just never imagined my demons might be the ones to pay for my obsession. Would I have done this if I had?

Her stomach turned.

People shouted at her as she ran through them, knocking into bags and shoulders. A truck honked as she darted out into traffic, and she rolled over the hood of a car that nearly hit her.

But she didn't slow. She couldn't. Because she had no idea where her demons were. She had no clues as to who took them. She could only hope this angel knew something, *anything* that could help her find her missing people.

Even as I child, when I was afraid, I would run like this, run as if moving fast enough would turn back time.

Someone grabbed her and pulled her roughly into an alley. Her back slammed against the wall and for a second, she couldn't breathe.

"Don't say a word. There isn't time."

Marval. She recognized the ancient vampire's voice before she spotted him. Then, her gaze focused on his face, and she gasped. He had been badly injured. Badly. His entire face was swollen, bruised, and streaked with blood. It was like a grotesque mask of pain so bad it hurt to see.

How is he still breathing?

"What the hell—?"

"Stop!" he ordered her, glancing behind them. "They're following me. There's no time."

Prickling moved down her spine. *Who's following him? Who did this to him?*

She wanted to ask a million questions, but she forced herself to remain quiet, even while her heartbeat pounded in her ears. Marval had seen a lot of awful things in his life, and until that moment she couldn't imagine one thing that could frighten him. But right now, he looked terrified.

"You need to go. Now! Listen to me... there's a place you've dreamed of. A place you thought wasn't real. You've seen it, in the forest, surrounded by angels. Go there, and you'll be safe."

My dream? The image of a place glowing with golden magic came and disappeared in a flash. She shook her head to clear away the picture.

Hide? Like hell! "My demons—"

"Doesn't matter!" he hissed, his voice frantic. "All that matters is that you get to safety."

She stood straighter, putting force into her words. "What happened to you?"

He squeezed his eyes closed. "You have to believe me. The fate of everything relies on you leaving town right this instant and going into hiding, do you understand me?"

Images flashed in her mind of her headquarters, of the evidence that a fight had taken place.

"No!" Her voice rose. "No, you're the one who doesn't understand. Everyone in headquarters is gone. There was blood everywhere."

His eyes popped open. "Their lives mean nothing compared to yours. If they die, they die. But you need to live."

"Like hell!" she snarled.

"Sharen, at least go to the refuge. Stay behind the protective barrier. They won't be able to catch you unprepared."

She stood taller, shoving his hands off of her. "Do you really think I'm just going to run and hide?"

He shook his head and winced. "You have to know if any

of them are still alive, they're only keeping them that way to get to you."

"I don't care."

"But—"

"I'm going to save them, and nothing you say will change that."

He stared back at her, and suddenly, it was as if her words really sank in. His expression crumbled, and his shoulders sank. "I risked everything to tell you. To get you to safety."

"Why?" Her pulse raced. "Did you find out what I am?"

He nodded. "Listen to me. Your powers, they're tied to hope. When you feel hopeful, when you feel connected to the faith of others, you become strong. And when you feel defeated, your powers wane. You're influenced by the emotions of others around you. It's a weakness and a strength, because you're capable of impossible, amazing things."

She took a small step towards him. "What am I, Marval?"

His mouth opened.

A shadow darkened the sky above her. The flurry of angel wings blocked out the sun.

"Go!" Marval shouted. "I'll distract them!"

"Not a chance!" She reached for the sword at her back and pulled it free. "Let the bastards come!"

He grabbed her shoulder and shoved her back. "There are things worse than death, and they've planned those things for you. Run, now!"

Her hands tightened on her sword. "You should know me better than that!"

In moments, the angels shot down toward them. Hitting the ground, the massive angels surrounded them. She slipped Marval a dagger and was grateful when he took it. They stood back-to-back, staring without speaking at the angels. They were all men, wearing normal clothes, but even without their massive, white wings, they wouldn't have looked human. Something about the angels marked them as immortals... they were too beautiful. And there was a dreamlike quality that made them seem unreal.

"Sharen." The one directly in front of her spoke, cocking his head to the side in a movement that was strangely creepy. His deep brown eyes glistened as his gaze ran over her, and his long brown hair fell almost delicately around his shoulders. "You will come with us."

She grinned, even though her stomach turned. "Where to?"

The angel raised a brow. "To a place you'll never escape from."

"Well now, that doesn't sound like a place I want to go, so I think I'll pass." Her grip tightened on the hilt of her sword.

The angel's mouth pulled into a frown. "I wasn't giving you a choice." Then, he looked to the others. "But first, let us kill the troublesome vampire."

A glowing soul-blade appeared in the hand of an angel with harsh features, and he took a step toward them.

Please let my powers be here. She thought she felt stronger, but she was never entirely sure. And she had no chance if she had only the strength of a normal human.

Marval slashed his dagger in front of him, but even the movement was weak.

The angel swung back his sword, and she acted. Moving in a flash, she severed his head from his shoulder. His body hit the ground with a thump.

Silence surrounded them.

That's right assholes, look who has super strength and speed too! She almost grinned. Almost.

"How the hell did you do that?" the first angel growled.

She looked at his angry face, but to her surprise, she also saw a touch of fear in his eyes.

"What are you?" he whispered, holding her gaze.

Show no fear. "I'm the woman who's going to kill all of you, if you don't let us go."

He laughed and a soul-blade appeared in his hand. "I'm not afraid." Looking over her shoulder, he gave the orders. "Kill the vampire. Leave her alive."

Time seemed to speed up, and blood rushed into her ears.

The angel dashed toward her. Their swords clashed. Behind her, there was a shout.

She spun away from her opponent, and plunged her sword into the stomach of one of the angels behind her. There was no time to think. Two angels were playing with Marval. He had a slash on his arm and one on his leg. And both the bastards were grinning like it was Christmas.

A roar filled her ears, and she attacked, catching them by surprise.

She knocked one of their swords away. It flew, clattering against the alley wall. Before the angel could react, she kicked him in the chest. To her surprise, he went flying back, hitting the ground on his back. Spinning to the other angel, their swords connected. Once, twice, a third time. Sweat trickled down his forehead.

He moved to strike again and she sensed movement behind her. Darting to the side, she just barely avoided the blow from behind, while at the same time, avoiding the sword from the opponent in front of her.

Both angels suddenly struck at once. She moved again, but the painful burn of metal caught her arm.

She hissed as blood poured from the wound, and held her blade in front of her. Four angels stood looking uncertain, their gazes darting between her and Marvel.

Keep them focused on you.

"So the great Caine didn't tell you what I am?"

The leader of the group glared. "He doesn't need to tell us anything. We're his soldiers; our job is to obey him."

"And you're such good, mindless soldiers," she mocked, sickly sweet.

She felt wind on her head one second before the angel descended behind her. A massive arm wrapped around her throat, choking her. Someone knocked her sword away, and then she was being lifted into the air.

Digging her nails into the arm at her throat, she struggled, her legs kicking at the air. Below her, the angels surrounded Marvel. He banished his dagger, and a second later, an angel behind him severed his head from his body.

No!

The angel carrying her flew higher and higher. Passing the top of the building, her thoughts cleared. If she didn't escape now, there would be no escape. Grabbing her other dagger, she pulled it free of her sleeve and stabbed it into the arm that held her.

A scream came behind her. The arms released her. And suddenly, she was plummeting to the ground. Reaching out, she grasped the ledge of the building as she fell past. Hitting the brick, she gasped in a deep breath and pulled herself to the top of the roof.

I'm so sorry, Marvel!

She had no weapons and powerful enemies who wanted her dead. She had no choice. Turning, she ran.

3

SHAREN CLIMBED DOWN THE FIRE ESCAPE ON THE SIDE OF THE building, watching the skies, even though she'd seen no sign of the angels for over an hour. When she hit the ground, she started running once more. Not looking back.

No matter how much she wanted to.

She raced down the sidewalk, the city a blur of colors around her. Marval was dead. The angels were searching for her, and she had no idea where her demons were. She had to... she had to do something, but what?

Take a deep breath. Think. Don't just run blindly.

She froze. A car honked. Turning slowly, she realized she was standing in the middle of a street. She moved without feeling her feet. When she reached the sidewalk, she stared numbly.

I have to save my demons. I have to save my people. But how? What can I do?

Closing her eyes, she willed her terrified thoughts to calm. And it hit her. The first thing she needed to do was get weapons. Without weapons, she was far too vulnerable. After that she could figure out her next move.

I need help. And I know just who to call.

Pulling her phone out of her pocket, it took her three tries with shaky fingers to dial Lily's phone number.

"*Yello.*"

"Lily." Sharen couldn't seem to find the words.

The teasing note immediately left her ex-student's voice. "What's wrong?"

"Someone... someone attacked headquarters while I was in the portal."

Her words were met with silence for a brief moment. "How bad is it?"

She swallowed around the lump in her throat. "Everyone was gone. And there was blood."

"Fuck. Any idea who did it?"

Sharen shook her head until she remembered the woman couldn't see her. "Maybe the angels."

"Where are you?"

"A street. I don't know. The angels attacked. They killed Marval."

"Shit. Okay. Can you get to your place?"

"Yeah, I think so."

"Go there and wait for me. Do you understand? You're in shock. We're going to take care of this together, but we can't be stupid."

"Okay." She felt the smallest stirring of hope within her.

"Whoever took them is going to pay. I promise you that."

"Thanks, Lily." Her voice was barely louder than a whisper.

"Get to your place. I'll see you soon."

The phone grew quiet. Slowly, Sharen stuffed her phone back into her pocket. Blinking, the world came into focus. The street was busy. And loud.

Her gaze moved to the street names. Damn it. She was

halfway across town from her apartment. She flagged down a cab, and when he pulled over, she got in. She muttered her address and sat back in the seat.

She couldn't stop from shaking. And she hated how much of a mess she was. How was it that even after all she'd been through, she still couldn't handle death?

Her parent's faces flashed in her mind, and she shuddered. Did it ever get easier?

Why the hell couldn't she be the kind of person who just told the world to fuck off and faced things like a bad ass? *Because you're only human.*

She laughed.

The cabby looked back at her, raising one brow.

Better be careful, or he's going to think I'm nuts. Hiding her smile, she felt a sense of resolve come over her. She could do this. She may not know what she was, but she knew that she wasn't human. And even though she wasn't good at handling death, she'd handle it too, because she had to do. Her people were counting on her.

And because if I stop fighting for one second, I'll lose my demons forever.

Her heart constricted as she thought of Kade, Alec, and Ryder. She felt like such a fool. Like this was karma for not appreciating them more. They'd done everything in their power to support her and her cause, even when it came at the price of their own happiness. Had she showered them with gratitude? No. At times she might have even acted like an ungrateful bitch.

But I'll make it up to them. The second I find them.

"We're here," the driver said.

She looked up and handed him a bill from her pocket.

He took it, frowning. "You got blood on the seat."

Glancing beside her, she saw that her bloody arm had

soaked the seat on one side. How had she forgotten about the wound?

"Sorry," she murmured. Reaching into her pocket, she pulled out the entire wad and shoved it toward him.

His look of annoyance vanished. "No problem at all!"

She nodded and opened the door.

"Are you okay?"

Meeting his gaze, she forced a smile. "I've had worse."

She slammed the door and hurried to their penthouse suite. Now not only did she need to suit up with weapons, she needed to wrap her damn wound. Her sporadic powers might help her heal, but even they had their limits.

As the elevator opened onto their private floor, she froze. Someone was lying on the ground at her door.

Heart racing, she ran to the man and knelt down, pulling him back to see his face.

Gasping, she fell backwards. Shit! The man was beaten so severely that there was no chance he still lived. Blood coated his shirt, his pants, and the carpet beneath his body.

And there was something stapled to the bare skin beneath his ripped shirt. Hand shaking, she reached for the blood soaked note and opened it.

RUNNING *from the angels was a mistake. We're going to get you. How many dead bodies will it take? Tick Tock.*

BILE ROSE in the back of her throat. And then, she saw the slightest movement. Reaching forward, she touched the man's chest. There, so slow she almost missed it, was the lightest rise and fall of his chest. She felt for a pulse and found it, weak and slow. She didn't know who the hell he was, but he was still alive!

Typing in the code on her door, she dragged the man inside of her apartment, leaving behind a smearing path of blood. Unsure what else to do, she dragged him all the way to their shower and put him inside. Turning it on, she watched as the blood washed from his flesh and turned the water to a dark red.

In seconds she had another shock. "Alderon?"

The fae Hunter said nothing. His eyes remained closed. Kneeling down, she pushed back his blood-stained pale hair, overwhelmed by the sight of his many, many wounds.

What should I do? Could she bring a fae being to a human hospital? Did he just need time to let his own body heal? Or should she try to stitch his wounds closed?

She felt... lost.

And then, her doorbell rang.

Jerking to her feet, she looked between the Hunter and her bedroom. God, she hoped that was Lily, but what if it was yet another enemy?

Moving through her room, she felt steel run through her blood. Taking a sword from off their dresser, she drew it from its sheath. She walked with sure steps toward her door with determination rising within her.

No matter what waited on the other side of the door, she would handle it. *One way or another.*

4

Sharen clenched the hilt of her sword harder and looked out the peephole. Lily stared back at her.

Unlocking her door, she threw it open.

Her student was staring down at the blood streaks on her floor. "This doesn't look good."

Sharen nodded, and the woman did her best to step around the blood and enter into her apartment. Lily looked... energetic.

God did Sharen envy her. Lily was only a few years younger than her, but she looked like a model just walked off the runway. With gorgeous white-blonde hair, high cheekbones and full lips, her skin practically glowed with health. Her eyes shone with something... maybe even excitement.

Who would have thought she was a half-demon? And more than that, a half-demon working in The Department but secretly fighting for The Rebellion?

Sharen wasn't sure whether she loved her for bringing the energy she didn't have, or hated her for not being as beaten down by the world as Sharen felt.

"So, what's going on?" Lily asked.

Sharen shook herself back into the present. "There's a wounded fae Hunter in my shower. I'm not sure what to do with him."

Lily cocked her head and pulled a dagger from beneath her leather jacket. "I can kill him if you don't want to."

A shudder moved through her body. "No—no. He was helping me with something. I think they figured it out."

And then everything hit her at once. "And since they left his body here, they know where I live."

"Which means we can't stay long."

"But we can't just leave him to die."

Lily nodded and put her dagger away. "Let me see him. Then we'll figure out what to do."

The blonde's boots seemed too loud as she hurried toward the running shower.

Sharen scrambled after her, hating how lost she felt.

They came to stand over the fae man, who was looking better with most of the blood washed away, but still bad. Very bad.

"He should live, but he's going to need some help."

Sharen took a deep breath. "But I can't... I need to find the others. My demons..."

Lily turned, her eyes wide. "They were taken too?"

She nodded, feeling her throat squeeze.

"Oh boy, someone is going to die for that mistake."

Sharen was suddenly able to breathe easier. "You don't think it's hopeless?"

"Fuck no." Then she smirked. "So, you need to figure out where they were taken, fix up this Hunter, and—"

"Check on the demons at the refuge."

Lily shrugged. "Okay, you track down your demons. I can bandage up this guy and drop him off at the refuge."

Some of the pressure left Sharen's chest. "Thanks."

"So, how are you going to find them?"

"No idea, but I'll think of something. I always do."

"All right. Well, we had better hurry before we get caught here. I'll stitch you up and then the fae."

Sharen frowned. "He's worse off."

"Yeah, but he's already healing. You need to get a quick patch job before you bleed out. Then you can get the fuck out of here before your trail goes cold."

"My trail." For the first time, she realized what she needed to do. "I need to go back to headquarters."

Lily nodded. "If they left that kind of mess, they probably wanted you to find them. I bet there's something that will lead you straight to them."

Sharen almost ran for the door, but caught herself. *Bandages and weapons first.*

She led her ex-student to the living room and typed in the code to open up her weapons chest. Lily whistled in appreciation behind her, but she ignored the other woman, pulling open the drawer of first aid supplies.

"So, how did you get so good at all of this?" Sharen asked, selecting what she thought they might need. *Because even though I'm a Hunter, these things don't come naturally to me.*

The young woman shrugged. "My job in The Department is to investigate disturbances that might point to half-breeds and demons who have crossed over into our realm. I've gotten good at getting inside other people's heads and figuring out what drives them and how to track them."

And I'm sure she's saved a lot of lives by being better than the other Hunters.

Sharen handed her the supplies. "We're lucky to have someone like you in The Rebellion."

She grinned. "Stop stalling and go sit down."

God, it's weird when my students grow up. But the thought warmed her heart.

Lily directed her to the couch and started laying out the stuff to stitch her arm up and wrap it. She smelled the alcohol before she felt it on her wound and she gritted her teeth to keep from crying out.

"Sorry," Lily said as she knelt down beside her and gently cleared the blood from her arm.

"It's fine," Sharen said, even though the alcohol burned like hell. She wasn't sure if her stupid powers meant this was all a waste, but she wasn't willing to bleed-out or grow weak when she had work to do. She would sit and cater to her human side.

No matter how much it hurt.

"You're just going to need a few stitches," Lily added.

Squeezing her eyes shut, she forced herself to take deep breaths and not think about the needle weaving through her flesh. She told herself to be the woman her demons needed her to be as her body ached as it was pulled together. This was nothing. Just skin. She could do this.

"All done."

Sharen's eyes flashed open. "Great, thank you."

Lily wrapped her arm. "Do you want me to meet up with you when I'm done at the refuge?"

"No," she said, too quickly.

Lily slowed. "You're going to need help."

Sharen spoke without thinking. "I'm not exactly sure what I'm going to be facing, but I'm not dragging you into this... any more than I already have."

"Mrs. Bran—"

"I'm just Sharen now."

"You're not *just* anyone. You're leading this Rebellion,

whether you know it or not. They need you. If what you're doing is going on a suicide mission, you need to keep that in mind, because this might just be one fight you can't win."

Can't win?

She met her ex-student's gaze. "This isn't about the Rebellion anymore. It's about the three men I love more than anything in this world. I dragged them into this mess. I made them give up their peaceful chance at a second life, and if I have to save them from the very depths of the demon-realm, I will."

After a second, Lily nodded. "Okay. But I'm here if you need me."

"I appreciate it."

"And I can contact the others if you haven't yet and update them."

"Shit." Sharen ran a hand through her hair. "I forgot."

"It's been a few hours," Lily said with a humorless laugh. "Don't be too hard on yourself."

She's right, but I need to do better.

There were many, many people working for the Rebellion. Small groups of rebels lived in cities all over the world and they looked for signs of demons who had crossed over into their realm. Their job was to offer them help and keep them concealed from the Hunters.

When she'd joined the cause, she had completely changed the way everyone searched for demons and how they helped them. She had also changed how they avoided the Hunters, mostly due to her insider information on The Organization. At first she'd just felt like an important source of information, but things had quickly changed when she'd presented the idea of trying to save demons before they had to crawl through all the realms.

By the time she and her demons had secured the

demon-stone and soul chalk, she had suddenly found herself being the go-to person for everything related to the Rebellion... so it bothered her that Lily had been the one to remind her of her responsibility.

"It's okay," her ex-student said. "I know you're a control freak, but you can count on me."

Sharen couldn't help but smile. She took a deep breath. If she had learned anything from losing her demons, it was that her focus needed to return to her husbands. That would mean releasing some control.

"I don't know what I'd do without you."

Lily smirked, rising and heading back to the injured fae, her first aid kit in hand. "Well, you don't have to worry about that. I'm damn hard to get rid of."

Another thing I can be thankful for.

Sharen stood and stretched out her injured arm. She decided it would have to do. She hurriedly changed into clean clothes, and then went back to the weapons' chest. Loading herself up, she at last felt more like her old self. If she ran into any more angels, at least she had a fighting chance.

"Mrs. Bran!"

Sharen spun and ran to the bedroom. Panting, she stared at her student. "What is it?"

"He spoke."

She looked down at the severely beaten face of the fae Hunter. *There's no way he spoke.* But then, his lips moved.

"Alderon?" Kneeling down, she leaned just over him. At first his words were nothing more than sounds. "I don't understand," she said.

"Water," he rasped.

Lily hurried from the room and came back with a glass. She put it to his lips and helped him drink. He choked several times and spit water, but finally seemed to calm. When she pulled the cup from his mouth, he licked his lips.

He didn't open his eye as he spoke slowly. "The Department... is corrupt. Y—you were right. Someone new is hunting you."

None of that sounded good. "I'll take of it. You rest."

"Sharen," her voice was almost a sigh. "The Hunter... don't underestimate him."

His breathing grew even once more, and she and Lily exchanged a look.

"Well, this fucking day keeps getting better and better."

Sharen forced a smile. "Where did the sweet, obedient girl I trained go?"

Lily smirked. "Being a half-demon in an organization that hunts demons means playing my role and playing it well. You didn't suspect what I was, and neither did anyone else."

"Well, I think I might like the new Lily even better than the old one."

Lily's smirk widened. "Take care of your demons. I'll be fine here."

"Thanks again. And get out of here as fast as you can."

"Will do," Lily said, laying out her first aid kit.

She'd better. Whoever left that message is probably watching our house. Hopefully they'll lose interest when they see me leave.

As she headed for the door, she paused and looked back. Lily was slowly drying off the fae man on her bedroom floor. She felt a pang of regret for bringing him into this. If he died, he was one more person who'd died because of her. And if he lived... well, she still owed him. She wasn't sure how he'd been found out, but she was sure he'd be safe right now if he'd killed her when he had the chance.

I wonder if he'll regret his sense of right and wrong after this.

Lily looked up, nodded solemnly, and went back to drying the fae Hunter.

Taking a deep breath, Sharen turned and headed for the door once more. She had no doubt headquarters was being watched too and that she was probably walking straight into trouble.

But that was the thing—facing trouble was better than nothing. At least it meant she might have a chance of finding out what happened to her demons.

No matter the risk.

5

RYDER HAD DREAMED OF SHAREN LONG BEFORE SHE STUMBLED into the demon-realm that brought them together. It wasn't exactly her face that haunted him, but a sense of her. A smell that lingered on his flesh when he awoke. A taste on his lips.

Too many nights he and his brothers dreamed of the human woman, a creature who was tough as hell on the outside, but soft and in need of their protection within.

And when they finally had her? There had been so much chaos, so much darkness and fear.

It wasn't what he'd wanted for her. It wasn't what any of them wanted for her, but he'd never been happier than when she was in his arms.

Lying cramped in the bottom of the dark cage, his mind was full of her. His memories helped him ignore the weeping, groans of pain, and the screaming that came from the darkness. It even helped him ignore his own pain.

He shifted and bit down a hiss. The wounds on his stomach and arms were already healing, but the angels' fists and swords hadn't been gentle. His body still felt sore and tight as it worked to knit his injuries back together.

One thing about lying here uselessly is that I'm healing faster. He moved again and felt a sharp stab of pain where one of his ribs had been cracked. Shadows drifted before his vision, but he refused to give in to them, to simply slip back into unconsciousness.

Sharen had brought him out of the darkness. She filled him with hope and kept him from slipping back to a place without fear or pain.

He knew from the little he'd heard from the guards that she was safe, that they'd tried to catch her not long ago and failed.

He didn't know why they hadn't just waited outside the portal for her, but he was damned grateful for their stupidity. It meant that she was safe.

His Sharen, his beautiful wife, was still safe.

Closing his eyes, a small smile touched his lips.

"THIS ISN'T how we celebrated Christmas," Kade growled.

Sharen laughed, stringing more tinsel on the large tree in their apartment. "Well, then you weren't doing it right."

Kade's glare darkened as he leaned back further on the couch. He took another slip of the spiked eggnog in his mug and winced. "This crap is awful."

Ryder punched him in the arm and jumped over the back of the couch, hurrying to Sharen. "Need help?"

She looked back at him, her smile making every cell in his body expand. "Sure."

For a minute he couldn't look away. She was so damned beautiful. Tonight she wasn't wearing her hoodie and jeans. She wasn't donned in weapons, with an aura of a woman just trying to get through the day. Instead, she wore pajamas. A white top that was criminally see-through, pants with reindeers on them, and slippers with reindeers with light-up noses.

In other words, she looked perfect.

Reaching out, he pushed her long, dark hair off her shoulders and buried his hand in the back of her hair. Instantly, her green eyes lost their merriment, darkening with arousal.

"Ryder, the tree," she whispered, but there wasn't a hint of scolding in her voice. Just arousal and anticipation.

He leaned closer. "The tree might just have to wait."

The tinsel in her hands fell to the floor.

A SOUND JERKED him back from his memories. Lights appeared in the darkness.

Rising to his knees, he peered through the bars of the cage. If he were human, the light wouldn't have been enough to see a thing, but with his superior vision he could see the many cages spread out in the massive room.

Yet, I don't see my brothers' massive forms among them.

Ice ran through his veins at just the thought, but he pushed it aside. His brothers were safe. Somewhere.

The light moved closer and closer until it was blinding in its intensity. For one second he couldn't see the person who held the lantern, but then his vision came into focus.

It was the creature from the battle. A man with purple skin, so dark it was nearly black. Cracks of gold like lightning appeared across his skin. And the cracks seemed to move in and out with each breath he took, causing his wet skin to shimmer with every movement.

The being stood before him for several long seconds before speaking. "How are you feeling, Ryder?"

"Fuck you." Anger rolled through him in waves. "And Darla, for betraying us!"

Instantly, his mind went to the young witch. Never in his life would he have expected her to open the door to their base and sneak in Caine's angels, or to kill their guards before she did it. How could he have been so wrong about her?

"I don't know anything about this Darla," the demon said. "But Caine has a way of getting to us all."

His thoughts skittered away from the young witch to the man before him. He couldn't do anything about Darla. He needed to focus on this man and why he was here.

"What did they give you to betray your own kind?" Ryder snarled.

The demon's golden eyes glowed softly. "They gave me the only thing that would make me join the side of evil... my freedom."

Ryder gripped the bars of the cage tighter and forced down his rage. *Get information. You don't know when you'll get a chance like this again.* "We're fighting for freedom. You could have joined us."

The demon sighed and then sat down on the ground, just far enough away that Ryder couldn't reach him. When he settled the lantern next to him, Ryder saw that his clothing was torn and filthy, and he didn't have any shoes. "I'm a poison demon whose touch is deadly even to my own kind. Believe me, I could endure the demon-realm. I could endure the loneliness and the darkness, but I could not endure Caine's prisons, nor his careful torture."

Poisonous even to his own kind? Is such a thing even possible?

Ryder would have felt sorry for him, if he hadn't been the reason they were all captured. "Demons are made to be beaten and harmed. We are strong beings capable of—"

"Beatings I can handle, my friend. But Caine is not so kind." His gaze held Ryder's for a painfully long time before he spoke again. "Caine brought his enemies before me... many innocent lives, and forced them upon me. My touch bringing them death." His voice grew quiet. "And not all of their deaths were fast. Instead, he would leave them in my prison cell as I watched the life leave their bodies."

"Why?" Ryder asked, unable to stop the question. "He kills whenever he wishes. Why kill them like that?"

His golden eyes met Ryder's. "Because there was a prophecy that I would help the victor win the war."

A shiver moved down his spine. "And I guess you did."

The poison demon grinned, his lips moving as if unaccustomed to forming a smile. "I will."

Looking around in the darkness as if afraid of the shadows, the demon slowly withdrew something from his pocket and laid it on the floor between them. The item was wrapped in a stained cloth.

Ryder frowned, opened his mouth to ask what it was, and stopped. The poison demon slowly opened it to reveal a key.

His heart raced. "What is that?"

"It's for your cage door."

Is he really freeing me? And can I trust him?

"Why are you doing this?" Ryder's hand twitched to reach forward and grab it, but something made him remain still.

"Because the Fate has said I will help the victor win the war... and Caine cannot be the victor. You see, it wasn't just freedom that made me agree to help our enemies. It was also a need for revenge. I helped Caine when I entered your headquarters and ended the battle with my poison, knocking you all unconscious, but I never intended to simply help him. It was my way of gaining Caine's trust."

Shit. This might actually be the thing that saves us from whatever hell Caine has planned!

And then something made him freeze. "Will this key open all the cages?"

The poison demon shook his head. "Just yours."

Damn it. His chest tightened. "And have you seen my brothers."

He shook his head again. "Sorry, it was actually harder than you can imagine to secure that key and get in here without being seen."

And he took a great risk to do this. To help someone he doesn't know. It doesn't matter if he had his own reasons for doing it, his actions might save us all.

"Well, thank you." Ryder reached for the key.

"Wait!" The poison demon cautiously picked up the cloth, then flipped the key out of the stained material and onto the ground. The sound it made seemed to echo through the darkness. "I was careful not to touch the actual key."

Ryder nodded and tore the bottom of his shirt, then reached forward and wrapped the key in the new fabric. Just to be safe.

The poison demon rose. "I don't know what you're going to do, but if everything goes according to my plans, I'll never see you again."

Ryder looked from the key to the demon. "I wish you the best." And then a thought occurred to him. "What's your name?"

"Golgoth," he whispered, his voice strangely soft and with a touch of vulnerability.

"Well, thank you, Golgoth."

The demon gave his strange smile again, opened the lantern and blew, swallowing the room in darkness once more. "One more thing. Whatever you do, do it soon. The Judge left all of you alive for one reason only, to use against *her*. If you don't act fast, she'll be caught in his trap."

Sharen. God damn it. I can't let that happen.

Ryder settled back in his cage, the key in hand. Things might seem simple now. He could escape, but if he couldn't break open the other cages of the others, he'd have to abandon them here.

Even the idea of it made his stomach turn. There had to be another way to warn Sharen and save their people. He just hadn't thought of it yet.

Minutes ticked by as he racked his brains, desperately trying to find a scenario that didn't involve leaving innocents in Caine's hands. But no matter what plan he came up with, everything led to them getting caught again.

I have to leave them behind. He felt sick, even while he knew it was the only way.

But sometimes there is no good choice, just the better of sucky ones. He began to unwrap the key, moving to the front of his cage.

And then, he heard another strange sound. Was someone else coming? Gathering up the key, he stuffed it into his shirt.

Fuck. Why do I think that isn't another unexpected person coming to help me?

6

SHAREN STOOD IN THE DOORWAY OF THEIR HEADQUARTERS, her heart aching. Blood was everywhere. On the floor. On the walls. Splattered on the supplies. And many of the lights had been shattered overhead, while others flickered as if afraid. The broken lights left much of the room in shadows, and the flickering gave it a spooky quality that made her clench her sword tighter.

Taking a step forward, she made the mistake of taking a deep breath. Bile rose in the back of her throat. The room was filled with the coppery scent of death... a heavy, revolting smell she never grew accustom to.

Note to self. Breathe through my mouth.

She continued inching forward, her pulse filling her ears. Her gaze clung to every shadow and corner. She felt sweat drip along her spine. The blood on the walls had dried nearly black, and the effect was like something out of a horror movie.

What could cause this kind of violence?

Whoever had attacked, they'd been powerful, and her people had fought hard.

In her heart, she felt that her demons were still alive, but she couldn't imagine what could have stopped a battle like this without someone taking their lives.

Goose bumps erupted on her arms. Moving slowly through the building, she searched for clues. The library nook, where all her precious books on magic, demons, and angels were kept, was a disaster. The shelf had been thrown. The books were scattered everywhere. And every drop of peacefulness had been stolen from the space.

She went on to the research area, where their computers had been tossed and broken. Scanning the debris, she searched for something, anything that seemed out of place.

Again, there was nothing.

She moved through the entire warehouse, her hope fading with each step. If they wanted her to find them, wouldn't they leave a clue that was a bit more obvious?

And what if they didn't want her to find anyone? What if they'd simply slaughtered them all and left her behind to suffer for her mistakes?

Fuck. Don't think like that.

Yet, she was beginning to panic. She felt it in the way her knees shook, and the way sweat gathered at her brow. She reminded herself that she'd been a fucking Hunter. That she'd been trained to withstand any emergency situation.

And yet, no amount of training could have prepared her for the possibility of losing her husbands.

She brushed at her stinging eyes, refusing to cry. Refusing to give up as she hurried to her office. That had to be the place! Of course! They must have left her a clue there.

Exploding into the room, she found it... perfectly organized.

She scanned her desk, pulled open the drawers, and

then just stood in the room, wondering what the hell to do next. Had no one actually been in her room?

And then she heard the slightest sound.

Pulling her blade from behind her back, she whirled to her small closet. What the hell was in there? Her mind raced to a thousand different things... none of them good.

Creeping forward, she took a deep breath, grabbed the handle, and yanked it back.

Her jaw dropped and her heart shattered into a million pieces. It was Darla, a bloody, broken mess of limbs. She lay unmoving on the bottom of the closet.

As she leaned down, she thought of the young witch with her beautiful strawberry blonde hair, her big eyes, and her eagerness to help The Rebellion. Why had they done this to her? And why, out of everyone, did they leave her body behind?

Then, she thought of the sound. Her heart raced as she leaned forward and touched the woman's throat. There was no pulse. Of course there wasn't.

And then, Darla's eyes opened.

A shriek exploded from Sharen's lips, and she leapt back. Darla's eyes were black swirling pools of magic.

Her voice came, jerking and emotionless from the mouth of the creature. So like Darla's, and yet, not at all.

"Beware. There is a betrayer among you who wears my face. A shapeshifter, Caine's own child. It is a creature of darkness and cruelty. It can take on any face and it has taken your people. It cares nothing for them, but only to capture you. Only the Immortal Ten can save them now, only a being more powerful than Caine." And then, the body slumped over.

She pressed her knuckles to her mouth and swallowed

back a sob. They'd killed Darla, but somehow, she'd left a message behind. *Which must have cost her so much to do.*

The young woman didn't deserve this. She didn't deserve to be a dead body with a message. She had so much life to live.

"God damn it. Damn it. Damn it!"

And there's a shapeshifter?

The thought held back her hysteria. She hadn't realized they were real. Of course, if vampires, werewolves, demons, and angels were real, it made sense shapeshifters were too. But how could she defeat an enemy when she wasn't even sure who it was?

And did the others think Darla was to blame for all of this chaos?

Just the thought made her teeth grind together. *Fucking bastards!*

She rose on legs shaking with rage. This trap they'd laid out for her? They might be surprised to find she wasn't such an easy target. Her demons were counting on her. Her people were counting on her. Darla and Marval deserved revenge.

Magic flared around her fist. Her eyes widened, and she stared at it. This had only happened in the human-realm once before. She squeezed her fist tighter. If this power stuck around, she might have an even better chance at destroying the enemy.

Looking at Darla's crumpled body, her magic faded away. Kneeling down, she whispered. "You've delivered your message. You can let go now." With a gentle touch, she closed the young woman's eyes.

Instantly, the body seemed to sink in, the magic used to animate the dead body gone.

Rest well, Darla. If you find yourself in the demon-realm, I'll come for you.

Rising, she started back through the warehouse, and then her brain turned to the Immortal Ten. She knew something of them, although the immortal beings sounded like more legend than reality. Could they actually exist?

Pulling out her phone, she dialed the number of the angel who secretly worked for The Rebellion.

Surcy's voice came, soft and filled with power. "Sharen?"

She took a deep breath. "I received a cryptic message about the Immortal Ten."

"We can't discuss this over the phone," Surcy rushed out. "But we're working on that as we speak."

"So they do exist? The Immortals who are prophesied to overthrow Caine?"

"I can't say more. Just that we're working on it. We'll stay away from headquarters. We can't afford to be caught right now when we're so close."

Sharen realized she was right. "Do you have any idea where Caine would take a bunch of prisoners in Shady Falls?"

Silence followed the question for so long Sharen worried she'd been disconnected. But then, the angel's voice came again. "The only place I can think of is a farm they own just outside of town."

Her pulse raced. "Can you text me the address?"

"Of course."

They said their goodbyes and she ended the call.

For the first time since her demon's disappearance, she felt like she knew what she was doing.

Which was exactly when the angels walked in.

7

RYDER HID THE KEY JUST IN TIME. DARLA WALKED STRAIGHT to his cage, surrounded by angels. Her cruel gaze swept over him.

"Time to come out, little demon."

"When I get my hands on you, bitch, you're going to wish—"

She laughed. "Save your anger, because I don't give a shit. I just wanted you to know that your girlfriend is walking right into our trap as we speak."

His stomach clenched. "You'll never get your hands on her."

Darla's face was twisted in a strange way that reminded him nothing of the sweet witch. "The Fate has decreed her death and soon it will come to pass."

"I thought your master wanted her alive?" he asked, trying to ply the traitor for answers.

"Oh, he doesn't plan to kill her quickly. First, he'll get what he wants from her." She smiled. "I just wondered if you could tell me which of you demons she loves the most."

Ryder spit at her in response.

She wiped the liquid from her cheek, not looking amused. "Well, then. I'll have to go with my own choice by personal observation."

Ryder tensed, prepared for what was to come.

"Men," she said, gesturing to the angels behind her. "Go get Alec. Lay him where we need him, and be ready to severe his head.

"No! Take me... I'm... I'm her favorite."

Darla smiled. "Sorry, but the choice was made long before I asked you."

"Then, why did you even ask? What the fuck game are you playing?"

Her brows rose. "I came because I get a little bored putting all my father's chess pieces into place, especially when it'd be so damn simple just to kill your human. *And,* because I have a message for you." Again, she waved to the angels.

Something wet and bloody dropped to the ground, partially wrapped in cloth, just outside his cage. It was a finger... one that could only belong to the poison demon.

He swallowed the bile that rose at the back of his throat.

"See, unlike your people, we're good at ferreting out traitors. Now, Ryder, will you give us the stolen key, or do we have to take it from you?"

For a minute he considered lying, but what was the point. "Come and get it. Unless you're scared?"

Darla smirked, pulled another key from her pocket, and unlocked the door.

Ryder leapt toward her, determined to tear out her throat for her treachery. But the angels were on him in an instant. He fought like a madman, but there were too many of them. They pulled him down, piled on top of him, a sea of punches and kicks that he registered somewhere in the back of his mind.

Damn it! I'm not going to win this! My only chance is to do something unexpected!

He gathered every drop of strength within him. Picturing his brothers. Picturing Sharen's sweet face.

With a roar, he stood, throwing the angels off of him. Barreling between the cages, he ran toward Darla, whose eyes were wide with fear.

But instead of pummeling her as he longed to do, he raced past.

When he exploded into the sunlight, he didn't give his eyes a chance to adjust to the light. He just kept running, no matter that his body screamed in pain. Within seconds, he realized that he was running through broken down farm equipment, and then he was in a field of dried corn.

He heard the angels shouting and knew soon they'd take to the air and easily reach him. He pumped his legs with all his might until he reached the woods, and then he kept going.

The trees were old, thick, and provided the perfect cover. The angels wouldn't be able to reach him by air. Their only chance was to follow him into the shadows of the forest.

And Ryder was a demon, accustomed to the shadows. Accustomed to hunting his prey in darkness.

The angels wouldn't stand a chance. And the second he finished with them, he'd find a way to get back to his people. He would rescue them and warn Sharen.

He just hoped that wherever his brothers were, they were safe.

And that I get to Sharen before she falls into their trap.

8

SHAREN STARED AT THE SIX MASSIVE ANGELS. THREE MEN AND three women, all had white wings. They stared at her with absolute hatred in their eyes.

"The Judge expected you back sooner than now. But maybe he overestimated your love for the demons?" The angel who spoke had long blonde hair and wore a red dress, as if she had just stepped from another world into theirs.

A strange sense came over Sharen as she stared at the angel with her unyielding face. There was something under the woman's skin. Something she hid deep inside. But what was it about her that made every instinct within Sharen scream to life?

Not all demons are good and not all angels are bad. Surcy is an example of that. Give her a chance. She stood straighter. *I can't defeat six angels... but maybe with an angel by my side we could defeat five of them.*

Sharen took a deep breath, deciding on a tactic none of them would ever have expected. "He didn't overestimate my love for them. No one could. I love them more than life."

She said the words confidently, but gently, as if speaking to someone other than her enemies.

The blonde angel's brows drew together. "Demons? How could you love such violent creatures?"

"Violent?" Sharen shook her head, forcing herself to remain calm and speak honestly. "Everyone is capable of violence, but the demons I've known have been kind... even gentle."

"That must be a lie." The angel said. "Caine told us—"

"Why are you talking to a demon-lover?" A male angel shouted behind her. "Caine forbids it."

The blonde whirled on him. "Information isn't dangerous unless we've been lied to."

The male angel punched her, sending her flying back against a box. The wood splintered beneath her, and she lay half inside the box, her limbs sprawled around her. When her eyes opened, shock and horror filled her gaze.

Sharen held the hilt of her sword more tightly and moved to stand in front of the injured angel. "I've never seen a demon hit a defenseless woman before."

The male angel smiled. "Perhaps your demons don't know how to demand respect. We take the respect we're due. Now, Sharen, it's time you come with us. If you don't, we'll kill your people, starting with your precious demons."

He had to be bluffing. If she went with him, they would all be doomed. The only other solution was to make sure these angels couldn't report back to Caine.

Clenching her fist, she thought of Marval's words. She must embrace hope. She must feel the support and love of her demons and her people. Even as she thought of all of them, she felt herself growing stronger and more powerful. She knew magic surrounded her fist before she saw it.

Without waiting, she punched her hand out, sending the

magic toward the collection of angels. To her shock, the magic struck them like a wave, lifting them into the air and cracking them down onto the ground.

Her legs shook as she stared, waiting for an attack. None of the angels moved. *It's like before, but this time I didn't hear the voices whispering to me. So was I able to do that because others made me stronger, or was that just me?*

"Shit," the female angel muttered, gingerly climbing out of the broken box. "You have magic?"

"I guess so."

There was an awkward moment of silence. "May I ask you something?"

Sharen nodded.

"Caine is The Judge. The most powerful person in all the realms. How do you intend to defeat him?"

"We have a plan." Sharen held her gaze. "There's a war coming, and you're on the wrong side. You had better start thinking about whether or not you want to keep blindly following Caine."

Turning, she headed for the door.

"I can't let you leave."

She looked back. The angel had her glowing soul-blade in hand.

Disappointment flared to life. "You know there's truth to what I'm saying. Caine is corrupt. He's putting innocents in the demon-realm and allowing thugs to become angels."

She looked uncertain, but her blade didn't waver. "I'm sorry, but this is the way it has to be."

Sharen held her sword out before her, ready to fight. She didn't have to wait long. The woman's sword struck her own, sending a vibration through her arm. The angel was powerful as she rained blow after blow. Sharen staggered beneath the attack, but met each strike without wavering.

When the angel rushed her, she moved with lightning reflexes, leaping from the ground and flipping over the other woman.

Whoa! How did I do that?

The angel was panting. "Can't you just fucking stay still? If I return without you, Caine will have my head!"

Am I getting stronger and faster? Or is this angel weaker than the other ones?

"Grow some fucking balls then! Stop working for an asshole!"

The blonde glared. "Haven't you ever seen those damned posters with the cat saying, *Hang in there?* that's my life right now, except I have a boss who likes to torture and kill people. So, excuse me if I'm not just willing to jump ship!"

"We all have problems, but sometimes we got to grow a pair." Sharen lifted her blade again, waiting.

The angel frowned. "Sorry, but I have to do this."

"You don't have to do anything but be a badass chick."

To her surprise, the blonde laughed, her blade lowering ever so slightly. "This is the most bizarre fight I've ever had in my life."

Sharen shrugged. "That's because you're fighting for someone you're afraid of, and I'm fighting for the people I love. But in another life, I think we would've been friends."

The angel's smile wavered. "I never did have a lot of friends."

"I just had a few, but they were everything to me."

Lowering her sword to the ground, the angel shook her head. "I think I must have eaten some crazy soup this morning. But here's what I'm going to do. I'm going to go lay in that pile of unconscious angels and pretend you got me too. But if we ever meet again, you're going to keep this to yourself, and understand that I'm not switching sides. I'll fight you to the death right then and there."

"Agreed."

Her sword vanished, and she went to the pile of angels, wrinkling her nose but finally lying down.

Sharen didn't put away her sword, but she inched around the bodies and headed for the exit.

The angel's voice made her pause. "But you know, if I thought you had a chance of succeeding, I would go with you. The problem is, your enemy is expecting you, and you have to go straight to them if you have any chance at saving the people you love. In other words, right now, they're holding all the cards, and you've got nothing."

She looked over her shoulder. "I don't have nothing. I have the knowledge that I'm fighting for the right side. I have people worth dying for, and I have hope. You might not believe it, but that's a hell of a lot more than your side has."

The angel said nothing more.

Sharen turned and raced for the car still parked somewhere outside. Today she'd gotten an angel to show her mercy. *Anything was possible.*

9

SHAREN SPED TOWARDS THE FARM IN THE SPORTSCAR, PUSHING it to its limit. Somewhere in the back of her mind, she sensed time ticking away. A strange sensation fluttered in her heart, one that made her think her demons were running out of time.

But her thoughts moved faster than the car. What the hell were the angels were doing? Why had they come to collect her, just to bring her here? Caine didn't plan to kill her, so what did he want?

It didn't make any sense. The shapeshifter. The Immortal Ten. Even the angel. None of it was adding up. And she had a feeling if she didn't get good at math really quickly, she'd get worse than a failing grade.

Turning off the main road, she moved down the bumpy dirt road but stopped long before she reached the farm. Even from this distance, she could see the specks in the sky. Angels circled the farm.

Hiding her car beneath a massive tree, she climbed out and raced through the woods toward her destination. The sun was starting to set, painting the sky in reds and oranges.

For some reason, it reminded her of all the blood in her life. Of all the death. Her parents. Too many friends to count. The wounds her foster family inflected. And little Brian and his family.

The truth was, she sensed secrets deep within her. What she was. And why The Department had spent so much money paying every person in her life. All of it was tied to what Caine wanted from her, but she couldn't understand what it could be. A being as powerful as him couldn't possibly care so greatly about her.

Unless you are his child, as the fae Hunter suggested.

Her stomach twisted. No, there had to be another answer.

The smell of pine invaded her senses as she ventured further and further into the woods. There were no sounds other than the pounding of boots against the earth and her own breathing filling her ears. The birds and creatures of the woods remained silent, as if afraid.

She stopped as she reached the edge of the treeline. There it was. The farm. Within that barn, her lovers and her people waited to be rescued.

A movement caught her eye on the hill just beside the barn. People were moving about. Something large was set on top of the flat, grassy hill.

She lifted her hand to cover her eyes from the glare of the setting sun. What was it?

A guillotine? She slid through the shadows, moving away from the barn and closer to the hill. Dread built within her. A body was hauled and tossed beside the deadly contraption. A big body.

She felt sick. It couldn't be. It just couldn't be.

Alec? Ryder? Kade? Don't worry, I'm coming!

Unsheathing her sword, she held herself still, counting

her enemies. There were only three of them: two who had carried the body and one who stood looking out over the sky.

A second later, a white winged angel flew to the hill. It took Sharen a second to recognize the blonde. *Fuck.* It was the angel who had let her leave. She had no doubt the woman was warning the people of her approach.

Why the hell did I trust an angel?

Her demons always said she trusted too easily, and yet again, they were right. She'd made a mistake. Now, she just needed to make sure no one but her paid for it.

A minute after the angel arrived, the people on the hill began to move frantically. Grabbing the body on the ground and putting it on the guillotine.

Sorry, assholes, but no matter how fast you move, it won't be fast enough.

Sharen clenched her sword more tightly and started up the hill with measured steps. She no longer had the benefit of surprise, but she couldn't wait and risk one of her demon's lives while coming up with a better plan.

For several long seconds, no one saw her. Eventually one pointed to her, and then the others turned to face her. No one made a move towards her. They didn't need to. She was coming straight at them.

A dark cloud moved above her, hovered above the hill, and then stretched out. The sky above the farm grew as dark as night, and a frigid wind blew. The air stunk of powerful magic.

She shivered and rounded her shoulders, trying not to let the wind cut beneath her jacket. But the wind was unlike anything she'd seen before. It plucked at her clothes and flesh, leaving her in pain. *What kind of magic is that? And why do I have a feeling I'm not going to like it?*

She continued until she was halfway up the hill and then she paused. Grey and black clouds spread out above the sky, and a tunnel of black rose up just above the hill like a slowly moving tornado. She spotted Darla standing next to the guillotine, or at least the shapeshifter who wore the young woman's face.

Her teeth clenched together. Unable to help herself, her gaze slid to the man whose neck rested in the guillotine. *Alec.*

Tears stung her eyes. With the smallest movement, they could take his life. They could easily send him back to the demon-realm, where it would be years before they had a chance to save him again. Perhaps longer without his brothers to help.

How could she stop his death?

And then, she knew.

Two big angels with cold eyes shifted to stand on either side of her Alec. One rested a hand on the handle of the guillotine.

She refused to look at the blonde angel, afraid to waste her energy on the spineless woman who had helped her only to ruin her anyway. Instead, she focused on the bastard pretending to be the witch.

"Sharen," the creature called, its voice eerily similar to the young woman.

"Shapeshifter."

Its eyes widened. "I—I'm not—"

"Let's not play this game. I know what you are, and I know Darla is dead."

The creature stared, then, at last, something came over its face. "Fine. No games then. Today this demon is going to die, and there's nothing you can do to stop it."She stared.

"You didn't lead me up here to kill him. You brought me here because Caine wants me."

His expression gave nothing away.

Her voice rose, taking on a slight desperation. "I'll give myself up willingly in exchange for his life and the lives of the others."

The shapeshifter smiled. "That would be so simple, wouldn't it?"

Her palms sweat as she held her sword. Why wasn't he agreeing to the trade? This is what they wanted, right?

"None of this makes sense if it wasn't to lure me here. Not taking my people or trying to capture me."

"That's because Caine is much smarter than you are."

She glared. "If he doesn't want me, what does he want?"

"He wants what's inside of you," the shapeshifter said, shouting over the wind.

"Inside of me?"

He nodded. "And do you know how he can get it?"

"I'm guessing if he's the psychopath we all know he is, he plans to cut it out of me," she said, striving to hide her fear behind bravo.

The shapeshifter tilted his head. "No, I'm afraid Caine has something worse for you planned."

Worse than cutting something out of me?

And then everything happened so fast. One second they were talking, and the next the angel had moved. The blade in the guillotine was a flash of silver, and then Alec's head was severed.

Her scream tore from her lips.

The female angel screamed.

Rage blinded her. Raising her sword above her head, she ran toward her enemies. A male angel grabbed the shapeshifter, and they all lifted into the air, just out of her reach.

"Get down here and fight me!" she screamed, her voice filled with tears.

"Afraid not," the shapeshifter said, and then, the male angels began to carry the treacherous creature away.

She collapsed onto her knees beside Alec's body. The female angel stared at her with terrified eyes.

"Fight me," Sharen said, but instead of it coming out a threat, it was a desperate plea.

The angel shook her head of blonde hair.

"Renata!" the shapeshifter shouted. "Come!"

"I'm so sorry," the angel whispered, and then she too flew away.

Sharen watched them leave. Her sword tumbled from her fingers and she turned to Alec. Tears streamed down her cheeks. Her breathing came in and out.

She climbed across the grassy hill top, her knees sinking into the bloody grass, and gathered his big body into her arms. Beneath her hand there was no heartbeat. *Nothing.* Just a stillness that seemed to echo through her own soul.

And the demon whose skin was always warm? It was cold.

"No! No!" she held him close, moving him, shifting him, as if it might somehow not be true, as if she could somehow turn back time.

Rubbing at her face, tearing at her hair, she couldn't seem to stay still. It was as if her body was no longer in her control. This was Alec. The man she loved. Her husband. A demon who changed her life forever.

And he was dead *because of her.*

He was dead because of her damn cause. Her selfishness. Her need to change the world.

He hadn't wanted any of this. He hadn't deserved any of this.

And he'd been killed. To get to her.

It didn't make sense. It couldn't be true.

And then, his body began to fade away, turning to ash within her grasp.

"No!" she tried to grab for it, to hold onto any part of him. But the ash slid between her fingertips, swirling around her as every last part of him changed.

At last, even the ash was gone.

She stared without seeing on the hilltop. The wind tearing around her. The dark cloud looming above her. There was no hope left. No goodness remaining in this world. Not with him gone from it.

Her sobbing grew hysterical, ripping from her belly as she collapsed onto her side. He was dead. Her Alec was dead. The man who made her laugh. Challenged her at every moment, and who made her feel like life was worth living was dead.

Dead.

It was impossible. Impossible that he died while she would continue living.

She sobbed harder. Her hope was gone. Her joy and love were gone. She was alone.

Who knew where Kade and Ryder were? Who knew if they had already been sent to the demon-realm?

I've lost them all.

Time slipped away from her. She didn't know how much when she realized that the wind had picked up speed. That it was swirling around her.

Suddenly, a man appeared before her. He had dark hair, cruel eyes, and an inhuman beauty that made her skin crawl. He stared down at her with a gaze as cruel as the wind. It seemed to slice into her flesh, with a possessiveness that made every hair on her body stand on end.

"Sharen," he whispered her name, but the sound seemed to come from all around her, repeating over and over again in the wind.

He moved toward her, and she watched him closely.

Her heart ached. Her emotions felt numb, and yet, she feared this man so instinctually that it shook her from her grief.

"He's dead, Sharen. And he will not return."

"He will," her voice shook.

"Only one person decides where a soul goes when it dies. And also which souls are too dangerous to return to any realm. Alec is simply too dangerous."

"No," her heart caught in her throat.

"Yes," he said, and the word seemed to seal her demon's fate.

Her grief suddenly had no end. No break. It swallowed her, never to free her again.

She blinked as more tears filled her vision. Alec would never return to her.

Someone tilted her chin up. It was the creature. Her skin crawled beneath his touch, and his eyes bore into hers. "There is no hope."

And she felt it. Something being pulled from her. Something shimmering and golden. It swirled in the wind. Releasing it didn't hurt, but it felt like the end of something. Something important.

The immortal being smiled. "That's it, Sharen."

Alec is dead. There is no hope.

"Sharen!" A voice tore through the darkness.

She jerked her head from the being. There, at the bottom of the hill, was Ryder.

He would know what to do! He would know how to save Alec!

She felt warmth fill her body.

"No!" The creature screamed.

He jerked her head up to him. His eyes had turned to red. "I will not lose your powers! Not when I'm this close!"

The gold left the wind, tangling back into her like a spool of golden thread.

Her hands clenched.

He yanked her toward him, and suddenly, she couldn't breathe.

She was dangling in his unyielding grasp. His fingers clenched around her throat.

Grasping her sword more tightly, she stabbed out, burying it in his chest.

The being dropped her with a tortured scream that filled the swirling magic.

And then, Ryder was standing above her, his soul-blade burning with orange flames. He struck out, burying his blade deep into its chest, before yanking it back out.

Sharen rose on trembling legs, and Ryder wrapped one arm around her shoulder, even while he held his sword out toward the creature.

The creature looked down at his body, where her blade still lay buried within him. But instead of blood seeping from his wounds, dark wisps like spiders crawled out. He looked from his wounds to them, his expression furious. Her sword exploded out of his chest and hit the ground.

"This isn't over."

Darkness like a cloak of shadows surrounded him, and then, he was gone. The winds and clouds slowly disappeared, and the day grew eerily calm.

It was... over.

Ryder's blade vanished, and he pulled her into his arms. Which was exactly when everything hit her at once.

"Alec is dead," she whispered into his shoulder with a sob.

"Dead?"

The words poured out of her. "They killed him. Severed his head with a guillotine on this hill. And I have no idea why. But they did."

Ryder pulled back from her. "What are you talking about?"

"They—"

"Alec isn't here. I overheard them talking. They have him in another location."

She stared. "I saw him..." She spun, pointing toward the guillotine. But there was nothing there. "I don't understand."

How was that creature able to make me see something that never happened? And why would he do it?

Ryder's voice came, harsh and cruel. "I think they wanted you to think Alec was dead."

Of course!

They had said they planned to do something to her that was worse than death. They wanted something inside of her, but didn't want to kill her. Somehow, making her believe Alec was dead was the only way to get her powers.

"Marval said my powers are tied to hope. Maybe the only way to take them from me is to make me feel hopeless."

Ryder placed his hand gently on her back. "I'm so sorry they did that to you. But Alec is still alive. And I think Kade is too. We just have to find them."

She hugged him tightly, her relief so overwhelming she couldn't speak.

They remained that way for a long time. Until, at last,

Ryder broke the silence. "Our enemies are still around us, and a lot of our people are being kept in cages in that barn over there."

She took a shaky breath, drawing on her last reserves of strength. "Then we better hurry and save them."

They walked down the hill together. She picked up her sword on the way, and he called his soul-blade back. Then, they linked hands, squeezing each other tightly. Taking that one moment to be grateful they were back together.

In her mind, she felt different. She might be facing another impossible fight ahead, but at least she wasn't doing it alone. At that exact moment,

Which was exactly the moment when the barn exploded into flames.

10

SHAREN AND RYDER RAN TOWARD THE FLAMES. SHE DIDN'T know what she could do to help, but she had to do something. She and Ryder froze as shapes appeared in the doorway.

Tensing, she clutched her blade in front of her, ready for the next battle.

Which was when the demons in The Rebellion came rushing out of the fires, carrying other members of their team.

She looked to Ryder.

He shook his head, his expression as confused as her own.

Henry led her team, holding her assistant Riverly in his arms. "Sharen," he greeted her.

She almost laughed. "You have no idea how glad I am to see you!"

He smiled back.

"Did everyone make it out okay?"

Her gaze ran over the others. Kade and Alec were not among them, but she didn't expect them to be, even though her heart ached with the realization. There were only a few missing faces among them.

Riverly spoke, her face pale, and her glasses missing. "Kim, Renolds, and Jake were killed in the battle. Everyone else—other than Kade and Alec—is here."

"Does anyone know where Kade and Alec are?"

Her question was met with silence. *Damn it.*

Sharen pushed back her sadness. "How did you get out?"

Riverly answered, her voice filled with amazement. "Henry came in. He'd stolen the keys and let us all out when no one was guarding us."

Finally, something went right! She looked to Henry. "We owe you, big time."

He nodded. "Don't even think about it."

Ryder squeezed her arm. "Our enemies are still around, and this fire will lead them straight to us. If it doesn't, my soul-blade will."

She nodded. "Put your blade away for now, and let's head for the woods." Turning to the waiting crowd, she raised her voice. "Are you all able to run?"

Their voice came together. "Yes!"

Her people looked beaten, bloody, and exhausted, but their strength against such impossible odds amazed her. She felt relief and gratitude fill her heart, and strength pushed away her exhaustion.

Turning, she led them back through the woods even though she knew not everyone could fit into her car, or that they could make it back to town on foot. But a quick call, when it was safer, could bring them the help they needed. And that was enough to keep her going.

She knew the only way she was keeping up with the demons was that her powers fueled her movements yet again. Even calling Lily and giving a quick explanation didn't slow her down. As they moved through the woods, she hoped like hell that their enemies wouldn't find them too soon.

But even though she kept looking to the sky, there wasn't a single angel to be found.

By the time they reached the road, the reds and oranges of the sunset had been entirely swallowed, and the moon rose slightly on the horizon. Lily was leaning against the side of a bus near her car, her stance that of a woman who did this every day.

"Mrs. Bran—"

"Sharen," she corrected her student for the millionth time, then threw her arms around her. "I'm glad I can always count on you."

The woman laughed. "Me too. And I'm glad you caught me before I starting boozing."

Sharen pulled back, laughed, and shook her head.

Her people gathered behind her, and she took a deep breath, turning toward them. "Lily will take you to the refuge. Stay there and try to stay alert. Our enemies likely know about the refuge."

Riverly spoke, her voice nervous. "Are you sure?"

"We suspected they planted an old man name David there a while ago, but no one has seen him since." *The shapeshifter! No wonder we couldn't find the old man, he must have shifted faces!* The realization hit her like a ton of bricks. "In fact, we might not be looking for the old man at all. One of our enemies is a shapeshifter, so be aware of any unusual behavior in any of our people."

A hundred questions rose at once.

She raised a hand, and slowly everyone descended into silence. "I know there's a shapeshifter. Darla never betrayed us. He killed her and made himself look like her. I... I found her body."

"I knew she wouldn't have betrayed us," Riverly whispered, and tears filled her eyes. "That bastard really killed her?"

Sharen nodded.

"Was her death at least quick?"

Sharen thought of the young woman's body and shuddered. No, it hadn't been.

"The bastard!" Riverly exclaimed, as if reading her mind. "Don't worry. We won't stop until we catch him!"

Sharen was amazed by how brave the quiet woman had become. "Yes, we will. We're a strong team, and now we know what to expect."

She answered a few more questions from the group before, at last, everyone seemed more tired than curious. It was time to go.

As the people began to load onto the bus, she caught Henry's sleeve. "Keep an eye out on them. Not everyone has the training that you do."

"Of course."

"No, 'commander?'"

He looked confused for a moment. "Sorry."

I don't need to hear it, but usually he ends every sentence with it. "It's okay. It's been a long day for all of us."

As Henry quickly climbed onto the bus, Ryder surprised her by hoisting her into his arms. A little cry escaped her lips, and then she wrapped her arms around his neck, grateful to hold him again.

"Ready?" He carried her to their car, just a short distance away, his expression far too satisfied.

His playfulness warmed her heart. God, had she missed

him! "So, you're going to carry me right over there? But not the whole trek through the woods?"

He laughed. "I'm a gentleman like that."

She reached up and touched his face. "I'm glad to have you back."

Leaning down, he pressed a soft kiss to her lips. "Me too."

If only we were all back together.

He heart gave a painful squeeze. "Now, to find Kade and Alec and kill the bastards who took them."

Ryder's brow rose. "Why does it turn me on when you go all badass Hunter?"

She shook her head. "Because you're a freak."

They both laughed, even while she could feel the tension singing between them. Yes, they were safely back together, but they could never be happy. Not when the other parts of them were still missing. Maybe even hurt. So they would need to keep going, keep searching for clues. They had no choice.

There's no rest for the Hunters.

11

THE SHAPESHIFTER STOOD ON THE OUTSKIRTS OF THE DEMON refuge. He kept his shape firmly in place as he called for an angel. Within moments, Renata teleported close to him. She was one of his father's favorites, a blonde angel with unexpected powers.

Renata looked at him, her expression guarded. "You called."

"Bring me to my father."

She nodded. When she took his hand, he felt a tremble run through her body. Interesting. As powerful as his father thought she was, she still feared him.

The world shimmered around him, and then he was standing in the hall just outside of his father's chambers. His brow rose at the closed doors.

"Why didn't you bring me inside?"

"He's meeting with someone," she said, her gaze avoiding his. "I must return to my post."

When she opened the massive doors, instead of allowing them to fully close, he slipped his booted foot between the doors, leaving a small space. Peering through them, he could barely make out his father's throne room.

A man knelt before the massive, curling black cloud of power that concealed his father from sight. There was something... wrong about the man. Something that bothered even him.

"I thought the angels could handle her without my Hunters. I'll do better next time," the human said, his voice shaking.

His father's anger seemed to swell the room. "Sorcerer, I gave you three days. Three days to walk the earth as an undead before your body falls to pieces. Just a short time to prove that you deserve to be given immortality among my angels. And yet, already, you fail me."

"I didn't expect her magic."

"You should expect that Sharen is capable of absolutely anything."

The man's voice shook. "I thought I was just to capture an ex-Hunter. I heard rumors she was your child... but I didn't know to expect abilities like that."

"Daughter?" His father repeated. "Interesting."

He tensed. *Sharen is my sister? Is such a thing really possible?*

And if he wants her powers, will he want mine too?

"Please, just give me another chance." The sorcerer whined, drawing him from his thoughts.

There was silence for too long. "I am not a man who gives chances, but since you are the only one with something to lose, I will let you live. But do not fail me again, sorcerer. My son will serve you her people on a silver platter. You and your Hunters need only to destroy them."

The man on the ground rose. "I won't disappoint you again."

"Good," his father's voice was filled with mockery. "Because if you do…"

His father pointed to the black awning pit in the back of the room. A shiver ran through his body as he stared at the place his father seldom used. If a soul was thrown into the pit, it could never be reborn again. It could never have any kind of afterlife.

The Soul Destroyer was made to be used against people too dangerous to even become demons. There was no worse fate.

"My son has already earned himself a place in the pit. Will you?" Caine whispered.

He stiffened. *My father intends to destroy my immortal soul?*

That's worse than I ever imagined.

Cautiously he allowed the door to close all the way. His father had a plan to finally take what he needed from Sharen. And once he did, he would be even more powerful than before.

And then, he won't need me anymore. Is that when he'll destroy my soul?

The plan his father had laid out was flawless, but without his shapeshifting abilities it would fall to pieces.

That's one way I can stop him from becoming more powerful.

And yet, if he failed his father, it would end in his death. *Either way he'll destroy me.* So what could he do?

He moved through the fortress, ignoring the angels he passed. The only way to ensure his survival was to destroy his father. But as far as he knew, such a thing was impossible.

Freezing, an answer hit him at once. *The Fate.*

He hurried through the fortress and down the many steps into the dungeons.

As he rounded a corner, he came to the guard. "Show me the Fate."

The angel raised a brow. "The Fate?"

He struck the woman, and she smacked back into the wall, sliding to the floor. Waiting with annoyance, he allowed her to climb unsteadily to her feet.

"Let me say that again, bring me to the Fate."

The angel hurried to obey, and he gritted his teeth. He was the son of Caine. He may have never visited the Fate before, but no one was to question his authority.

No one.

She led him past the demon's cell, and her keys jangled as she pulled them from off her belt. With annoyingly slow movements, she unlocked the door and pushed it open.

The shapeshifter grabbed a torch from off a wall and held it out before him as he moved into the stinking darkness of the Fate's cell. At first he didn't see her, then spotted the dirt-covered creature cowering from the flames, beside her blanket, which was equally dirty and spread over the ground.

He strode into the room and stared down at her, then glanced back at the guard. "Close the door. I'll rap when I'm done."

The angel looked concerned, but closed the door without complaint.

"I have a question for you, Fate."

The tiny woman raised her head from off her knees and peered at him with hostile green eyes. "Anything for the disgusting son of Caine."

He kicked her. Once. Twice. A third time, until she lay, little sounds of suffering coming from her like music to his ears.

"I have question for you, Fate," he repeated.

Her breathing came in pants. "Ask away."

"You told my father the answer that changed everything. That allowed him to finally get what he wants. Now, you'll answer the same sort of question for me." He took a deep breath, knowing that there would be no going back now. "How do I kill my father?"

Those eyes of her appeared again above her legs that she'd curled to shield herself from his blows. He saw pure hatred in her gaze, but knew she could do nothing. The Fate could not tell a lie.

"You cannot kill him."

His rage flared to life, and he drew back his booted foot.

"But Sharen can," she hurried out.

He froze, listening.

"At the battle, she can kill him. You need only to betray him to ensure his life is forfeit."

The shapeshifter stared. "It can't be so easy."

She smiled. "All it takes is one death. Just not the person you imagine."

He knelt down, clutching the torch more tightly. "Tell me everything."

12

ALEC'S EYES OPENED AS THE SOUND OF A TRAY CLATTERING jerked him from his restless sleep. His soul-blade lay on the ground, the orange flames lighting the cell.

Clenching his teeth, he rose and moved to the tray. The food was disgusting. Moldy bread, a bowl full of God only knew, and a cup of water. But he picked it up and sat down, with his back against the wall and ate every last bite, and drank the disgusting stale water, because he had to. If he didn't eat, he'd grow weak. And he refused to. Sharen and his brothers were out there somewhere. It didn't matter that he couldn't see a way out of his situation, he'd figure one out, and he'd save them all.

Tossing his tray to the door, he felt only a little satisfied at the loud clatter. He wanted to break something. To destroy something. Especially the fucking shapeshifter and its master.

A strange sound came, like scratching. He tensed and looked around. He could see nothing to explain the sound. *Where had it come from?*

The scratching came again, this time louder and longer.

He stood and moved around the cell, trying to find the source. At last, he knelt and stared at a spot on the dirt floor. Was it coming from underground?

Hurrying across his room, he grabbed his metal cup and returned to the spot. Using the tool, he started to dig. Minutes ticked by. The scratching continued, and so he didn't slow.

At last, the earth caved in.

He heard coughing. Acting on instinct, he reached into the small hole, and grabbed whatever was inside, then hauled it out.

A tiny woman, entirely covered in dirt, coughed and coughed as he set her on the ground next to the hole. He stared in shock, not sure exactly what he was looking at. And not sure at all how she'd come to be beneath the ground.

Reaching for her, he began to dust the dirt from her face, scooping it out of her closed eyes, and brushing it from her hair. At last, as the cloud around her began to calm, her eyes opened. Two bright pools of green stared at him from a face thin, to the point of starvation.

"Alec?" she whispered, and her voice cracked.

He frowned. "How do you know who I am?"

She held out one small hand, and he reached out and shook it without thinking. "I know a lot of things. Too many things."

"You sound like a damned witch, with that kind of meaningless babble."

A small laugh escaped her lips. Her big eyes widened. "Did I just laugh?"

He nodded, his frown deepening.

She touched her mouth as if in awe. "I can't remember the last time I laughed. I forgot what it sounded like. What it felt like." She closed her eyes, and her mouth twisted into a smile.

Fuck. His demon-heart was made of God damn steel, but he felt an immediate protectiveness flair to life. Someone had hurt this child-like woman. *Caine.* It just gave him another reason to tear the bastard limb from limb.

"Are you alright?" He was surprised by the gentleness in his voice.

"Yes. I've just been his prisoner for so long.... and there's no joy in this place. No light. No happiness." She looked to his sword. "I'd give anything just for that. A light in the darkness."

Damn it. "Well, as long as I'm here, you have it."

Her big eyes focused on him again. "I've seen you so many times. I know what you will do and how you will do it, and yet, it's different to actually meet you. You're kind. And handsome. And—"

"Married." He held up his hand, moving the finger with his wedding band, and feeling remarkably uncomfortable with where the conversation was going.

The woman laughed, touching her lips again. "Don't worry, Alec. I know about Sharen, and I know she holds your heart. I'm meant to be something else to you. A figure representing innocence, and the cruelty of Caine. A shadow that will haunt your thoughts in a way that turns your stomach."

What the fuck? "I don't understand."

"I'm Lachesis, but everyone calls me Lachy."

He stiffened. "Uh, Lachesis like the Fate who knows the future?"

She nodded. "I've been Caine's prisoner for longer than you can imagine."

His stomach turned. "Is that how he always seems to be one step ahead of us?"

"A little," she hung her head, her voice growing soft. "I try to fight him. I throw him off every time I can. But being a Fate, I can't lie."

Alec felt a sting of regret for making her feel bad. Reaching forward, he gave her shoulder an awkward pat. "I'm a demon and the bastard got me, so no need to feel bad."

She looked back up at him again and smiled. "Sharen really is lucky to have you."

He winced and dropped his hand. Sharen. Where was she? And was she okay?

Then, an idea hit him. "You're a Fate. Can you tell me about Sharen? Is she safe?"

The Fate, Lachy, shrugged. "I'm not the Fate of the present, so I can't say. But I can see her future."

"And..."

"I can't tell you."

His brows rose. "Why?"

"Because it would change the course of fate."

He sighed and leaned back against the wall of his cell. "Of course."

"But there are things I can do."

His eyes snapped open. "Like what?"

"Like help you to escape."

"Shouldn't you be trying to help yourself escape?"

The look of pure sadness that struck her face made him regret his words. Fuck, it made him feel like a complete asshole.

"Sorry."

"No," she said. "It's okay. The problem with knowing the future is that I can't quite see my own, but through the future of others, I know I won't be escaping any time soon. Maybe never." A tear leaked from her eye, leaving a trail in her dirt covered cheek.

"I can't imagine much worse than knowing you have a crappy future."

She gave him a wavering smile. "I don't think there is much worse."

A thought occurred to him. "And we can't change your future?"

"The future can always be changed."

"And would I ruin the future if I saved you?"

Her brows rose. "I don't think so... but I also don't think it'll happen."

He smiled. "Well, that might be because you don't know me too well. In this escape plan of yours, let's adjust it so we both make it out?"

There was something in her eyes that he couldn't quite read. "Okay."

"So how will this happen?"

Instead of answering him, she crawled over to his sword and stared into the flames. "I miss light. I miss warmth." Raising her hands over the flames, she made a soft sound of contentment and closed her eyes.

Even though he was desperate to return to Sharen and his brothers, he clenched his teeth and remained silent. This poor woman deserved so much. The least he could give her was a moment to feel warm.

"I remember the time before Caine was in power."

He stared intrigued. "What was it like?"

"It was... wonderful. No one can see it, but there are ten thrones in the throne room. That was where the Immortal Ten sat. They worked together to send the souls to the right places. The good people went to the angel realm. The people who made bad choices, but had good souls, went to the demon realm. There, they were given a chance to move up. During their journey, if they learned enough to do better, when they reached the human realm, they were given another chance at life. A chance to be reborn and try again. And the truly evil... they were locked in the darkest pits of the demon realms, never to return." She sighed. "This place wasn't a fortress. It was a palace. The Immortal Ten weren't chained to their thrones. They lived lives. Had relationships and children. And... things were fair. Death wasn't a bad thing, just the next phase of life."

"So how did Caine become so powerful?"

Her eyes opened. "He is an immortal being with one horrible power. He can influence people's minds. He erased their memories... the world's memories too. And he took over."

"Fuck."

She nodded. "Yeah, fuck."

He rubbed at his face. "But how do we take down someone like that?"

"We all have our roles."

He sighed. "If I can get out of here."

She crawled toward him, and he watched her wearily. "Thank you, Alec."

"For what?"

"For talking to me. For reminding me of the goodness. And for letting me share your light and your warmth."

He felt uncomfortable. "You're welcome to use my sword as long as you wish."

"I wasn't talking about your sword."

"Uh, okay." He felt so sorry for her. She must really miss company if she thought he was something special.

"Are my brothers safe?"

She continued to stare at him. "None of us are safe."

Shifting back from him, she stood on legs that seemed to tremble. Then, after a moment she went and picked up his sword. She swung it around, her gaze glued to the flames as she smiled. Then, she handed it to him.

He took it, watching her with pity.

"Are you fast, Alec?"

"Fast?"

"Can you outrun the angels? Can you outrun the burn of metal? The kiss of arrows? The shadow of death? Can you run through stone and dirt? Can you cross the border between worlds?"

He stared at her.

"For Sharen?"

"For Sharen I would do anything."

She smiled. "Then, Alec...," her voice lowered. "Run, and don't look back."

"What—?"

Suddenly, he heard the scrapping of a key in the door. Spinning to his feet, he tensed. The door swung open, and he knocked down the surprised guard. Two other angels waited behind the first. Without thought, he sliced their heads off, then started up the stairs, shouting, "come on!"

He heard the feet of the Fate behind her, but he followed her advice and didn't look back.

Every angel that crossed his path met the sharp end of his sword. He didn't know quite where he was going, but saw the light of a window staring out at clouds. Grabbing an angel by the throat, he dragged him to the window. Then, moving behind him, he shifted so his arm was against the angel's throat.

"This is our exit," he turned to the Fate.

She looked uncertain.

Sending his sword away, he grabbed her around the waist, then pushed them all out the window. The ground was far below, as he expected. The Fate shrieked, and the angel struggled as the ground grew closer and closer.

Come on, bastard, before we all die!

Suddenly, the white wings of the angel began to flap. They slowed but continued downward. When they were feet from crashing into the ground, Alec released the angel and braced himself for impact.

His feet hit hard, sending a vibration through his legs. But because the angel had slowed their descent, his bones stayed intact. Not releasing the Fate, he started to run for the border, calling his soul-blade back.

Overhead, he sensed the flurry of angels, even in the early morning light. Running as fast as his feet could take him, he had to skid to a halt in the desert sands. Six angels had landed in front of him.

Backing up, more angels appeared behind him.

"Let me go," the Fate whispered.

His instincts screamed not to, but he obeyed. She did know the future, after all.

He expected many things, but not for her to start running between the angels.

His enemies looked confused, most started after the woman. A few remained.

"Luchy!" he shouted after her. *What the hell was she doing?*

"Go!" she shouted back. "For Sharen!"

His heart twisted, his protective instinct burning, but he did as she commanded. He ran toward the angels, barreling into them before they had a chance to attack. He continued on, his legs pumping.

Arrows hit the ground around him, but none struck

their target. Angels tried to pluck him from the ground, but he swung his sword into the air, keeping them at bay. Ahead, he saw the shimmering of the border that kept Caine's lair from the rest of the world. Putting his last ounce of strength into his legs, he did what he promised he wouldn't.

He looked back.

The Fate was surrounded by angels. Her expression that of absolute sorrow. He wanted to save her, to go back for her. But there was no chance that he'd be able to take on that many angels.

He hit the magical border, her face, streaked with tears, the last thing he saw.

No matter what happened for the remainder of his life, he would not forget the woman who sacrificed herself for him.

Her words came back to him, like a whisper of wind, as magic tore around him. *"I'm meant to be something else to you. A figure representing innocence, and the cruelty of Caine. A shadow that will haunt your thoughts in a way that turns your stomach."*

Sure enough, the Fate was right.

She would haunt him. But he'd try to push her to the back of his thoughts. Sharen and his brothers needed him, and he had no idea how to reach them.

13

SHAREN FOLLOWED RYDER, BARELY NOTICING AS HE STOLE A truck from the farm and drove them across town. It wasn't until they came to an unfamiliar building that the full impact of their situation hit her. They couldn't go to head-quarters or to their home. So where were they going?

"Some place safe," is all he said, a response that would have irritated her if she wasn't so exhausted.

Right now I'd sleep in a trash can, if it meant I could recharge just a little.

He led her inside and down the stairs to a basement apartment. His every movement screaming of a soldier on the alert. She walked behind him, muscles tense, ready for any danger that might come their way. Ryder might radiate the strength of a demon, but he was battered and bruised. And even though he tried to hide it, she could sense his exhaustion growing with every step.

If something attacked them now, they'd be in a lot of trouble.

But to her relief, the hallway was silent. Nothing more than a stretch of blank walls illuminated by dim bulbs.

When he typed in the code on the keypad by a door, she half expected to find a roach-infested, hole-in-the-ground. But when he opened the door and turned on the light, she was surprised to see a more basic version of their home. It was sparsely decorated, but had a relaxed feel that spoke of her demons' touch.

"Nice—what is this place?"

He grinned. "A demon has to keep some secrets... This place has everything we need for a few days, and even better, *a lot* of weapons."

She felt her tense nerves relax ever-so-slightly. "Sometimes I'm thankful you three are so damn paranoid."

Walking in slowly, she gazed around in gratitude. The one bedroom apartment was set up efficiency style, with a small bedroom to one side, and a main room containing a tiny living room, dining room, and kitchen.

Basically... a slice of paradise after all they'd been through.

Without another word, he ushered her into the bedroom and led her straight to the bathroom. She felt like she should probably protest... but for the life of her, she couldn't think of anything better than getting clean and crawling into bed.

He turned on the shower and undressed them both. When he moved her beneath the warm spray of water, he touched her bandaged arm. Pulling back the wrap slowly, they both stared at her perfectly healed, smooth skin.

She ran her hands along his body. The fight at their headquarters had been as brutal as she imagined if he still carried the evidence. The dark bruises decorating his skin looked painful, and the slashes from the angels' blade had left raised scars over most of his body.

Kissing each wound, she touched him, worshipping him

with her lips. She kissed him for every ounce of pain he'd gone through, and because she'd thought never to hold him again.

They cleaned each other with gentle touches, rubbing shampoo in each other's hair and soap over their bodies. They remained in the water as long as they could, letting it work their aching muscles. When it grew cold, Ryder switched it off, and they dried each other.

Then, she stretched out beside him on the unfamiliar bed, her head on his chest and their hands locked. "I missed you so much."

He kissed the top of her head. "I missed you too."

Her heart squeezed. "What are we going to do? They have Alec and Kade. We have to save them. How can we ever be safe with Caine's angels constantly surrounding us?"

Silence stretched between them for far too long. He finally answered. "How about we kill all of them?"

"Alright, let's go with your plan," she agreed.

He laughed, a soft sound. "Now that we have that figured out, I'm going to make love to you."

Lifting her head, she stared at him.

"Sharen, I need to. I need to be inside of you. I thought —I thought I might never see you again."

Something within her stirred, a longing to take away the loneliness and fear she'd felt since first seeing the headquarters covered in blood.

Leaning up, their lips met. At first the kiss was soft, tentative, as if exploring each other. And then, it grew harder, deeper. Her lips parted, and his warm tongue swept into her mouth.

She felt her body come to life. It sung beneath his touch. And when his hands moved up to cup her naked breasts, her skin tingled and her nipples hardened. His hands brushed her breasts, lifting her mounds as if to feel the weight. When he moved to her nipples, she gasped as his fingers pinched the peaks, sending heat shooting straight to her core.

He moved so that he was on top. Then, he broke their kiss, moving down her neck.

He sucked a path down her body, making the hairs on her body stand on end. When he came to her breasts, he took her nipples into his mouth and worshipped them with his lips.

She dug her hands into his hair, and leaned her head back, enjoying ever flick of his tongue, every spark of pleasure his touch brought.

When he started to kiss her belly, her body tensed, knowing what was to come. Her legs spread, and he shifted beneath her thighs. First his fingers teased her, stroking her bare mound. Then, he parted her folds and his fingertips slid along her folds, making her inner-muscles tighten in anticipation.

One finger buried inside of her, drawing a gasp of surprise from her lips. And then, when a second finger joined the first, his mouth lowered to suck her clit.

She never grew tired of this. This feeling that made her remember that she was alive. That made her feel as her demons wasn't just a part of her heart, but part of her body too.

She pushed against him, rotating her hips to take him deeper. She moved against his mouth in a rhythm, her thoughts scattering with each incredible touch. When he sucked her clit deep into his mouth, she cried out.

This was what she wanted. This was what she needed.

Her orgasm came like an explosion, rocking through her

body. Her hands suddenly dug into his hair, and she rode his face and fingers as if her life depended upon it.

When at last her orgasm calmed, he withdrew his fingers and mouth. Moving to lay on top of him, she wrapped her arms around his back, needing his closeness.

His big cock sunk deep into her ready channel, and the feeling, after her orgasm, was both pleasure and pain. But she knew. Knew this man could bring her to the edge again. And she was ready for it.

Her legs wrapped around his back, and his panting filled her ears. His big cock filled her so fully that her tight body seemed to shudder around him each time he pulled out and then slammed back in.

His movements grew more frantic. Her nails dug into his back, and then they were both coming. His hot seed spilled into her body as he roared his release.

She cried his name, over and over again, as her inner muscles squeezed him tightly. Her thoughts spun away, and her toes curled. For too long it felt as if the explosions of pleasure would rip her apart, but then, at last, her muscles relaxed, and the world came into focus.

Holding him closer, she buried her face into his shoulder, breathing in his spicy scent. This man was a part of her. She had missed him as desperately as air.

And then, she started to cry.

She felt silly, but Ryder only stoked her hair.

"I miss them too," he whispered. "But we'll get them back."

She cried harder, everything hitting her at once. She might have Ryder back, but she'd never feel complete until they saved Kade and Alec.

Who would argue with her if Alec weren't around? Who

would sulk about everything but secretly enjoy it if not for Kade?

They were... hers. Hers to love and laugh with. Hers to touch and kiss. Hers forever.

And she didn't know where they were, if they were hurt, or worse, if they were dead.

We need to find them. No matter what it takes.

When her sobs slowed and finally died away, she felt a little better. "Thanks."

"Any time."

He pulled off of her, and tucked her under his arm, wrapping the blanket around them.

"So," she began, her eyes already closing. "What do we do next?"

Maybe he answered. Maybe he didn't. She wasn't sure, because sleep tugged her under.

14

SHAREN SHOT AWAKE, SWEAT DRIPPING DOWN HER FOREHEAD.

"It's just a nightmare," Ryder whispered sleepily, rubbing her back in the darkness.

"No, it wasn't." She struggled to form the words around the tears that choked her throat. "It was a memory."

He sat up, instantly the grogginess fading from his voice. "Of what?"

She closed her eyes. He doesn't know, but he deserves to. And yet, it was hard for her to speak. The nightmare brought everything back to her in a rush of fear and pain. "When I was in the portal, we were attacked by Hunters. They killed most of the demons... women, children, they didn't care. They slaughtered them."

Ryder's touch stilled on her back. "You did your best."

"We were losing. So I did the only thing I could do..." she pressed her face in her hands and a sob exploded from her lips. "I used a spell to slow the Hunters. Those young people who didn't have a choice, my ex-students, many of them were torn apart by demons. I killed others. Even Rorde. It was—"

"War."

She nodded, her face still in her hands. How had she not understood this before? The Rebellion she cherished so fully wasn't just going to be her saving innocent lives. Sometimes she would have to kill to. And after being a Hunter, she had to accept that the lines between good and evil were blurred. Some deaths would not be so simple.

"The first time I saw death was when we killed the men who raped my sister." Ryder's voice came soft and vulnerable. "I would have never thought I was capable of something like that. I respected life so much. When you spend as much time in the ocean and with nature as I did, you start to see the world in a different way. And it's value changes. So to take a human life? I never would have imagined it."

He began to rub her back again. "You'd think killing would get easier after that. But even as a demon, I didn't like it. Even when I felt myself changing... losing the human parts of myself, I wasn't like my brothers."

She lifted her head and looked at Ryder in the darkness. Even in the shadows, she could see him. His expression was open. He held back nothing in that moment, not even hiding behind his usual smile or jokes.

"When the attack came in the warehouse, I fought, Sharen. I fought like hell. I killed angels like I was slaughtering sheep, but it wasn't enough. Seeing everyone surrounded, I'd realized that we were all going to die. And everything went red. All I wanted was to kill as many of them as I could before I died."

"So what happened?" She whispered the one question that had been plaguing her since they disappeared.

"They brought a demon in... a poison demon. A black cloud covered us, and then... everything faded away. We were knocked out." He shook his head. "I woke up in a cage and my brothers were gone."

She crawled into his lap and wrapped her arms around his neck. "It's okay."

He buried his face against her throat. "It's not. But it will be. I swear to you, Sharen, one day I'm going to take you surfing. I'm going to take you scuba diving and show you the world underwater. We're going to live normal, happy lives."

She brushed his hair back from his face. "Is that all you want?"

"More than anything."

"Then, I promise you'll have it."

He laughed. "After all the demons are saved, of course."

She shook her head, frowning. "We'll figure something out. Something that gives you guys the lives you deserve. Because I've been a complete idiot."

"Sharen—"

A chill ran down her spine, and every hair on her body stood on end.

"You felt it too?" Ryder whispered.

She nodded. The mood in the room had instantly shifted, and every instinct screamed within her that something was wrong.

They dressed in silence and equipped themselves with weapons. Shoving her phone into her pocket, they stepped out of the bedroom and cautiously headed for the front door.

A second later, it exploded inward as Hunters raced into the room.

Spells came hurling toward them. Sharen muttered something on instinct, and a red shield leapt into place around her and Ryder. A spell that she'd only ever welded in the demon realm. Yet, there it was. Magic that she shouldn't have been capable of in this world. Magic that she'd never had in the human realm. Hers to command.

Thank God for these strange powers, she thought staring through the chaos of the exploding spells that couldn't reach them.

She and Ryder both pulled their swords free as spells continued to hurl towards them. Hunters encircled them, but to Sharen's surprise, the shield held, and she didn't feel her energy wavering. Within her, the knowledge hit yet again that her powers were growing.

After several long seconds, the magic attack stopped. The Hunters still pointed their splicers at them, but their expressions were uncertain. Their circular blades glowed with the magic that only the most powerful Hunters could wield in the human-realm, but Sharen had stood strong.

A shadow suddenly moved to block the door.

"Mrs. Bran," he greeted.

She stared in shock, blinked, and looked again. Sure enough, it was her ex-student, Rorde. *How the hell is this possible? He's back from the dead already?* And yet, he didn't have angel wings.

And... he looked wrong. His skin had a strange green tint to it, and he was thinner, almost weak looking. Black, sunken circles under his eyes made him resemble a corpse more than an angel or a human.

"I killed you," she whispered, her sense of unease growing.

His eyes grew hard. "Yes, you did."

"But it doesn't appear you were given wings."

Rage came from him in waves. "No, I was not."

This doesn't make sense. "So what did the great Caine do for his good, little soldier?"

"That's none of your concern."

That doesn't sound good. And yet, she couldn't think of an explanation for how he'd returned without becoming a demon or an angel. It was... impossible.

Her gaze moved to the other soldiers. Guilt made her heart ache. None of the faces were familiar. Hopefully the few of her students who hadn't been killed were safe somewhere.

Because this animal is capable of anything. Like what happened to Alderon...

She leveled her gaze on the sorcerer. "Were you the one who left a message at my door?"

It took him a second before realization dawned on his face. "Ah, yes, the fae Hunter. The traitor. I'm glad you found him."

In that moment, she realized what she could do for the fae man who had helped her. She could make sure The Department could never hurt him again.

"Next time you need to send a message, how about using something better than a dead body?"

He laughed. "Well, he wasn't dead when I left him there."

Ryder sent her a confused look, but she ignored him. She'd explain about the Hunter and the message later.

"So, what can I do for you?"

Rorde raised a brow. "You know what I'm here for, so let's stop fucking around. How about you and that demon turn yourselves in? Look around you, you're out numbered. You have no shot at defeating us."

She laughed. "If you haven't noticed, I'm not the same Hunter you knew."

He glanced at her shield. "I've never heard of a Hunter learning to harness magic in the human realm later on in life."

Now is the time. A chill ran over her flesh. *Use your powers to convince them. To get them to see the truth. There doesn't need to be another bloody battle. Perhaps I can even save some of these young people's lives.*

She held Rorde's gaze. "That's because I'm not a normal Hunter."

"No?"

"I don't know what I am, but I'm sure The Department does. Based on what they told me and the paperwork I've found, they've been controlling every aspect of my life from the time my parents were killed."

Some of the Hunters shifted in their stance. She caught their concerned expressions, but tried to stay focused on their Leader.

"They've also paid almost everyone I've interacted with. My abusive foster parents. The man who raped me. Everyone. So, excuse me if I've lost faith in The Department and their cause."

"Why would they pay those people?" A young woman asked, her bright blue eyes filled with concern.

"According to The Department, they wanted me to join their cause. They orchestrated most of it to turn me into a victim, to make me feel like I could do something about my world."

The young woman lowered the splicer in her hand. "I joined after I was jumped by a gang and beaten."

A man next to her, with shaggy hair and the build of a linebacker, lowered his splicer too. "I joined after my parents were killed by a drunk driver."

A murmur rose up among the people who surrounded her.

"Shut up!" Rorde shouted, and they all grew silent.

A sense of déjà vu came over her. Just a short time ago

she was surrounded by Rorde and his team. She'd managed to convince some of them to believe her, but the results had been deadly for one of her students.

Her chest tightened as she remembered the young woman's face.

"Oh yes, they haven't forgotten. Anyone who disagrees with you dies, right Rorde?"

His gaze grew angry. "Samantha brought it on herself. Traitors deserve nothing but death."

"Being a traitor and questioning what you've been told are two different things. My people can question me all they want. They can leave my cause any time they want. Can yours?" A shiver traveled down her spine. "I was a Hunter. A Leader. And I believed in this cause more than I believed in anything. And then I realized it was all a lie. Demons are not all bad. Angels are not all good. But more than that, I learned that The Department is corrupt."

"She's trying to manipulate you!" Rorde shouted. "She knows she's outnumbered. This is her only chance at getting away. Turning us against each other!"

Sharen lowered her weapon. "I don't think you understand. My powers... they're unlike anything you've seen before... well, perhaps you've had a taste of them. But I don't need to convince your team to believe me in order to escape. I just *want* them to know the truth."

"Oh yeah, do you plan to freeze us and unleash your demons on us again?"

The energy in the room shifted. She was losing their faith. And she needed to fix things. Quickly.

"The king of the demons allowed me to take all the innocents from his realm and return them to earth. Your people came... they attacked. Women, children, the elderly. They attacked them all!" She whirled onto the Hunters. "Ask yourself, really ask yourself, what do children do to deserve the demon-realm? Huh? Can you think of an answer? What about babies? What did they do?"

"What are you saying?" the young woman asked.

"The system is corrupt. Caine, the immortal being who decides who lives and dies, is wrong."

And she saw it. In their faces. Some of them believed her.

She felt it. Energy flowed from them to her and from her to them. The air felt charged, just as if lightning was about to strike, and the air seemed to crackle.

Her head spun. Whoa! This magic... it was what was trying to escape from her all along. Marval was right. Her ability to convince others was a power. It was a skill.

And it could change everything.

"Look into your hearts. See the truth. And take action." Her powers vibrated in the air, and she saw a glow surround the Hunters.

All but two of them believed her. And they would no longer walk this path.

"I'm done." The young woman said, throwing her splicer to the ground.

She knew what Rorde would do before he did it.

A whirling black magic leapt from his hand toward the woman.

Sharen sent her magic out. It hit the black spell and shattered it, sending the dark pieces falling like glass to the wood floor. The sound echoed through the room.

The Hunters looked at floor, then back at their Leader.

"You were going to kill her?" the man beside the young woman said. His jaw tightened, and he threw his splicer. "I'm done too. And if you try use a spell against me, you'll wish for death."

To her surprise, she felt a more powerful spell building within Rorde. He lifted his hand, and she sent her magic out. It hit him, knocking him to the ground. His gaze moved, but he lay, no longer in control of his body.

"You don't need to fear him," she told the Hunters. "Do what you feel is right."

They began to file out. The two Hunters who seemed to glow with a red light, looked at her. "We don't believe you. But we're not working for someone who would kill us without thought."

They left the room. After a moment, she dropped her shield and walked toward Rorde, kneeling down next to him. "Tell me, what made you decide to become a Hunter?"

His expression changed.

"I know you had a rough past. I know you did some awful things. But I wonder what it was that triggered those choices. I can't change your mind, but if I were you, I'd do some digging. I wonder if you also have a folder of people in your life who were paid."

In an instant she saw a flash of far too many emotions all at once. Fear. Regret. Guilt. And hopeless. Then, his emotions faded, and his expression became guarded once more.

"I know your secret," he murmured, his lips barely moving.

She stared. *Secret?*

"Your Caine's daughter."

Ryder inhaled behind her. "Lying bastard!"

She caught Ryder's fist before he could use it, her heart racing. Then, she turned to the sorcerer. "What makes you say that?"

"Your powers. They aren't normal."

"That doesn't mean I'm his daughter."

Rorde's cruel eyes focused on her. "Do you want to know why Caine brought me back? He's given me a time limit. My job is to make you remember who and what you are."

She felt cold. "I know who I am."

"When your memories come back, you'll abandon your demons and your precious cause, and you'll take your rightful place at Caine's side."

Bile rose in her throat. "No. He tried to take something from me already. My powers. My memoires. I don't know what, but he tried. He isn't trying to remind me of something. That I'm sure of."

He stared at her. "If I can't do my job before my time is up, he'll destroy my soul for eternity. So, I don't care what you say. I'm going to do what I've been asked to do."

She rose, staring down at him with pity. "Yet another person in charge who has to rule with fear, huh? I guess you don't have a choice then... other than to do one good act before your death."

"Sorry, but I prefer eternal life."

"Then, until we meet again."

"Just kill him!" Ryder exclaimed.

"Caine will just bring him back." She looked away from the young man, pity growing in her heart.

Rorde shouted after them as they made their way down the hall, but it wasn't until they started up the stairs that Ryder spoke.

"Are you really Caine's daughter?"

Her muscles tensed. "I don't know."

15

ALEC FOUND HIMSELF OUTSIDE A TINY TOWN IN THE MIDDLE OF nowhere. After asking a local, he determined that the part of the border he'd exited out of had brought him to somewhere halfway around the world from where he needed to be.

Of course!

Not only did he have no money or identification for a flight back to their city, the angels would be on his tail soon enough. He couldn't afford to sit around trying to figure out a way to get home on his own.

Which left him with only one choice. One he detested.

He borrowed a phone and called the angel named Surcy, even though it bothered him to do so. Although she had helped Sharen and was now working for The Rebellion, it went against every instinct within him to ask an angel for help.

Or is she an ex-angel now? I'm not really sure. Either way, he didn't like it. And he didn't like her cocky demons either. Sharen said they were having a hard time, but he thought they were just assholes.

Only a few moments passed before she appeared near him, her demons behind her.

"Thank you for coming," he said, knowing how formal and stiff he sounded.

One of her demons, a tall blond-haired man named Daniel, gave an arrogant smile. "So, you still hate angels, but you don't mind calling her when you need a little teleportation, huh?"

Alec's fist clenched. "I'm fucking trying to save Sharen and all the God damn demons."

He shrugged. "Just saying."

His rage coursed through his like a wave. "Well, pretty boy, how about I shut you up with a fist to the—?"

"Enough!" Mark stepped forward, adjusting his glasses and drawing attention to the dark shadows beneath his eyes. "We don't have time for this. We don't mind helping, but we need to move quickly."

Alec tried to push down his anger. "Understood."

Surcy moved forward, her dark eyes filled with interest. Her large, black wings folded on her back, and she smiled. "Okay boys, stay here. I'm going to bring Sharen's missing man back."

Triston, a massive man, with mismatched eyes moved forward. "We can't keep you safe if we aren't with you. And we have enough trouble without getting dragged into theirs."

Surcy placed a small hand on his shoulder, and the man's harsh features seemed to melt. "It's for Sharen."

Her demons watched her with pained eyes as she moved forward and took Alec's hand. "Where do you wish to go?"

Where should I go? Headquarters wasn't safe. Would Sharen be at their home? Or somewhere else? "The demon refuge."

"You got it." Then, she winked at her demons. "Don't worry, I'll be back."

He felt the strangest sensation... almost a prickling along his flesh. And then, trees came into focus around them. She released his hand, and he stumbled a bit, feeling off-balance.

It took him a second to identify the road that led to the refuge.

"I can't take you inside. It has a protective shield around it."

He shifted awkwardly. "Uh, no problem. Thanks for taking me this close."

She smiled. "Of course. I better get back to the demons before they go completely nuts."

He nodded. "Thanks again."

Within moments, she teleported away.

Alec took a deep breath, curling his hands into a fist. Now, time to see who had survived the battle, how many demons Sharen had saved, and most importantly, whether Sharen and his brothers were here.

Please, let one thing go right. Let them be here and safe.

As if in answer, he heard thunder roll through the sky. He glanced up at the cloudy day. Was it really going to fucking rain?

16

SHAREN LAY BUNDLED IN ONE OF ALEC'S OLD SWEATERS, sitting in a room in the refuge manor. She'd been alert for anything suspicious since arriving, looking for the potential shapeshifter, but everything appeared normal, especially considering all the new demons that had arrived.

The spirit of her people amazed her. They'd gone out of their way to welcome the newcomers and to make them feel at home. Some of them had been dead for a long time, and seeing things like cellphones and televisions had concerned them.

But with such an amazing group of people, I'm sure they'll come around in no time.

There was a knock at her door.

"Come in!"

Elle entered the room. For once, she wasn't holding her baby, and Brian wasn't tagging on along behind her. *The little ones are probably already asleep.*

"Everything okay?"

Elle nodded, giving a tight smile. "Can I join you?"

"Of course."

The woman walked across her room in bare feet, her shoulders sagging, and her steps measured. Sharen had come to realize the woman walked the same way, no matter the time of day. She walked as if she was someone who had lived a long and exhausting life... which she had.

When Elle settled on the window seat next to her, Sharen waited until the woman spoke what was on her mind. "I wanted to talk to you about something."

"Sure, what's up?"

Elle stared down at her hands. "I'm so glad to be back on earth. You have no idea how much. It's not an endless sea of white desert. It isn't so hot it's god-awful. And I hope I never again have to pull children with me through that black tar that we are born into in the demon-realm." She shuddered. "There's no way to describe that kind of darkness. That feeling of trying to swim for fresh air, but not lose my children as I do. It's truly a miracle we made it out twice."

"But?"

Elle looked up. "But many of us don't feel we belong here either."

She frowned. "What do you mean?"

"We already lived once. Earth feels... wrong. Not for all of us, but for some of us it feels like we're wearing clothes that are a size too small."

Sharen leaned back against the wall, troubled. "I was worried about this."

Elle held her gaze. "You were?"

She nodded, deciding to screw it and just be honest. "I don't know if what I'm doing here is right. I mean, none of you should be left in the demon-realm. You were meant to be angels... but not Caine's kind of angels. So as things are, there's really no right place for you."

The woman sighed and rubbed her face. "We just can't keep going like this."

Sharen's stared at her hands hanging over her knees. "Everyone keeps telling me that."

There was an awkward silence before Elle continued, her voice softer. "Are you going to keep doing this after you find Alec and Kade?"

There's no point in lying.

"I don't know. I have to do something, but I can't continue putting them at risk."

Elle leaned back against the other wall beside the window seat and looked out at the falling rain. "If it helps, I don't feel the way the others do. I didn't feel like I had a whole life with my kids before my husband killed us. This is a second chance to not repeat past mistakes."

Sharen's heart squeezed. "That wasn't your fault."

"I knew he was abusive. I didn't leave because he said he'd take them away, but I should have found the strength to run anyway. To start over somewhere he'd never find us."

"Evil has a way of making us feel hopeless." She remembered her foster parents, her rapists, and The Department. "We can't do better until we know better."

Elle's mouth twisted into a smile. "I've heard that somewhere."

"Damn, and I thought you'd think I was really clever."

They both laughed.

And then Sharen took a deep breath, there would never be another chance to ask her question. "I found the place the angels killed you and the kids."

Elle shuddered, gripping her arms. "That death was even worse than the first."

Sharen felt her stomach tighten. "And I found the body of the old woman in the apartment."

Please don't make me ask if you killed her. Please.

The woman's hand came to her mouth, and her brown eyes, the same color as Brian's, widened. "Grandma Lu is dead?"

"Grandma Lu?"

Tears filled her eyes. "She was this nice old woman who was helping me watch the kids. I was working at that secretary job you guys helped me get, and she just adored them."

"I'm so sorry." *Thank god, I was right. She didn't hurt the old woman.* "Do you know what happened to her?"

She shook her head. "I picked the kids up that day, and she was fine. We started walking home, and the angels ambushed us. I can't imagine why anyone would hurt her."

Sharen rubbed her face. She didn't know either, but at least she knew her demons weren't turning into bloodthirsty monsters. "Probably the angels."

"But have you ever heard of them killing humans before?"

No, she hadn't, but she didn't have another answer.

"Someone was probably watching us."

Sharen glanced up. "What do you mean?"

"I don't believe in coincidence. She was killed because we got involved with her." Elle rubbed a tear off her face, her voice growing angry with each word. "I guess this is a lesson about involving as few humans in our troubles as possible."

Unable to help herself, Sharen reached forward and squeezed the woman's knee. "We're going to figure this out."

Elle gave a short nod and rose. "I should get back to my room in case the littlest wakes up and needs to nurse."

"Everything will be okay," Sharen reassured her, even though she wasn't certain herself.

"Of course." Elle left the room as quietly as she had come, closing the door softly behind her.

Sharen stared out at the rain. *What the fuck is the right solution here? What am I not seeing?*

Something stirred in the darkness. She narrowed her eyes. Henry and Ryder were out walking the refuge, checking to make sure everything was in order. Was it one of them?

The figure moved closer and closer to the manor. He was big... but who?

She froze. *Alec?*

Her thoughts flashed to the horrible trick Caine had played on her mind. How she'd watched Alec die. Could it actually be him? Or was it the shapeshifter pretending to be him?

Rising, she ran to the door, flung it open, and ran down the stairs. Not slowing, she barreled open the front door, leapt down the slick steps, and stopped. The rain poured down on her and she was instantly soaked, but she didn't care. She couldn't care about anything accept the man who stood just a short distance from her.

He opened his arms. He had taken a severe beating—she could see his injuries even though the rain, and his clothes were torn and muddy.

She didn't move. "Alec?"

His expression changed. "Sharen?"

She took a step closer. "Prove you are who you say you are!"

"Sharen..."

"Prove it!"

And damn it, she was crying, shaking uncontrollably. If this was the shapeshifter, she would kill him for stealing her lover's face. And if it wasn't... a sob built in her chest.

"I'm Alec." He took a step closer. "Your husband. Your demon."

"That's not enough!" she shouted, holding out her hand as if to ward him off.

He moved even closer. "The instant I saw you I knew you were mine. Even though you're stubborn. And crazy. And a badass. Even though you're always wrong."

"I am not!' she shouted.

He laughed, the sound rich and inviting. "What else do you need to hear?"

"Something only you would know."

He was close to her now, only a few feet away. Almost close enough to touch. And God did she want to touch him.

"You take way too much sugar in your coffee. You're obsessed with Christmas." He took another step closer. "You think you're damaged because of your past, but every bad thing you've ever gone through made you who you are... a woman who's absolutely perfect." He closed the distance between them and pushed her wet hair back from her face. "And I love you more than anything in this world."

Her gaze drank him in. His normally perfectly manicured dark hair was a soggy mess. The stubble that usually hugged the lines of his square jaw had grown into a slight beard, and his cheek had a still-healing scar.

When he leaned down and kissed her, her heart soared. Something inside of her opened, pouring out every moment she feared he was lost to her forever. Over and over in her mind she pictured his death. Curling her arms around his neck, she pulled him closer. She needed to know this wasn't a dream. That he was really back and alive.

When he grabbed her hips and pulled her roughly to him, she jumped and wrapped her legs around his back. Their kiss grew harder and more desperate.

She was barely aware that he'd carried them up the stairs until they entered the foyer. He kicked the door closed behind them and carried her up the stairs to their room.

Inside, he tore her clothes off, leaving the shreds to fall onto the carpet. She broke the buttons on his shirt, pulled it from his shoulders, and swore as she tried to work the wet button on his pants.

He laughed, pushed her hands away and ripped his pants open, struggling out of the wet fabric. And then, she was in his arms again. Two wet, naked bodies pressing together. Rubbing against each other, struggling to get closer.

When her legs wrapped around his back once more, he spun her so that she was pinned between him and the wall. His hard cock pressed between them. She whimpered as his mouth tore from hers, but then he took one of his nipples in her mouth, and she moaned, arching to give him better access.

Rubbing against him, bouncing against the hot shaft she wanted so desperately inside her, she struggled to pull him inside. But he refused. Moving between her breasts and heating her cold nipples with his warm breath.

She was begging for his cock. Begging for it. And still he refused.

In desperation, she reached down and grasped him.

He groaned, cursed, and commanded she stop. But instead, she held his iron rod tightly and started to stroke.

Roaring, he pushed her hand away, and then, he was inside her, his hard shaft filling every inch of her. But he wasn't gentle, or slow. Instead, he barreled into her over and over again, thrusting like a wild animal. And she was fucking grateful for it as she dug her nails into his back and met him thrust for thrust.

Her orgasm built and built growing in intensity with each of his thrusts until a scream tore from her lips, and she exploded. Her inner-muscles clenched him as she soared over the edge. He made a guttural roar, and came, his hot seed filling her even as she continued to ride him.

They continued moving against each other for too long before finally slowing and clinging to each other. The sounds of their breathing filled the room.

When at last he drew back and looked at her, he grinned. "So I guess you missed me?"

"Not half as much as you missed me," she said, but her tone was sad rather than teasing.

He frowned. "What's wrong?"

"They made me think they killed you."

He cupped her face and kissed her forehead, cheeks, and finally her lips. "You should know me better than that. I could never leave you."

She laughed.

"You're crying," he said, kissing her wet eyelashes.

"Because I thought you were dead, you ass!" she punched him lightly in the shoulder.

He chuckled. "Come on my little Hunter. I'm going to shower us off, and then go see my brothers."

She stiffened.

"What's wrong?"

She opened her eyes. "Kade's still gone."

Anger like a blanket came over his face. "They still have him?"

"Yes."

The way he smiled sent chills down her spine. "Well, when I'm through with them they'll wish for death."

"Good."

17

SHAREN PUSHED ALEC DOWN IN THE BATH. "YOU LOOK exhausted. Why don't you let me do all the work?"

He put his hands behind his head and grinned. "I love this fucking giant tub."

She laughed. "And here I thought you'd tell me you loved me?" She lowered an inch onto his cock. His eyes widened. "Or that you loved when I did this." She sunk deeper.

He swore.

"Or," she leaned forward and bit his bottom lip before taking him fully inside of her. "this."

"Damn it," his hands started to move to grab her.

But she pushed his hands back. "I'm doing all the work, remember?"

"You mean torturing me?"

She smiled, and shifted on top of him. "Maybe."

The door to the bathroom opened. "Didn't you already take a—?"

Ryder's eyes widened. "You're okay."

Alec shrugged, even with his hands pressed above his head. "I'm doing a little better than okay."

Ryder looked overwhelmed for one painful second. "I'm glad you made it, brother."

"I am too."

"And I wish the first time I saw you wasn't when you were buck naked." Ryder grinned. "You know, because naked hugging is awkward hugging."

Alec threw back his head and laughed. "Rain check!"

Sharen felt her heart warm. Two of her husbands were home safe. *And one isn't*, a soft voice whispered in the back of her mind. She closed her eyes, refusing to give in to the sadness. She didn't appreciate her men when she had them. Never again would she repeat that mistake.

"Is there room for one more?"

Her eyes flashed open, and she shifted in the warm water. "Always."

He stripped slowly, and she watched him with bated breath. She would never tire of his eight-pack of hard, delicious muscles, or his flat stomach and corded arms. And god did she love seeing his big erection. It filled her with pride to know it was all hers, and to know exactly how much pleasure it would bring her.

"A guy could get an ego with you always staring at his junk," Ryder joked.

She met his gaze, losing herself for a moment in the happiness in his pale blue eyes. "Why don't you put your money where your mouth is?"

He raised a brow. "I'd rather put my cock where your mouth is."

She licked her lips. "Try it and see what happens."

His smile faded. He moved across the room and stood just in front of her, his tip inches from her mouth. Very slowly, she leaned forward and pressed a kiss to his tip. His eyes darkened. And she moved pressing one kiss after another along the underside of his shaft.

When she knew both men were watching her every move, she ran her lips back to his tip and then took him in her mouth, sucking hard.

Alec swore and bucked under her. She continued to take Ryder in and out of her mouth in a rhythm she knew would drive them both mad. And when she could feel the tension singing through the air, she reached up and grabbed his shaft, braced herself on Alec's shoulder, and started to ride her demon.

Both men groaned as one.

She increased her speed, her body awakening again. Never did she get tired of this. Maybe there was something wrong with her, but she could fuck her husbands all day, every day, and never get tired of the pleasure they brought her.

Then, she froze. Alec swore. She slowly withdrew Ryder from her mouth, licked him again, and grinned.

"That's going to cost you," he whispered.

Pulling his cock from her grip, he moved behind her, stepping into the Jacuzzi-sized tub.

She waited in anticipation as he pushed her forward and thrust a finger inside of her from behind. Sighing in anticipation, she rubbed her breasts against Alec's chest, teasing them both.

In answer, Alec reached between them and started to fondle her breasts. She shuddered, her inner-muscles tightening around his cock.

Ryder added a second finger to her from behind. "You missed me?"

She swore. "Yes."

"Did you miss me inside of you?"

"Yes."

He added a third finger, and she bit down on a cry a pleasure. "I'm going to fuck you so hard, Sharen. I'm going to fuck you until you can't remember your own name."

She whimpered as he withdrew his fingers, and then, she felt him behind her. Gritting her teeth and digging her nails into Alec's shoulder, she braced herself as Ryder eased inch after inch inside of her.

When he came to his hilt, she knew her eyes had rolled back in her head, and her mind had turned to sludge. She couldn't think of her own God-damned name as they began to thrust into her as one. All she could do was ride them, hard and fast, until she was coming again, and they were filling her with their hot seed.

Only then did she sag between them, feeling better. Not complete. But better.

They showered, dried each other, and climbed into bed.

An unspoken tension hung between them. Tomorrow they had a lot to deal with, not the least of which was to find Kade. But they didn't know what other new horrors the day would bring, so they'd try not to ruin their time together by discussing them.

And they didn't, even though she was sure none of them slept a wink.

18

KADE OPENED THE ONE EYE HE COULD STILL SEE OUT OF. There was a sound in the darkness. He was sure of it. Straining against the chains that kept him standing, spread and vulnerable, he tensed in preparation.

The shapeshifter moved through the darkness, still wearing Henry's face. His expression was as dark and cruel as ever.

Without a word, the creature went toward his table of torture tools.

Kade flinched as the man's hand ran over each of the many things he'd already used on him. Tools he'd never imagined in his wildest nightmares.

"I can't decide if you really don't know or if you're just this stubborn." The creature looked back at him, his hand curling around the handle of a whip. "So, which is it?"

Kade took several deep breaths, pulled at his reserves of strength, and spit.

The man's lips curled in disgust. "What a fitting response—from a demon."

He pulled the whip from the table and flicked the long,

black weapon. Kade tried not to flinch again. His back still burned where the crisscrossed marks decorated his flesh.

"Here's the thing, demon, I no longer need to know how to extract her powers. My father showed me... and he failed."

Is this good or bad?

"My goal has changed, because I've come to realize that perhaps you and I should become allies rather than enemies."

"In your fucking dreams."

The shapeshifter chuckled. "Demons have never been accused of being overly wise. Why don't you try listening first, beast?"

"I'm not interested in anything you have to say."

"Even if it could overthrow Caine and save your little wife's life?"

Kade stiffened.

The man leaned closer to him from behind, his hot breath disturbing as it puffed on his neck. "I believe that I've outlived my usefulness to my father. Now I'm no longer concerned with helping him achieve his goal. I've created my own. I plan to destroy my father and take his place."

"And how do you intend to that?"

"I intend to kill him."

Kade's mind raced. Was the shapeshifter telling the truth? Or was this another lie?

"It seems to me a lot of people have tried to kill him and failed."

The shapeshifter moved from behind him and circled to stand just in front of him. "But no one knows his secrets the way I do. Or his weaknesses."

I'm not sure about this, but let's see where his plan goes. "So what do you suggest?"

"It's simple really. You're going to call Sharen and help me spring my plan."

Trust the shapeshifter? "No."

The creature's hand tightened on the whip. "You'll do as I say. Because if you aren't a good little demon, you're going to be a dead little demon."

Fuck. Now what?

19

SHAREN WALKED THE REFUGE IN THE EARLY MORNING, breathing in the scents of the forest. Henry and Alec were asleep after guarding the grounds all night, so she'd taken over. So far, there was nothing the least bit suspicious.

Which was just how she liked it.

Moving to the edge of the protective barrier, she stared out at the rest of the woods. She could feel the pull of the magic this close to it. She was grateful that her witches had been reinforcing it daily to ensure it was strong enough to keep their enemies out. Suddenly, her phone rang. Sliding it out of her pocket, she frowned at the unfamiliar number, but answered.

"Hello?"

"Sharen!"

Her heart lurched. It was Kade. "Are you—are you alright?"

"No, that sick fucking shapeshifter has been torturing me." He sounded breathless. Pained in a way she'd never heard before.

"Where are you?"

"I escaped. I'm coming for the refuge."

Her pulse sped up. "I'll come and get you. Just tell me—"

"No, you've got bigger problems. The shapeshifter is in the refuge. He's going to kill the witches and take down the shield."

"No... Kade!"

"And then, Caine and his angels will attack. You need to prepare the demons for a final battle. And you need to use your magic. Do you understand me? You're capable of ending this, once and for all."

"How? How do I end this?"

"Set things right. You know how to do it. Deep inside. You might not remember, but instinctually you know how."

She felt the magic of the protective barrier fluctuate.

Turning, she started run. She thought she had more time. She had to save the witches. But the magic was fading at an incredible speed, drifting into the heavens as wisps of multicolored light.

"Kade, the barrier is coming down!"

"Hang up, Sharen. I'll be there soon. Trust me. Just prepare the demons for war!"

The call ended. She dropped her phone into her pocket and pulled her sword free.

When she exploded out of the woods, dozens of demons littered the lawn in front of the manor with looks of horror on their face.

"The shield's failing!" Elle shouted, clutching her children against her.

Someone else ran out of the manor. "The witches are dead. Their rooms are a blood bath!"

Alec and Ryder came out of the manor, swords in hand, their expressions wild.

She reached them, her voice carrying above them all.

"The angels are about to attack. The shapeshifter is in the refuge. Warriors, prepare to fight! Everyone else, go to the basement of the manor and hide."

More demons had begun to flood out of the manor as she spoke, but instantly, everyone shot into motion. Some of them were running inside, some of them were pulling blades free and joining her on the lawn.

Alec caught her by the arms. "How do you know?"

"Kade warned me. He's coming here now. He said I need to use my magic. That I can save all of us, but I don't know how."

He stroked her cheek, his gaze holding hers. "You'll figure it out.

The sparks of magic that were the shield faded to nothing. Within moments, shadows darkened the sky.

"Use your soul-blades!" she shouted. The angels already knew where they were.

There were perhaps three dozen warriors with her. And in an instant, they clutched swords that leapt with flames.

She took a deep breath, reaching for her magic, for her belief that they would succeed. Strength filled her, and her people turned as if feeling the wave of magic that moved over her flesh.

Clenching her jaw, she raised her sword into the air. "They might think this is a battle they can win, but they're about to find just how dangerous we can be!"

They shouted, raising their swords. "Yes, commander!"

The angels gave no warning as they shot down toward them. Instantly, swords clashed against swords and the sound of battle filled her ears. An angel flew toward her, but she ducked and rolled.

He landed in a crouch and gave her a wicked grin. "Ready to die, demon-whore?"

Her lips curled. "Try it, batboy!"

He came at her with all the recklessness of someone who fully expected to overpower her. To her surprise, she easily avoided his blow. Her quickness was a blur. She struck, moved, danced around him, struck again, and then severed his head.

She stared in shock, but didn't have time to think further as the next angel attacked.

Her demons were close, fighting their own opponents. It scared her, catching sight of them out of the corner of her eye as she fought. They were still healing and exhausted from their capture, as were many of the demons.

They aren't in any shape to take down dozens of angels.

So, I need to end this. And fast.

When she killed her next opponent, she looked out at the battle. They were outnumbered, at least two to one, and her people were falling with a quickness that terrified her.

What do I do?

And then, spells began to strike the demons as they fought. She turned in horror, only to see Rorde and a dozen Hunters exploding out of the woods.

If I don't figure out how the hell to use my magic, we're doomed!

She reached for her powers the same way she'd done in the past. She felt it warm and strong within her, but it was like sand, slipping between her fingertips. She couldn't grip it, couldn't use it.

Not for a spell as powerful as I need to end this.

Her pulse filled her ears. The screams and cries of battle slices within her heart. Her people would die if she couldn't save them.

Raising her hand, she formed a wavering red shield around them.

Instantly, the Hunters spells hit the shield and disappeared. At least if they wanted to attack her people, they'd need to get closer. They'd need to make it a fair fight.

But all I did is buy us more time.

And then, above them, the sky darkened. The familiar black and grey swirls told her that Caine was joining the battle.

She swallowed, sweat dampening her body.

An angel attacked and she killed him with the efficiency of a master swordsmen. Her mind focused elsewhere.

Reaching again and again for her magic, she tried to find the source of it, but it remained just out of her reach.

Rorde was suddenly before her. He stood with his hands glowing, and his expression dark. She gasped. His green flesh was peeling in chunks, and his eyes were sunken.

"Rorde?" His name was filled with pity.

His partially exposed teeth moved. "My only chance at becoming in an angel is to destroy you. To open you so that Caine can take your magic. And believe me, I'll be successful."

"Is that really what you want to do?"

Again, she saw the flicker of something. "It's what I have to do."

She tensed, allowing magic to flow into her hand. A Hunter's spell, simple, but effective.

Rorde sent the swirling mass of black magic out, but instead of hitting her, it flew behind her. Turning, she stared at where Alec stood. His eyes were widened in shock, and his sword tumbled from his fingertips.

Screaming, she sent a powerful spell toward Rorde and his Hunters. They leapt out of the way as it exploded, sending earth flying. Running toward Alec, she caught him as he fell.

Touching just beside the deep burn on his chest and stomach, anger filled her.

"I'll be okay," he whispered.

She touched him. A red glow slid over his skin. He would be safe. For now.

A spell hit her. She flew back, her head striking the hard earth beneath her. For a second she couldn't see, couldn't breathe. She looked up and saw Caine coming for her, not far above her.

A mass of swirling blackness cloaked him from the view of the others, but he stood just above her, looking down. His dangerous beauty chilled her to her core.

"Your demons are losing," he said. His words were whispered, but carried on the wind that swirled around her, as if part of nature itself. "They will die. Your lovers. Your friends. All of them."

"No."

She tensed, knowing she could rise, but she remained lying down, feeling her powers coursing through her. Something was changing within her, something familiar and strange.

Perhaps it was seeing his face... it was as if incased in them were memories she'd lost long ago. She could do things. She knew. She could stop him, but how? The solution was right there at her fingertips, but her memories swam away.

Caine flew lower over her, and the sounds of battle died away. Soon, his face was just inches from her own. "Give me what I need, Sharen. Release it. And all this can end at last."

"What do I need to do?" she whispered.

He smiled. "The simplest thing in this world. Accept that you have lost. Accept that there is nothing left for you in this world anymore."

She closed her eyes and reached out, touching his face.

His eyes widened. Memories flowed into her as cracks of light came over his face. Within him, he hid the truth of what she was and what she could do, and she began to riffle through his stolen memoires, grasping the pieces she needed.

He shouted, breaking free from her. "That was a mistake! You've become too dangerous for your own good, and now, I must lose what I wanted. But you too will lose Sharen... your life. At least this one. But be ready, I'll be there in your next life, waiting all over again."

She smiled, knowing what she must do.

Her thoughts filled with an image. The solution to everything. Time froze. And she imagined it, with tears falling from her cheeks, getting caught in her lashes. She imagined what she never could before. The solution to it all.

She had to put everything back into its rightful place. That's all it would take. She had to embrace the hopes and dreams that her demons didn't even see. The possibilities they didn't know existed.

And she needed to make things right.

She felt her magic like golden water spring from within her heart. It ran out, flowing over the battle field, flowing over her people, and the angels, and the Hunters.

Things would be right at last.

Time moved slowly. Caine's expression of horror filled her sight.

He withdrew back from her golden light, further and further. And she knew he intended to escape. Yet if she tried to stop him, she would lose focus on her task, which she refused to do.

And so, he'll escape. To attack us another day.

Ryder suddenly leapt over her. And before she could react, his blazing sword sliced Caine's head off.

Her mouth dropped open in shock. Ryder hit the ground near her, breathing hard, his expression intense.

Within moments, Caine's body turned to clouds, and faded, disappearing into the darkness. Not turning to ash like the demons, but simply transforming into nothing.

She didn't know what she imagined would happen with Caine's destruction, but not this. It was as if the man never even existed.

And yet, he's finally gone.

It's over.

But it wasn't. Caine's death was just the beginning. She still needed to set things right.

Climbing slowly, carefully, to her feet, she felt her magic continuing to flow out of her. And to her surprise, the fighting had stopped. Everyone was staring down at their bodies covered in gold.

And then, the angels and Rorde began to scream. Their swords vanishing. Their bodies melting. And where once they stood, demon-like creatures crouched upon the ground. They were red, two foot tall beasts, with horns, and an inability to speak. Beings she recognized as Level One and Two demons. These were the forms the worst kinds of people took.

Their rightful forms.

The ground rumbled, caving beneath the low level demons as her people scrambled back. And then, the creatures were gone. The earth shook again, and the gaping holes closed, leaving no traces that the low level demons had ever existed.

The Hunters looked between where the angels had

stood and where her demons waited, ready to take them on. Without a word, the Hunters turned as one and fled.

She had no doubt they would never see them again.

But she wasn't finished. Not yet.

Her people emerged from the basements of the manor. The old, the young, the women, the children. Everyone was covered in the golden light.

They moved across the grass to join the wounded warriors who had fought so hard to protect them. In the air there was sense that everything was about to change, that a miracle was taking place.

Taking a deep breath, she willed her magic to finish what it had started. To finish making things right.

And there, before her eyes, they changed. Dark wings sprouted from their backs, and an inhuman beauty lit their flesh.

Now, things are right once more. My people are the angels they were always meant to be.

Everyone stared down at themselves in wonder. And she wondered if they too felt as if the world was finally the way it should be.

Her gaze swept over them. In one corner, to her surprise, one of Caine's angels remained. The blonde who had rescued her, only to betray her.

Sharen watched as fire leapt onto her wings, burning spots as she cried out.

When the woman looked up, her gaze met Sharen's, and then she turned and ran. Disappearing into the woods.

She's been given time to prove herself still.

She looked out at her people. They had gathered together, and they looked both amazed and confused.

She smiled, wishing she had all her memories. Wishing

she knew more than that her magic wanted to make things right.

And then, she caught a movement in the woods. Kade came limping out. His body a broken, bleeding mess, a blade clenched in his hand.

She smiled and ran to him.

Everything was right once more. Everything was being put back into place.

She reached him, gently pulling herself into his arms. He held her for a moment, and she pulled back.

"You've missed everything, but I'm so glad."

His blade dove into her stomach. Her eyes widened. He pulled it out again, and stabbed over and over. She fell back, the sword still buried inside her. Her golden magic faded. Her warmth faded.

A numbness swept over her.

"Shapeshifter," she whispered.

Kade's mouth curled into a smile.

And then, Alec severed his head from his body.

Before the shapeshifter's body even hit the ground, Alec and Ryder knelt over her. Their black wings spread behind them.

"Sharen!" Alec exclamined. "Sharen, it's okay. You're not human. This won't kill you. You'll be fine."

And yet, she knew she wouldn't be. She'd used her power. Her magic was tired. Gone. She no longer felt the strength of being something else... she was merely, mortal. And this wound would kill her.

"Sharen!"

She turned her head.

Kade was crawling towards her. Black wings on his back. He kept trying to rise, but couldn't.

It seemed to take an eternity to reach her. And then, he

was there, tears streaming down his face. "I tried to beat him here. Damn it, I tried."

Her husbands gathered above her. She looked at each of their handsome faces. Her heart swelling with love.

I have them back. Safe. Now everything is right with my world.

Coughing, she felt the blood that rolled from her mouth.

Ryder wiped it away, his tear filled eyes above her.

She felt Alec trying to stop her bleeding. She heard someone shouting for help.

Reaching up with hands covered in blood, she touched each of their faces. "It's okay. You lived. I put things right. That's all I needed."

Darkness filled her vision. She was falling, somewhere cold. Somewhere she'd never been before.

And she knew, that was the end of her life.

KADE HAD DONE EVERYTHING HE COULD TO REACH SHAREN before the shapeshifter. But it hadn't been enough. He'd run until he couldn't run anymore. He'd walked until he could only crawl. And then he crawled without stopping.

Just on the edges of the forest he'd felt her magic sweep over him and felt confused when the wings had sprouted on his back. But still, he hadn't slowed. He needed to warn Sharen.

But even after everything, I was too late.

He and his brothers held their wife, their tiny human wife. She didn't breathe. She didn't have a heartbeat.

The others said she was dead.

They wouldn't hear them. There was no way that the woman they loved with every ounce of their hearts could no longer be alive.

It was impossible.

And so, they held her, not caring as the day faded to evening. They held her.

The others moved about them, but Kade couldn't see anything except her face. Her pale, expressionless face.

Her blood cooled. Her body was like ice. And yet, they couldn't let her go.

"What—what now?" Ryder whispered, breaking their shocked silence.

After several moments of silence, Alec answered. "She wasn't human. I don't know if she was part angel or demon, or witch... I don't know. And without Caine to pass judgment on souls, I don't know where she'll go either."

"But we'll get her back." Ryder said, the words filled with certainty.

And they would. If they had to pluck her from the heavens, or from the pits of the demon-realm, they would save her. They wouldn't stop searching until she was with them again.

A strange feeling overtook Kade.

He stiffened. Looking up. His brothers had the same look. It was if a jingling was filling their ears. A calling.

The demons... who now wore angel wings, stopped in their tasks.

"We need to go," someone said.

And then, everyone began to flap their wings.

He had the urge too. The overwhelming urge to go. To follow the call.

Looking to his brothers, he asked the question without words.

"Let's go," Alec whispered.

Kade gathered Sharen in his arms. And although his body ached, it was nothing in comparison to his soul or his heart.

They lifted into the air, dozens of dark-winged angels. They flew toward the horizon, and then like an instinct, they teleported. In a new place, far from where they started, they rushed forward and passed through a magical barrier that shimmered like Sharen's golden magic. They traveled down toward the earth until they hovered just above a small temple hidden in an ancient woods.

"Where are we? And why did we come here?" Ryder asked.

They settled upon the ground around it, and the instant Kade's feet touched the ground the building began to glow. A golden light, so like Sharen's magic, spread out covering the building, the ground, and running over the angels. When it reached Sharen, the magic shuddered.

And then, her eyes opened.

Kade gasped and watched as the golden light streamed into her wounds, through her eyes, her mouth, her ears, and her nose. And then, in shock, he watched her take a breath.

The light vanished.

And they all stood staring at Sharen.

She blinked. She reached forward and touched where her wounds were no longer visible.

"This isn't how it's supposed to happen," she said.

Kade choked back tears. "How what's supposed to happen?"

She frowned. "I should have been reborn in another body."

"Reborn?" he repeated, confused.

She looked up at him, holding his gaze. "I don't know everything, but I know this. I'm one of the Immortals. The Goddess of Hope... and this was not what was supposed to happen."

For some reason, he laughed and gathered her to him. "I don't care how it was supposed to happen, just that you're alive!"

Alec and Ryder were there in an instant, and they held her between them. There was a lot of kissing and touching and more laughter. It was as if every step they'd taken since meeting Sharen had been meant to lead to this.

When at last she insisted they put her on the ground, she stared at the temple, frowning. "It's like my dream... but why are we here?"

The others looked at her.

Elle spoke, cradling her angel baby in her arms. "We thought you might know."

After a second, Sharen's mouth curled into a smile. "It's because things are not ready for us yet. I can't take my place as a judge of mankind yet, for some reason. And you guys can't join the angels because they're still corrupt. This is a place we will be safe, for a time, until it's ready for us."

Kade expected the others to have questions. To have fears, but instead, they started to walk into the temple like her answer made all the sense in the world.

He frowned. They were just supposed to accept this?

He squeezed his fist and felt his dark wings curl around him. And then, it struck him. None of this felt strange.

"We were always supposed to be angels?"

Sharen smiled beside him. "Caine has screwed the whole system up, but yes, none of you were meant to be demons. Things won't change overnight, but this is the first step toward setting the world right."

Kade shook his head, feeling a wave of exhaustion come over him. "If Caine's dead, why can't we just put things right?"

Her smile faded. "I don't know. I have pieces of my memories... but not enough. I just know the world isn't safe yet."

He nodded. *I guess that has to be enough for now.*

They moved into the temple and were met by druids who welcomed them with confused, but open arms. The temple ran deep underground and had been created as a safe place for immortals in trouble.

It was strange. Kade had more questions than answers, but he also felt safe for the first time in longer than he could remember.

21

SHAREN STOOD AT THE VERY TOP OF THE TEMPLE, STARING OUT at the sea of forest. She knew in her heart that she and her people would not be safe here forever. This was only a temporary resting place. But there was nothing more she could do now. Being one of the Immortals meant that she could no longer fight.

The idea pained her more than she would ever tell the others.

If Caine had succeeded in gaining her powers, he could have stolen hope from the world. And such a thing would have made it impossible to ever destroy him. She had been reckless not to go into hiding as Marval has warned her. Even though if she could turn back time she'd do it all over again.

But this time things were different. Her demons were with her. Her people were with her. And they were all safe, for now.

She could no longer fight this battle the way she had been doing. She had to wait and be patient. One day it would be her time to battle again.

Because that was the other thing. The thing she told no one.

Caine wasn't dead.

"Sharen?" she spun to find that Kade had walked the steps to her little tower. "Are you coming to bed?"

She smiled and moved to him, taking his hand. They moved down the many stairs until they reached their room. Throwing open her door, she smiled again at the lovely room filled with everything she could need, a massive bed, and her three demons.

Or were they simply her angels now?

They'd discovered they could hide their wings with glamour, but at the moment, their black wings were spread wide. And the combination of big, half-naked men with dark wings was strangely... sexy.

Alec and Ryder looked up at her as she approached. Then, they closed their wings tightly to their backs. And within seconds, their wings had disappeared.

She smirked. "How does it feel to be angels?"

Alec scowled. "We're not angels. Angels are winged bats. We're demons with wings."

"Demons with wings?" she couldn't contain her laughter.

"Yes, he exclaimed, yanking down his boxers to fall around his ankles. "Demons with wings and big cocks."

She threw back her head and laughed.

He was on her in an instance. "Hasn't anyone ever told you not to laugh at a man when he says he has a big cock?"

That just made her laugh harder.

Suddenly, she was swept up and tossed on the bed.

"Apparently our wife needs to be taught some manners," Alec said.

Kade grinned and tugged his own boxers down. "I'm all for it."

Ryder stripped and leapt onto the bed next to her. "How is it that we always say we're teaching her a lesson, and then she ends up owning our asses?"

Sharen laughed, curling her hand around his erection. "Because we all know who's really in charge.

She knew what would come next. And for the first time since her marriage to the demons, there was nothing else they had to do. There was nothing else to focus on. Tonight, she'd make love to her husbands, and the next day, and the next day. There would be no more Hunting or fighting or running.

They would just have... peace.

For now.

And that was enough for her.

22

CAINE PUNCHED THE STONE FLOOR OF HIS THRONE ROOM. HE was damned weak. He'd died and been born again, which meant he had to gain strength over his powers once more. Dragging himself across the room, he sunk into his throne.

The moment he'd arrived in the throne room, he'd commanded his angels not to interrupt him, and he would not allow himself to be seen by them until he was strong.

A great deal of his forces had been destroyed in the battle, sent into the demon-realm and out of his grasp forever. He would need more angels. *More warriors.*

Because even though he no longer sensed Sharen's magic and she was no longer under his thumb, there were nine more Immortals.

As he closed his eyes, he sensed them. His angels worked tirelessly to break them down. This would be their last lives, he'd decided. Since discovering the secret of how to take their powers, he was determined to have what he desired most in this world.

Yes, it would take time. And yes, killing them was far easier.

But he grew tired of simply torturing them. Of watching them being reborn over and over again. Because that was the thing with the Immortals, they could die, and they couldn't be judges.

Yet now that he knew how to take their powers from them, he could finally kill them for good. And what was more? Once he absorbed their powers, he would be unstoppable.

Sighing, he looked to his throne room. It was crowded with the tiny glowing wisps that represented souls. Far too many had come to gather since his death, without him there sending them away with his judgment.

Annoyed, he sent all but the most defined of the wisps screaming into the demon-realm. He didn't care if they were good or bad. He just didn't want to stare at them any longer.

When those were cleared away, a dozen remained. The wisps that still took human form were more powerful. He would look at these more carefully and determine which would make good, obedient soldiers to join his forces, and which were too dangerous to become angels.

Out of the corner of his eye, he caught sight of one and stood up.

It was his son, the shapeshifter.

Fury overtook him. His son had one job at the battle. To kill the demon called Kade in front of her. To make her feel hopeless so that Caine could take her powers.

Instead, he'd watched his father die. And even knowing that his spirit still remained, waiting for an opportunity to use Sharen's powers to take shape once more and become even more powerful, his son hadn't destroyed her hope. Instead, his traitorous son had killed the woman herself.

Because he believed it would destroy his father.

My son wanted me dead. And now, he'll pay.

Calling the shape to him, his son's eyes widened as they focused onto his father.

"You thought I was destroyed forever."

"No," the shapeshifter lied, crumbling to his translucent knees.

"Yes," he hissed.

"It was simply a mistake." His son's voice was filled with fear.

He knows his fate, and yet he can do nothing to stop it.

"You killed her, thinking you were sealing my fate." He smiled. "How could you know you were sealing your own?"

"Father, please, I beg of—"

With a flick of his wrist, he sent his son's soul to the black pit on one side of the room, something he rarely used. The place where soul's deemed too dangerous to continue living were thrown into... to be destroyed and never reborn again. The Soul Destroyed.

His son's soul screamed and screamed, the sound echoing in the room as every tiny piece of his soul was torn and burned until nothing remained.

And then, his throne room was blissfully silent once more.

Caine pressed his fingers together and rested his forehead on his hands. *Now back to what matters.*

I have to destroy the rest of the Immortals and ensure I'll rule for eternity.

He smiled. Already he could sense the Immortals suffering.

This will be too easy.

WANT to find out what happens to Surcy and her demons? Find out in Supernatural Lies.

ALSO BY LACEY CARTER ANDERSEN

Guild of Assassins

Mercy's Revenge

Mercy's Fall

Monsters and Gargoyles

Medusa's Destiny *audiobook*

Keto's Tale

Celaeno's Fate

Cerberus Unleashed

Lamia's Blood

Shade's Secret

Hecate's Spell

Empusa's Hunger

Shorts: Their Own Sanctuary

Shorts: Their Miracle Pregnancy

Dark Supernaturals

Wraith Captive

Marked Immortals

Chosen Warriors

Wicked Reform School/House of Berserkers

Untamed: Wicked Reform School

Unknown: House of Berserkers

Unstable: House of Berserkers

Royal Fae Academy

Revere (A Short Prequel)

Ravage

Ruin

Reign

Box Set: Dark Fae Queen

Immortal Hunters MC

Van Helsing Rising

Van Helsing Damned

Magical Midlife in Mystic Hollow

Karma's Spell

Karma's Shift

Infernal Queen

Raising Hell

Fresh Hell

Straight to Hell

Her Demon Lovers

Secret Monsters

Unchained Magic

Dark Powers

Box Set: Mate to the Demon Kings

An Angel and Her Demons

Supernatural Lies

Immortal Truths

Lover's Wrath

Box Set: Fallen Angel Reclaimed

Legacy of Blood and Magic

Dragon Shadows

Dragon Memories

Legends Unleashed

Don't Say My Name

Don't Cross My Path

Don't Touch My Men

The Firehouse Feline

Feline the Heat

Feline the Flames

Feline the Burn

Feline the Pressure

God Fire Reform School

Magic for Dummies

Myths for Half-Wits

Mayhem for Suckers

Box Set: God Fire Academy

The Icelius Reverse Harem

Her Alien Abductors

Her Alien Barbarians

Her Alien Mates

Collection: Her Alien Romance

Steamy Tales of Warriors and Rebels

Gladiators

The Dragon Shifters' Last Hope

Stolen by Her Harem

Claimed by Her Harem

Treasured by Her Harem

Collection: Magic in her Harem

Harem of the Shifter Queen

Sultry Fire

Sinful Ice

Saucy Mist

Collection: Power in her Kiss

Standalones

Beauty with a Bite

Shifters and Alphas

Collections

Monsters, Gods, Witches, Oh My!

ABOUT THE AUTHOR

Lacey Carter Andersen loves reading, writing, and drinking excessive amounts of coffee. She spends her days taking care of her husband, three kids, and three cats. But at night, everything changes! Her imagination runs wild with strong-willed characters, unique worlds, and exciting plots that she enthusiastically puts into stories.

Lacey has dozens of tales: science fiction romances, paranormal romances, short romances, reverse harem romances, and more. So, please feel free to dive into any of her worlds; she loves to have the company!

And you're welcome to reach out to her; she really enjoys hearing from her readers.

You can find her at:

Email: laceycarterandersen@gmail.com

Mailing List:

https://www.subscribepage.com/laceycarterandersen

Website: https://laceycarterandersen.net/

Facebook Page:

https://www.facebook.com/authorlaceycarterandersen

Printed in Great Britain
by Amazon

16112342R00254